"Has the ring of truth on every page … Hill is giving us a timeless panorama of life and death in an English town, one in which a murder investigation is only one drama among many."
—Patrick Anderson, *The Washington Post*

"Hill is a fine writer … brooding, downright ominous."
—*Entertainment Weekly*

"Crime fans on the lookout for intelligent examples of the genre will enjoy." —*Time Out*

"Fans of P.D. James and Ruth Rendell can rest easy, knowing that those authors' tradition of fine storytelling will move forward at least one more generation." —*Bookpage*

"For the first time in years, P.D. James has serious competition."
—*Literary Review*

"A mystery with literary leanings … A controlled, impressive piece of work … *The Various Haunts of Men* is a book about how suddenly mortality can enter everyday life and how people do or don't deal with it." —*Newark Star-Ledger*

"A gripping and unusual procedural … A must-read."
—*Kirkus Reviews* (starred review)

"A hugely satisfying, highly entertaining, masterfully written book in which Hill is once again at the top of her game."
—*Booklist* (starred review)

"Exhilarating … These books succeed in harnessing all the genre's addictive power while maintaining a complexity and fascination entirely their own." —*Independent*

THE BETRAYAL OF TRUST

A Chief Superintendent Simon Serrailler Mystery

SUSAN HILL

THE OVERLOOK PRESS
New York

First published in paperback in the United States in 2012 by
The Overlook Press, Peter Mayer Publishers, Inc.
141 Wooster Street
New York, NY 10012
www.overlookpress.com

For bulk and special sales, please contact sales@overlookny.com

Cataloging-in-Publication Data is available from the Library of Congress

Manufactured in the United States of America
ISBN 978-1-4683-0065-9
1 3 5 7 9 8 6 4 2

Acknowledgements

My thanks to Dr Jill Barling and Dr Giles Bointon, who have both given me the benefit of their medical expertise.

Barrister Anthony Lenaghan has been faithful and wise counsel on the changing legal aspects of assisted suicide, and kept me well briefed with up-to-date information and judgements.

Thanks also to the anonymous source who has kept me abreast of the likely effect of cuts on the day-to-day running of police forces.

Barbara Machin, who, as creator and sustainer of the BBC TV series *Waking the Dead*, knows more than most about the investigation of cold cases, has been unfailingly helpful in sharing her knowledge and experience.

Antonia Fraser solved the small problem I put to her by giving me Rachel Wyatt, thereby putting both Simon Serrailler and me in her debt.

I have been cheered on during writing by the encouragement, support, all-round kindness and jokes of my friends on Facebook, quick visits to which during the course of the working day are a solitary writer's equivalent of brief chats around the office water-cooler. Thank you, therefore: Alex Massie, Amanda Craig, Andrew McKie, Anna Brooke, Bel Mooney, Carol Drinkwater, Caroline Sanderson, Charles Cumming, Chris Ewan, Claire Rutter, Curzon Tussaud, Danuta Keane, Elizabeth Buchan, Emma Barnes, Emma Lee Potter, Eugenie Teaseley, Fiona Dunn, Gill Poole, Helen Hayes,

Helen Nicholson, Jack Ruston, James, Malcolm Hugh, Richard, Ivo, Lydia and Berry Delingpole, Janette Jenkins, Jenny Colgan, Jess Ruston, Jo Crocker, Josie Charlotte Jackson, Kitty Hodges, Lesley Jackson, Liam Pearce, Linda Grant, Liz Parmiter, Lynne Hatwell, Mark Billingham, Meg Sanders, Naomi Alderman, Nicholas Daniel, Nicholas J. Rogers, Nick Harkaway, Nicole Roberts Hernandez, Philip Hensher, Polly Samson, Ray Hensher, Rosa Monkton, Rosalie Claire Berne, Sam Leith, Stephen Gadd, Trisha Ashley, Val McDermid, Valerie Greeley, Veronica Henry, Will Wyatt and Zaved Mahmood.

To the carers of this world

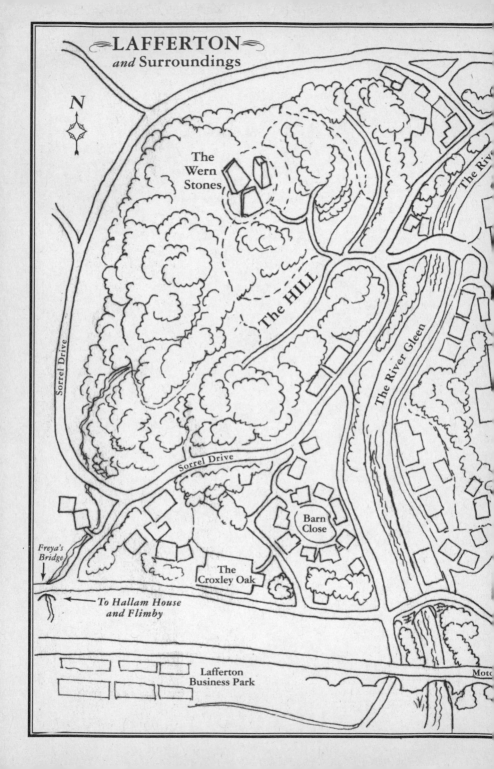

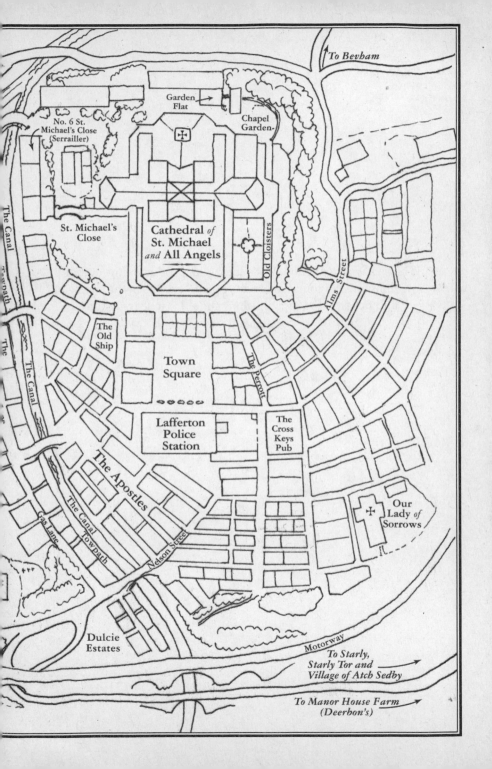

To Bevham

Garden
Flat

Chapel
Garden

No. 6 St.
Michael's Close
(Serrailler)

St. Michael's
Close

Cathedral *of*
St. Michael
and All Angels

Old Cloisters

The Canal

Towpath

The Canal

The

The Canal

The
Old
Ship

Town
Square

The Perrott

Alms Street

Lafferton
Police
Station

The
Cross
Keys
Pub

The Apostles

The Canal Towpath

Gas Lane

Nelson Street

Our
Lady *of*
Sorrows

Dulcie
Estates

Motorway

To Starly,
Starly Tor and
Village of Atch Sedby

To Manor House Farm
(Deerbon's)

One

SEVERE WEATHER WARNING

The Met Office has issued a severe weather warning for much of south-west England from noon today. Storms will affect the whole region. There will be torrential rain and high winds, reaching gale force at times, with gusts reaching 80 miles per hour in exposed places. There is a risk of flash flooding in many areas and drivers are warned to take extra care. Flood alerts are now in place for the following rivers in the south and south-western region . . .

The rain had been steady all afternoon as Simon Serrailler drove home from Wales and the wedding of an old friend. Now, as he poured himself a whisky, it was lashing against the tall windows of his flat and the gale was roaring up between the houses of the Cathedral Close. The frames rattled.

He had spread out some of his recent drawings on the long table, to begin the careful business of selection for his next exhibition. The living room was a serene, secure refuge, the lamps casting soft shadows onto the walls and elm floor. Simon was no lover of weddings but he had known Harry Blades since university, after which their paths had diverged, Harry to go into the army, Simon to Hendon, but they had kept in touch, tried to meet every year, and he had been happy to play best man on the previous day. He was even happier to be home in his own calm space, sketchbooks open, drink in hand. For his last birthday his stepmother had bought him the Everyman hardback of Evelyn Waugh's *Sword of Honour* trilogy and later, after making an omelette, he was going to settle down on the sofa with it, plus a second whisky.

The storm blew louder and a couple of times made him jump as a burst of hail spattered against the glass and a razor blade of lightning sliced down the sky at the same time as thunder crashed directly overhead.

'Spare a thought for those who have to be out in it,' his mother would have said. He spared one, for police on patrol, the fire and rescue services, the rough sleepers.

It was not a night to let a cat out.

In the Deerbon farmhouse, the cat Mephisto slept on the kitchen sofa, head to tail-tip and deep in the cushion, with no intention of venturing out of his flap into the howling night.

Cat pulled back the curtain but it was impossible to see anything beyond the water coursing down the window. Sam was in bed reading, Hannah was writing her secret diary, Felix asleep. It was not her children but her lodger Cat was worried about. Molly Lucas, final-year medical student at Bevham General, had come to live with them five months ago and slotted straight into their lives so easily that it was hard to imagine the place without her. She was out during the day but always glad to look after the children any evening, was tidy, quiet, cheerful and anxious to learn as much from Cat as she could in the run-up to her exams. She relaxed by baking bread and cakes so that there was usually a warm loaf on the table and the tins were full. The children had taken to Molly from the start. She played chess with Sam and shared a mystifying taste in pop music with Hannah. Felix was in love with her. It had taken Cat a while to feel happy about inviting someone into the house. Even just having a lodger felt like too big a change. She knew she was afraid that somehow it would move her on yet another step from the old life with Chris. But once Molly had arrived she realised, not for the first time, that when something new came about, the old was not therefore obliterated. Less importantly,

2

she no longer had to rely on her father and Judith to look after the children if she was on call or at choir practice. Once or twice recently, she had also accepted invitations to supper with old friends. Going out was not only good for her spirits but a different kind of freedom for the children – she had clung to them and it had been a long time after Chris's death before she had stopped waking in terror that one of them was going to die too.

It was after nine and she was worried. Molly had been working in the med. school library. She biked to and from the hospital, a well-equipped, fast and efficient cyclist, but this was no storm to be out in on two wheels and the severe weather warning had gone up a grade since the last time Cat had tuned in to Radio Bevham. She had rung Molly's mobile but it was switched off, tried the hospital but the library closed at six on Sundays.

She went upstairs. Hannah was asleep, her diary with its little gilt lock put away in the top drawer of her chest, its key on a chain round her neck. Cat remembered the need of an eleven-year-old to keep a diary private, and the fury she had felt when her father had mocked her about her own. How much it had mattered.

The wind sent something crashing. Rain was coming in through the cracks around two of the bedroom window frames and the ledges were full of water.

The storm seemed to be trapped in the roof space and roaring to be let out. Thunder cracked, startling Felix, who shouted out but barely woke and was easily settled again.

'This is how the world will end,' Sam said casually, looking up from *Journey to the Centre of the Earth* as she went past.

'Possibly, but not tonight.' Cat did not wait for him to ask how she knew that, nor did she tell him to put his light out. He would debate until dawn if she let him and she had no need to worry about the reading – when he was tired, he simply fell asleep, lamp on, book in hand, and either she or Molly sorted him out when they went upstairs.

Molly.

Cat picked up the phone again.

Just after midnight the river burst its banks. The car park of the supermarket on the Bevham Road was underwater within minutes, the streets and the lanes around the cathedral filled up, and in the grid of roads known as the Apostles water roared up through back gardens and pushed its way under doors into the terraced houses. The fire services were out but could do little in the dark, and it was too dangerous to try installing flood-lights in the high wind. The storm washed a ton of debris down from the Moor onto the road below, causing a lorry to overturn. The road that skirted the Hill was impassable and the houses nearby now at risk.

'Si, were you asleep?'

'You're joking. Are you OK?'

'We are, but Molly isn't back and she's not answering her phone.'

'Which way does she usually come?'

'Depends . . . at this time of night probably the bypass – it's quiet and it's quicker. What should I do? I rang the hospital but they don't think she's there.'

'Could she have gone home with a friend rather than risk it on her bike?'

'She'd have rung me.'

'Right, I'll put in a call . . . there's a red alert now and there'll be plenty of people around. If she's had an accident they'll find her.'

'Thanks, I'd be grateful. Molly's so reliable, she'd always let me know. How was the wedding?'

'Fine.'

'How did she look?'

'Who?'

'The *bride*, duh.'

'Oh God, I don't know . . . fine, I guess, beautiful, all that sort of thing.'

'Not going to ask what she was wearing.'

'No, no, I can tell you that. It was white. Now go to bed – I'll ring if I hear anything.'

But she would lie awake until she had news. She made tea and settled down next to Mephisto, who had not stirred for several hours. The rain was still drumming on the roof. She had been reading a book about the lives of women in oppressive regimes, but after a couple of pages set it aside and got a battered paperback of a favourite Nancy Mitford novel from the shelf. Reading that was like eating porridge and cream, and slipped down in a similarly comforting way.

Ten minutes later, Molly fell through the door, soaked and exhausted, having waded through flooded roads and then been blown off her bike. She had a badly cut hand and was shaken, but Cat gathered from her usual grin that it would take more even than this to crush her spirit.

Jocelyn Forbes turned on her radio hoping to find some light music but it had given way to alarming weather updates, and she only needed to listen to the storm to know all she needed. She clicked on the bedside lamp and reached over to turn the dial. She tried for several minutes before giving up in frustration. It had happened again. Yesterday she could not twist open a bottle top, now this. Arthritis, like her mother, like her aunt. Age brings arthritis.

She lay back on the high pillows.

Her bedroom curtains were always left slightly open and she could see lights in the windows of the two houses opposite. People would be awake tonight, up making tea, checking windows, hoping there were no slipped tiles on the roof.

But it was not the rain and wind that troubled her. She wished she could pick up the phone and talk to someone. There was no one. Penny would be asleep, her alarm set for six thirty. Her daughter liked plenty of time to get ready in the mornings, to eat a proper breakfast and dress with care, whether she was in court or chambers. There were a few friends but no one close enough to telephone after midnight, except in an emergency. Was this an emergency? No, though the thoughts she had were as urgent as anything that could come to disturb her from outside.

She had never worried about ageing. It took something minor, like not being able to turn the radio dial, to make her see what it might be like to become incapacitated and need care, to lose independence, have to move, to . . .

She told herself to snap out of it. It was the middle of the night, when everything blew up out of proportion, it was stormy, the news was terrible. Stop it.

The thoughts came back. They were not thoughts about pain or the loss of consciousness, nor even frightening or confused thoughts. They were clear, calm, rational. Jocelyn Forbes was a calm and rational woman. But it would have been pleasant to talk to someone now, not about the thoughts and where they had led, but about a programme watched or a bit of gossip, a crossword clue that was defeating her, an exhibition worth seeing. The small cogs in the wheel. Things she had been able to talk to Tony about, even if he had only grunted, half asleep. Things she used to ring her sister to share. She could always ring Carol any time. Carol had only been twenty miles away and would cheerfully have driven over here at two in the morning if she thought Jocelyn needed her. Or just chat on the phone for half an hour. Carol. It was almost three years.

The rain was steady on the roof though the wind had died down a bit.

Rain.

Rain.

The wind got up again, banging a gate.

Rain.

But doctors could help with arthritis now, they had all sorts of tricks up their sleeves. New medicines meant that people were not crippled so soon or so much. Crippled. It would be a long time before she needed to use the word about herself. All the same . . .

She wished there was someone to talk to.

Thunder rumbled but in the distance.

Rain.

Sleep.

The storm water was still rushing off the Moor and now it was bringing stones, soil and branches along with it, washing earth away from the outcrops of rock and exposing the tree roots that clung to the slope. The outspread hands of giants had gouged the surface and hurled it down, gathering speed, rumbling like

6

an underground train as it went. With nothing in its path it slipped and slithered on until it hit the road below and spread out over the tarmac, leaving a silt of branches, earth, boulders, mulch and more.

Two

'Guv?'

Serrailler's watch said six twenty. He hadn't got to sleep until after two.

'Morning.'

'Sorry, sir. We're sending a boat.'

'You're . . . ?'

'Town centre's underwater . . .'

'Right.'

'Can't say exactly when – the fire brigade and our diving lot are out now and the lifeboats are deploying a team . . . we're among the worst hit. They're evacuating as many people as they can and one of the dinghies will divert to you. Thought you'd want to be up and waiting, guv.'

'You read my mind.'

Simon went through to the sitting room and looked out of the window, but even before he did so, took in the strangeness of the light on the white walls and ceiling, silver-pale and wavering in the reflection of the water below. It was like being transported to Venice. The Cathedral Close, as far as the gate at the end, was underwater, but the wind had died down now, so that there was a strange calm and stillness about the scene. The cathedral rose above the water, the tower reflected in it and seeming to sway slightly. No one was in sight.

The dinghy arrived soon afterwards and then there came the most surreal half-hour of his life, sailing down the centre of the Cathedral Close and out under the arch into the water-filled streets of Lafferton. Other orange inflatables with outboard motors were carrying the elderly, children, dogs, even a budgerigar in a cage; firemen on turntables were being swung up onto rooftops. The whole of the area in and around the Lanes was so deeply underwater that the shops were only two-thirds visible. It was not until they reached the outer roads beyond the town centre that it was possible to get out and wade through the shallows. The station yard was crowded with rescue vehicles and press wagons. Doors were banging to and fro as more people came on duty and others went out wearing waterproof gear.

'I take it the interviews are cancelled?'

'Right, guv. Rescheduling for Friday.'

The station had been in a state of upheaval for several months after the suspension of two CID officers and the resignation of the DCI. Morale was at rock bottom, no one felt like trusting anyone and the Chief Constable had been threatening serious reprisals. None of it was Serrailler's fault, but he still felt to blame. If there were bad apples in the barrel he should have spotted them and got rid of them.

But things had calmed down, those who remained had pulled together well and worked overtime, and today the interviews for a new DCI had been scheduled. Serrailler was not involved; the Assistant Chief Constable, the Superintendent from Bevham and two officers from outside were the panel.

He would be relieved when there was an appointment. The shortlist was said to be a strong one with several good applicants from other forces. They needed fresh input.

But that, like every other routine matter, had been put to one side.

It was barely seven thirty but as he headed along the corridor to his office DS Stuart Mattingley was coming out of it.

'Looking for me?'

'Guv. It's bones.'

'Bones.'

'The storm brought half the Moor down onto the bypass. Couple of JCBs just got started clearing when one of the drivers spotted remains, guv.'

'They'll be animal. Plenty of foxes and badgers up there, sheep –'

'Apparently they don't look animal, only no one can get out there until the water goes down a bit. Soon as there's a chance forensics will send someone, do a recce.'

'Meanwhile . . .'

'There's been a report that a couple of youths in a canoe are looting shops in the Lanes and they've found a body in a bedroom on St Paul's Road. Old lady. Forensics on way.'

'By coracle?'

The DS looked blank.

None of it had much to do with Serrailler directly unless the death turned out to be suspicious. He headed for the canteen and his first coffee of the morning, wondering as he went whether he would get a lift home by dinghy later.

So far as the rest of Lafferton was concerned, the day was written off. Schools were closed, shops shut, traffic non-existent. The skies cleared as the storm moved away and shafts of sunlight touched the flood waters. The rescue boats went on ferrying people from their water-filled houses. Television cameras shot the scene from helicopters.

Simon caught up on a backlog of admin until shortly after eleven when a head came round his door.

'The bones, guv. Definitely human. There's a skull as well.'

'Have they started clearing again?'

'No.'

'Don't let them. We don't know whether there are any more remains, where they came from, how old they are. This will be a slow job, sifting through a few tons of embankment.'

'Problem is, if they can't reopen the bypass and traffic can't get through the town . . .'

'You said it. Any chance I can get out there?'

'You'll have to wade to the main road, get picked up there and dropped off by the roundabout. Walk along the bypass from there. The landslip is about half a mile down. Forensics are out there now and they'll get a couple of small diggers to start shifting the debris bucket by bucket. Move it to the other side, check, then scoop it away if there's nothing in it.'

10

'Slow job.'

'And too many bods are still tied up in the rescue and clear-up op.'

'I need boots.'

'You need waders and a hard hat, sir.'

He went down the concrete stairs to the basement and the equipment store. An hour later he was standing on the empty bypass looking at a small hill of soil and rubble, beside which tarpaulins had been laid out. Two forensics in their white jumpsuits were bending over some pale grey bones, dirty with earth.

'What have we got?'

'Most of a body – that's limbs, skull, ribcage . . . there was some damage as it all tipped down. We're missing a foot, pelvis –'

'Same person?'

'At a guess. But until we get it all onto the table and fitted together we won't know for sure.'

'Roman soldier?'

The young woman shook her head. She was pretty, short dark hair, nice smile. Shelley Churcher. Simon knew her well from many a crime scene over the last five or six years. She had once told him she had wanted to do this job since she was twelve and watched an American detective series every Saturday night.

'No,' she said quietly. 'Much more recent.'

'How much more?'

'Can't tell you that yet. But categorically not your Roman soldier.' She looked down at the bones.

How appalling, Serrailler thought, to have what remained of someone who had been flesh and blood, life and breath and laughter, finally spread out on a tarpaulin under the sky. To have been pitched down from some hole or ditch or grave along with tons of earth in a howling storm and then to lie being scrutinised by strangers, waiting to be fitted back into something that once again resembled a human body. It seemed wrong simply to stare at the bones, wrong to see what should never be seen, wrong and lacking in all respect and sensitivity – though forensics, he knew, always treated the dead as respectfully as they could, even while doing their job with medical detachment.

11

'Cause of death?'

'Come on, sir, you know better than that.'

'How long has he been dead then? Can you give me anything?'

'No,' Shelley said. 'Not yet. Nothing at all.'

They both stood for a moment longer. On the empty bypass, the diggers were still. Clearing the mounds of earth and debris would now have to be done slowly and carefully, everything sifted in case there were any further remains. The road would not reopen for several days, adding to the traffic chaos around Lafferton in the aftermath of the storm.

But the logistics of all that were someone else's job. Simon glanced down again at the skeleton, laid out on the tarpaulin.

'Poor bloke.'

Shelley shook her head. 'That's one thing I *can* tell you,' she said. 'This is a female.'

From the *Bevham Gazette,* 21 August 1995

Fears are growing for the safety of 15-year-old Lafferton schoolgirl Harriet Lowther who went missing last Friday afternoon after playing tennis at the house of a friend. Harriet left the house of Katie Cadsden, in Lea Close, at around four o'clock and was last seen walking towards the bus stop on Parkside Drive. She was due to catch a bus into Lafferton and meet her mother, Lady (Eve) Lowther, at La Belle hair salon. She never arrived.

Police are conducting house-to-house enquiries and are also combing undergrowth and woodland, a playing field close to Parkside Drive, together with nearby allotments and towpaths, and divers are searching the river.

Drivers and regular dog walkers and joggers in the area are being handed leaflets and asked if they remember seeing Harriet, who is a pupil at Freshfield College for Girls.

'Her disappearance is completely out of character,' Sir John Lowther said.

He stressed that there was no reason why Harriet, an only child, would not have wanted to meet her mother or return home. 'We are a close-knit family and there have been no arguments or problems. Harriet is sensible and she would never fail to come back on time or to let us know if she was in any trouble.'

Harriet, who is five feet four and very slim with blonde hair, was wearing shorts and a white T-shirt with a pale blue sweatshirt over it, and carrying her racket in a navy zipped bag.

Lafferton Police are continuing searches. Detective Inspector June Whybrow, who is leading the investigation, said: 'We remain hopeful that Harriet will return home safely. We are following all lines of inquiry and are keeping an open mind at this stage.'

From the *Bevham Gazette*, 26 August 1995

SEARCH GOES ON FOR HARRIET

Lafferton residents joined forces with more than 100 police officers this week as the search for missing 15-year-old schoolgirl Harriet Lowther intensified.

Police and firefighters from across the county were joined by volunteers as they scoured wasteland, woods and playing fields in a bid to find the daughter of prominent local businessman Sir John Lowther and his wife, Eve, of Up Starly near Lafferton. Harriet disappeared after leaving the house of a friend, to catch a bus on Parkside Drive.

Officers have also carried out extensive searches of the towpath and river areas and police helicopters have circled the region.

Detective Inspector June Whybrow of Lafferton Police said: 'We're still hopeful that we may find Harriet but as each day passes the search becomes more difficult and frustrating.'

Members of the public who think they may have seen Harriet in the vicinity of Parkside Drive, Lafferton, at the bus stop, on the 73 bus or who have any other information that might be of help are asked to call the dedicated line at Lafferton Police HQ or to contact any police station.

From the *Bevham Gazette*, 19 September 1995

Lafferton Police today confirmed that a 37-year-old local man has been arrested in connection with the disappearance of 15-year-old schoolgirl Harriet Lowther, daughter of Sir John and Lady Lowther. Harriet has been missing since leaving the house of a friend on the afternoon of 18 August . . .

From the *Bevham Gazette*, 22 September 1995

Police in Lafferton said that earlier today they released a 37-year-old local man, without charge. Neil Marshall was arrested on 19 September in connection with the disappearance of 15-year-old Harriet Lowther . . .

From the *Bevham Gazette*, 18 November 1995

Police today confirmed that the body found in Lafferton Canal, close to the town centre on Monday morning, was not that of 15-year-old schoolgirl Harriet Lowther, who has now been missing since August . . .

Three

It was four days before Jocelyn could get an appointment, partly because of the floods and their aftermath, partly because Dr Deerbon now only took two surgeries a week and as she was still very popular these booked up well in advance. But the receptionists and Cat had an understanding that patients she was concerned about, anyone with a serious condition or who just sounded more worried than seemed normal should be given one of what the practice manager called the 'secret slots'.

There had been no more rain, the water was going down quickly and the flood alert had been lifted, though the bypass was still closed and the town centre was filthy with the silt and rubbish left as the water receded. The shops which had been flooded out were mostly still closed as proprietors tried to clean up.

For a couple of days after the storm Jocelyn had been too busy helping Penny, whose ground-floor flat had suffered water damage. Penny had a big case about to start at Bevham Crown Court and little time to organise anything, which meant that Jocelyn had had no space in which to worry about herself. She had made the doctor's appointment and now felt foolish. She shouldn't be taking up surgery time. Her panic about being incapacitated had only come on because she was alone, it was two in the morning and the storm had seemed to be heralding the end of the world.

She would have cancelled the GP appointment if she had not

16

let slip to Penny that she had one. That had been that of course. Penny was insistent, Penny the competent one, Penny the barrister, Penny who took charge and was irritated that she had had to leave her mother to sort out the flat.

'I don't think I'll bother, Pen. Someone else needs the appointment more than I do.'

'How do you know that?'

'It's obvious. I'm perfectly fit.'

'You must have made it for a reason, Mother.'

'Yes, well.'

'What are you frightened of?'

That goaded her, as Penny had known it would.

'I am not frightened of anything.' She met her daughter's eye. 'Fine, fine, I'll go, waste Dr Deerbon's time.'

'It's what she's paid for.'

Now Jocelyn sat in the waiting room looking at a magazine for young women under thirty and feeling pleased that she had no need to starve herself or binge drink or worry about unfaithful men or wear skirts no wider than a hairband. By the time she was called she felt extremely cheerful and even more of a fraud.

Four

'Makes a change,' Gordon Lyman said. The pathologist stood at the head of the dissecting table looking down at a sheet of heavy-duty plastic on which the set of bones was assembled into an almost complete skeleton. Serrailler had a momentary shock at not seeing a dead body, whole and entire.

'Let me show you why I've got you in.'

Like most of the pathologists Simon had known, this one managed to combine efficiency and enthusiasm with a laid-back air.

'It's been surprisingly straightforward actually. Pity. I don't often get a build-your-own-skeleton kit to play with.'

'They seem to have sifted everything out of half a hillside pretty quickly.'

'Thing was, it had pretty much stayed together – clods of damp earth formed a protective mould around it.'

'How long has it been there?'

'Well, sixteen years, give or take. These are the remains of Harriet Lowther.'

'Right. No doubts?'

Gordon shook his head. 'Firstly, we know Harriet wore a brace on her front teeth, even without accessing her dental records, and these braces always fit pretty snugly. It's still there . . . see?'

Simon leaned over and looked at the jaw. The brace, discoloured but undamaged, was still firmly fixed to the upper front teeth.

18

'But we have her dental records as well. Perfect match. One other thing is the clincher . . . Harriet only had four toes on her left foot. Congenital thing.' He pointed again. 'Everything else fits – height and so on.'

'One hundred per cent sure?'

Gordon shook his head. 'With a skeleton there always has to be a sliver of doubt, but what are the chances of the body of a girl of fifteen with a tooth brace, and only four toes who disappeared near the burial spot sixteen years ago –'

'I get it. Right, thanks for the heads-up. The press are already panting at the door but we can let them pant a bit longer. There's enough here for me to alert the Chief and reopen the case.'

He looked round the cold-tiled room under its blue-white light. Harriet Lowther had been found but it would be some time before she could be laid to rest in a place of her family's choice, not of someone else's.

It was still well before nine o'clock when he slipped the Audi into his parking space. The pathologist had been on the ball in alerting him, as they always were. It was a fascinating job, he thought, going up the stairs two at a time, he could see its attraction. You needed to have a certain detachment, an eye for minute detail, an orderly and meticulous nature with a flair for interpretation, the ability to solve puzzles logically yet allow for the occasional flash of understanding or enlightenment – inspiration even. If he had become yet another doctor in the Serrailler line, he could see that the career might well have suited him.

The Chief Constable, Paula Devenish, was on sick leave following an emergency appendectomy and a post-operative infection, so he had to put in his call about the identification to the ACC.

'Thanks, Simon. All systems go then. I'll authorise the reopening of the case now. You head it up, get a team together.'

'Sir. The first thing is for Harriet's family to be informed. I'll do that myself this morning.'

'Parents live in Lafferton, don't they?'

'Nearby, but only the father, Sir John Lowther. Her mother died about four years ago and there were no other children. I've met him a couple of times – family connections.'

'Helpful. These things are never easy. And the interview board meets today to appoint your new DCI so you'll have another pair of hands, make it easier for you to focus on the case.'

Simon wondered about taking DS Ben Vanek with him but in the end decided it would be better to go alone. The Lowther house was in a village four miles out of Lafferton and to reach it he would drive past Hallam House. A word with his father might be useful – Lowther was in the same Masonic Lodge and Simon thought they had also been on a hospital committee together. Lowther had made a fortune in pharmaceuticals, and both before and even more since his retirement had given a lot of time and business expertise as well as money to Lafferton. He and his wife had retreated from the public eye after their daughter's disappearance, but John Lowther had thrown himself back into the swim after being widowed and become involved in a number of causes.

There was a broken-down vehicle holding up traffic and Simon was about to turn round and make a detour when his phone rang.

'Serrailler.'

'Guv – Dave Keys. The station said you were out and about. You anywhere near us?'

Dave was heading up the search team that had sifted through the debris on the bypass. Everything had now been put back and the road reopened; the team was clearing up and should be leaving by the end of the day.

'I wasn't but there's a traffic block so I'm making a detour.'

'Better come over.'

Simon had pulled off to take the call but now he sped towards the bypass, wondering as he did so about the new DCI. The internal candidate who had made the shortlist was not strong and he prayed it wouldn't go to him, but he knew nothing about the rest. While he was going to be occupied full-time on the Lowther case – and who knew for how long – the ACC was right, he needed someone at the station to head up CID who would hit the ground running and keep the team and its still fragile morale together. Before she had been taken ill, the Chief had talked to Simon about it. He was sure that she would be gunning for a woman in the job. There were too few in senior positions in the force and Simon, who knew Paula Devenish well and liked her, was fully aware that she sometimes felt beleaguered. Although she herself was based at Bevham HQ, she would appreciate a woman DCI on her side in Lafferton. Did he mind either way? There were two women on the team in CID but both sergeants and the DI were men. Uniform had a bigger female complement. If the DCI was to be a woman, so long as it was one with a strong personality as well as all the other necessary qualities, Simon would be happy, and he knew that to balance his own liking for working alone – not to mention being a maverick occasionally – the new DCI needed to be a team player. It wasn't going to be the easiest job to come into.

He turned into what was left of the car park at the bottom of the lower slopes, found a space near the forensic vans and got his rubber boots out. The team was on a temporary ledge above him, one of their green tents erected over a section of ground. A couple of them were moving a huge tree branch out of the way, another was stamping the earth down to pack it hard. The usual scene, but he had not expected so many of them still to be there.

Dave Keys watched him climb the last few yards. The ground was very wet and it was not easy to get a proper foothold.

'What's that?' Serrailler nodded at the tent.

Dave shook his head. 'Take a look. Mind your feet.'

He held one side of the nylon tent up for Simon to duck under. There was barely room for his six foot four and he had to stoop but there was enough light for him to see a hollowed-out area some seven or eight feet long, shallow and marked out with the forensics' small metal stakes and flags.

It was a grave and it held a skeletal body, entire this time and pushed slightly to one side, the left leg bent.

He stared at it for a moment before backing out again and stretching upright.

21

'That wasn't opened by the force of the storm.'

'You're right. A tree root had come up like a tooth out of a socket and when we were checking over this part the corner of the grave was just visible. We almost missed it, but then Lyn Pearson went back – she had a hunch something looked not quite right. Only took a bit of careful scraping away.'

'Could Harriet Lowther's body have been buried in it as well? Looks to be a bit of room.'

'No. Harriet came down with the landslip. She must have been further over there.' He indicated the gouged-out area of hillside fifty yards or so away to the left.

'This one might be our Roman soldier then.'

Dave looked blank.

'It's OK, I had this theory.'

'You wouldn't find Roman remains as near to the surface as this. They sink a long way over time. Often find them when a farmer does some deep ploughing.'

'Pity.'

'You an archaeology buff then, sir?'

'Nope. Just thinking how much less hassle there'd be if it was a thousand years old, that's all.'

'Cold case then.'

'Stone. But probably still not cold enough. Thanks, Dave. You moving it?'

'When Lyman's had his turn. He's on the way.'

'We can't close up here now. Any sense of how wide an area you might have to start trawling through?'

'We can't dig up the whole Moor, if that's what you're thinking. But in point of fact, this is a pretty self-contained section. Off this level area and you've a steep climb for quite a way – nobody's going to have dug a grave on that incline. We'll cordon off around here and take it inch by inch, but my guess is there may well not be anything else.'

'I hope to God you're right,' Serrailler said, turning and almost slithering backwards on the churned-up ground.

Dave Keys made a grab for his arm and hauled him up. 'It's the rubber soles,' he said with disapproval.

'If I'd known I was coming mountaineering I'd have brought my climbing boots.'

He left forensics to their job and drove away. It was just after eleven and he needed to see Sir John Lowther. No one working on the Moor would have alerted the press – it was more than their jobs were worth – but in Serrailler's experience everyone in the media on crime desks had a sixth sense for this sort of news. Once he had spoken to Lowther, he would call a press conference – always give them something, always keep them in the loop, always be one step ahead of them and never the other way round. Those were his rules when dealing with the media and he had a good relationship with the press office, who mostly went along with him.

He had not been out to Up Starly for a long time. It was one of the most unspoilt of the villages in the countryside around Lafferton, with a pub, the Oak, which his mother had liked. Meriel Serrailler had not been a natural pubgoer, or indeed someone who had had much time for lunch outings of any kind, but she had occasionally come out here with Simon – and Simon only, never Richard, never any friends. It hadn't been more than two or three times a year but he had loved spending the time with her, loved to have her to himself, away from his father's sarcastic and often disapproving company. Simon had not been since her death. He did not think he would want to again, but as he turned out of the lane into the village, he saw that the pub, on the other side of the green, was a pub no longer. Its signs had gone and what had been the entrance was now the front door of a private house.

He slowed down. The Oak was now Greenview. A picture came vividly to mind of Meriel, turning round to say something to him over her shoulder as they went in through the pub door. Smiling slightly. She had been wearing a violet-coloured pashmina over her left shoulder. Stylish. Beautiful.

The pub was no longer there, and yet it was still there.

He felt as if some final link with her had been roughly cut off, a link he had not even realised still existed.

He wound down the window and took a deep breath of the mild, damp air. He was not here to remember his mother fondly, or to think about himself and the past. He was here for the job.

The village was compact, the small houses and cottages spread out around the green and down two lanes leading off to east and west. There was a close of pebble-dash council houses and behind them a recreation ground with football posts in place.

A woman walking her dog slowed to peer at him. If he had been a potential burglar, she would have remembered everything about him. He stuck his head out of the window and asked for the Old Mill.

'I'm . . . not sure.'

She was sure. He pulled his warrant card out of his inside pocket and flicked it open.

'Ah, the police. I see. You go down that lane, Binders Lane, to the far end, and it's on the left. Concealed entrance. I won't say you can't miss it because you can.'

She stood watching him until he turned.

How long was it since police had regularly called at the Lowther house? Years. The village must have changed – people had died or moved away, others had arrived, the pub had closed – but Harriet's disappearance would not have been forgotten and the arrival of the police, even a solitary detective in an unmarked car, must be of interest. It would be round the village by lunchtime.

The Old Mill was exactly that. The fast-flowing stream ran through the garden and under the house. The water rushed towards the old wheel and paddles before emerging at the back of the house, which overlooked the wide mill pool. Simon got out of the car and went over. The recent floods had given a great surge to the stream and the noise it made was like the sound of an incoming tide. He wondered if it ever stopped, and how anyone in the house ever slept.

But the main door was on the other side, and as he went round to it, the noise faded to an agreeable, silky sound. A dark blue Jaguar was parked on the drive. An uneven lawn sloped away from a terrace and a flight of stone steps. The windows were closed and, in the upstairs ones, two or three blinds were half down.

He took a couple of deep breaths. It was a long time since he had been the official bringer of bad news but his stomach had the old knot of apprehension. He had been here so often in his past, as a young constable with the Met and then a uniformed sergeant. You never forgot. They crowded into his mind now. The Jamaican woman in her barricaded tiny ghetto of a flat in a tower block, opening her arms, throwing back her head and letting out a long wail of anguish when he told her about her son who had been stabbed. The Polish family, sitting in white-faced silence, until the grandmother went to a stoop of holy water placed before a picture of the Virgin and crossed herself with it. The woman with a toddler clutching her leg and a couple of boys, huge-eyed, standing behind her on the stairs, who had told Simon, and loudly enough for them to hear every word, that she was glad her waste-of-space husband was dead, he deserved anything he got, serve him right, we're better off without him, and no, I won't come and identify him, I never want to see him again, and now bugger off. The man who had walked out of the farmhouse kitchen in which he and his wife, Serrailler and a fellow officer had been standing while the news of his murdered daughter was broken, and had shot himself a few minutes later, for them all to hear and Simon to be the first to reach his body.

That had been the last time. Now this. Before, the news he had brought had always been of a recent death. This was very different. Yet he wondered if, essentially, it would be any different at all.

'They always know,' his army friend Harry had once said. He had several times been to the homes of men killed in action in Iraq and Afghanistan. 'They know the minute they open the door to you – no, before that, the minute they see your shadow through the glass. They always know.'

Simon rang the bell of the Old Mill, wondering if Sir John Lowther would see him and know.

But it was a middle-aged woman who opened the door. The housekeeper. He gave his name and stepped into a large, rather

25

dark hall. There was an empty feel about the house, as if it were somehow hollow inside. It smelled of polished furniture and cleanliness.

He only waited a moment.

'Simon – how nice to see you . . . but I hope nothing is wrong with your sister?'

'My . . . ?'

'Cat – we've a hospice trustees meeting at two o'clock. Is she all right?'

'Ah . . . yes, thank you, Cat's fine. I'm sure she'll be there.'

'That's a relief. I have a lot of time for Dr Deerbon. Please, follow me.'

He was a tall man, stooped, with thinning grey hair and anxious, deep-set eyes.

He led the way into his study, a long room overlooking the side of the garden away from the mill. The desk was set about with papers in neatly ordered piles, an open laptop, a small Georgian clock.

'Can I offer you a cup of coffee? Mrs Mangan will be making some for me any moment.'

He was oblivious to the reason for Serrailler's visit. They did not always know.

'Thank you.' Sitting down with coffee might help.

He watched Lowther leave the room and, as he did so, caught sight of two photographs on the bureau. One was of a pretty woman with hair coiled up behind her head, marked eyebrows, a pleasing smile. The other, next to it, was of a young girl of fourteen or fifteen, with the same eyebrows, a high forehead, smiling slightly but with her lips firmly together. Because, Simon thought, she was self-conscious about the brace on her teeth.

Sir John came back, talking about coffee as he did so, but although Simon had looked away he had not done so quite quickly enough. Lowther followed his gaze. And then, as he glanced between the photograph of his daughter and Simon, he knew – the split second *when* he knew was clear on his face. It was as if a curtain had dropped down over his welcoming expression, replacing it with a terrible blankness and he seemed to go not pale, but grey, the lines around his mouth and at the

26

corners of his eyes deepened, the flesh sagged. A brisk man in his early seventies had been replaced by an old one.

'You've found something,' he said.

'Yes, I'm afraid so.'

Lowther sat down slowly in the desk chair. For a moment he stared ahead of him, but then straightened his back and turned. As he did so, the door opened on the housekeeper bringing their coffee, so that they had to wait until she had set it down, though as she did so, Simon saw her glance at Lowther with a flash of concern. But she said nothing.

'Tell me, please.'

The coffee pot and cups stood untouched on the desk between them.

Simon told him. Lowther did not interrupt, and did not look at him, but at a point somewhere above the fireplace. It was quickly said and then there was silence.

Simon poured coffee for them both. Handed Lowther his. He took it, but did not speak until he had drunk half the cup quickly. Then he said, 'I'm grateful to you for speaking directly, Simon. For telling the full story.'

'There is never any point in not doing so.'

'No. I won't ask if you are absolutely certain because you have indicated that you are and you would not be here –'

'I have to be guided by the pathologist. He has no doubts at all.'

For a second, Lowther's face crumpled, and as he bent his head, Simon thought he was going to cry. He always felt helpless in the face of other people's tears. But, instead, the man walked across to the bureau and looked not at Harriet's photograph but at that of his wife.

'I never thought I would thank God that Eve died. But at this moment I do.'

'I understand you.'

'She could not have borne this.'

'But the not knowing . . .'

Lowther turned to face him. 'Yes. It was terrible. Unthinkable. After several years one lives with it but hope never quite fades and . . . well. One lives with it. She lived with it. She hoped. I

27

always knew deep down that something like this would happen. I don't think my own hope was alive after – what? – a year, perhaps less. But Eve hoped. This would have killed her.'

Serrailler drank his coffee. It was best to let Lowther talk.

'Is there any chance you'll find out more, do you suppose, or is that hopeless too?'

'Absolutely not. The case has been formally reopened and I am the senior investigating officer. I'll get a small team together and we'll start from the beginning – but now we have rather more to help us.'

'Harriet's skeleton. Yes. We can hardly call it a body. I presume she won't be able to rest in peace for some time?'

'I hope it won't be too long. You need that. I'll press the pathologist to find out everything he can and see if we can have her handed over for a funeral – and burial.'

'Thank you, Simon.' He shook his head vigorously as if to shake off water after a shower.

'I must get back,' Simon said. 'And get on. I'm sure it's what you want me to do. We can provide a family liaison officer, someone from uniform – they'd come and stay here, listen to you, support you in whatever way . . .' He trailed off.

'I think not. Thank you.'

'I had to ask.'

'But perhaps – you yourself would keep me informed if there is any progress?'

'Of course. It goes without saying.'

'I have a meeting of the hospice trust this afternoon . . .'

'You'd like me to cancel it for you? I'll ring my sister.'

'No, no, naturally I will go. Life cannot stop. I will not let this – this person – this – I will not let them do any more.' Lowther clenched his fists briefly. But his eyes showed already that he had accepted the truth. Shock was there, and grief, and there would be more of the same to leave their mark. 'I wonder though – will they know? When will people find out?'

'I have a press conference later today. We've kept the media away from it until now, but I must tell them, otherwise there will just be wild rumour and speculation.'

'Do you think reporters will come here?'

'Almost certainly. But you don't have to see them and you have absolutely no obligation to comment. If you do want to say anything you can issue a statement through our press office. Or if you feel you want to be interviewed, let them guide you on that too . . . some papers would be fine, others not so fine.'

'I would prefer not.'

'I'll tell the press office – and if anyone comes here, just turn them away.'

'Thank you. Thank you for coming, Simon.' He hesitated. How little it takes, Serrailler thought, to etch fresh lines onto a man's face, to add a hundred years. But it was not 'little', this news that he had had to bring Lowther. 'I think,' he said now, 'that before long this will prove to be a relief. Sixteen years is a long time to wait and not to know. Anything is better than that. At least, I hope it is.'

Simon put a hand on Lowther's arm. Perhaps it was the last straw. He could not tell. But as he walked to his car he saw the man turn away, unable to hold back his tears.

Five

'Just lift up your right arm, will you?'

Jocelyn did so.

'And the left. Fine. Now, stretch both arms out and rest them on my desk, hands spread.' Cat looked carefully. Turned Jocelyn's hands over one by one, and back. Touched her forefinger to the knuckles. The joints were not swollen or reddened.

'Where is it most painful? Hands? Knees?'

'No, no, my knees are fine.'

'Have you had any mobility problems at all? Going upstairs?'

'I can do that.'

'Walking – stretching and bending?'

Jocelyn hesitated. Cat Deerbon was being so thorough, so careful, but she didn't know how much was relevant, whether to bother about . . .

She said, 'I – this is going to sound weird.'

'No, go on.'

'I sometimes feel as if I'm walking a bit sideways . . . or even shuffling. I sometimes feel – it's as if I'm drunk. But I almost never drink. I had a gin the other night, at a friend's house. I can't remember the time before that. Glass of wine at Sunday lunch? Really.'

Cat smiled. 'Don't worry. Can you just walk over to the door and back again? Slowly.'

Jocelyn got up. Walked there. Walked back.

'Again. Do you mind?'

She did not.

'Tell me what happened with the radio knob. Here – try this.' Cat held out a small tablet bottle. 'No childproof top, you just twist it.'

Jocelyn took it. She knew what she wanted to do, was trying to do, but her hand wouldn't cooperate.

Cat watched. 'Does it hurt when you try to do that?'

'No. My hand just doesn't work.'

Cat asked about her general health.

'I get tired. But I'm seventy-three. I'm bound to get tired, aren't I? I remember my mother being tired when she had arthritis.'

Cat stopped herself from looking at her computer screen. It was too easy a way out. 'Look at your patient.' She had had it dinned into her by a consultant on her first ward rounds. 'Look at your patient, listen to your patient. They'll tell you what you need to know.'

She looked at her patient. 'You don't have arthritis,' she said. 'You're not in pain; your joints aren't swollen or tender to touch.'

'Oh. All right,' Jocelyn said. 'Both my mother and my aunt had arthritis.'

Cat waited, said nothing.

'I think I can work it out for myself . . . I have multiple sclerosis, don't I?'

'No,' Cat said, 'I don't believe you do.'

Jocelyn was visibly taken aback.

'You haven't been wandering round the Internet, have you? I know it's tempting, and there's plenty of helpful information there, but self-diagnosis via Google is a dangerous occupation.'

'No. Not really.'

'Not really.'

Jocelyn laughed. 'So, it isn't anything and I'm sorry I've bothered you, Dr Deerbon. I should have more sense at my age.'

'Do you think of yourself as old? You're only seventy-three. That isn't old these days.'

'No, but my daughter reminds me about it a lot. Perhaps that's it.'

31

'Well, tell her not to.'

'You don't know Penny.'

'OK. You don't have arthritis, and I'm pretty sure you don't have MS, but you *do* have something. You did right to see me.'

'So what is it?'

Cat hesitated. 'I'm not absolutely sure. I'd like you to go for an MRI scan – just to eliminate a few things really. And I'll get you an appointment with a neurologist.'

'Oh good heavens, is that really necessary? It isn't troubling me much, you know. I really don't think I should take up a specialist's time.'

'We need to get to the bottom of this, but don't worry, an MRI is painless and I'll send you to someone new at Bevham General who comes highly recommended. Let's sort you out. You'll get the usual appointment through the post but it might be a while, I'm afraid.'

'How long?'

'Hard to say. I can try and push it through – unless you've got private insurance?'

'Yes,' Jocelyn Forbes said, 'I do. I've paid a fortune into it over the years – so did my husband – and never had much need to call on it. Is now the time?'

'Now,' Cat said, 'is indeed the time.' She turned to her computer screen with some relief.

Private health insurance would ensure an appointment within a few days. And after that? If she was right about her diagnosis, time would make absolutely no difference. Sometimes, Cat wondered if the old ways had not been the best, when a GP suspected that a patient had an untreatable, incurable illness and for those reasons delayed telling them so for as long as possible. 'You cannot and must not lie to them,' her father had always said. But was withholding the truth for a while really lying?

When Jocelyn Forbes had gone, Cat made a note on her pad and rang for the next patient, but Kathy came through on the intercom. 'That's it – one cancellation, two no-shows. Can you sign a batch of forms?'

'Give me a minute.'

She went back to her screen, did a search. Read. Read more. Then spun her chair round and looked at the patch of curdled grey sky through the top window. Once, she could have gone through to Chris, asked his opinion, compared notes. She had a flash image of him, frowning, listening to her, tapping his pencil on the desk. His coarse brown hair standing on end where he had run his hand through it over and over during the morning's surgery. Sam had the same hair, made the same gesture. She clenched her hands tightly.

Go and talk to Russell then, see what he thinks. No. She had been a GP for fifteen years longer than Russell Jones, so how would it look if she confessed to doubt over a diagnosis?

Instead, she picked up the phone.

'Dad?'

'Good morning, Catherine. Why aren't you attending to patients?'

'Finished. I've got something I'd like to run past you if I may. Can I come over?'

'Now?'

'If it's convenient.'

'It is.'

He replaced the receiver. Judith might have worked miracles in softening Richard Serrailler's abrasiveness but she had had no success with his telephone manner.

Jocelyn had planned to walk into Lafferton and browse around the new Lanes bookshop, have coffee, pick up something for supper from the deli. Instead, she asked the surgery receptionist to call her a taxi. She felt drained, as if her legs had been filled with sand, and there seemed no time, now, for a relaxed morning in town, no time for anything but to get home and confirm it. Dr Deerbon had been as helpful, concerned, friendly as she always was, and what she had said was right. Quite right. But she did not understand. Not fully. How could she? Waiting to find out the official way would be agonising. Jocelyn did not intend to wait. She had guessed in any case, of course she had. Guessed. Knew. She had only to remember her father, who had died of it, at forty-six.

The taxi drove slowly and the roads were still in a mess, this or that one blocked off, diversions here, no through roads there, caution, repairs, potholes. She closed her eyes. Her thoughts swirled around but they would clear later. She was quite calm; she felt purposeful. She had plenty of self-control and soon she would be in charge again, decisive. Cool.

She wondered how Penny was faring in court, Penny, with her brilliant insight, clever and rational line of argument, persuasive manner. Penny was cool. Coolness itself. She was prosecuting in a child abuse case, something so distressing Jocelyn did not want to know any details. How her daughter managed to remain so detached, so unemotional about such things was a mystery. Cool.

Does she get it from me? Some of it, yes. But I can be detached about myself only, not about the pain and misery of others. 'I could never do your job,' she had said.

'No, Mother. You could not.'

Home. She looked at the outside of the house as she turned away from the taxi. White-painted pebble-dash. Detached. Bow windows downstairs and up. Wooden gate. Path to the front door. Porch. Side path to the kitchen door and on to the garden. Privet hedge, clipped low so that she could see into the street. Wide avenue. Neighbours in similar houses on either side. Pleasant neighbours, but she did not know them as she had known their predecessors. The world had changed. Her world was different.

How much did she love this house? This avenue? Those neighbours? This place? This world? The different world?

Love?

Not at all, she thought, getting out her front-door key. Not at all.

She tried several times to turn the key in the lock. Tried again. In the end, the pleasant neighbour she barely knew came to her rescue. 'These locks,' she said, pushing open Jocelyn's front door. But looked over her shoulder as she went away.

Six

There was a news-stand.

'LANDSLIDE GRAVE SKELETON IS MISSING HARRIET.'

Cat looked at it, registered. Oh God.

She pulled up. But Simon's phone was on voicemail. She didn't leave a message.

'Lowther,' her father said, as she went into the kitchen at Hallam House. 'Poor devil. Is it better to know?'

He stood for a second, his hand on the coffee percolator, looking out of the window. Judith had gone to see her son and a new grandchild, in Ludlow, for a couple of days.

'It's a sort of closure, I suppose.'

'Not unless they find out who and how and when.'

'And why. No. Is Simon involved?'

'I imagine so. We've got a hospice trustees meeting this after-noon – important one too, financial crisis report. No one's rung to cancel but I can't believe John Lowther will be there.'

'Why not? He's not a man to duck. Staying away won't help matters.'

Cat had always wondered if his absolute reasonableness was just that, or if he was as cold and hard as he seemed. He had been a distant father, yet he had loved them, she had never doubted it. He had expected a lot – demanded even – been ambitious for all of them, reserved his deepest feelings for the child who had been unable to fulfil a single one of his hopes. Listening to him now, rational as always, she still wondered.

And of course he was right. Staying away from a meeting would not help. But attending it might hurt.

He poured her coffee and led the way into his study. Kitchens, in his view, were for cooking.

His computer was open on a page of the online medical journal he still edited, papers beside it, and those on the table neatly ordered, magazines stacked, books carefully arranged. Simon, she thought. It is the only thing Dad and Simon have in common – this tidiness and order. Or was it? No. They were more alike than either would care to admit.

'You wanted to ask me something?'

No small talk.

'Yes. A patient.'

'I'm not very up to date clinically.'

'Enough. Right, a woman of seventy-three, generally been in good health. I don't often see her. She's presented with one or two vague symptoms – sudden disorientation, weakness of her legs, a bit of trouble walking normally . . . she described it as feeling the need to shuffle. But mainly, she can't grip things – couldn't turn the dial on her radio, unscrew a bottle top. I've sent her for an MRI . . .'

'That isn't diagnostic.'

'To exclude MS.'

'Correct.'

'I've got her a neuro appointment.'

'Well, that will confirm it. I don't see why you have any doubt – this is almost certainly motor neurone.'

'I know.'

'You know.'

'I just needed to run it past someone. I would have asked Chris.'

'But you can't do so.'

She did not reply. Had she been looking for sympathy? No, but if she had, she would not have got it from her father.

'It seems to me that you are suffering from a loss of nerve. What I do not understand is why.'

'No.'

'You are a sound doctor, you have a special diploma in

36

palliative care, you have varied experience. Is it because you now do too little general practice? Think. Think of the responsibility you carried as a young doctor, out on night calls alone, having to make decisions, be self-reliant. Now – you do a surgery or two. Your work in the hospice is quite different and much more limited.'

'So what should I do?'

'Why ask me? You decide, Catherine. It's your career and your life. So – your decision.'

'You always handed everything over to us.'

'I happen to believe I did the right thing. Meanwhile, your patient with probable motor neurone. Grim prognosis.'

'Five years?'

'No more than three. MN is a bugger. Nothing to be said for it as a way to die.'

She rested her head against the chair back and closed her eyes. When she opened them, her father was looking at her. She saw a quizzical look on his face, and something more. Something like concern. Something like tenderness?

Seven

'No appointment.'

'Sorry?'

'We didn't appoint a new DCI.'

'Good God, that bad?'

The ACC sighed. 'Well, it wasn't the strongest list I've ever seen. But before the appointments committee we had an emergency budget meeting.'

'Ah.'

'We have to lose 25 per cent in the coming year. That's drastic.'

'Cut the civilian staff.'

'Oh, we will, but police earn a lot more than support staff, you know that. It might even come to losing Lafferton – or rather, only keeping it as a satellite to HQ. But that's all in the air . . . for now, no DCI. Freeze on new appointments with immediate effect. Blame the coalition.'

'I bloody well won't, I'll blame the last lot for spend, spend, spend.'

'Yes, well, it's all coming home to roost.'

'What about my team?'

'We're not making anyone redundant.'

'No, the team I need to reopen the Harriet Lowther case.'

'Hollow laughter. Team? That's you.'

'I can't do the entire thing on my own and run CID.'

'No. You can't . . . you'll fit this in with whoever's free at the time.'

'That's nonsense . . . you know how many hours it takes trawling through old files – it's sixteen years ago. We're talking box files and pieces of paper.'

'Which anyone can go through. Come on, Simon, a heck of a lot of this is routine stuff.'

'Great news then. Thanks, sir.'

He had barely replaced the phone before it rang again.

'Lyman. Want to drop by?'

'I can't, Gordon, there's too much on. You'll have to give it to me this way, much as I love to see your handiwork.'

'Right. Second skeleton. Is female. Age – difficult. Adult, anywhere between twenty and forty . . . prime of life. Nothing unusual at all, no dental brace or four toes this time. Cause of death interesting . . . the neck's broken. Could have been done post-mortem though . . . anything can happen, but they found this one still *in situ* – not chucked down with half the Moor in the landslide. There's a bash to the back of the skull but I doubt if it caused death.'

'Nothing at all to identify – are you sure?'

'You're asking a lot. You were lucky with the last one.'

Lucky.

'You can circulate dental records – might get something. Teeth pretty healthy and whole which means she's on the younger side. Probably narrow it down to between twenty and thirty then. I'm having another good look.'

'Let me know, Gordon. I'll need to get as much out to the press as I can.'

'Did another girl go missing at the same time as Harriet Lowther?'

'No other local one, I'm sure.'

'Could have been a year or two later – or earlier.'

'Even so. But obviously we're checking. If we don't turn anything up, we'll widen it to a national search.'

Simon sat back in his chair, hands behind his head, listing what had to be done. The Harriet Lowther files reopened and gone through line by line. Follow-up interviews with any witnesses still living in the area, last known movements worked out carefully, contact made with every living relative, friend, neighbour, chance acquaintance, pupil, teacher. The sort of routine that had to be meticulous and painstaking, that took nothing as read, nothing for granted, made no assumptions. Sixteen years of life and change muddied the waters. Sixteen years meant memories faded, events became confused. People had died, moved away, grown up, changed jobs, had families. Sixteen years of events and everyday routine had altered everything. Suspects, if there had been any, must be located, re-interviewed, their subsequent lives gone over in fine detail. Anything like suspicious behaviour, let alone arrests, charges, imprisonments, would have to be examined in the light of the Lowther case and an individual's relation to it.

The second body was a second inquiry. Not a cold case because at the moment it looked as if it had never been a case at all. A new inquiry then. But the body was of a girl who had gone missing somewhere, her absence reported by someone, surely. Young girls, unless they were on the streets of a city, did not vanish without someone wondering why and where and how. Young girls had families, friends, childhoods, previous lives, they had lived here or there, they were remembered.

It was a huge amount of work. He had hoped for a team – a deputy, and a close-knit group of three or four, working side by side, talking, bouncing things off one another, propping one another up. At the moment, it looked as if he would be lucky to get anybody.

He sat upright. No, he thought. No, he would not 'be lucky to get anybody', he would get a team. He was SIO on what was no longer a Missper from sixteen years ago but a definite murder inquiry. There was a second inquiry which would have to be opened, another murder, and probably related to the first. Somewhere out there was a person or persons who had taken the lives of two young women and buried their bodies.

The Chief – or in her absence, the ACC – had a duty to provide him with a full support team, cuts or no cuts, and although he was perfectly prepared to put in extra hours himself and take on the work of others, he was not going to be hamstrung by lack of officers. A team he needed and a team he was bloody well going to get.

He reached for the phone.

Eight

John Lowther took the papers out of their folder and arranged them neatly on the conference-room table in front of him. He had glanced around the room on entering and nodded, but in general, not catching anyone's eye. There were eight of them, eight men and women well used to difficult meetings and differences of opinion, well versed in what to say and how to say it, eight in prominent positions in various areas of public life. And not one of us, Cat Deerbon thought, has any real idea of how to handle this.

There was none of the usual murmur as they waited for him to begin. The silence was perhaps the worst of it.

At last, he moved a typed sheet of paper slightly to his right. Looked down at the agenda sheet. Looked up.

'Mr Chairman . . .'

Pamela Vaughan, the hospice chaplain, was looking directly at Lowther. His face had changed, Cat thought, even in a few hours, it was all registered there, in the pallor, the way the flesh seemed to have fallen in, the lines deepened. His eyes had a deadened look. The waiting, the strain and anxiety and fear of sixteen years had fallen away, to be replaced by grief and weariness and more dread, more dread. There was an answer, but that had only raised new and dreadful questions. She felt great sorrow for him, sorrow and some of the same dread.

'Before we begin, I know I'm speaking for everyone when I say that you have all our sympathy and our prayers today. It's

41

very courageous of you to be here. And it goes without saying that if we, together or individually, can do anything for you, you know you've only to ask.'

There was a murmur round the table.

'Thank you,' he said. 'I do know that and your words mean more than I can say. Thank you. Now, we should make a start and get through a few small matters before turning to the main item on the agenda, which I'm afraid, is financial. We shall need to discuss it at length so may I just approve and sign the minutes of the last meeting and move on?'

The early business was out of the way and tea had come in. John Lowther's chairing of the meeting was no different from usual. He was courteous, businesslike, well organised. The best chairman they had had, Cat thought, and they were lucky to get him.

'Finances,' he said now, glancing down at his agenda paper. 'To put it bluntly, the hospice is in a very poor financial state. It's a combination of things, as always – expenditure is up considerably, income is down considerably. We have a large deficit. We have been dipping into our reserves and living beyond our means, though not in any sense of being profligate. But however justified every penny of our spending may be, the fact is that we can't continue to lay out more than is coming in, so we must either cut our costs or bring in more money, or both, preferably both.'

The meeting gathered energy and determination, proposals flew round the table, suggestions were discussed, strategies examined. After listening and noting, Lowther asked them to consider appointing a fund-raising committee – not, as he put it, to discuss coffee mornings but to find ways of accessing serious financial support from major donors, trusts and grant-making bodies.

'Don't we need a professional fund-raiser?' someone asked. 'This is a competitive area. Funding is big business.'

'Fund-raisers command high salaries. I do dislike the idea of paying over a lot to someone before we even start.'

'We can't make an appointment of that kind,' John Lowther said. 'We simply don't have the money.'

'This isn't something for amateurs – as you say, it's competitive

42

and it's time-consuming. A new committee would be drawn from where? Some of us? It's difficult enough to find time to attend trustees' meetings every month.'

Everyone spoke, everyone had an opinion, but there were no positive suggestions.

'Perhaps you'd allow me to reiterate what a really desperate financial situation we find ourselves in.'

Lowther looked round at them all slowly.

'It ought to focus our minds. It took the effort and will and strength of so many people to build Imogen House – and money. Without that, I doubt if we would be here at all.'

'We absolutely need to be here,' Cat said. 'To lose the services of the hospice is unimaginable. The calls on us are increasing month on month.'

The meeting continued for an hour and a half longer, until everyone was exhausted. They broke up with the decision having been made to establish a separate working party with the sole remit to come up with ways of bringing in money.

Cat was leaving to do a quick ward round before going home when John Lowther beckoned to her.

'May I have a word? I want to ask your advice.'

She wondered if it had to do with the discovery of Harriet's body.

'Have you by any chance met Leo Fison?'

'I don't think so. The name doesn't ring a bell.'

'Leo is someone I knew years ago. He was a doctor but retired when he had a spell of ill health in his fifties – a cancer but all clear for some time now – and he has been wanting to find a way back into working again, though not in ordinary practice. He inherited some money and he has come down this way – his wife has family in the county. He's setting up a small care home specifically for people with dementia – no more than eight or so patients at a time. The emphasis, as far as I can gather, is on individual care and one-to-one therapy.'

'It's very much needed,' Cat said. 'A lot of new work is being done on dementia care. There isn't a cure but some of the ideas are quite positive.'

'I knew you'd be up to speed with this. I told Leo as much.'

'Oh?'

'We were talking about things here. I'd like you to see what he's doing – the house has been renovated and updated, made fit for purpose. But they plan to take people in quite soon.'

'Then I should go over. It's important to see what's available – people expect an honest report from their doctor.'

'I did have another thought. Leo will be running the home with his wife, Moira – and of course staff – but I think he will have some free time. He's always had business interests, via a family firm, as well as being a doctor, but those don't occupy him much nowadays and he would make a first-rate chairman of our new committee. Leo knows a lot of people.'

'Not what you know . . .'

'Indeed. He has a way with him, lots of contacts, but he's also new to this part of the world and so without prejudice, if you take my point. That can be a positive asset.'

'It needs someone with energy and a real commitment to the work of a hospice. Not going to be easy, John.'

'We should show him round – you're the best person to do that, I think. Initially I would sound him out – if he says he won't do it there'd be no point in wasting your time. But if you feel it would be worth my making the approach . . . ?' He put a hand briefly on her arm. 'Though you may have someone in mind already. Forgive me.'

'Absolutely not. I can't think of anyone who isn't already very committed.'

'This is where we miss your mother so much.'

'People found it hard to say no to her.'

They left the conference room together and then, as she turned to the ward area, Cat glanced at John Lowther's back as he went down the corridor. He was stooped and walked slowly, as if he had given everything he had to conducting the meeting and, in order to do so, had somehow set aside what had happened, but now, remembering it, he was cowed under the weight of his grief, all over again.

Nine

Now, she had said to herself. Do it now. Don't wait. Don't dither. You know what you want, you have thought about it, gone into every aspect of it, lain awake thinking about it, written it all down to try and make it even clearer.

You haven't any doubt and you know what the specialist will say without needing to wait for the appointment and the scan. So tell her now. Ask her now.

Penny's case at the Crown Court was likely to continue for another week. The amount of evidence, she had told Jocelyn, was considerable and difficult for a jury to follow and there were a larger than usual number of witnesses.

Laying the small table by the French windows for their supper, she wondered again if she ought to have postponed this – not for her own sake but for Penny's. Was it fair to give her this news and then to tell her what she hoped she would do, while she was the defending barrister in a major criminal trial?

Anyone else would have spared their daughter from all of it for another few weeks. What stopped Jocelyn was Penny herself, the person Penny was. Competent, organised, controlled, frighteningly capable of putting a dozen things into separate compartments of her mind, her emotions, her life, and never letting their boundaries blur. Penny would walk out of the court at the end of each day and set the trial aside, once she had done any reading and preparation for the next day. She would not let it keep her awake, she would not worry about it or dream of it.

That was the only reason Jocelyn was not putting off what she had to say. Penny would be annoyed if she delayed. Penny had stood on her own two feet and fought her own battles, no quarter given and none expected, since she was two years old.

There was home-roasted ham with baked potatoes and salad. Penny did not eat any form of pudding so Jocelyn spooned coffee into the cafetière and took out a bottle of Beaujolais, hesitated, tried to work the corkscrew and failed, as she had guessed she would. Left it for Penny.

Then she went to sit down on the wicker chair in the conservatory. There was a little warmth still left in the sun. This, she thought. There is this and it is now. The minutes were separating themselves and taking on a new significance.

'Are you out there?'

Penny. Tall. Hair pulled back so tightly it gave her a facelift. Wide-apart eyes. The eyes she got from her father, like the colouring, but where had the height come from? Jocelyn supposed it was useful, for a woman barrister in court.

She loved Penny. But she had never felt entirely comfortable with her, always been anxious to keep her happy, not to annoy her, since she was a child – kowtowing to her, she sometimes thought. Not that Penny had been spoiled, or had tantrums if she had not got her own way, but she had had an air of seeing through her mother, seeing through an argument, seeing through a fudge or an evasion, a rationality about her from the start. Jocelyn had been head of a Civil Service department for years, as competent and authoritative in her sphere as Penny, but the moment she arrived home that authority had always seemed to fall away. When she retired, it had gone altogether, though when alone she felt confident enough. She had done an Open University degree, then an MPhil, and had planned to continue, until she had woken one morning wondering why and could find no satisfactory reason. Since then, she had felt increasingly overtaken by her daughter, overtaken and overlooked, she occasionally thought in self-pity.

'Did the carpet people come?' she asked now as Penny came through with a glass of wine for them both.

'They did, all sorted. I realised I never liked the colour of the old one anyway. Thank you, Mother.'

'I didn't do much. Once I'd found the cleaning firm and the carpet people . . .'

'All the same.' Penny raised her glass.

'How's the case?'

She shrugged. Talk about it, Jocelyn willed her, talk about the case, the court, the jury, what you think the outcome might be. Talk.

'Did you see the doctor?'

Jocelyn got up. 'I'll just put the ham on the table. Could you get the potatoes out of the lower oven?'

'Don't change the subject, Mother.'

'I wasn't. I was postponing it. I'm rather hungry.'

Postponing it. Yes.

'Anyway, did you?'

'Let me say what I have to say when I want to say it, which is not yet. I want to eat.'

Penny held up her hands.

The sun still shone. They took coffee into the conservatory. Two comfortable chairs. A neighbouring cat. An early butterfly.

'The doctor,' Penny said.

Now that it had come, she felt entirely calm. And quite sure.

'I have motor neurone disease,' she said.

She had not imagined Penny's immediate reaction but would have assumed a moment's silence to digest the information and then a battery of questions and cross-questions, requests for second opinions, statement of medical options. Penny had been born with a lawyer's mind.

Instead, after a split second, she simply burst into silent tears. Jocelyn was so taken aback she got up and went into the kitchen, where she stood looking out onto the bricks of the side wall, counting them, making her eyes trace the lines of mortar – along, down, across, down, down, along . . .

Penny would need the time to compose herself. She had not, to Jocelyn's knowledge, cried since childhood and the circumstances that might make her do so were unimaginable, other than in reaction to sheer physical pain.

But when she went back, Penny was still sitting with tears on her cheeks, head bent. Jocelyn put her hand tentatively on her shoulder.

'I'm sorry. I couldn't think of any other way but to – tell you.'

'Oh, it's the only way.'

'Yes.'

She sat down and poured them both more coffee. Waited. A small breeze rustled the bushes.

'What did Dr Deerbon say? What has to be done?'

'A scan. I see the neurologist. But Dr Deerbon knew. And I knew the minute she ruled out both arthritis and MS. Then, as soon as I got home, I looked up the symptoms.'

'Mother . . .' A flash of the usual Penny.

'I know, I know. I'm not a fool.'

'It's the worst thing I can imagine. Worse than cancer, worse than – anything. I knew a brief with it when I was a student. He taught us for a couple of terms, constitutional law, he was brilliant. Just a couple of terms.'

'Drink your coffee.'

'I'll move back here of course.'

'You will do no such thing.'

'We won't argue.'

'We will argue.'

'Of course I must.'

'Neither of us could stand it, as you well know. Besides . . .'

'Well, you couldn't stand being in a home.'

'I could not.'

'You would hate having a stranger living in here.'

'Yes.'

'So . . .' Penny waved a dismissive hand. The tears had stopped now. She blew her nose. Drank her coffee. 'What's happening to you at the moment?'

Jocelyn smiled. The cross-examination.

'A few irritating things.'

'Irritating?'

Jocelyn did not reply. She was trying to compose the next

48

sentence which would somehow tell, explain, ask, defend – all in the same few words. But there were none. Penny was looking at her, eyes tearless now, the usual faintly challenging expression back, and for a second, Jocelyn thought that she would neither tell nor ask after all, would find someone else. Who else? She lacked courage not in the face of her decision but of her daughter's reaction.

'The sun's gone,' she said. 'Are you cold?'

'No. Is that a symptom? Feeling cold?'

'I don't know. I suppose it may be eventually. If one can't move . . .'

'How long does it take to develop? Did the doctor say?'

'I've read –'

'Not Google. The doctor.'

'I have to see the neurologist, I told you.'

'I'll come with you.'

'No. You're in the middle of this case.'

'Well you won't get an appointment straight away, will you? The trial will be long over.'

'It's this coming Wednesday.'

'Ah. Then put it off.'

'I don't need you to come with me, I'm perfectly able to drive myself.'

'To Bevham General?'

'The Manor.'

Penny did not approve of private medicine, private health insurance, private anything, so far as Jocelyn could see. Where had she got all that socialism from?

'There is one thing I'd be very grateful for.'

'Which is?'

'Please don't interrupt until I've said everything. Please hear me out.'

And Penny would. She was a good listener when she wanted to be. It came with the job.

'At the moment, this is not bothering me very much. I'm in no pain or discomfort – it's just tiresome. But that won't last. The specialist will probably tell me more but I know what course it will take. I have been independent and I have enjoyed my life

49

and what I do. The idea of old age hasn't troubled me because I've assumed I would remain hale and hearty. How foolish. But now I know I won't, I cannot face that sort of decline – cannot and will not. And while I am still able to decide and to act, I intend to do so.'

Alarm flickered across Penny's face but she said nothing.

'I am planning to go to Switzerland, to a clinic where I can end my own life while I still have the ability and before the worst overtakes me. I have read a lot about it and I need to read more. When I have, I'll get in touch with them. What I have to ask you –'

Penny said very quietly. 'I know what it is.'

'Let me say it myself. Let me ask. I don't want there to be any misunderstanding.'

'There won't be.'

'I'm asking if you will come with me. Take me to the clinic.'

'And help you kill yourself. Help you die.'

'No. Watch me. You would do nothing but be with me while I take my own life. That's all.'

'That's *all*?'

'Penny –'

'A little thing like that? Hardly worth asking, is it?'

Penny stood up quickly and went out through the open conservatory doors into the garden, to stand at the end by the low stone wall and the raised flower bed, her back to Jocelyn straight and absolutely still. After watching her for a few moments, Jocelyn got up and took the tray of coffee pot and cups into the kitchen.

Ten

Serrailler came out of the station with an armful of paperwork. It was just before six and he had had enough of his office, the file stores and canteen coffee. He was going to drop into the farmhouse and hope for a beer and maybe an early supper before heading home to go through notes on the Lowther case. He would work in the flat tomorrow if he possibly could, to get more done in a shorter time. There was yet another drug offensive on, with a fancy operation name, dawn raids and a side serving of armed response. He would be glad to keep out of it.

Lights blazed from what seemed like every room in the farmhouse, and although Cat's car was not in the drive the smell of braising meat reached him as he opened the kitchen door and Wookie the Yorkshire terrier came tearing towards him, barking and turning round and round in mad circles.

'This dog is uncivilised.' He bent down and let the puppy jump into his arms and lick his face. As he did so, Mephisto leapt off the sofa and banged out through the catflap.

'Please don't interrupt,' Sam said, glaring at him. He was sitting at the table with a book open in front of him and Molly opposite, head down. 'I'm testing her.'

'Don't blame me, blame the untamed beast.' He put Wookie down.

'He ghost-watches,' Sam said. 'He stands at the glass door onto the terrace at night and stares and stares. He did it for

51

almost an hour last night. There's deffo something out there.'

'Why don't you let him go and find it?'

'We've tried. He just races round a bit and comes back inside to go on staring. Right, you ready, Moll? Next. Brachial.'

'Runs from the shoulder to the elbow and –'

'Where on the shoulder?'

'What do you mean, where?'

'I mean where on the shoulder.'

'The shoulder's the shoulder.'

'No.'

Molly sighed.

'This isn't going well,' Sam said. 'The anterior of the shoulder. Next – carotid.'

'Neck.'

'Which side of the neck?'

'Both.'

'Correct.'

'That's all twenty.' Molly jumped up.

'Mum's gone to supper with Dr Finch.'

'Oh.' Simon pulled the cap off a bottle of lager.

'Sorry,' Molly said, 'the casserole is for tomorrow and we've had egg and chips but I could easily do you some more.'

'They were only oven chips,' Sam said.

'How's the revision, Molly?'

'I'd kill a lot of people if they let me qualify now.'

'She needs to sort out the names of the major arteries. Talking of killing, how are the skeletons? Dug up any more?' Sam looked round at him. He had done a growth spurt and his face was changing. He would be fourteen next birthday, a Serrailler in shape, long-legged and -backed. But the small boy lingered. 'There could be a mass grave of skeletons.'

'I doubt it.'

'Are you digging? With bare hands?'

'I hate to put a dampener on things, Sam, but this isn't something out of a horror film, these are the remains of real people. They were probably murdered. Not a joke.'

'Sorry. Doctors make gory jokes. Molly told me that when they were cutting up a corpse for practice, someone –'

52

'Shut up.' Molly threw a tea towel at him. 'I told you, if you said anything you could get me into trouble.'

'Why, it wasn't you who took out the –'

Simon grabbed his nephew in an armlock. 'You heard the lady. Shut it. Now come quietly.'

'Ha, not even uniform say that any more. Can I have a slug of beer?'

'No. Where are the others?'

'Hannah's at Stupid Samantha's and Felix is in bed. And I'm in the county hockey second 11 team – can you come to a match next Thursday?'

'Second 11? I'm impressed, Sambo.'

'Huh, more than Grandpa is. He just said, "Why not the first 11?" OK, I could do ten more minutes, Moll, but then I have to do Latin homework.'

Simon felt the momentary chill of not belonging. Sam picked up the book from which he was testing Molly, the beer was finished, the casserole for tomorrow, his sister out. He hesitated, then walked to the door.

'Tell Mum I'll call her.'

Sam nodded but did not look up. 'Right, let's carry on,' he said. Molly sighed.

She was very pretty, Simon thought. Dark curly hair. Heart-shaped face. Intelligent. Smiley.

'Femur,' Sam said.

Simon left.

His mobile rang as he drove through the close, and when he got up to his flat the message light was flashing on the landline.

'*Simon, Paula Devenish. Can you ring me at home?*'

'*Simon, Paula, I'm leaving this on both phones. Ring me when you have a moment would you?*'

Ten minutes later he was driving through the southern outskirts of Bevham. It was getting on for half past seven by the time he reached the house, which was set back from what had once been a quiet country road. There had been a tall Scots pine in the front, he remembered, and as he pulled into the drive he saw that it was lying on the garden. Something else uprooted by the storm.

Paula Devenish had been married previously, and had two grown-up sons; five years ago she had married again, apparently with great success.

Her husband opened the door now, a bearded, broad-shouldered property developer who, Simon knew, had lost his wife and son in a violent attack when a burglary had gone wrong. He himself had suffered severe injuries and lost the sight in an eye. They had only met formally but Serrailler had taken to Malcolm Innes. He had a solid calm and steadiness about him, and he smiled a lot.

He smiled now, showing the way into the sitting room.

'I can't keep her down,' he said. 'Any suggestions?'

'I wouldn't dare.'

'I'm going stir-crazy,' Paula said. She was on a sofa with her feet up and it was clear that the illness had taken some of the stuffing out of her. She looked thinner in the face, and older.

'Have you eaten, Simon – and if not, will you join us? It's just family supper.'

'I'd like that, thank you.'

'Good. I could do with some police talk.'

'Which she is not supposed to have.' Malcolm Innes held up a glass and a bottle of wine. 'Or a beer?'

'Beer please. So what am I allowed to chat about? – I can do holidays, politics, weather –'

'You'll do police.'

Malcolm went out, laughing.

'He cooks,' she said, 'nothing else, wouldn't know where the washing machine is or how to fold a shirt, but he cooks.'

Malcolm brought in Simon's beer. There was a fire burning low in the grate, smelling of damp wood.

'Sorry about the urgent-sounding messages. Not urgent at all really.'

'You have withdrawal symptoms.'

'For about a week I honestly didn't care if the force fell to bits, but now I'm afraid it's all going to slip through my fingers. Am I a control freak?'

'All chiefs are.'

'We're supposed to be brilliant at delegating.'

'I'm supposed to be that and look at me. We're alike – we can delegate the boring stuff but when the job gets exciting we want to be in the thick of it.'

He was surprised how easy it was to talk to her as an equal, not because she had been ill but because a domestic setting and the absence of uniform made the essential difference. She was not the Chief, not his boss, she was a fellow police officer and a friend.

Paula Devenish was a formidable woman, decisive, in control, her finger on every detail of what was going on around her at work, but in spite of what he had said, he knew that she was also better than he was at standing back and giving other people responsibility. She did not, in fact, find it hard to delegate. She knew it was vital or a force would never survive. Nevertheless, she always wanted to be kept in every loop and Simon could imagine how frustrating an enforced convalescence was for her. They had always got on well, but sitting opposite her in the quiet sitting room, he saw her for the first time as a middle-aged woman and twice-married mother of adult sons, who might be a neighbour, his sister's patient, his stepmother's friend. Not the Chief. Not a police officer at all. Somehow, he needed to start all over again, discover what kind of person this was.

They ate a kitchen supper of fish pie and French beans and a plate of excellent cheeses, bought, Malcolm Innes said, from the Deli in the Lanes.

'I love my cheese,' he said, 'and I don't want to see that nice little shop close. I go there a lot.'

'The shops on the Lanes were hit badly by the storm – most of them flooded out. A friend of my stepmother's was due to open a new bookshop there and she's had to postpone it; the clock shop lost a lot of valuable stock. Is that a goat's cheese?'

Malcolm pointed out each one, describing, recommending. When they had finished eating he gave Paula his arm back into the sitting room, saying he would clear up and bring coffee through.

'Harriet Lowther,' she said.

He waited.

'It's some sort of resolution, I suppose.'

'Yes, in a way. Her father thinks so. But . . .'

'Too many unanswered questions. What are your thoughts?'

'I don't know if I have many yet. She was murdered and buried in a grave on the Moor, by a person or persons unknown. I've taken all the files home. Maybe they'll yield something. I'll know more when I've gone through the lot. But after sixteen years? Long time.' He hesitated. 'The second skeleton complicates the picture considerably of course.'

Simon knew what he wanted to say. But he also knew it would be unprofessional and unfair. Yet he felt frustrated, his hands tied and a job not being properly done.

'What will it take?'

She knew. He knew.

He shrugged but remained silent.

'My name's still on the door, Simon. Tell me.'

'I need a team. Not necessarily a big team but I've got to have a couple of people working on this. Especially on the second body. I'm not going to let that gather dust in a file because of Harriet, though obviously Harriet takes precedence.'

'Has Brian formally authorised the case to be reopened and a new investigation for the second murder?'

'Yes.'

'Leave the rest with me. But you won't get as many bods as you should have.'

'Understood.'

Malcolm brought in the coffee and the conversation moved away from police business. But as Simon stood up to leave, the Chief said, 'I wonder if you could do me a small favour? It would get me out of a spot.'

Payback then.

'Of course.'

'The Lord Lieutenant is giving a dinner on Tuesday. It's in the castle and I'd accepted of course, but I'm really not up to this sort of formal do yet. Would you go in my place? Brian can't, he's got an ACPO meeting in London, and there isn't anyone else senior enough. Are you free?'

He was free.

'Will I need a partner?'
'The invitation is for two, yes.'
'Fine. It will be a pleasure.'
The Chief gave him a sharp look.

Eleven

Harriet Lowther had been at a school twelve miles from Lafferton. She was popular and hard-working but not an academic high-flyer, played tennis for the school and at a local club where she was rated higher than average. She also played the piano very well and had lessons at school. She was near-sighted and wore glasses for reading the blackboard. She had recently had a brace fitted on her teeth, about which her mother and several school friends said she was a bit embarrassed and self-conscious. She had signed up to take a Duke of Edinburgh's Award.

Simon had half a dozen photographs of Harriet Lowther on the table. Harriet as a six-year-old with missing front teeth. Harriet at eleven, proud in her new school uniform, a shot taken in the garden of the Old Mill. Harriet with the tennis team, holding a trophy. Harriet playing with a friend's puppy.

Harriet. Normal. Cheerful. Neither pretty nor plain but certainly growing into prettiness. Harriet Lowther. So much like a thousand other middle-class girls at middle-class schools. So entirely herself.

Harriet Lowther.

Simon looked into her face, at each photograph but most of all at the last, taken six months before she disappeared, as if she might tell him something. Might? Could? No. Just a cheerful, bright-faced girl. No secrets. He was as sure as he could be that she hid no secrets.

He got up and stretched, lay on the floor and did a couple of dozen press-ups, then rolled over with his knees bent up to his chest several times. His back had always caused him problems, partly because of his height, but in the last few months it had become much worse. Cat had suggested he see an osteopath – 'GPs are no good at backs' – but he had not yet made the time.

'Psychosomatic,' his father had said, typically, without sympathy and without elaborating, which had annoyed his stepmother.

'You have only to look at him to know he'd have back problems,' Judith had said, 'and even if they were psychosomatic, what difference would that make? His back still hurts.'

One more reason to be pleased that Judith was now in their lives. She had recommended an osteopath. Simon had the name and number. Somewhere.

He got up carefully, swung himself to and fro, then went to make coffee. His father and Judith had bought him a Nespresso machine for his birthday, streamlined, smart, efficient. He thought it might be the thing he would grab if the flat caught fire.

Harriet Lowther. One Friday afternoon sixteen years ago she had left a friend's house for the bus stop less than a hundred yards away and, after turning round to wave at the corner, had walked out of sight for good. Now her skeleton had been found among earth washed down from the Moor in a storm.

In between, silence.

In between, sixteen years of inquiries, interviews, searches, notes, files, sixteen years of anguish and hopes raised and dashed, parental grief and then death and, now, terrible shock. Sixteen years of unanswered questions.

It made Serrailler feel as if he were ageing himself as he went through everything carefully, painstakingly, as if he were doing a fingertip search of the ground, but it also roused something in him which he recognised as the original passion he had felt for joining the force and moving to CID. It was difficult to pin down. Curiosity. Determination. The need for answers. The need to close ends. To make sense. To find not only solutions but explanations. The need to be ten steps ahead and several miles cleverer than those who committed appalling crimes. Day-to-day routine, too much desk time, meant that inevitably he lost sight of it but it was still there, and now he had it again, the focused passion to discover what had happened and put the whole puzzle together from a thousand small pieces. It was a cool and rational determination – if it had not been it would not have been of any use. But there was a spark too. His feelings had to be engaged in some way. The first spark had been lit when he had seen Harriet Lowther's pathetic skeleton in the mortuary; the second, even fiercer one, when he had broken the news to her father. And now the third. Harriet was alive to him, in these old photographs and newspaper reports.

She would have been thirty-one, an adult with her growing up behind her, possibly married with her own family.

He made more coffee and a ham sandwich then went back to stand at the window looking down on the close. People were walking about – lawyers and accountants going out to lunch, a couple with a pushchair, a woman carrying a pile of filing boxes. Cars driving slowly up and parking in front of various houses, some of which still belonged to the cathedral but were now mostly offices. It was odd to be here in the middle of a weekday.

Cat had phoned to tell him how John Lowther had been at the trustees meeting.

'He's seems broken. He's been living with it for all this time, not knowing. He must have felt in his heart that she was dead but there was always a thread of hope.'

'And I cut that.'

'In a way.'

'Oh, don't worry. I wouldn't be where I am if I ever blamed myself for being the messenger.'

And yet he did. Some part of him felt guilty.

He went back to the table and opened the file that contained the first interviews.

The mother of Harriet's friend Katie Cadsden.

Katie herself.

A man who had been clipping a hedge a few houses down from theirs and remembered Harriet walking past – he had moved his ladder for her and had smiled.

A van driver on the main road who had seen her standing at the bus stop.

60

The bus driver.

Passengers on the bus.

One of the passengers thought there had been two people at the stop, Harriet and a middle-aged woman. The bus driver did not remember.

The van driver a second time. The man clipping the hedge again. Sir John Lowther. His wife.

Harriet's teachers. Headmistress. Friends. The hairdresser. It was the usual stuff.

He leaned back and finished his coffee.

Mrs Frances Cadsden, age 44, Alflyn, Lea Close.

'Harriet often came over. We're lucky enough to have a tennis court – it's not in a very good state but they can get a game. She'd arranged to come that Friday and her mother dropped her off at about ten, I suppose. They went straight out to play. The dog was being a nuisance, chasing the ball, so Harriet brought him back into the house at some point. She had a drink of water and they played again.

'They had lunch. I made a cheese salad and there was some fruit cake and apples. Harriet was her usual self. Quite chatty. She's always very helpful, you know, clears the plates, puts things away. I like having her – some of Katie's other friends are pretty casual, never think of doing anything. Not Harriet. They went up to Katie's room with cans of Coke. Played music and so on. I could hear them talking. They had another game of tennis, and then Harriet had to go. She said she was catching the bus on Parkside Drive – they come about every half an hour – she'd done that before plenty of times. It's a handy bus, takes you right into the square. She was meeting her mother at the hairdresser, and they were going to buy a couple of things for school – I know she wanted a new cover for her tennis racket too, she was hoping they'd get that. But Harriet wasn't spoiled. She didn't just ask and get. I saw her off – stood and watched her go down the road . . . the man a few doors along was clipping his hedge and he moved his ladder for her to get by. She turned round and waved and then I went in. I didn't see her reach the corner. Well, I didn't need to. She's fifteen, they don't want to be made to feel like little children again, do they? That's all. She was fine, absolutely fine. Didn't seem to have anything on her mind, or to be worried. But she never does. She's just a normal girl. Like Katie. Just a lovely, normal girl.'

Ronald Pyment, age 60, Haven, Lea Close.

'I remember it all right. I was taking up a bit of the pavement with my ladder and I'd laid some tarpaulin on the ground to catch the hedge clippings. I was a bit in people's way but I was trying to get a move on and it's a quiet sort of road, not many walking by. Then she came along, been at the Cadsdens'. I'd seen her with their Katie. She had her tennis racket and bag – at least I think she had a bag. Wouldn't like to swear to that – could be wrong. Fair-haired lass, hair tied back. Nice sort of girl. Like Katie. I moved the ladder quickly so she didn't have to step into the road. She didn't say anything – I don't remember that she did – but she gave me a lovely smile, you know, a thank-you smile. Then she went on down the road and I went back to my hedge. I hope she's all right. Lovely girl. Hope nothing bad's happened to her.'

Neil Anthony Marshall, age 37, 20 Cherry Road.

'I drive for Reynard's Wholesale Greengrocer, Pitts Road, Bevham. I've been driving for them for about four years. I was in my van, taking a delivery of potatoes to Lafferton. I remember having to wait for a petrol lorry coming the other way down Parkside Drive and there was a post van at the kerb so I had to give way. I was near the bus stop opposite Lea Close. There was a young girl waiting at the stop, I remember seeing her, I remember she had a tennis racket and a bag. I think she had her hair tied back. I've seen the photos and I think it was her. It looks like her. But definitely she had a tennis racket and a bag. The bus wasn't there. I didn't see it in my rear mirror but I wasn't looking out for it. I just remember the girl. There was nobody else waiting at the bus stop when I saw her.'

The interviews with the Lowthers were painful to read, but as he did so, Serrailler felt Harriet emerging as a distinct person, not just a fifteen-year-old girl with blonde hair and a tennis racket. They had been sad that she was an only child but after various problems Eve Lowther had been unable to have more and they seemed anxious not to stifle Harriet, or to spoil her.

There were detailed photos of her room from every angle, full lists of her possessions down to the last hair clip, notes made by every officer who had talked to the Lowthers. The tension and strain mounted as every day went by without news. Simon could sense the strong thread of hope weakening. Then he came to the recordings of all the phone calls made to the special unit set up after Harriet's disappearance, those from people who were sure they had seen her in different parts of Lafferton, in a car, on a bus, on a train, in the town centre, with friends, with a man, with a group of men. The mad were there, and the vicious – easy to pick out, as were the sexual deviants. There were numerous friends of Harriet's anxious to say something, anything, that might be useful. 'She said she wanted to meet Rod Stewart one day. Maybe she went to London? Just thought I ought to say.' 'She met a boy. He goes to Roddington. I'd better not say his name – but Alistair Foster knows. Ask Al.'

A couple of weeks after Harriet's disappearance, the delivery driver, Neil Anthony Marshall, was interviewed again. There were discrepancies in his story, his van had been searched and a small stash of cannabis resin found, plus two boxes of new electrical spares which were identified as having been stolen. His employer said that although it was true Marshall had taken out a potato delivery, that had been on the Thursday. He had had no deliveries on the Friday at all.

Forensics had crawled all over the van but found nothing else and nothing to link Marshall to Harriet Lowther, but, probably because panic had started to creep in by then and the SIO, an Inspector David Clumber, wanted to show that they were being proactive, Marshall was again called to the station for questioning.

Simon pulled out the transcript of the interview.

But it was quarter to one and he had been reading the files since before nine.

Ten minutes later he had thrown on his running gear and was driving towards the Moor.

Twelve

It cost a lot of money. She had not expected it to be free but the amount was startling, and that was before she paid for her flight.

One-way ticket, Jocelyn thought, so that's a saving.

If she had been talking to Penny, to a friend – to anyone – she would have made that a joke. Gallows humour. But sitting alone at the small desk with her chequebook in front of her, and all the papers they had sent, the rows of printed facts, it was not a joke. Not funny. It was not possible to be flippant. She did not have to pretend to herself or put on a brave face. On the contrary, it seemed important not to do so.

The truth. That was all she had to hold on to and she must hold fast.

The truth.

The truth was that it cost a lot of money, but what else would she spend it on if she did not write this cheque?

A care home. Far more expensive.

A live-in help.

Not so expensive but absolutely out of the question. She had considered the idea of a nursing home or whatever else might be available and had found that there were indeed some things to be said in its favour as well as many against. There was nothing in favour of a live-in help. Some people might prefer it to moving into a home, but this house was so much her centre, almost her life, not just a roof and four walls. She could never share it with a stranger however discreet and pleasant.

Every time, she came back quite smoothly to where she was now, at her desk, in front of the wad of papers from Bene Mori, their website on her computer, her chequebook and pen.

The clinic put out everything in German so that you had to search for an English version. At first Jocelyn had used the auto-translation but that had converted some of the information into nonsense. Eventually, she had found 'English' written small, in a list of technical information at the bottom. She had downloaded the brochure and printed it off. She read it thoroughly several times before sending a cheque for 'membership' and a request for the 'Restricted' information.

After it had arrived, she had a new lock fitted on her desk drawer, and put the key inside the battery section tube of a broken electric toothbrush.

Penny had not phoned or been to see her, but that morning an email had come from her.

It has taken me these few days even to write this, I have been so shaken and upset. I wonder if you had any idea what effect your request would have. To be invited to supper by your mother, only to be told that she has an incurable illness is a shock, but at least you did tell me, when you might have tried to keep it to yourself. But how could you calmly sit there and not only say that you planned assisted suicide, but ask me to go with you, to be that 'assistant', that 'companion'? Some daughters – or sons – might bring themselves to do it, though I really don't know how. It made me sick even to think of it. The other objection, which I'm pretty sure didn't occur to you, is that I am a criminal barrister and what you propose to do is against the law here, though not in Switzerland. But accompanying someone, in the full knowledge that they intend to commit suicide on arrival at this clinic, is a criminal offence and although to date charges have not been brought, or if brought have been dropped, a member of the Bar would be struck off immediately if they undertook such an action. Did you know that?

I am too upset to write more now but please, Mother, please reconsider. You will have every help of any other kind

66

from me as you face this wretched illness but never that. Never, ever that. Put all this from your mind.

My case has another couple of days or possibly three but as soon as it's finished I'll come and see you. There will have been time for you to think and we can talk more calmly with this nonsense out of the way.

Much love, P

Nonsense.
Jocelyn looked calmly at the papers.

For legal reasons we do not give you the precise address of our clinic until just before you depart. You will be sent all details and also instruction of friendly hotels to stay at before and then of suitable taxis for your journey. You should not take any taxi, only these.

Our clinic is set in rural surroundings with beautiful tranquil woodland near to hand, Photo 1, and is well appointed and furnished for comfort and peace, Photo 2.

The image of the fields and small belt of trees with mountains in the far distance was pleasant but could be anywhere. There was, understandably, no photograph of the exterior of the clinic, but there was one she had looked at again and again – the Peace Room.

There was a bed, neatly made. A carpet. A rug. A window with the distant mountain-top view. A vase of what looked like wild flowers and branches on the sill. A small table with a lighted candle. Sunshine touching the wall.

Peace Room. She felt the tranquillity coming to her from the picture. There would be music playing softly – you were encouraged to take a CD of any music you chose, though there was a note that perhaps 'heavy rock' would not be very fitting, but it was up to you.

She would take her time in choosing. The right music would matter. The last music she would hear. Music to die to, she thought. But that did not sound right, that was disturbing, rather than comforting.

67

She looked not so much at but into the heart of the Peace Room on her computer screen now. The colours were right. The bedcover was violet blue, the walls a pale rose. The flowers were violet, blue, pink. But the overall impression was of the violet blue. The colour of hills in the evening.

All this peace and reassurance would be within her reach and her control. There would be no haste, no shock or distress, no anguish of a race in an ambulance, a clattering hospital ward, the scrape of curtains round a metal rail. Pain. Other people in charge. None of that. The time would be of her choosing, before she had lost her dignity and her will.

And Penny called it a nonsense.

Jocelyn pulled her cheque book nearer and picked up her pen, but writing was becoming difficult. She could not grip. The pen fell. She picked it up again and it fell again.

This was what she faced – and worse, so much worse. She had all but fallen that morning, her left leg suddenly heavy and not obeying her mind properly but shuffling itself over the step into the kitchen. How she had not pitched forward she did not know. She had grabbed at the wall and somehow managed to stay upright, but another time she might have crashed onto the tiled floor and knocked herself out, broken an arm, lain in agony or even unconscious. It was the dread of all the elderly living alone and becoming frail or unsteady, but this was nothing to do with age, this was IT. She had started to call her illness IT.

She had a card on the desk. An MRI scan and an appointment with the neurologist.

Was there any point in going? She already knew what was important to know – what IT was and that there was neither treatment nor cure, just a railway track on which she would be propelled forward. No getting off. No stops. No relief. Nothing. Just on, steadily, relentlessly on down the preordained route.

She was worth more than that. Her life was worth more. Worth a better death.

But she could not go to Switzerland alone. She would not be admitted, even if she had the courage. Penny could not go, of course – it had not occurred to her that she could be struck off for doing so and how could she ever be responsible for that?

Could not go, would not go. So who would? How in the world could one ask this of even the closest, dearest friend? And she had no close, dear friends. All her life, she had had a few people she liked, whose company she enjoyed, with whom she kept in touch, went to the theatre or on a day's outing. They were friends, she supposed, but not close. Not what she had heard called 'friends of the heart'. She had not quite known what was meant by it, but now she needed to find out.

Thirteen

Fretfield was a village that had grown, as many around Lafferton had, but its centre was still recognisable as belonging to the country rather than the town. Maytree House was on the southern edge, and as she drove towards it, Cat remembered that it had once been a small convent school – she had had a couple of friends who went there and whose days were subtly different from her own, marked out by the angelus bell, catechism lessons and fish-on-Fridays. She had once stood inside the front hall and been riveted by the sight of the colourful statues of the Virgin Mary and the Sacred Heart.

'Yes, it's all quite fun being an idolater,' her father had said when she had described them. 'Apart from Hell of course.' She had not dared to ask more.

It looked superficially the same as she approached down the long drive, but the evergreen trees had been felled and the laurel and other dark shrubs cleared so that the whole place was now open to the fields and the distant view of Starly Tor. The school and convent signs had long gone, the whole place had been painted and the ugly prefabricated classroom extension at the side demolished. The gravel tennis and netball courts had gone too. She realised what a handsome house it was without the utilitarian trappings.

But the outside area was a mess of builders, vans and equipment, with half-built walls, cement mixers and a site office occupying most of it.

As she walked from the car, Cat saw that a man was standing in the open doorway. Behind him, an empty hall, ladders, painters, light.

'Dr Deerbon?'

He was totally bald, not, she thought, from ageing or being shaved but from alopecia. He was handsome, though, enough to distract from his baldness within a few seconds.

'Leo Fison. Come in – it isn't as bad as it looks from here. The builders have almost finished actually.'

She remembered somewhere dark and wood-panelled but now the house was full of light. Walls had been knocked down and in the main sitting room a wide bow window opened out onto the garden. The place was empty and smelled of fresh paint.

'We want it to be as little like an institution as possible. There will be smaller rooms down here – a separate one for television, one for crafts and memory activities . . . several occupational therapists.' He led the way into a new conservatory which looked towards the Tor.

'I wish everyone with dementia who needed to live somewhere like this, could.'

'I know. Cost. Money. I've been talking to people in the local authority but the chances of getting any fully funded places are growing smaller every day. I dislike the idea that I will be caring only for the well off.'

'But the well off are still people and those with dementia have equal needs. Look at it that way.'

His smile was immediate and had a great sweetness. 'I try to. And you're right.' They were heading towards the staircase. 'Up here are patients' rooms, staff quarters, nursing station. Utility rooms are all on the ground floor – we've built an extension on the back for kitchen, laundry, all of that. And a big staffroom where I hope they will be able to relax and switch off, even during a tea break. It's vital.'

There was the sound of banging and the smell of new carpet as they walked along.

'When will you open?'

'I hope we can welcome the first residents by the end of

71

the month. Once the decorators are out of the main house, we can get the furniture in – it'll come together very quickly. The builders will just have a bit of outside work to complete. Would you like some coffee? There isn't much more to see but I would like to know if you've any suggestions – I'm trying to see as many GPs as I can and people from the hospital too if they can come over. Your input will be important. The point is that there are any number of general care homes but this is the first to cater solely for dementia sufferers and to focus on their very specific needs. It's a growing problem . . . well, I don't need to tell *you*.'

He led the way back to the ground floor and down a side corridor.

'We've bought the house next door – you can see it from here. We moved in a month ago so at least home is now a home. This is my office – shambles still.'

He pushed papers off a chair.

John Lowther had suggested that she come here, see the new facilities, and at the same time form an opinion about Fison as possible head of the new hospice committee. She watched him as he made their coffee, talking all the time about what he called his mission, not only to provide dementia care but to move practical work with sufferers forward. From what he had been saying Cat gathered that he saw himself as a specialist and even something of a pioneer.

Given all of which it seemed unlikely that he would have the time or the inclination to take on another role. Whether he would be right for that role she decided she could not tell. Fund-raising on a professional level was not her area of expertise.

But she liked Leo Fison, she thought, as she drove away, and she liked what she had heard of his plans, as well as the potential of the house. It had a good feel.

She was still thinking about it as she headed back, first to do a grocery shop, then to Imogen House after lunch, for a clinical meeting. The country road wound round the Moor, single track in places, and as she stopped and reversed a few yards into a gateway to let a tractor pass, she saw Simon and hooted.

He had already slowed to a jog.

72

'Hey! Why aren't you at work?'

'Same to you.' He opened the car door and got in. 'I was heading over there.'

Cat looked at fluttering tape stretched between the plastic posts.

'Have you got a few minutes?'

She parked beside his Audi, and together they scrambled up the muddy section of track.

'Is this a crime scene?'

'Officially. But forensics have combed it for days and pretty much done – there won't be anything else to find, especially not after the rain we've had since.'

They reached the area where the soil had been flattened down. Below, out of sight, came the rumble of traffic on the bypass. Above them, two buzzards soared lazily, wings flat, like the sails of a windmill. They were on the edge of the first clumps of trees.

Simon stood looking down, then turned and looked up at the Moor. Turned back.

Cat put a hand on his arm. 'It's gone, Si. It can't tell you anything else.'

'It has to. I've got that feeling I've had so often before. If I stand long enough I'll know. It will tell me. Do you understand? Somehow it's here. I need to hear it or see it . . . what I have to know is here somewhere.'

'No. It was once. If there were any secrets, they'll have them.'

He sighed. 'It gets me every time.'

'It's also a long time ago. You were lucky they could identify her at all.'

'I know.'

'What about the other body?'

'There's a request out. Girls gone missing around the same time as Harriet, and still unaccounted for. Every force will check. Something could come out of it. Not that discovering who she is will necessarily move us forward to who killed her and why.'

The wind blew fine rain into their faces.

'Time for a quick pub lunch?'

She was going to say no, that she ought to do the supermarket run before her meeting, but then she looked again at her brother's face. He was troubled by this case, beginning to be obsessed by it, as he sometimes was, fiercely determined to focus on nothing else until he reached the solution and could close it for good. It would eat into his sleep and dreams as well as occupy most of his waking hours.

'Yes,' she said. 'Where's nearest?'

'Churchill Arms. Race you to the cars.'

He was well ahead of her, long legs taking the slope easily. Cat had no intention of slipping on her backside by trying to outrun him and he was putting on his warm kit by the time she reached level ground.

The pub was quiet. They had bowls of thick lentil and tomato soup, with grated cheese, doorsteps of home-made bread. Simon leaned his back against the bench and eased his shoulders forward a few times.

'Why don't you take a holiday? Your back always plays up when you need a break.'

'Ha. But there's a treat coming up – feel like helping me enjoy it?'

'I don't think I trust you.'

'Wise woman. Next Tuesday night. Big banquet given by the Lord Lieutenant. The Chief has appointed me to go in her place.'

'Since when did you need your sister to hold your hand at deadly social functions? I can't – you know Tuesday night is choir night.'

'Oh come on, you go every Tuesday.'

'Precisely. I need to. We're doing some Berlioz and it's hard. Ask a proper date.'

'Do you think Judith would come?'

'And your stepmother is a proper date? Are you losing your touch?'

But seeing the closed expression drop down like a portcullis over his features, she bent her head to her soup and said nothing more.

They drank their coffee and Cat got up. 'Chores beckon.'

'So do cold case files.'

'Don't let it get to you, Si.'

'What, that I'm getting too old to pull?'

'I didn't say that and you know it.'

He kissed her on the cheek and turned away. Damn, Cat thought. In spite of their closeness, one chance remark and he shut her out. Dear God, why don't I learn?

All the same, she was not going to try to win him round by agreeing to give up St Michael's Singers to be his partner at a banquet of dignitaries.

As she got her supermarket trolley a text message came through.

What's Molly's Mob no?

She cursed as she pressed reply. *Don't even think it.*

There was no answer.

He smiled to himself most of the way home, knowing he had wound Cat up and that she would fret all the way round the supermarket in case he had been serious.

Had he? The thought of taking Molly to the banquet was a pleasing one, but he drew the line at a twenty-four-year-old with a boyfriend, even as his partner for a single evening.

It was his sister's dig at his single status that annoyed him. It was a while since Kirsty on the Scottish island, Kirsty now married to Douglas – he had had a cheery email and a wedding photograph. Simon wished them well and was entirely without envy.

He ran up the stairs to his flat, changed, showered, made coffee and then rang into the station. The message about the second skeleton had gone out and replies were coming in from other forces, detailing young women who had gone missing around the same time as Harriet Lowther and who had never been found. There were enough of them and each case would have to be followed up. Tomorrow, he would go in and try once again to get a team together, now that he had the nod from the Chief.

Today, he was still on his own, so he worked through the rest of the files on Harriet, then listed people he wanted to interview himself.

He wrote:

John Lowther
Cadsdens
White van man
Bus driver
Hedge clipper
Who else?

Needle. And not even much of a haystack.

Fourteen

Pam started to cry, and after a few moments Jocelyn had to hold the receiver away so as not to hear her stumbled words buried in sobs and odd little choking noises.

She had written it all very carefully in a letter, reading it over twice and then rewriting it in what they had called 'best' when they were at school together. She and Pam went as far back as that.

The phone call had come in the early evening. Pam had had the day to think about Jocelyn's request but in fact she had not, she said, been able to think about it at all, she had torn the letter into pieces and thrown it in the rubbish, then retrieved and burned it instead.

'I have never been so upset. I honestly don't believe I have. I've been shaking all day.'

'My dear, you should have rung earlier, or just come here. I didn't intend it to upset you like this.'

'So what did you intend?' But the crying had begun before Jocelyn could answer.

'I'm sorry. Let's just forget it, forget the whole thing, Pam.'

'You ask me to . . . as if you wanted us to go out for a day in the country or something. You've changed our entire relationship . . . you've destroyed a friendship of over fifty years. Doesn't it occur to you?'

It had not, but clearly for Pam things between them would never be the same.

Somehow, she blurted out a few more apologies and came off the phone. She made a pot of tea and took it out to the conservatory, though it was a grey and dismal outlook.

She would ask no one else. If her daughter and her oldest friend had reacted so badly, leaving her feeling both guilty and disturbed, there could be no more attempts.

But she was not going to change her own plans. She had burrowed deeper into the Internet and braced herself to read some personal accounts of those who had had relatives die of MND – what its progress had been, how they had worsened, how they had died – and they had only served to strengthen her determination. Waiting until she could no longer speak or swallow, and then breathe, was out of the question. She was not brave enough. Yes, she thought now, that's what it was. A question of bravery. What she planned required far less courage.

It was not until later that she found the newspaper, on the floor with a pile others to be put out for recycling. As she bent to move them she saw the photograph and the headline, which she must surely have read at the time without much interest. The paper was several weeks old, from what she had come to think of as 'the time before' – the time before the symptoms had appeared. In her old life.

SUICIDE DOCTOR KILLED IN ROAD ACCIDENT
Dr Thomas Thorne, a retired GP who accompanied a number of patients to a Swiss clinic and helped them commit suicide, was killed yesterday in a multiple accident on the M4. Dr Thorne had freely admitted to going to the Bene Mori clinic and said in an interview, 'I would do it again, if I was asked. So long as I am satisfied that the patient is of sound mind and suffering from an incurable terminal illness, if they wish me to go with them and help them, I will gladly do so. My conscience is quite clear.' Dr Thorne, who was 72 . . .

She went upstairs. She took great care now when having her bath, aware that her balance or the movement of her legs could let her down, not filling it too full or allowing the water to be too hot.

But tonight, she had no trouble, and she managed to turn the taps on and off without too much of a struggle. For how much longer?

Dr Thomas Thorne was in her mind the whole time. She could not ask him for assistance now, but she could surely find someone else, somewhere, a doctor or someone similar who was willing to help people in her situation. It relieved her mind. Presumably it would be a business arrangement – certainly all fares paid and probably a 'fee' – and she felt much happier about that, she realised, than she had about asking someone she knew.

What could be simpler or more efficient? It did not much matter to her that she would travel with a stranger and that she would draw her last breath among strangers, see strange faces last of all. They would not show distress or have any reason to try and deter her at the last minute, she would not feel guilt or face their tears. Problem solved. She slept.

And woke at four thirty. Problem solved? So what must she do? Advertise?

'Congenial companion wanted to travel with terminally ill lady to . . .'

'Friend wanted to assist . . .'

'Wanted. Discreet person to . . .'

She got up and went downstairs. The house was silent. She looked through the curtain at the outside. It was never very busy but now, deserted under the street lights, it looked like a street in a black-and-white photograph.

Once, she had had a cat, never especially affectionate or companionable, but a presence in the house, something else that moved and breathed, and she longed for it now, sleeping curled on the kitchen chair, or at the foot of her bed.

The kettle whistled.

A moment later, boiling water was all over the floor. She was not badly scalded but only because she had jumped back as she had dropped the kettle, out of a hand that had suddenly ceased to work.

She sat at the table, frightened. Something else. She was not safe to make tea in her own kitchen.

She knew that the progress of her disease was unpredictable but that at any time she might find that a particular symptom had become very much worse very quickly. Today, her grip was weakening, tomorrow, she might find her walking much more unsteady, or that she had difficulty speaking or swallowing. No one could tell her what exactly would or would not happen next or how long it would all take, but, sitting here at the kitchen table, with hot water dripping onto the floor, Jocelyn knew that if she was to make arrangements to travel, it had to be done soon.

She went into the sitting room, noticing that she was shuffling slightly. Was that because she was afraid to trip over the carpet and so shuffled deliberately, or because she could not now walk any other way?

It took twenty minutes of working her way through the wrong websites to find what she needed. She had to register, re-register and then be sent from one site, which was clearly just a front, to another, where she registered again and had to enter and confirm two passwords. But in the end, she was a member of the forum, joined by those who wanted to share information, as well as feelings and thoughts, about assisted suicide. There were people who had already been to Switzerland and who had said goodbye to friends on the forum, others who had taken relatives and were returning to share the experience. She read one or two posts but then went on searching. It was some time before she found a protected area, for which she had to register again.

But then, she was there. She had found it.

Q. I have terminal cancer and I am planning to end my life with dignity and at a time of my choice. I cannot ask anyone in my family to accompany me. Does anyone know of a doctor or nurse who might travel and assist me?
Sandra

A. Hello, Sandra. There are several members of the medical and caring professions who are members here and would be able to help with your enquiry. Please send a private message (PM) to the forum administrator quoting the reference number beside this reply.
Mike (Moderator)

She was suddenly overcome with tiredness and a great wave of relief. She bookmarked the page, closed down, and went back to bed. There was no light in the sky yet.

She slept until after nine o'clock and woke with a feeling of having settled her future.

Fifteen

Dougal Crawford and John Fryer, two of the oldest DCs at Lafferton, were both accepting the early retirement package and leaving within a month. Fryer would not be greatly missed. He kept his head down, was rarely to be found away from his desk and never took the initiative. If anyone had routine paperwork they wanted to escape from, Fryer would always take it on. He had transferred from uniform as a keen young officer and the keenness had evaporated the moment he walked into the CID room. Dougal was an old hand, experienced, methodical, but with a nose for a crime and a suspect, and Serrailler had hoped to persuade him onto what might eventually be a team investigating the cold cases. Now there was little point. Dougal would be gone just as he dug into the inquiry.

This morning, after exchanging files, Simon found the CID room empty except for DS Ben Vanek and Fryer, face, as ever, at his computer screen.

'John . . . any chance you could do a bit of digging for me? I'm trying to trace a man who drove a van sixteen years ago.'

Fryer shook his head without glancing round. 'Sorry, guv, got this known dealers file to sort.' Which meant checking old addresses and prison records and updating them, and Fryer would rather plod along doing that than be given a new, more complicated task.

'I'm free,' Ben Vanek said, pushing his chair back. 'I slipped chasing a villain down the underpass in the rain and I'm on desk duty, only there doesn't seem to be much going on. Everyone's out crawling over the Dulcie estate, except Steph, and she's waiting at BG for someone either to come round or to die.'

'Thanks, Ben. Honestly, these blasted drug ops drain our resources and for what? How much difference do we make? How many kids do we stop from getting hold of them? OK, subject for another day. If you can trace this guy, find out if he's still on our patch, at the same address and so on . . . If he is, you can come with me to talk to him. Could take you five minutes, could take all day.'

Simon opened up his computer and checked out a few things, then headed down the stairs, wanting coffee but not from the canteen; as he reached the main doors, though, he heard Ben Vanek call him. Simon shouted for him to follow over the road and round the corner to the Cypriot café.

'Word the other day was that canteen takings are right down,' Ben said, catching him up.

'The day they make the Cypriot out of bounds is the day I hand in my warrant card. Canteen would buck up its profits if it didn't serve muck out of that urn.'

There were usually two or three CID in the small, busy café but today it only held two mothers with pushchairs.

'Double espresso, one cappuccino, coming up.'

They went to the table in the window. Ben Vanek had been with the force a couple of years now and he had shaped up well. Serrailler had thought him naive at first and had been irritated when the sergeant had followed him about like a puppy. But his romance with DC Steph Mead had blossomed and they had moved into a flat together. Some of her feistiness and ambition had rubbed off on him, though not, Simon was pleased to note, any of her attitude. And Vanek had stopped wearing weird ties and had abandoned his terrible black leather jacket.

'You got something?' Serrailler sipped his coffee and scalded his lip. The Cypriot brothers did not serve anything weak or lukewarm. 'Or just fancied a halloumi cheese butty?'

'You said maybe five minutes and it wasn't much more. Neil Marshall, white van driver. Aged fifty-three now. 20 Cherry Road, Langlands.'

83

'That's handy. Still work for the wholesale greengrocer?'

'Doesn't say, but I doubt it, guv. He's on the Sex Offenders' Register.'

Serrailler whistled. 'Is he now?'

'Went down for kiddie-fiddling seven years ago. Cautioned once before that but not charged. On the register since 2004.'

'Surprised he still lives at the same address then. They usually get as far away as possible – neighbours hate them, they never feel safe.'

He filled Ben in on the Lowther case as they had their second coffees. A couple of the civilian staff came in but no other officers.

'Can I work on this with you, guv? I'm cheesed off with sitting at my desk all day filling in forms for other people.'

'But not cheesed off with the drugs op?'

Ben made a face.

'Good. I've got the nod from the Chief for a team – trouble is, I can't get one together, there aren't enough spare bods. You're a start though. Get the file and read up the interviews with Marshall from '95. Then we'll nip over and see if he's at home.'

'There's a nasty rumour going round, guv,' Ben Vanek said as they drove out.

'Let me guess . . . we're losing half of uniform and two-thirds of CID.'

'We might close altogether, merge with Bevham.'

Serrailler was silent.

'Guv?'

'Listen, I don't know any more than you.'

'But what do you reckon?'

'It'd be a last resort. How could a place the size of Lafferton not have its own station, and be served from a city fifteen miles away?'

'Public wouldn't buy it?'

'There'd be riots in the streets.'

Ben relaxed in his seat.

'Set the rumours flying and they'll find an open window.'

Simon, though, was less sure than he sounded. A merger with Bevham was unlikely, but after what he had heard about the savings that had to be found, he wasn't fool enough to rule it out. But if it ever happened, he thought his own police days might be over.

'Not so long ago, I'd have had half a dozen bods on these cases and now it's all I can do to get you for a morning. Still, if things really hot up the Chief has promised she'll find a way to give me what I need.'

'Looks like they might be hotting up. This Marshall guy has to be in the frame again now, doesn't he?'

'One man on the SOR doesn't make a summer. Right, it's somewhere in this maze of bungaloid streets.'

They toured around for several minutes, swinging right and left, backing out of cul-de-sacs. No one was about apart from a window cleaner and a couple of dogs.

'How's Steph liking the drugs op?'

'No accounting for taste. She loves it. Getting dealers off the streets and kids off the drugs is her mission. Reckon she'll head up the squad before she's thirty. She made herself unpopular with a couple of uniform though – they were apparently all for making drugs legal and she got into a bit of a strop.'

'There is an argument for decriminalising them. Not sure I support it but there's a case to be made.'

Ben shook his head. 'Thing is, guv, there's the soft drugs and – that was Cherry Road, you just passed it – back, then first left.'

'Discreet,' Serrailler said. 'Out of sight of nosy neighbours.'

But Marshall had seen them draw up. The front door opened and he all but hustled them inside.

'Thought you'd be here,' he said. He led them into a cramped front room, made more cramped by a bulky leather sofa and armchair, and a table on which stood a large half-completed balsa-wood model of St Paul's Cathedral. More pieces were piled around on sheets of paper, with tiny pots of enamel paint, a jar of brushes, glue, card. The room smelled of it.

Serrailler had his warrant card out but Marshall waved at it. 'You think I don't know you lot a mile off? What is it? Way you walk maybe.'

He was a nondescript man, average height, mid-brown hair,

rimless glasses. The only notable thing about him was his thinness. Ben Vanek was reminded of a character in a children's book he had had, a boy so flat he could slide under doors and post himself in an envelope. If Marshall stood sideways, he almost disappeared.

He gestured to them to sit down, then went to the table, picked up a knife and piece of balsa and bent over the model. He studied it in silence for a few seconds, then placed the wood delicately to one side of the great roof.

'Glue dries,' he said, 'if I leave it.'

'You've got a lot of patience.'

'Have to.'

Serrailler studied the model. As far as he could see there was not a hair out of true. It was a painstaking piece of work, apparently done entirely from an enlarged photograph of the cathedral that was laid out on the table.

'I know what you've come about,' Marshall said, meeting his eye. 'Well, I would.'

'Yes.'

'I've never forgotten her, you know. Might have been yesterday. Clear as yesterday. It just doesn't happen, does it? You see a girl at a bus stop – next thing, she's vanished off the face of the earth. Just doesn't happen.'

'Unfortunately, it does.'

'Still, it's something, I suppose, finding her body. Something for her family.'

'Something. But not everything.'

'Do you want a cup of tea?'

'No thanks.'

'I knew you'd be round here, even without me being on the register. Got nothing to do with it though.'

'Hasn't it?'

Marshall looked up and met Ben Vanek's eye this time.

'Nope. Done my time, learned my lesson. Only it's like tar rubbed into your skin. Never leaves you. Every time I go out.'

'Is there a Mrs Marshall?'

'Buggered off with my best mate, once it all came out.'

'Do you work?'

86

'Who employs people like me?'

'Forget all that,' Serrailler said. 'You say you remember Harriet Lowther very clearly . . . that day you saw her at the bus stop.'

'Vivid. Close my eyes, she's there.'

'Describe it.'

Marshall cut across a triangular piece of balsa, then laid down the knife. But he did not move from the table.

'I used to drive for Reynard's Wholesale Greengrocer. Drove for them, what, twelve years? It was a Friday. I was in Parkside Drive . . . there was a traffic hold-up, not sure why . . . that's one thing I'm not so clear about. Bit blurry. I mean, I drove all day, every day. But I was held up. And she was at the bus stop, by herself. I can see her now.'

'You noticed young girls a lot then?'

Serrailler shot Ben a look.

Marshall bent over the model and with a pair of tweezers, laid the triangular piece of balsa onto the roof. 'Haven't you been through my record with a nit comb, then?' He stood upright. 'Because if not, maybe you should.'

'What are you trying to say, Mr Marshall?'

'Back to the bus stop.' Serrailler interrupted quickly. 'Can you describe her?'

'Oh yes. Clear as clear. About fourteen, fifteen – young teenage. Fair hair, really fair, like Scandinavian, you know, and tied back. She was carrying a tennis racket in one of those covers. She might have had another bag, I'm not sure. It was her face I remember. She had this look.'

'Look?'

'Listen, this'll sound – well, after the event, you know? I mean, when I saw the photos of her in the papers. But I don't think it is. She had – an expression. Happy. You don't see people look happy, just plain happy, do you? They look worried, they look worn down, they're frowning, or maybe laughing out loud . . . but this was – just happy. I remember it.'

'Did she catch the bus?'

'Not that I saw. Next thing, road was clear and I was on my way.'

'Thought no more about it?' Vanek said.

Marshall shook his head. 'You're wrong there. I thought about it. I had her happy face in my mind on and off all day. Just this blonde-haired girl with a happy face. Kept me going, you know? And not in the way you're thinking. Not in that way at all.'

'And you didn't see anyone with her, approaching her, talking to her?'

'No. She was on her own.'

'Did you see the bus draw up?'

'No.'

'Is there anything else at all you remember?'

'No. Just her. I wished I bloody well had. When I read about her. Wished I'd seen her get on the bus or not get on the bus – wished I'd seen anything. But I didn't. What happened to her?' he asked Serrailler. 'What the hell happened to the poor kid?'

'It's my job to find out.'

'Wish I'd seen something else.'

'You didn't stop and talk to her?' Vanek asked.

Marshall turned. 'No. I did not.'

'Give her a lift, maybe? Pretty young girl who caught your eye, couldn't get her out of your mind. Didn't maybe go back and pick her up?'

'No. I did not.'

Serrailler put his card on the table beside the model. 'If you remember anything else – even something very small and you think of no significance – please ring me.' He bent again to look closely at the model. 'It's good,' he said. 'From just a photograph.'

'Yes, well, I have a lot of time on my hands, don't I? Started doing it inside. It got to me.'

'Keep them all in the attic, do you?' Vanek asked.

'I don't. They get auctioned. Raise money.'

'Oh yes?'

'Children in Need. Nine thousand pounds in six years, if you want to know.'

'That's sick,' the sergeant said getting into the car. 'Children in Need!'

'So what would you rather he did? Stuff them in the attic like you said?'

'Might choose a different good cause. You know, cancer or something.'

'Maybe he thinks he's still paying. Still trying to make it good.'

Vanek sniffed. 'I shouldn't say it, but I hate paedophiles.'

'That much,' Simon said, putting his foot down, 'is obvious. Don't let it cloud your judgement.'

'So you reckon he's in the clear?'

'I don't think he killed Harriet Lowther. I don't think he went back or spoke to her or gave her a lift. But that's just my hunch. He's still on my list.'

Vanek's phone rang. He made a face. 'Can you make a detour to the Eric Anderson, guv? Drop me by the underpass?'

'Am I losing you to this bloody drugs op?'

'Nah. Don't forget my bad foot. Only they want me to do an ID.'

'Get them to bring you back then.'

As they pulled up, Ben said, 'Sorry.'

'What for?'

'I was a bit out of order there.'

'Listen, Ben. Paedophiles are a grubby bunch. But don't turn a distaste into a blind prejudice, that's all.'

'Guv.'

At the station, it took Serrailler only a few minutes to find details of all the charges against Marshall. He had been convicted on four counts of indecent assault, and asked for a number of others to be taken into consideration. He had pleaded guilty on all counts. Each one of the offences was against boys, aged between eight and twelve.

Simon sent an internal email to Ben Vanek, picked up more files, and left, not driving straight home but to Hallam House, where there was an unfamiliar car parked next to Judith's blue Polo in the drive. He was about to leave again when he saw his stepmother at the kitchen window, waving.

'Are you here for lunch?'

'No, I'm off home to get my head down to work, but I wanted to ask you something.'

'Well, at least have a drink – beer? Whatever. Come into the sitting room and say hello to Emma.'

Emma.

She stood up and held out her hand. A small, very slender woman with pretty features, pretty auburn hair, a pretty smile. Her eyes were thoughtful.

'Do you want a beer?'

'Better not. Is it too late for coffee? I'll do it.'

'No, talk to Emma about her new bookshop in the Lanes.'

'Will you excuse me?' he said to Emma. 'I need to ask Judith something before I forget.'

He would not have forgotten. But somehow he did not want to be alone in the sitting room with this disturbingly pretty woman.

In the kitchen, Judith said warningly: 'Simon?'

'No, listen. Could you do me a huge favour?'

'Try me.'

He told her about the banquet.

'I can't get out of it, Cat won't give up her choir night –'

'And we're going to stay with the Devereux in Oxford – they're taking us to see *Iolanthe*, which, as you know, always makes your father twenty years younger. I just can't.'

'Bugger. Sorry.'

Judith nodded in the direction of the sitting room.

'Divorced,' she whispered.

He made a face at her, but, when his coffee was ready, took it through and chatted to Emma.

'Lafferton,' he said, 'needs a good bookshop. Waterstone's closed, the old independent closed – all we have is one anti-quarian and W.H. Smith. But you're brave, aren't you?'

'I'm terrified. But I was manager of a branch of Blackwell's in Edinburgh for seven years. I wouldn't forgive myself if I didn't give it a serious try.'

'Which premises?'

'Where the expensive shoe and handbag shop used to be. I gather it didn't last long. I'd have been open now but of course the floods have set everything back. Thank God I hadn't moved in any stock – just some shelving and that will be OK with fresh paint. The floor suffered though. I've had to replace that.'

'Will you specialise?'

'No. But I'm going to have a book club, some author events, children's story mornings. And try to stock books you don't find everywhere. I'd like to surprise people – challenge them even.'

She was very relaxed, with a confidence he found attractive. And she was pretty. How old? Late forties?

He wondered about the banquet.

Judith called, 'Are you staying for lunch?'

Was he?

He stood up. 'Thanks, but I mustn't. I'm short-handed and I've got six hours' worth of files in the car.'

'Are you on the inquiry into the bodies of those poor girls? Sorry, you probably can't answer. I don't know about police protocol.'

'It's fine. Yes, I am.'

'It makes me want to weep. Some young woman disappears for years and no one notices she's missing? That can't be right. Surely to God there's a parent, a partner? How old was she?'

'Probably a bit older than Harriet Lowther.'

'Is there a connection between them?'

Simon shrugged and put out his hand. Emma's was very smooth, and cool.

Could he ask a woman he had barely met to a banquet?

He said, 'I'll come in and buy some books.'

'Please do. I'm opening Tuesday week, assuming no further floods.' She smiled. A nice smile.

As he kissed Judith at the door, she gave him a sharp look but said only, 'Lovely to see you, darling. And I wish I could have come with you.'

'I'll find someone,' Simon said.

Sixteen

Did the house smell of cat? Lenny went outside. It was drizzling a bit and she held onto the rail so as not to fall. Falling was one of the few things she feared, falling and lying there undiscovered, perhaps for days.

She filled her lungs with the damp air and went back into the cottage.

There was the faintest smell of cat. But female cats only smelled if you did not remember to let them out. She must remember. She had read about cat flaps but disliked the thought of having an entrance to the house that she could not control.

And then the telephone started. She was on her way into the music room and had to go all the way back.

It stopped as she reached it.

She returned to the music room. It was still called the music room though no one played there now apart from herself. But she played. So she would continue to call it the music room. Yes.

She closed the door and drew the velour curtain to keep out the draught, switched on the lamp.

There was a Beethoven sonata on the stand but she rummaged in the pile on the floor. The floor, the piano itself, the table, the window ledge. Satie. She wanted to play Satie. Where was Satie?

The phone was ringing again. Then stopped again. She'd been told there was a way you could find out who had rung you, but what was it? Who knew?

It did not ring again but the doorbell did.

'Leonora Wilcox? Packet to sign for.'

Miss Wilcox to you, she would have corrected once upon a time. But you gave up. She couldn't be bothered.

The package was music but not Satie.

The phone rang.

'Miss Wilcox?'

The cat was weaving round her ankles.

'This is Sister Moss from Babbacombe House.'

Sister Moss. They called themselves Matron this and Sister that, Nurse the other. But were they?

'Yes?'

'Is this a good time for us to have a word? It's about Olive.'

What else would it be about?

'Is she all right?'

Lenny knew there was trouble.

'This is not very easy, I'm afraid.'

'What's she done?'

'We need you to come down here. To discuss everything.'

'Everything? How can we do that?'

'It isn't really very suitable to talk about it on the telephone, but . . .'

Lenny listened. Just let the woman talk. She had known it was trouble.

Trouble.

The woman who called herself Sister finished at last and Lenny put the phone down. It was tiresome. They were paid enough and now they couldn't cope. She knew what was coming.

'We're very much afraid . . .'

. She had said she would drive down there tomorrow. So that was what she would do.

She found Satie and started to play and could not stop playing and suddenly it was afternoon. That was what happened. But she felt calmer. Better. Satie did that. She wasn't angry now.

Lenny ate a tin of pilchards and a tomato and went to sleep.

Seventeen

The man clipping the hedge had died ten years earlier.

'Don't think he was going to give us anything new but it would have been tidy. Cadsdens?'

'Found them. They divorced and she moved to Angus Road. No other occupant on the electoral roll.'

'The bus driver?'

'Retired to Scarborough to live near his daughter. Still there.'

'Scarborough.' They had not been far from there when he had stood on a rock with a fierce tide coming in and he had clung to a child murderer for what had felt like days while the 202 Squadron Sea King helicopter had hovered overhead and the pilot tried to determine how dangerous it would be to winch them aboard. Simon could close his eyes and feel the spray on his face, hear the roar of the chopper engine above his head. Cliffs. Cliffs and caves and fast incoming tides.

It was not a part of the country he was anxious to visit again.

'Nice trip,' Vanek said.

'No money for seaside treats. Phone.'

'Oh, guv . . .'

'If the bus driver saw Harriet get into a blue Vauxhall Astra driven by a man in dark glasses we'll go. Otherwise, phone.'

'A blue Vauxhall As—'

'Oh, for God's sake.'

'Ah, I get you.'

'For a bright-ish DS you can be very slow.'

Ben Vanek looked embarrassed. 'Shall I go and talk to Mrs Cadsden?'

'No, *we* will. But I'll call the bus driver myself – what was his name? Johnson. Charlie Johnson.'

'I've just emailed the number across to you.'

'Thanks.'

Simon went back to his office. He hadn't meant to come down so hard on the sergeant and he was annoyed with himself.

'Good morning. My name is Simon Serrailler – Detective Chief Superintendent Serrailler from Lafferton CID. I'd like to speak to Mr Charles Johnson if that's possible.'

A woman had answered. Middle-aged. Yorkshire accent.

'Where did you say?'

He told her again.

'Well, Dad hasn't lived down in Lafferton for seven going on eight years.'

'Yes, I do know he retired and moved away. Who am I speaking to?'

'Ann Sharp. Mrs Sharp. I'm Charlie Johnson's daughter.'

'Mrs Sharp, I do need to speak to your father if I may. If he isn't with you perhaps you could give me a contact number? I'm investigating the –'

'No.'

'Sorry?'

'You can't speak to him. Dad had a stroke four months back. He hasn't left hospital. He can't speak, he can't move. He understands, and he knows us. He's not – he's all there. But he couldn't answer any questions, and apart from anything else, I wouldn't let him. I wouldn't let him be upset by anyone from the police.'

'I see. I'm very sorry. But it just might be that we would need to talk to your father at some point, Mrs Sharp. It depends on the progress of our inquiries. If it were necessary, I might need to ask him just one or two questions . . . you say he can under-stand? Just a nod or a movement of his hand, for yes or no — '

'What's Dad supposed to have done, for goodness' sake?'

'Nothing at all. But he was a witness some years ago now. A

95

young girl was waiting at the stop for a bus he was driving and —'

'But he hasn't driven a bus for eight, nine years.'

'I know. This was sixteen years ago. A young girl went missing – she was due to catch his bus but she didn't.'

'Well, that can't have been Dad's fault, can it?'

'No. There's no suggestion of that.'

'Was he not spoken to at the time? How come you're ringing now?'

'Yes, he was, he gave a full statement.'

'Then he wouldn't have anything else to say, would he? Dad's an honest man and he's very ill too and I wouldn't give any sort of permission to you to come mithering him. You could kill him. Have you thought of that?'

Simon fished out the original interviews with Charlie Johnson. They were simple, straightforward, without interest. He was sure that Harriet Lowther had not got on to his bus and he had continued his journey into Lafferton. Nothing had happened. No one had looked back. Why would they?

'Guv? I've got a hospital appointment, check on the foot.'

Simon waved Ben away. He felt irritable and at a dead end with the investigation. The sergeant couldn't help.

There were three people left on his main list – Mrs Cadsden. Her daughter Katie who had been Harriet's friend. And John Lowther. Serrailler did not want to have to interview him formally again but it was probably unavoidable.

Before he saw him, though, he needed to hold a press conference. Harriet's disappearance was still recent enough to be remembered. He wanted memories jogged, wanted people to start talking to one another, looking back, checking over things they might suddenly realise could be relevant after all.

When Vanek returned they went through the plans together.

'What about a reconstruction? I know it's a long time ago but it's amazing how they jolt people's memories. I had two in my old force and they both led to convictions.'

'If it were even just a couple of years ago I'd have organised one, but I doubt if I can balance cost against the very slight chance of success. Not at the moment. We'll have to explore other avenues first. Did the hospital sign you off by the way?'

'No. Got to go back for another X-ray in two weeks.'

Simon smiled. 'So you can't possibly be expected to hang around underpasses, let alone chase after pushers.'

Ben shook his head, drawing his breath in sharply.

'Good stuff. Come on – let's call on Mrs Cadsden.'

But the phone rang first.

'Gordon Lyman. About this second skeleton.'

'Have you found something?'

'Not on the skeleton itself, but I've got a bit of time owing me and I'd quite like to do some work on this. You know about computer-aided facial reconstruction? I'm rather keen to get more practice. A colleague at UCH, Declan Devey, is something of an expert. He's going to help, teach me a few tricks – via computer. Should be interesting and we'll end up with a likeness you can put out there.'

'How long will it take?'

'Depends. But we'll get something.'

Angus Road was a cul-de-sac of 1920s semi-detached houses with bow windows. Number 52 was almost at the end. The street was quiet when they got out of the car, but the sound of children in a school playground nearby gave it some life.

'Most people are at work,' Simon said. 'Can't you tell? Our Mrs Cadsden will be too.'

But she was not.

Frances Cadsden was now a smart, young-looking sixty.

'I was made redundant eighteen months ago,' she said, showing them into a kitchen/dining room at the back. 'I was a PA – do you know Dramboys Estate Agents? I quite liked the job. I'd never worked – well, not after I married and had the girls. Would you like some coffee?'

'Thank you.' Serrailler believed in letting people make hot drinks. It was friendly, it made them relaxed – and once they relaxed, they usually talked.

'I imagine this is all about poor Harriet. I read the news of course. I can't get my head round it. Poor little girl. Do you know how she died or anything like that?'

'Not really, I'm afraid. Though obviously it was unlikely to have been accidental, given the circumstances in which she was found.'

'She was a nice child. Goodness, listen to me – they weren't children, were they? She and Katie were fifteen. But I think of them as being children then.'

'What's Katie doing now?'

'She's a sister on the cardiac ward at Bevham General, married to a haematologist. No children. Louise has – that's Katie's younger sister. Two boys, so I'm a granny.'

She set down a cafetière.

It was a tidy, slightly bleak kitchen, used by someone who lived alone. There were photos on the shelves. Two young women. Two weddings. Two small boys.

The coffee was excellent.

'I've read through the statement you gave when Harriet disappeared, obviously, and it's very helpful. I know it's a long time ago . . .'

'It could be yesterday, Superintendent. That day is etched on my memory. From the second we heard that Harriet was missing, somehow everything seemed to be – I don't know – as if it was underlined. That sounds silly.'

'Not at all. It's surprisingly common.'

'Little things – the music the girls were playing, something Katie said, a nasty scratch Harriet had on her arm, all that. I can hear them shouting as they played tennis . . . we had a court at the side of the house. I can hear the sound of the ball pinging off their rackets. It was a day like any other day – Katie often had friends round to play, and it was often Harriet, too.'

Frances Cadsden looked down into her cup. Her eyes had filled with sudden tears. 'I remember feeling so awful – so guilty. If I'd have walked with her to the bus stop . . .'

'But she was fifteen, as you said. Not a small child. You wouldn't usually have done that, would you?'

'No. No, of course not.'

'It's entirely understandable that you feel somehow to blame

– if you'd seen Harriet onto the bus, she might not have vanished. But we don't know when she disappeared – we only know she almost certainly didn't catch the bus, though she'd been waiting at the stop. You're not to blame and I think you know that.'

'Rationally, I suppose. I know I felt guilty that we had Katie, that she was safe. I went into her room in the middle of every night for months. Every night. I was terrified she wouldn't be there. Mad.'

'No, it isn't.'

She smiled at Simon. 'You're very understanding,' she said. 'And of course I know why you're here. Do I remember anything new?'

She drank her coffee and they were all silent for a moment. Serrailler thought she had been going over it in her mind for days, that if there was the slightest thing that worried her she would have picked it out and pulled it apart.

'Harriet was quite young for her age,' she said. 'She certainly wasn't likely to have a boyfriend for instance – say a boy she'd arranged to meet that day without telling anyone. Even if she had, I think Katie would have known. But it would have been completely out of character. She was an only child – a bit old-fashioned maybe?'

'But popular?'

'Very. No one disliked Harriet – not just her friends, but their parents, her teachers. Well, there was nothing to dislike.'

'Was she clever?'

'She did fine, but as far as I remember she wasn't an academic high-flyer. She loved sport and music – she sang, she played the piano well, she told me she wanted to learn guitar but she'd have to win her parents round to the idea. They would think she didn't have time, more music would get in the way of studies – you know the sort of thing.'

'How did you find her parents?'

'We didn't really know them. I only met Sir John once – he brought Katie home after she'd stayed with them. Her mother was quite a shy person, you didn't get to know her well. She seemed very – self-contained. She was musical too. That's where

Harriet got it from. The sportiness seemed to be all her own.'
She looked up at Simon and he saw the tears still in her eyes.
'None of this is any help, is it?'

'Yes. Everything helps us to build up a picture. We'll be talking
to Katie too.'

'Morris, she is now. Katie Morris.'

'Thank you.' Ben made a note.

'I know you're divorced, Mrs Cadsden.'

'Seven years ago.'

'Are you in touch with your ex-husband?'

'Not really. He lives in Bevham, and I have his contact details,
but he remarried, he has a second family.'

'Was he at home that afternoon of Harriet's disappearance?'

'No, he was working.'

'What time did he come home that day?'

'He didn't . . . he was at a conference in London – he didn't
get back till the next afternoon. He heard about Harriet being
missing on his car radio as he drove home. So there wouldn't
be any point in talking to him, really.'

'Probably not – but if you could give us his address?'

'Daffern Road, number 23. I've got the phone number
somewhere.'

'We'll find it.' Serrailler stood up. 'One other thing – your
neighbour, the man who was cutting his hedge that day . . .'

'Ronald. Ronald Pyment. He died a while ago. Had a heart
attack. He was so distressed about Harriet, you know. He might
have been the last person to see her or talk to her. He came
round to us . . . he was really upset. I think it affected his health,
personally. He brooded about it so much. He never really got
over it.'

She showed them to the door, and as they left, said, 'None of
us ever did, you know. None of us has ever got over it. And I
honestly don't know whether finding her body has made it
better or worse. Is that a terrible thing to say?'

'No,' Serrailler said, 'it isn't.'

'She didn't have anything to do with it,' Ben Vanek said in the
car.

'No.'

'Nice-looking woman though.'

'Was she?'

'Oh come on, guv.' But he saw Simon's expression and moved on. 'Where now? The ex-husband? House-to-house?'

'They knocked on every bloody house in Lafferton in '95. Nothing.'

'Look, someone, somewhere, saw her. If she left the bus stop and walked for a bit, maybe to the next one. If she got a lift. If she went back to the Cadsden house. If she went to meet someone. It was broad daylight, it was the middle of the afternoon. There were cars, buses, people looking out of windows, people on bikes . . . just people. So, let's say a friend passed, offered her a lift – maybe the parent of a girl at her school, someone she knew. They'd pull up, speak to her, she'd get in, they'd drive off. Now somebody saw that. If it happened. The chances of that main road being deserted are zero.'

'Agreed. If that happened someone saw it – but they didn't remember because it was a perfectly normal occurrence. No one dragged her into a car – somebody would have noticed *that* and come forward.'

'Not sure that a car slowing beside a bus stop, where a pretty fifteen-year-old girl is waiting, and then her getting in, is what you'd call perfectly normal, guv. Might have an innocent explanation. Might not.'

'Problem is, we have no evidence that any car slowed down or that Harriet got into one.'

'*Crimewatch.*'

'What about it?'

'Wonder if they'd do an item about it. Reconstruction-type thing.'

'Too long ago for them.'

'I could call them.'

Simon started the engine. 'You could call them.'

101

Eighteen

The woman rang a week after Jocelyn had posted her enquiry on the forum. Her name was Hazel Smith and she would give more details when they met, if that was what Jocelyn still wanted.

She did still want.

'It's a good idea to see one another for the first time on neutral ground. Do you know Victoria Park?'

She did.

'There's a nice café by the pond. It's quite quiet before eleven o'clock and if it's pleasant we can sit outside. Are you still able to drive?'

She was.

But as she put the phone down, she realised that she might not be for much longer. How long? Would she realise when she became unsafe? She did not think she was unsafe yet.

The phone rang again almost at once.

'I thought you might like to have lunch,' said Penny, who never had time for it.

'Today?'

'No, I've got a summing-up to prepare. But I can take an hour tomorrow. I'm not in court.'

'I can't.'

'Why?'

Did other people's adult children interrogate their parents? But that was Penny's training – cross-questioning became a way of life.

'I'm already having lunch with someone.'

'Who?'

'Margaret Dean.' She plucked the name out of the air.

'You fell out with Margaret Dean years ago. You said you wouldn't mind if you never set eyes on her again.'

'Well, perhaps I need to mend some bridges now.'

Penny sighed.

'I'm sorry, Pen. Next week?'

'It's never easy finding a free lunchtime.'

'Come here on Sunday then.'

'I'm in the West of England Bridge Tournament, I did tell you.'

Had she? Jocelyn did not recall it but having memory lapses was nothing to do with having MND, she knew that perfectly well. Everyone had what they now called 'senior moments', a term she disliked.

The next morning, before their meeting, Hazel Smith rang again. She had a pleasant voice. Steady. Not too matey, not too businesslike.

'I'm just ringing to say that if you would rather take a bit longer, not meet quite yet, then that's fine. I shan't mind in the least.'

But she did not need longer. She would be there.

If Hazel Smith had been chummy or had spoken in the way carers sometimes speak to the elderly, she would not have wanted to meet her. Or if she had sounded brusque, as if this were purely a business arrangement. That would not have done. There had to be something – what? She supposed she just meant, well, human.

It puzzled Jocelyn that she still felt determined, clear-minded. Calm. Ought she not to be nervous and full of second thoughts and questions, ought she not to be lying awake going through what would happen step by step, imagining? Dreading?

No. All her imaginings, all her dread, were for how it would be if she did not do this but had to let her illness run its course, until she was helpless, trapped inside a body whose every function but consciousness had been gradually taken away. Going into a beautiful, tranquil room, however, lying down on a soft, freshly made bed, with a view of sky and trees beyond the window, and swallowing a small glass of liquid before drifting off to sleep, with an understanding companion sitting beside her – what was to dread in that?

She took care with her appearance that day. She had had her hair set. She tried on a couple of things before settling on the taupe jersey suit with a chocolate silk blouse and a long scarf in browns and blues that Penny had brought her back from India. Plain court shoes. She took time over her make-up.

Getting into the car, she realised that she did not feel nervous so much as excited, as if she were setting out for a holiday. Which was madness.

She backed out of the drive.

Madness.

It was warm enough to sit outside at a table against the wrought-iron railing that separated the café from the path. A couple of the inevitable mothers with gargantuan pushchairs were at the other side. No one else. The park had been refurbished and replanted over the past year in a fit of municipal pride, the flower beds spruced up, turf relaid, pond cleaned out, playground renewed. The bandstand was freshly painted. Even the ducks looked cleaner.

They got coffee and Danish pastries. The sun was creeping round to them. Hazel Smith had a husband. Two adult sons. She and Jocelyn would be thought simply friends. Not unalike. Not dissimilar clothes. Hazel was a head taller.

'What would you like to ask me?'

Easy. She had had the question in mind from the start.

'Why do you do this?'

Hazel smiled.

'Is that something everyone asks?'

'It is. Understandably.'

'So why?'

'I went to the clinic with someone I knew – not very well but she had no one. No family at all. She lived near me, I used to pop in and see her when she became ill. And one day, she just asked me, point-blank. Would I go with her. I was shocked, to

104

be honest. But I knew her, I knew she was determined and I knew she had very little time left in which she'd be well enough to travel at all. So I agreed. Mainly because having no one – no one at all in the world – seemed so terrible. I was very glad I went. It's six years ago now.'

'It's against the law – well, our law. Doesn't that worry you?'

'No one has been prosecuted under it. Besides, they would have to find out about me first. They won't.'

Jocelyn thought.

'Or rather, they haven't so far and I am very careful. But if I were to be prosecuted, I'd defend myself all the way.'

'Yes. I can see that you would.'

Hazel sipped her coffee.

'What was wrong with the first person you took there?'

'She had an inoperable brain tumour. And she didn't have long.'

'I suppose I have months – or even years.'

'Months certainly, from what I know. But rushing is not a good way. You need time. She didn't, and she didn't regret it, but now I wouldn't consider taking someone who had so little time.'

'How many people have you taken?'

'A number.'

'And . . .' But she did not go on. She realised that she knew enough and did not want to know more. It was not her business. She was her business.

'Jocelyn, now that we've met, the next thing is for you to think hard and then decide in your own time. Any questions, please send them via email.' She took out a piece of paper. 'Here are all my details. I'll answer anything you want me to. And when you decide – one way or the other – let me know. If it's no, fine, but I'd be grateful for a message. Would you like another coffee? I think I would.'

Jocelyn had warmed to her. In another context, they could have become friends who went on a shopping trip or to London for the day or who decided to diet one last time. Or not to diet ever again. Talked about everything, disagreed sometimes.

They had more coffee. The sun came round. The café filled up.

The ducks bobbed and dived and swam for bread thrown by solemn toddlers. She was filled with rage and pain that it could not stay like this.

When she turned round from watching the ducks and the toddlers, Hazel had left.

They had not discussed money.

Nineteen

Lenny was a bad driver. She had been a bad driver all her life but it had mattered less when there were fewer trunk roads and thundering lorries. Nevertheless, she enjoyed driving and, when she got behind the wheel, felt a small surge of power and the need to behave recklessly, to take chances round bends, to over-take. Passengers closed their eyes. Olive sometimes let out little shrieks – or had, when she had been more aware of the danger she might be in.

It was a pleasant day and dry. Lenny would once have felt excited at the prospect of a thirty-mile spin. She could turn up the radio. She could put her foot down quite hard on the accelerator.

But she was not going out for fun, she was going to face the usual scene – people at the end of their tether and being firm, Olive having hysterics, the dreadful journey home as she screamed and cried and tried to open the van door, or wept and clutched suddenly, dangerously, at Lenny's arm.

Halfway there, Lenny pulled into a lay-by where a caravan with flags hanging out, like washing to dry, was selling 'Burgers, Sandwiches, 'Furters, Hot and Cold Drinks, Confectonairy'. Two lorries were pulled in as well. The caravan had an awning, a plastic table and chairs. She got her tea and a cheese roll and sat at the table, watching the traffic race by. The sun was on her face. And suddenly, a memory of sitting at an outside table in a French village, drinking coffee and eating slices of tarte aux pruneaux made with crumbling flaky pastry, came to her. How long ago? Twenty years? Twenty-five? More? Yes, more. They had both been teaching at Drivers Hill, had holidayed together, the first time of many. At the end of that summer they had decided to buy the cottage. Olive had been shy, still unsure of these new feelings, terrified that her father might find out. But underneath, there had been the determination Lenny had seen through to, as well as the infinite capacity for love. For admiration. For adoration. Who would not have responded to that? But she knew hers had not been a response – she had led. She had decided, during the previous term, in fact, when Olive had barely been aware of her.

The sun on her face. The cheese roll was not a tarte aux pruneaux, but she was hungry, it was fresh, with surprisingly tasty tomato and real butter, though the tea was stewed.

She wanted to turn back. Turn back the van, turn back the clock. Turn back. Olive had been alert and alive, husky-voiced and intelligent, quick-thinking, strong. That Olive no longer existed. The Olive she was going to see was an angry, foul-mouthed, occasionally violent stranger.

The sun on her face. Lenny closed her eyes. The French market square had been suddenly full of children, a long, bright kite-tail of them, graded in size, fluttering out of a primary school. Olive's eyes had brightened. The children had gone across the square, chattering, laughing.

They had asked for more *café au lait*. But no more pastries. They would save themselves for a long idle lunch.

The sun on her face.

Lenny opened her eyes and saw a bright red plastic tomato full of sauce, a bright yellow plastic mustard pot. A lorry roaring past. A plate of crumbs.

She did not buy a second cup of tea, just sat in front of the empty one, and the plate of crumbs, miles and years away.

An hour later she was sitting in the proprietor's office. The senior nurse, a man called Colin, was in a chair by the desk, looking down at a red folder. He had refused to make eye contact with Lenny when he had walked in and shaken hands, and now he looked at the file in front of him, at the floor or at the proprietor, Mrs Mulcahy. She wore no uniform but a bouclé suit with a gold-leaf brooch on the lapel. Her hair was bouffant and pale, like spun sugar. Lenny had seen her just once before, on the day she had brought Olive here.

'We try very hard but there are limits to what I can expect my staff to tolerate,' Colin said. 'Physical abuse.' He looked at the notes. 'Scraped her nails down Ignatia's face. Spat at a cleaner, Norah Dobson. Urinated in a pot plant. Screamed for fifty-five minutes, until sedated. Slapped Nurse Smailes across the arm, bit her hand, drawing blood.' He glanced at Mrs Mulcahy.

'And so it goes on,' she said.

'I'm sorry.'

'I'm sure you are, Miss Wilcox. So are we. I don't think I have ever found myself in quite such a disagreeable situation before, but I have my staff and other residents to consider. I wonder if you've thought that Miss Mills really needs to be in some sort of secure environment?'

'Secure environment? Do you mean kept under lock and key?'

'For her own welfare and safety. That's what I mean.'

'Of course you do. Can I see her now?'

Colin shuffled his feet.

'Miss Wilcox . . .'

'Can I see her?'

'I'm afraid there's rather more to it than that. We didn't ask you simply to pay a visit.'

She had known that all along.

She stood up. 'You're kicking her out,' she said to the proprietor and the nurse, Colin, who had not even had the courage to look her in the face.

'You're not entitled to do this,' Lenny had said, several times. 'I intend to speak to my solicitor.' But it made no difference to their bundling Olive into the van, strapping her in, putting her cases and boxes in the back. At the last moment, Colin had reached in and adjusted the seat belt under her coat collar so that it would not rub against her neck. Lenny had almost thanked him but did not, nor did she glance back as she turned out of the drive of Babbacombe House into the road.

The journey home was terrible.

Olive was silent and still for ten minutes. Lenny asked her if she was comfortable. If she was warm enough. If she knew they were going home. She did not reply. She sat stiffly with her hands together, eyes ahead.

And then it began, first the low moaning sound, and then the rocking of her body back and forth, and after a while, the tossing of her head up and down and from side to side, like a horse in a stable. The moaning became louder and changed to a cry and the cry to a scream. She screamed and shrieked and then fell silent, screamed and fell silent, struggled to get out of her seat belt.

Lenny pulled into a lay-by and took Olive's face in her hands. Turned her towards herself.

'This is me,' she said, as if to the small child Olive now was. 'This is me. Lenny. We're going home, O.'

Olive twisted her head and bit Lenny's finger.

She had to keep stopping because from time to time Olive lurched sideways, grabbed the gear lever or the steering wheel or Lenny's arm, tried to open the door. And screamed. She spat at the windscreen and banged her foot on the floor, *bang bang bang bang*, refusing to stop. It was like having a wild animal penned in the van with her.

'I'll put you out on the road if you scream again, I swear.'

Olive screamed and then began to whistle, and to sing in a high crazy voice.

But a couple of miles from home she fell silent again, and when Lenny glanced across, her head had fallen forward and she was asleep.

She woke quietly when the van stopped and allowed herself to be unstrapped from the seat belt, helped out and up the path. She looked round, as if she had no idea where she was, no recollection of having lived here for twenty-six years. She touched a bush beside the front door and then held up her hand to inspect it.

Lenny waited for her to go inside but she did not, and in the end, after trying to coax her and hold her hand and lead her, she had to half pull, half shove her into the hall.

At once, Olive opened her legs slightly, to pee for a long time, making a widening, warm pool on the rug.

Twenty

As he stood in front of the mirror unravelling his black tie and starting again with it, Simon wished he was not a snob about ready-tied, and so would not have to put himself through this ten minutes of stress every time he went to a formal occasion. He began to retie, slowly.

The Lord Lieutenant held the St Michael's Banquet every other year but Simon had only been once before. He had endured rather than enjoyed it, though the food had been excellent, and the wines too, for those who were not driving themselves home in their own cars. The Chief would have had her driver, he thought, flipping right over left. He would not be able to slip away unobserved from a banquet as from a reception.

That afternoon an email had come in to say the computerised facial reconstruction of the second skeleton was shaping up well. There would be an image for him to see in a couple of days.

Ben Vanek had been ringing a colleague in his old force whose wife worked in television documentaries and who might know a producer who would find the case of interest. But Simon held out no hope there. Cold cases going back sixteen years, girls who had gone missing – there was nothing unusual enough in it for the media. The local press report had been picked up by the online crime news of a couple of nationals but led to nothing.

His tie was right. He combed his hair, put on his dinner jacket and prepared himself to be bored for the next four hours.

*   *   *

Haxby Castle looked magnificent, the tower and the main residence floodlit and the courtyard full of lamps, the flight of steps up to the great doors red-carpeted. Sir Hugh Barr was rising seventy and would not be Lord Lieutenant for much longer. This might well be the last banquet he gave. His successor would not have a castle in which to entertain half the county.

'Detective Chief Superintendent Simon Serrailler.'

He walked along the receiving line. Barr. Lady Barr. Their son, Marcus. And then the daughter, whose wedding had caused the Lafferton Police Force such a headache, with royal guests and a crazed gunman on the loose, one with a habit of targeting brides. Emily Barr, now Lady Ravilious, was heavily pregnant, very beautiful.

'Ah, the man who kept me safe on my big day,' she said, taking Simon's hand and holding it between both of her own for a moment.

He was very conscious that he was without a companion, but for the next half-hour he was kept busy. He knew plenty of people or they knew him and as he was representing the Chief he had to circulate, listen to this or that comment or complaint – usually made laughingly. 'I do know this isn't really the time or the place, Chief Superintendent, but there is a singular absence of police on the streets/slow response to call-outs/lack of a sense of urgency . . .'

He smiled, defended, apologised, explained, and sipped a single glass of champagne, which grew lukewarm in his hand as he went round, and identified his place, relieved to see that he was not on the top table, though he was sure the Chief would have been. If he had had a companion, he might have been too, which was the bonus for having come alone.

The occasion was as glittering as the palace State Banquets, which the Lord Lieutenant was doubtless used to attending. Plate and glass gleamed and sparkled under the chandeliers and in the gently wavering light from candles in their tall silver sticks set down the centre of each table. Staff stood against the walls in motionless ranks, waiting. Slowly, everyone filed in, found their places, waited for the top table. The three speakers, the

High Sheriff, the Bishop and, finally, the Barrs. The buzz died down.

'Bless, O Lord, this food to our use, and us to Thy Service, through Jesus Christ Our Lord.'

The Amen.

Voices rising.

Chink of cutlery and glass.

Doors opening. Lines of waiters, bearing dishes.

Simon turned to his right.

Afterwards, he asked himself time and again what it had been first, what he had noticed.

Eyes. Deep violet blue. Eyes of that colour were rare. And skin. He remembered his mother saying that everyone who met the Queen noticed her beautiful skin, as she herself had.

He had known handsome women, pretty women, attractive women, women with rare individual features – a wide, appealing mouth, or hair like Jane Fitzroy's wild red curls. But of none could he have said, quite simply, that they were beautiful. How many women were?

Someone poured white wine into one of the glasses in front of him before he was aware of it. He pushed the glass slightly away.

The banqueting hall was settling down, conversations opening.

'I've never met a detective chief superintendent,' she said.

He tried to read her place card but it was obscured by the array of glasses.

'Rachel Wyatt.' She smiled. 'And if you prefer not to talk shop, please say. But you must know how it is – people love the chance to get the undivided attention of doctors and policemen.'

'You have my undivided attention.'

She hesitated, as if she would reply, then glanced too quickly away.

Plates of shellfish and smoked fish were set down in front of them. Langoustines. Crayfish. Prawns. Smoked salmon, trout and eel. The Lord Lieutenant was never mean. Half-lemons in gauze bags, black pepper, fine slivers of bread and butter, arranged on platters.

'Are you based in Lafferton?'

He cut gravadlax into small pieces. Handed her the plate of half-lemons.

'I am.'

'I read about the girl whose remains were found,' she said, 'and just now I saw her father's name on the table plan. Brave of him to come.'

'He'll think it's a sort of duty. And perhaps easier than brooding alone. But you're right – he is a brave man.' He realised that she had illuminated something for him.

'Have you anything to do with the case?'

He told her. She lifted her hand to reach for a pepper mill. She wore a wedding ring. But that might mean nothing. He had a strong feeling that it meant nothing.

How old was she? He thought younger than he was. Where was her husband? Partners were not seated together. He might be anywhere in the room.

Rachel Wyatt.

'Tell me more,' she said.

'About the Lowther case?'

'About anything. Tell me anything.'

Then he did look at her. Surprise. Bewilderment. Alarm. Amazement.

All of those things. And something else. The one true thing.

She lifted her glass. Simon saw that her hand was shaking.

He turned to the person on his left, a local councillor he knew slightly, and plucked a question from the air, about the cost of clearing up after the storm and whether there was an adequate emergency budget. It was dull and it was safe; the councillor predictably picked up the baton and ran on and on with it, giving Simon time to recover his equilibrium.

Roast fillet of beef with excellent vegetables. Rich gravy. Tiny, crisp Yorkshire puddings.

Eton mess.

A Cheddar, and a goat's cheese made by a small farmer in the county.

She had turned to her right, apparently engrossed in what her neighbour was saying, and did not turn back until the cheese was on the table, port was served, and the speeches were about to begin.

But as the Lord Lieutenant rose, she looked at Simon, and smiled, a deep, warm and conspiratorial smile, as if she were sharing an unspoken joke with him.

Two of the speeches were long and uninteresting, one short, intelligent, witty. Rachel Wyatt leaned slightly towards him. 'He should give lessons.'

'Yes, to the other two.'

She laughed. Her eyelashes were very dark, her hair fairer, swept back with a comb on either side of her head. He wanted to ask her if she had a job, if she had children, where she lived. Instead, she asked him.

'In the Cathedral Close. I have a flat at the top of one of the old buildings.'

'Do you play a musical instrument?'

He laughed now. 'No. Do I look as if I do?'

'You might be a pianist. Your hands are right. But I don't know of any piano-playing cops.'

He looked at his own hands. 'I draw,' he said.

'As in pencil? Charcoal?'

'Both.'

'And paint?'

'No. I did, but not for a long time now.'

'How good are you?'

How good? Who knew?

'You'd have to ask someone else that.'

'Who would I ask?'

'My gallery probably.' He hated himself for saying it. For sounding pompous. Or vain.

She blushed slightly.

'I'm sorry,' Simon said. 'That was rude.'

'Not at all. I should have known.'

'You couldn't have known. I use a slightly different name.'

They seemed to be skimming fast over some fragile surface and had to go on skimming, to stay out of danger. But they each had another neighbour and natural politeness came to their rescue. Simon listened to more comments and complaints about the police,

116

more advice about how to restore safety to the streets of Lafferton, did his best to respond, was rebuffed, listened again.

It was eleven thirty when the Lord Lieutenant rose and left the dining hall, followed gradually by the rest of the top table.

'Where is your husband sitting?'

It seemed very important to see the man and then he could draw a line underneath the evening.

'My husband is at home.'

She did not elaborate. They were moving slowly with the crowd towards the wide doors. Simon was afraid of losing her but when they reached the stairs she was still beside him. The Lord Lieutenant was outside bidding farewell. They each shook hands. Moved out of the floodlit circle. The car park was beyond the archway.

'I have a card,' she said, opening her bag.

For a second, he thought she meant a card to give him, but when she took out the oblong of paper, it marked her place in the rows of cars.

'G41. That's rather helpful – at least I hope it is. There are a lot of people.'

'We'll find it,' Simon said. He wanted to take her arm but did not, merely went a step ahead of her. There were plenty of attendants and the car park was very well lit.

'Row G.' The man pointed to his left.

There was the sound of engines starting, wheels turning.

'Careful,' Simon said as a Bentley glided almost silently forward, and then he did catch her arm.

She had a silver Passat.

'Thank you,' she said, the keys ready in her hand.

'Must you go?' he asked then.

She hesitated, not looking at him.

'Rachel?' Say no, he thought urgently, say no. Say that your going now isn't absolutely essential.

'I'm afraid I must, yes.'

'Wait.' He felt in his pockets for a pen. But he had not brought a pen. Nor his CID cards, but in any case, he would not have given her one of those.

'I know where to find you,' she said, not looking at him.

He wanted to stop her and could not.

Other cars were backing out, her progress to the exit gate was slow, he could still have gone after her, even walking. Stopped her. But he did not. She had said that she knew where to find him. He supposed she meant at the station. But he did not know where to find her.

He walked slowly across to his own car. The area was half empty now.

Of course he could find her. He was in the one job which made that easy enough.

She could find him. He could find her.

He remembered nothing about the drive home.

Twenty-one

Ring me when you've got a moment, Simon. I've got something for you.

He had slept badly, got up early, gone for a run in the drizzle. It was still only five past eight. The message from the pathologist was from late the previous afternoon but it was a good excuse to get straight out of the office again.

He went across to the Cypriot deli, which opened at seven. A couple of paramedics at the end of night shift were having breakfast, otherwise it was empty.

'Double espresso, scrambled eggs on toast.'

He sat in the window. There were morning papers on the ledge. He flipped through one, read nothing.

The previous evening filled his mind. What she had said. What he had said. How she had looked. Her hand on the glass. The coil of her hair around her ear.

I know where to find you.

The eggs were buttery and hot. He took fast gulps of his coffee and ordered another.

He had to focus on today. On whatever was waiting for him at the labs.

'Guv.' A couple of uniform nodded as they came in. Simon picked up *The Times* and kept his head down. As he called for a second round of toast, his phone rang.

'Did you get my message?'

'I'm on my way now.'

'It's looking even better this morning. I'll be surprised if you don't get some response from this.'

He cancelled the toast.

Half an hour later he was looking at the computer-generated image of a young woman.

'We get a better idea if I transfer it to – here. See?'

The plasma screen was on the wall behind them.

She had the android look of all such images but you could still see what she had been like.

'Early twenties – no more than twenty-five.'

'And not English?'

'Right. Difficult to say exactly what but possibly Eastern European – Hungarian, Czech.'

She had a broad forehead, eyes set wide apart, flattish cheekbones.

'Why have you given her long hair? Impossible to tell, surely?'

Gordon Lyman turned back to the computer. Within a few seconds, the image of the girl had short hair.

'Looks quite different,' Serrailler said.

'It's only superficial. The point is, we can play about but we've given her mid-length, mid-brown hair because it's the most neutral, the most common, and because it detracts least from the features. I can make her a blonde or a redhead – anything you like, scrape her hair back, pile it up . . . but that draws attention away from the face. And it's the face we want people to look at.'

All this from a skull, he thought. An expressionless but possibly very recognisable young woman.

'Are you happy with it?'

Gordon leaned back. 'Declan Devey, the chap I told you about, thinks it's as good as we'll get. So over to you. We can get you posters made, send the image to the media boys. Just say when and where.'

'Posters will have to wait.'

'Cash flow?'

'Yes, but if we get this onto the television news and in the papers it's a great start. Someone might spot her straight away.'

120

'In my experience, they often don't. Put up a poster, someone walks by it a dozen times on their way to work, and it sticks at the back of the mind. The subconscious does its work – bingo.'

'But if she was a visitor – girl on holiday, let's say.'

'Interpol?'

'In the long run. For now, I'll focus locally.'

'Well it's where someone buried her.'

'Though she could have been murdered anywhere and her body brought here, but why would anyone do that?'

'Yours to find out,' the pathologist said.

The drizzle had stopped and the sky was clearing. Instead of driving back to the station, Simon turned off the main road and wound his way up towards the Moor. The earthworks had been completed, the embankment shored up and propped with new buttresses and fencing. Saplings would be planted there in the autumn. But the area where the graves had been was still cordoned off, though there was nothing left to see and the ground had been levelled. He walked past it, clambering over the tussocky grass until he reached a stone outcrop facing towards the western hills. Sheep were dotted about on the lower slopes, their eerie cries coming to him now and then on the breeze.

He had to plan what to do next. There were a couple more people to interview about Harriet Lowther. He had to talk to her father again. The image of the other girl had to be sent out in a press release to the local media, then nationally. He needed to see the press officer and go over the wording, put her in touch with Gordon Lyman.

He thought about none of it.

I know where to find you.

Why would she bother?

Because she had felt as he had. He knew that perfectly well.

Yes, but she was married. She had a husband, and presumably a family too, so that was that. Or that ought to be that.

But she had not seemed like a woman with a husband and children and another life.

How did that sort of person seem then? Like Cat, he thought immediately. Even though she was now a widow, Cat came

121

across as married with children the moment you met her, though quite why he was sure of that he could not have said. But at last night's banquet, sitting next to a stranger, what would Cat have talked about? Her job. Her family – at some point, even if the conversation had subsequently ranged far and wide.

But what conversation had he had with Rachel Wyatt? They had both been too shaken by the feelings that had been there, between them, almost immediately, too overcome to chat, share information and opinions about this and that, as would have been normal, usual. But there had not been anything normal or usual about their meeting.

He shook his head. Did he believe in any of this? How could he not believe it? It had happened. If it had not happened why did he feel as he did? He was restless, he could not focus, he was uncertain what to do next because what he wanted to do was see Rachel. In order to see her, he had to find out where she was and he could do that easily enough.

So he should go back to his office.

He had to talk to the press officer. He had to make an appointment to see Harriet Lowther's friend, Katie Morris née Cadsden. He must interview Sir John again.

It was routine. But he had to focus because the break always came either quite by chance – a lucky strike, a fluke – or by such close attention that one small detail led to the result. But you did not spot that detail unless you were absolutely focused.

He made his way back down to where the police tape, torn and twisted now, showed where the bodies of the two girls had been. He willed the place to give up its secrets, something he had done so often before. But there was nothing, only the cry of sheep in the distance and the rumble of traffic below the embankment. No voices. No cries for vengeance from the dead.

What had happened and why, who the second girl was, whether the two had had anything to do with one another – all of it was in the past and that past was a box still closed to him. If he had the key, he didn't yet know it.

His phone had rung a couple of times while he was with the pathologist and halfway to the station it rang again. He realised that he had been so preoccupied with Rachel Wyatt that he had actually forgotten to pick up his messages and texts – a thing that was so routine he should do it on autopilot.

He pulled into a gateway.

DS Vanek had left a message. *'Guv, not sure when you're coming back but I've got some news. Call me.'*

He got off the country lane and onto the fast road into Lafferton.

Vanek was hovering on the stairwell.

'Right, what have we got?'

'BBC.'

'Let's grab a cup of tea.'

The canteen was half empty.

'So?'

'I got onto *Crimewatch* about a possible reconstruction but they only do current stuff.'

'Thought so.'

'However, they put me onto someone else, phoned me back this morning. They're doing a programme about young people who've disappeared – some of them are kids who've walked out of home, hitched a lift to the Smoke maybe, and then vanished. They want to try and track down a couple.'

'Do our job for us? Good luck to them.'

'I know. Anyway, the point is that they picked up on the Harriet Lowther case because she fits the format anyway, and now there's her remains, it's a murder inquiry. They want to focus on it for the last part of the programme – and do a reconstruction. They reckon it'll be a sort of test case – can it work after fifteen-plus years, can you get a response after so long? There's a researcher called –' he looked at some biro scribble on the back of his hand – 'Lorrie Mason. She wants to come here tomorrow, talk to you, see if they think it's worth giving it a go.'

'And what do you think?'

'Well, it's got to be, hasn't it? I mean, what are the chances of us having money to throw at that sort of job at the moment? This isn't someone walking down the high street, same as they

123

walked down it last Friday . . . cordon off an area, get a match for the person, couple of cameras, Bob's your father's brother.'

'No, it's pretty expensive . . . like filming a play set sixteen years ago.'

'Right cars, right buses . . .'

'A lot of fun. Chances of anything positive coming out of it all?'

'You never know.'

'You don't. I couldn't justify the spend, but if it's their money . . .'

'I think a lot of people will watch – it's different, it'll catch a big audience locally.'

'OK. So we meet this BBC bod tomorrow.'

'You meet her, guv. I've got an appointment at the fracture clinic.'

Serrailler swore.

Twenty-two

'This is such a nice spot. I should imagine you can be out here in the middle of winter and be quite warm.'

'When the sun is shining, yes, I can.'

They were in the conservatory. The tea tray was on the wicker table between them.

The previous night, Jocelyn had had a strange dream in which Hazel Smith had appeared, dressed exactly as she had been when they had first met, but without a face. She had had hair, a neck, a necklace, earrings. She had turned round and instead of a face there was only smooth flesh. When she had opened the front door to her just now, she had hardly dared to look.

But she had a face. Well, of course she had a face. A perfectly pleasant face. Just oddly unmemorable.

Jocelyn offered a plate of shortbread.

'Thank you. How delicious.' She nibbled it with her front teeth, neatly, like a rabbit.

Some blossom floated onto the grass, twirling as it fell.

'You said you'd . . .'

'Accompanied other people? Yes.'

'Why?'

Hazel Smith set down her tea. 'Various different illnesses. Multiple sclerosis – twice actually – and –'

'No. Not why did people go. Why you? Why do you do this?'

Because it had struck her just now, as it surely should have done earlier, what an odd thing it was to make a habit of, what a – she struggled for the right word, and came up with 'inhuman' which did not seem right. 'Impersonal'? No. Perhaps 'morbid' then?

Yes.

She wondered if the woman would reply that it was simply a way of earning a living, and that struck her as so bizarre Jocelyn thought she might laugh aloud.

'I saw that I was fulfilling a need. Not a very frequent need but a need all the same.'

Not an answer.

'How much will it cost?'

'You pay my expenses. The travel. Hotel for two nights.'

One single ticket. One single night in the hotel. The other, two nights and a return ticket.

'And five thousand pounds.'

As she said it, there was a voice in the hall. Penny had a key though she usually rang the bell too.

'Oh, there you are. Jury sent home so I thought I'd call in.'

Penny. Smart as usual. Dark work suit but with a vivid red and purple stole over one shoulder. Hair immaculate as ever.

'This is – Hazel, Hazel Smith. My daughter Penny.'

Penny summed up people in a single long stare but Hazel Smith was not put out.

'I'll make some fresh tea.'

'I'll do it – you stay there, Mother.'

But Hazel Smith was standing, bag in hand. Decisive.

'No, I must be somewhere else. Thank you so much, Jocelyn, let's be in touch.'

She might have been an official of some sort, a social worker, a woman from the council offices. It was in her manner.

'What's your case?' Jocelyn asked when Penny returned.

Penny leaned back in the chair and closed her eyes briefly. 'Nasty – woman cheating a very charming, confused old man out of his savings, getting him to make a new will in her favour . . . would probably have gone on to poison him if a family member hadn't been sharp. Don't you let yourself be chatted up by some stranger at a taxi rank, Mother.'

'Is that what happened?'

126

'Yes, but it was very carefully planned. She's an evil woman – done it before.'

'Are you defending her?'

'I am. For my sins. I hate it. Who was that? I didn't take to her either.'

'Just someone I met – she's moving into the street – bit further down.'

Penny opened her eyes. 'Really?'

Jocelyn burst into tears.

Her daughter had never been a hugger, even as a child. She disliked contact, kept her physical distance even from close friends, and Jocelyn was used to that, so she did not expect arms around her, she expected what she got. Penny went into the kitchen, made a pot of fresh tea and brought it out to the conservatory, by which time the tears were over.

'You'd better tell me the truth, hadn't you?' she said.

It didn't take long. When she had finished, Penny was silent for a moment, watching her mother pick up the teacup and hold it, with both hands. Jocelyn had no idea what she was thinking or what she would say, was only sure that her daughter would be angry and that she couldn't cope with anger. She was usually an emotionally robust person – probably Penny got more from her than she cared to admit – but the illness itself, as well as the stress of trying to do as she wished to see it to a conclusion, seemed to have left her vulnerable.

'I'd better move back home,' Penny said.

'No, absolutely not.'

'Why?'

'Because you don't want to. Of course you don't – why would you? And I would resent your doing it out of a sense of duty and so would you. Because we would fall out within the hour. Because it isn't necessary.'

'It soon will be.'

'No.'

Penny sighed. 'You heard what I said, Mother. Quite apart from doing something which is morally wrong and also illegal, that woman is very unpleasant and I think you know it as well as I do. She gave me the creeps.'

127

'Only with hindsight.'

'Look me in the eyes and tell me you would be happy to travel to the planned place of your own death with her for company. You can't do it.'

No, she could not. Hazel Smith's face came to her, bland, expressionless. 'And five thousand pounds,' she heard. She thought she had found her pleasant. Sympathetic. Someone who understood. There seemed no limit to self-deception.

'You're right, of course you are. But it doesn't change my mind. I know what I want and I know what I can face and what I can't. This illness – being trapped inside my own body, being wide awake and knowing everything that's going on, everything that is going to happen to me, being unable to prevent it and unable to get out of it . . . that's what I can't face.'

'And yet you can face travelling to this clinic.' Penny shook her head.

'Yes. I can.'

'Have you ever thought of me in all this?'

'You made enough of a fuss when I first brought the subject up. I had to. But you don't have motor neurone disease.'

'No.'

There was silence. They looked at the garden because they could not look at one another. I will miss this, Jocelyn thought suddenly. I will miss sitting here, maybe more than I will miss anything. Her heart lurched.

'Have you told me everything?'

'I'm not sure what you mean.'

'No more secrets – no more people about to crawl from the woodwork?'

'I wish you wouldn't speak to me as if I were five years old.'

'It's how you speak to me.'

'No.'

'A lot of the time.'

Was that true?

'Then I'm sorry.'

'Will you think about what I said?'

'I have. Penny, we couldn't live together at the best of times and these will not be the best.'

128

'All right. But don't ask me to go to the death clinic with you.'

The death clinic.

'I asked. You said no. I understand why. Leave it.'

'No more women?'

Jocelyn laughed. 'No. For a very short time I thought I rather liked her.'

Penny shuddered.

'So now what?'

'I don't know. Actually, yes, I do. Have you been to the new bookshop in the Lanes?'

'Meant to. Haven't had time.'

'Will you be in court tomorrow?'

'I won't know that until tonight. Possibly not.'

'If you aren't, let's go to the new bookshop, then have an early lunch?'

Penny opened her mouth to say something and thought better of it.

'Oh, I know, I know. But I shall need a couple of books at least, for the journey.'

Yes, she thought. Because strangely, in spite of it all, she knew that she would go. She knew. And so did Penny.

Twenty-three

'Morning, guv.'

Serrailler nodded. He was not in the best of tempers.

'Seen the press?'

The papers were laid out on the CID-room table.

DO YOU RECOGNISE THIS GIRL?

Police today issued a computer-generated image of this young woman, created from her skull. The skeleton was found in a shallow grave in an area just outside Lafferton, close to where the body subsequently identified as that of local girl Harriet Lowther was found.

Pathologist Dr Gordon Lyman said, 'Obviously this is not the same as a true photograph but these new computer images do create a remarkably good likeness to the person whose remains have been scanned and then carefully built up in our new systems. This is state-of-the-art stuff – I have been working with colleagues in London and we are confident of having produced a very good image of the young woman whose remains we found. She is likely to have been between 18 and 23 at the time of her death and possibly of Eastern European extraction. It is quite a distinctive bone structure.'

Two of the tabloids had picked it up, one on the front page. There was nothing in the broadsheets. He didn't hold out much hope of anyone coming forward to identify a young woman who appeared to have come from nowhere and had not been reported missing. But it bugged him. Why was she buried here if she had no connection with the area? If she had a connection, why had no one reported her disappearance? Or could it simply be a million to one chance that her remains had been found near to Harriet Lowther's?

'Of course it wasn't,' he said aloud.

'Guv?'

'Talking to myself. I just feel I'm missing something that's right under my nose.'

He went from the CID room to his office. This was the worst, this floundering around in the half-dark, trying to piece together bits of information from sixteen years before.

A couple of hours later, he was buoyant again. The BBC woman had been, listened, made a lot of notes, and was confident that they had a programme.

'It's news and we want to do it as soon as we can. People find cold cases fascinating – someone will have their memory jogged, or their conscience pricked, you see. Nothing like television for making it spring to life. Newspapers can't touch us.'

'Isn't it a fairly major undertaking – reconstructing the scene from quite a few years back? I know it isn't half a century but things have still moved on.'

'We've got all sorts of tricks up our sleeve, don't worry. And there's a lot more to the programme than that.'

Simon left her with the press officer, who would take her on an initial recce.

He went down to the CID room where part of the wall screen showed the face of the unknown girl, and as he walked through the door and it confronted him, Serrailler was struck by what the pathologist had said about her possible origins. Yes. Not an English face, not Celtic either. Eastern European. He was reminded of some of the faces you saw in Lafferton now, mainly Polish, sometimes Czech or Romanian. But those were all recent immigrants, come to work here in the last few years. There had been hardly any when Harriet and presumably this young woman had disappeared.

'Any calls?' He pointed to the screen.

'Usual "she lives next door", or "I think I remember someone like that just after the war".'

'And "they come over here, taking our jobs".'

'Someone rang to say that?'

'Always do.'

'But we haven't said anything about where she came from – mainly because we don't know.' Simon paced down the room and stared at the screen. 'We don't know. So do they? Did you log these?' He turned on his heel and looked at the DC – the room was full today, everybody writing up endless notes about the drugs op, presumably.

'I didn't log the nutters, never do. I mean, the call's logged but . . .' His voice trailed off, seeing Serrailler's face.

'Then get those numbers from the log and call them back. Ask some questions. Find out why they said what they said. If they recognise a foreign face then why do they? It isn't screamingly obvious.'

'Guv.'

'And get on with it.'

'Right, only we've –'

'I said get on with it. Never mind the bloody drugs op, there'll be pushers on the Dulcie estate and down the underpass next week and next year until the end of time. This girl was murdered by someone. Somewhere, she has a family. Somewhere, someone doesn't know what's happened to her, to their daughter or their girlfriend. She has as much right to our time, as much right to everybody's effort to find her killer, as much right to justice and then to rest in peace, as every bloody drug pusher out there. Just for once, forget them. I want this one sorting. Now pick up the bloody phones.'

He was in his car on the way to the Old Mill ten minutes later. He was going alone and he was going unannounced, taking his chance on John Lowther's being in. This was quite different from the morning when he had had to break the news. Lowther must not have time to prepare, and he himself had to step back and be both more formal and more neutral – no instinctive show

132

of sympathy, though no aggressiveness either. It wouldn't be easy but it was the kind of interview he got little chance to do these days and the kind he always preferred. He was trying to keep an open mind, but it was difficult. He had read the files. He had seen the man's reaction on hearing about Harriet's body and would have bet any money on his innocence. But the interview had to be got right – and got out of the way.

As he turned into the drive, he saw Lowther standing with the gardener beside an ash tree. One of its large lower branches was split. The gardener carried a chainsaw; Lowther was wearing cords and an old leather jerkin. He looked at the car with surprise and then with a marked tightening of his expression. Simon noted it but that was all. In his experience, people who had received appalling news were tensed forever afterwards to expect more.

'Simon?'

'Morning, Sir John.'

'Still clearing in the aftermath of the storm, as you see. I hope this is the last. I take it we should go inside?'

'If you don't mind.'

There was the sound of vacuuming. Lowther led him into the study.

'You have some news?'

'In a sense, yes.'

'But no arrest?'

'No. I do have something to tell you and I also have some questions.'

'I see. I apologise – may I offer you coffee?'

'Not for me, thank you.'

Lowther sat down at his desk. He looked different, Simon thought, as he took the chair opposite him, his face had had time to register the shock and the renewed grief; there was the familiar sunken, sad look about his eyes, and the lines at the side of his mouth had deepened. How they change us, he thought, change us and age us, how they leave their mark, these terrible things.

He said, 'Firstly, let me explain about a forthcoming television programme.'

Lowther listened without interrupting as Simon gave him the details.

'I don't have a transmission date yet but it will be soon and you're under no obligation to watch it.'

'Of course I shall watch. How could I not?'

'It will be difficult and painful.'

'You think I'm not used to that, Chief Superintendent?'

'Of course. But people sometimes underestimate the impact of a reconstruction – someone once described it to me as like being hit repeatedly in the face.'

'Will you need my involvement?'

'That's not my call. We supply information, the producer makes the decisions and the programme. It's possible they will want to talk to you and that could be on camera. But if they do, it's entirely up to you as to whether you agree or not.'

'Would it help if I did?'

'It's impossible to say but it can never do any harm.'

'You will give them my details?'

Serrailler nodded.

'And you say you have some questions?' Lowther looked at him steadily.

'Yes. I need to go back over your original statement after you reported Harriet missing. There are one or two things I'd like to clarify.'

There was a pause. Lowther did not drop his gaze. At this moment, Simon had to be polite but unapologetic, steady, unembarrassed. He also had to remember with every word he spoke that he was questioning a man whose only daughter had disappeared for sixteen years and whose skeleton had just been found and whose wife had died of a cancer possibly caused and undoubtedly exacerbated by grief, distress, despair.

'Am I being questioned or interrogated?'

'Questioned.'

'Am I obliged to answer your questions, Simon?'

'No, but it would be better if you did. And it would help us. I'm reinterviewing as many people as possible – this isn't personal. If you would like to have your solicitor present . . .'

'I would not.'

Lowther got up and went to look out of the window.

Am I now on the other side? Simon wondered. He treated me as a friend, for all I was bringing terrible news. He can no longer do that.

He will expect me to ask about that day, to go over it in the minutest possible detail, to account for his movements from the moment he woke.

Instead, Simon said, 'What kind of girl was Harriet?'

Lowther turned round. 'What . . . ?'

'What was she like? Describe her until I feel as if I'd known her.'

There was a long silence. Lowther sat down. Simon watched his expression change, become both thoughtful and tender as he pictured his daughter more clearly, bringing her to the forefront of his mind, looking at her, hearing her voice, smelling her even, feeling as near as he could to her. It would be extremely painful and also, in an odd way, though briefly, comforting and sustaining.

She would be returned to him for these few moments, closer and more vivid than perhaps for years.

'Quiet,' he said at last. 'She was a quiet girl. Always very calm. You didn't hear her come into a room. She played a lot of music – I mean, records, tapes, all that sort of thing, and played it herself, too – but it never seemed to be intrusive. She had a quiet voice. So did her mother. But . . . I'm not sure that gives the right impression – she wasn't shy or particularly self-effacing. It was just an inner quietness that came through to you – if you can understand that.'

Simon nodded.

'She had a . . . a very slow, delightful smile . . . it altered her face. Lit it up. But you didn't see it all the time – she was . . . thoughtful, I suppose. And then suddenly, she would smile. Even as a very small child it was like that.'

Simon waited. Interrupting, pressing another question, even encouraging – he knew he must do none of that. He just waited.

'She was fairly bright – but not anything out of the ordinary. She was about to do her GCSEs and she had perfectly decent predictions – some Bs, an A or two if she was very lucky. She worked hard and that was what would get her the right results.

Not one of the high-flyers. She liked sports – tennis, running – she was a very fast sprinter – netball. She was a cricket fan too. Knew as much about the countyside as I did. We sometimes went to cricket together. She was quite – self-contained, somehow. She had friends of course, they came here, she went to their houses – but if she was alone she was perfectly happy. She never seemed to be on the telephone to them half the night – I heard other parents complain about that – but . . . she liked her friends. She liked her school. But she had a – an inner life, I think. Does that sound ridiculous for a girl of her age? I think she'd had it since she was small. I used to come in late and go up to her bedroom to say goodnight – it might be nine or ten o'clock – and I'd find her just lying there, eyes open . . . thinking perhaps . . . perfectly content. She was . . . you see, I remember nothing . . . nothing bad about her, nothing . . . would you expect this? I suppose so. It's perhaps . . . she was never noisy, not rude, never needed to be reprimanded – I don't want to make her out as some sort of angel . . . we just rarely had to do more than have . . . you know, a word . . . never needed to punish her. She just got quietly on with her life . . . her ordinary days.' He put his hands to his face.

'Thank you,' Simon said.

Sir John sighed and after a moment wiped his eyes. Simon let him come to.

'When you're ready . . .'

'I am.'

'Thank you. I need to ask one or two questions about the few days before Harriet's disappearance. Had there been any trouble at all – even a few hot words between her and her mother or you, about something trivial – a messy room, bedtimes, not eating, boyfriends . . . the usual sort of teenage things?'

'None. There was nothing. I went over all this in my mind at the time – every detail, every conversation. There was nothing. But, you see, there never was.'

'Never?'

'She was such an easy girl to bring up.' Lowther's eyes were cloudy with pain. 'She was a bit of a noisy toddler at one stage . . . liked to bang things . . . spoons on tables, feet on the floor . . . it passed very quickly.'

'Had you seen her that morning?'

'I had, yes. I passed her on the landing as she was going to the bathroom just after her mother had woken her . . . I was on my way out. I said something to her.'

'Can you remember what?'

'No. But probably hello – good morning. You know.'

'What did you call her?'

'I'm sorry?'

'Did you call her Harriet – or Hattie? Something else?'

'Always Harriet. She was never Hattie to us, though some of her friends used it . . . she preferred Harriet. Occasionally . . .'

Simon did not prompt him.

'Occasionally I called her Alice.'

'Her middle name?'

'No. *Alice in Wonderland* was her favourite book. I read it to her night after night when she was six or seven. She played Alice in a school production when she was eleven. It was a musical version. She had quite a pleasant singing voice – tuneful. I liked to listen to her.'

'Did she sing a lot?'

'Around the house, yes. And she was in the school *West Side Story*.'

'Did you see her again that day she disappeared?'

'No. I heard her upstairs but she hadn't come down before I left as usual at around a quarter to eight.'

'You drove in to work?'

'Yes. I could have had a car . . . chauffeur. I hate all that. I like to drive.'

'How did Harriet get to school?'

'Usually one of us drove her into town and she caught the school bus from the square. Occasionally we gave her a lift all the way, if she had a lot of things to carry – sports gear and so on. But that day was in the holidays, of course.'

'The rest of your day?'

'I had meetings all morning, lunch with some clients.'

'Where did you lunch?'

'At the factory. We have – had – a dining room. A cook. Much the best.'

137

'And in the afternoon.'

'I worked . . . and I went for a walk. The factory is set in rather fine grounds. I often walked there. I hate not having some fresh air and space to think at least once in the day.'

'What time did you go out?'

'About a quarter past three.'

'Until?'

'I walked for around half an hour, as usual.'

'What kind of day was it?'

'Oh, it was a beautiful day . . . warm, sunny . . . it was a . . .' He cleared his throat.

'Did you walk outside the grounds of the factory?'

'No.'

'And so you came back inside at around four?'

'I think so. This is all in the original interview.'

'Yes. What did you do for the rest of the afternoon?'

'Worked at my desk. I think I made a few phone calls. I had a lot of papers to read about another company we were planning to take over.'

'Would your secretary have remembered the time you came back in? Did she bring you tea?'

'You know the answer to that.'

'Could you tell me?'

'My secretary was off – she was going to a wedding some distance away the next day.'

'And no one was standing in for her?'

'No. It was Friday afternoon. I didn't need anyone.'

'So you made your own phone calls?'

'Yes. I liked to do things for myself. My secretary, Gillian, was invaluable but I never wanted a secretary to wait on me . . . for the same reason I liked to drive myself. I still do.'

'What time did you leave your office?'

'Just before six. Perhaps ten to? I was reading some company reports. I put the rest of them in my briefcase to go through at home that weekend.'

'Had everyone else gone by then?'

'Not the security staff or the doorman. But the factory itself closed at four on Friday and the offices at five.'

'Did anyone see you leave?'

'Ernie – the doorman. There's confirmation of that in your files.'

'Yes. Did you drive straight home?'

'Yes. No – I stopped for a paper. I like to get the local paper. And some pipe tobacco. I had a rule only to smoke at the weekends. Eve never cared for the smell of my pipe. I stopped altogether some years ago.'

'Where did you buy the paper?'

'The newsagent's on Mercy Way . . . it's closed now. There's a confirmation of that too, I believe.'

'Yes. What time did you get home?'

'About six thirty. By then Eve was back – Harriet hadn't met her as arranged. Eve had been trying to call me at work and missed me. Of course nowadays I would have had a mobile phone – so would she. So would . . . Harriet.'

'Your wife had reported Harriet missing by the time you got home?'

'Your people were already at the house. I saw the police car as I drove in. Eve was at the door. I can see them now. They were very good. Their kindness . . . I know they had to ask me those questions . . . where I had been, what time . . .'

'Yes.'

They were both silent.

Simon did not return to the station after leaving the Old Mill but drove a couple of miles on, to a pub he sometimes visited when he didn't want to meet anyone he knew. The place was quiet – it was still short of twelve thirty – and he ordered a home-cooked-ham sandwich and a half-pint of the locally brewed ale called, for some reason, the Snoddy.

When the thick slabs of fresh bread and ham with mustard arrived, he sat quietly for several minutes, clearing his mind of the morning's interview with Lowther. He had come here in order to think about something else.

He drank, then took out his phone.

He had chosen a corner seat. To his right were two empty tables. The bar was at the far end, so the sound of voices was not going to disturb him.

There was nothing to disturb him.

He took another couple of draughts but did not eat. He would ring first. Eat afterwards. Once he knew.

It had been easy to find the phone number of course. He had the card on which he had scribbled it down in his wallet. He took it out. He finished his beer and picked up his phone.

For a few seconds there was no connection. A bad line, a wrong number? Why was he doing this?

Because he had sat next to a woman at a dinner and . . .

And what? For Christ's sake. And nothing. An attraction? A fleeting connection but nothing else because there had not been time, it had not been the occasion, and besides . . . He heard the dialling tone.

She came into his mind. Her face, her hands, the curve of her arm, the line of her mouth, clear and distinct, along with the glittering lights and the gleaming silver and the sound of a room of people talking, the smell of candle smoke.

How long had it been since he had experienced anything like this? Freya. He remembered Freya and with a sense of great sadness. But he could not bring her face to mind, could not remember her voice. Freya had gone.

'Hello. This is the answerphone for Kenneth and Rachel Wyatt. We aren't able to take your call. Please would you leave a message? Thank you.'

Her voice was utterly familiar, as though he had been hearing it all his life, and listening to the message unnerved him, so he disconnected quickly, leaving no message.

He left the pub and strolled up the lane in the cool, bright afternoon. A donkey stood by a field gate and he stopped to scratch its ears, thinking he might come back to draw it.

His phone beeped a text.

Come 2 supper? Steak pie. Not seen u 4 ages. X

He was answering Cat when the phone rang, but in the confusion of ceasing to text and then replying, he pressed the key but did not give his name.

'Hello? I think someone rang? This is Rachel Wyatt.'

'Yes. I rang.'

She hesitated a long moment then said, 'Simon?'

140

'Yes.'

'How did you – Ah. Yes. But you didn't leave a message.'

'No.'

'Are you at the station?'

'No. I'm in a lane near a pub. I just had lunch. Can I see you?'

'Now? No, it's –'

'Not now. I have to get back. This evening? Could we meet this evening?'

'I'm not sure . . .'

'A drink?'

'I'm not sure. I would have to . . .' She stopped.

'If you'd rather not, it's fine, of course.' Though it wasn't.

'No. No, I want to. Can I let you know a bit later? Or should I not ring you?'

'It's fine. I have to go and interview someone but you can leave me a message. Or send a text. Will you?'

'Yes.'

'I'll be back at the station around four. When can you ring?'

'Simon, I don't know. Just . . . I will if I can.'

'OK.'

'But . . . it's nice to hear from you. What a non-word that is – "nice".'

He laughed. 'I'm happy with nice.'

'I'll ring.'

'And meet me. Try and meet me.'

Twenty-four

He would have recognised Katie Cadsden – now Katie Morris – from the photographs of her in the files, though she had been fifteen then, was thirty-one now. She had small sharp features but a wide mouth.

The house was on one of the new estates that had sprung up in the past decade between Bevham and Lafferton. It was neat, clean, detached, pleasant, but with all the character of a show home. Perhaps it had been a show home, Serrailler thought, as she led him into the sitting room. It overlooked a small garden. Grass. No borders. An octagonal cedar summerhouse at the end. A fence.

'Please sit down. I was making some tea. I try to keep the day to its normal pattern even when I'm on night shift, otherwise there's no logic to your life. I don't suppose you do night shifts, do you?'

'Not officially but I still get called out.'

'How do you like your tea, Superintendent?'

He waited on the camel-coloured sofa, his feet on a cream rug. The walls were off-white with a couple of bland landscape pictures and a pale-framed mirror. Blonde-wood sideboard. Television tucked into one corner. A glass-topped table with a few magazines, splayed out in a fan. The sofa had coffee-coloured velour cushions. There was a tall plant in a china container beside the door. Show home. It was also very markedly a home without children or animals. It smelled faintly of vanilla.

He thought of his sister's farmhouse, tumbled with children, cat and dog, books and papers, folders and files, games and rugs and coffee mugs, always clean, never tidy.

Katie Morris came in with a handled tray of pale wood. China teapot, small china mugs, a plate of iced biscuits, arranged in a circle.

'How long have you been at Bevham General?'

She set the tray down. 'I trained there, did general nursing, then I went to the National Heart Hospital for two years and that was it. I became a scrub nurse, theatre sister. Then back home. I can't see me moving again. And of course I met Dave.'

She poured tea and handed it to Simon, then sat in the blonde-covered chair opposite to him.

'But you came to talk about Harriet, didn't you? This will sound awful but I'm just so glad you've found her – never mind the rest, I'm just glad. Not knowing, always at the back of my mind . . . Where is she? Is she OK? Can she be alive? If she's dead, where have they put her? All that. This is something else to get my head round but still . . .'

'I think her father feels the same way.'

'So would her mother. It killed her, you know. Indirectly, directly, whatever. Harriet disappearing like that killed her. I wish she could know. At least puts something to rest, doesn't it?'

'Would you mind telling me something about Harriet? What sort of girl she was?'

'I said all that – you can find it in the files, surely?'

'I can. But I'd like you to tell me about her now. Time can lend a different perspective and you gave that interview when you were shocked and upset.'

She set down her mug and leaned back. This was always the moment when Simon knew he must not prompt – must not say anything at all. He watched her. Her face took on a slightly distant expression as she brought Harriet Lowther to mind again and tried to organise her thoughts. He looked out of the window. A few plants in pots or even a climber up the fence would have made it look less raw. Perhaps they had not lived here for long and this time next year it would be rich with colour and foliage – but he somehow doubted it.

143

'Self-contained,' she said now. 'Everyone thought of Harriet as self-contained and maybe she was. In school, if she came to tea with us . . . she was quiet. She worked hard. She wasn't the cleverest by a long chalk but she was good at maths, though she couldn't get her head round languages at all, so she got tapes out of the library and listened to them till she got better. That's how she was. She loved music. And tennis. Most games actually but tennis was her real thing. Tennis. Music. Maths.'

She stopped and leaned forward to pour more tea, offering the pot to Simon but he shook his head. She was still with Harriet. He didn't want her to come back yet.

'She was pretty self-sufficient. I mean, I was her friend, probably her best friend, and she got on fine with most people, but you always got the feeling she'd be just as happy by herself. Or with . . .' She hesitated and looked at him.

'Go on.'

'It sounds funny but, well, with older people . . . she liked being with adults. She liked my mum and other people's parents, she liked most of the teachers. I don't mean she sucked up to them or anything . . . she just liked to talk to them.'

'Anyone in particular?'

'I'm not sure. You know, I haven't said this before . . . it's only looking back that I wonder. I just sensed there was someone, some particular friend.'

'A boyfriend?'

'I don't know. No. It wasn't that she ever said anything . . . the opposite really. But she'd say she couldn't come into town after school or on Saturday morning because she was "doing something". But she never said what. I don't think it was a family thing or she'd have just said, wouldn't she? I mean, she did sometimes say "I'm going to London with Mum and Dad" – that sort of thing. But I just got the feeling this was different. I don't know now. I could have imagined it. I probably did.'

'Did she ever mention a boyfriend?'

'Never. We all talked about boys – the ones at the Cathedral School, and at Burdon Hall – not at the Comp, we didn't really know anyone there. A few people had boyfriends, but she didn't. At least, if she did she kept it very dark.'

'So what makes you think there was someone – some friend she often saw?'

Katie shook her head. 'I don't know. I did ask her once . . . she said she wasn't going straight home, she was meeting someone in town, and I asked who but she just – I think she pretended not to hear. Maybe you'd better just forget it.'

He did not reply. But he would not forget it.

'I know you said everything about the day she disappeared and we've got your original statement, but I'd like you to go over it again, if you would. Think yourself back – and try to remember it as if this were the first time you'd had to tell anyone. I know it's difficult but –'

'No. I owe it to Harriet. Everybody does.'

She sat forward and stared out of the window, not seeing what was there, seeing a different day.

He listened, waiting, waiting for something else, something new, something previously forgotten, trivial, mentioned in passing, vital, but there was nothing and he knew it had been too much to expect otherwise.

Then she said, 'I did wonder for a minute though – she said she was meeting her mother at the hairdresser's in the square and they said it on the television, on the news. Her mother was saying it. "We'd arranged to meet up at my hairdresser's but Harriet never arrived." So it must have been true. But . . . no, nothing.'

He waited, knowing that she was going to venture it, even so.

'I just wondered if she was going somewhere else – meeting someone else. There was just something in the way she said it. Only – well, I was wrong, wasn't I?'

'Had she ever done that, to your knowledge? Told you where she was going but actually planning to be somewhere different?'

'If she had I didn't find out. I said she was quiet and that's true. But sometimes it wasn't just quiet – it was closed up. Oyster-like. You always wondered what was going on inside her head. She made you feel like there was something. I've met people like that since – you get a feeling they're carrying these huge secrets or have a fascinating other life. Well, they're not. They're just not. What you see is what you get.'

'But in Harriet's case, perhaps not entirely?'

'Perhaps.'

He always knew the precise moment. Something went click, as if they had come out of a trance, and that was it, back in the present, and you'd got everything you were going to get.

At the door, she said, 'I've thought about her, you know, probably every day . . . it's always been there. So now I don't have to wonder any more. If she's alive, where she's alive, why she . . . all of that. It's done. That's something, isn't it?'

'Yes.' Simon walked to his car, down the path beside the neat, hedgeless, fenceless, flowerless front garden.

And it was. But how much?

He glanced back as he reversed. Katie Morris had gone in and the tidy crescent of new dolls' houses was empty again. No cats, no dogs, no kids. Nothing.

As he reached the turn his phone bleeped. He had switched it off while he was at Katie's, knowing how a sudden ring could blow away something about to be remembered, or spoken, and then the whole interview was forfeited.

'*You have one message. Message received today at sixteen eleven.*'

'Simon.'

His hand tightened on the phone.

'Sorry, you're obviously busy. But . . . if you still want to . . . I could. Maybe you can ring back? I could meet somewhere at half six . . .' She paused, then said again hurriedly, 'If you still want to. Oh, and I'm on my mobile – if you call back would you use this number?'

He called back.

'*Hello. Rachel Wyatt. Please leave me a message. Thank you.*'

He didn't leave one. He needed to think where they could meet. Not anywhere in Lafferton. Not any of the country pubs he went to for the occasional lunch – there was always the chance of someone he knew being there.

Where? There had to be the right place. But he had still not thought of it when he turned into the station forecourt. Six thirty.

He checked his messages, looked in on the CID room, which was deserted, returned the files he had brought in and took out half a dozen more. Left again.

146

He was home just after five.

It came to him in the shower, a picture of the place clear in his mind. But not the name, not the damned name.

He took out a clean pale blue shirt, the dark blue needlecord jacket. No tie.

Burleigh Hall. It was like a coin dropping into a slot. It was a long time since he had been there.

'Hello?'

'It's Simon.'

'Oh. Yes.'

'If you'd still like to meet . . .'

'Yes. I would, yes.'

'That's good. Do you know Burleigh Hall?'

'I think so.'

'About three miles from Starly, going west. You drop down the long hill and after about a mile there's the sign. Turn left and that's the long drive up to the hotel.'

'All right.'

'There's a quiet bar on the first floor. Or there was when I was last there. Rachel?'

'Yes. Sorry.'

'But if you'd rather not, just say.'

'No. No, I wouldn't rather not . . .'

'Maybe when you see me you won't feel the same.'

'I don't think so.'

'No. Nor do I.' He hesitated. 'Is it OK?'

'Yes. It's good. Good feeling.'

'I'll see you soon.'

Good feeling. It was.

Twenty-five

Olive drummed her heels on the floor and when Lenny bent into the van for the third time to try and coax her to get out, Olive spat, first at the windscreen, then at Lenny.

For the past week she had refused to stay in one room but wandered about the cottage like a lost soul, from room to room, upstairs and down, and when Lenny had locked and bolted the front and back doors she had kicked them.

She would not, or could not, wash herself and, when Lenny tried, she beat her fists. But then, once or twice, she had suddenly gone limp and quiet and crumpled to the floor whimpering and so Lenny had managed to get her clean.

Dressing and undressing were battles, and she had to be fed with a spoon but at the last minute would turn her head sharply or push it away so that food spattered everywhere.

She followed her. In the end Lenny could no longer stand it. She had shut Olive in the back bedroom which had a lock and key. It gave her half an hour's respite but then the banging and shouting and crying started up again.

Lenny hardly ate, hardly slept. She looked at herself in the mirror and saw an old, sour-faced, withered woman and hated what Olive had done to her. Hated Olive.

And now she wondered if someone else might have to come and drag her from the van. But then, miraculously, Olive looked at Lenny and stretched out both her hands, meekly, and Lenny took them. Olive looked round but without interest or expression on her face. Just looked, holding Lenny's hand.

'Miss Mills?'

The woman's voice made Olive turn, and as she turned, she smiled and dropped Lenny's hand.

'I'm Moira Fison, the Sister here. Would you like to come and see the house?'

What was it? The pleasant, warm voice, the gentleness of expression, the way she spoke to Olive as if she was . . . was not . . .

Lenny watched.

'Don't worry about the bags and so on, someone will bring those.'

It was like arriving at a hotel. A tall young man in an overall was walking towards them and the Sister was indicating the old van. 'Miss Mills is in room 4, Andy.'

It smelled of new paint and carpet. The last place had smelled of urine and synthetic air freshener. It was quiet and seemed empty but very soft music played. Lighter Mozart. Lenny wondered if Olive would recognise it. She had come to hate music. When Lenny played the piano she made a droning noise, louder and louder and louder, until she had to stop.

They were going up the wide staircase, treading softly on the new carpet, Olive still holding the Sister's hand and looking at her occasionally, smiling.

Unfair. Unjust. Unkind. She had loved her and looked after her and helped her for twenty-seven years, and now, she was the one Olive kicked and spat upon and railed against and fought, and this woman she had met two minutes ago was allowed to hold her hand and lead her up the stairs, this woman was smiled at and trusted.

In the room, the bright, cheerful, comfortable room that smelled of the same new paint, new carpet, and had a window onto the garden, Olive sat on the bed and smiled, but not at Lenny. Smiled at the new woman and held out her hands and the woman took them. Lenny did not understand how this could happen, this instant trust, how Olive could simply abandon her and turn to a stranger and smile, hold out her hands, become calm.

149

She went over to the bed and touched Olive on the arm. I'm still here. I'm here. Look at me, look at me.

Olive bent her head swiftly and bit Lenny on the wrist.

The Sister took Lenny downstairs, washed her wrist and sluiced it with disinfectant, covered it with a dressing.

'This is what happens,' Lenny said, still angry, 'this is what she does. She'll do it to you too, she isn't always docile.'

'I understand. Is that comfortable?'

'Thank you.'

'Then let's go into the sitting room and have a cup of tea. Dr Fison – my husband – will come to meet you too. We can talk everything over.'

The sitting room was bright, with yellow curtains and sunny sofa covers. Pictures. Nice antique sideboard. Piano. Nice room.

Empty.

'There are only two other residents at the moment. But in any case we are never going to have more than eight or nine. So Miss Mills will have a lot of attention – nobody is going to be left sitting in a chair staring into space.'

'She quite likes to sit in a chair. She's not easy with food now. She was always interested. She cooked. Far better cook than me. Now she doesn't want to eat.'

'Miss Wilcox, we can't put the clock back and we haven't a cure but we can do a lot to stimulate and help everyone individually through each bit of the day . . . time doesn't mean anything to them but there can be advantages in that.'

'I didn't notice any. She gets very restless. She wakes in the night.'

'Please don't worry. We can deal with difficult situations. It's always easier for people outside rather than . . . family.' She looked at Lenny. 'No emotional involvement, no memories of how they were before it started. People come to us and we start there. We take them as they are. It helps. We have no expectations.'

'Just as well.' Lenny stood up. Said, 'Payments. The direct debit is all set up. Can I visit?'

'Of course you can visit ! Whenever you like. There's a guest room if you want to stay. Just let us know the previous day.'

'I won't need that.'

'She's in good hands.'

You would say that, Lenny thought. You have to say that.

It was a relief to get out of the place, get away from the new paint and the new carpet and the emptiness.

Her hand hurt. Let Olive bite them for a bit.

She drove the van home as badly as ever.

But it was too quiet. She had grown used to Olive's presence – for it could not be called company now – the restless movements in and out of each room, up and down stairs, the abrupt fits of laughter, the sudden wails or shrieks or bursts of tears. The rages.

Lenny made tea and took it into the music room. The furniture seemed to settle as she closed the door. The piano lid creaked faintly. She took out Schumann, played a few bars, but they sounded hollow in the room and she realised she was still half listening out for Olive, for sounds that meant distress or anger or accident.

Olive.

She took down one of the albums that stood in a matching line, dark blue backs arranged edge to edge.

1984.

Devon. Provence. Corfu. London.

Sunshine. Blue sea. Famous buildings. But mainly, Olive. Olive swimming. Olive in a small boat, waving. Olive on the Rialto Bridge. Olive on Exmoor wearing a headscarf. Olive holding her hand up against the sun. Lenny had taken them. Olive didn't like using the camera, she fidgeted about and claimed that she couldn't see properly through the viewfinder, didn't know which button to press. There were just a few without Olive.

Lenny turned the pages, remembering this place or that, the weather, the small hotel, the smells, the taste of the food. Had they been happy? Lenny no longer knew.

They had not been so young by then, but not old either. 1984. They had met the year before that but things had moved quite slowly. Olive had been cautious. Lenny would have preferred to plunge ahead, incautiously, preferred to be reckless in those days.

Not now.

She knew where reckless could lead.

Olive, close up, sitting on a pebble beach with her legs stretched out, face turned to the camera lens. Lenny could not read her expression but perhaps she was about to ask a question – or just to say something. Talk. Olive talked, asked, told, described, rarely waiting for a reply. It was like a small child chattering and it was one of the things Lenny had found lovable about her at the beginning. She was not used to someone who talked as she breathed. It was when the talking had begun to wind down, when there were long silences, when a sentence would stop and never be completed, another one started, about something different, unrelated to what had gone before.

The silences had grown longer. The forgetfulness become serious. 'What time is it?'

'Ten past three.'

'Thanks. What time is it?'

'Ten past . . .'

Lenny set the album down, open at the page on which Olive sat on the pebble beach. When had it all changed? What had happened? She knew the answers. But not why. Never why. Only that the Olive she had first met, first loved, first lived with, had vanished.

It was getting dark but she did not put on the light or return to the piano. The cottage was quiet. Once they had had an affectionate dog. Once.

It occurred to her that she could have one again. Her own dog. She could have what she wanted. Do as she liked. For two years she had had a feeling that everything was temporary. That the care homes would find it too difficult to cope and that Olive would come back to her. And Olive had. Only of course it was not Olive. Olive had gone.

However, the moment Lenny had walked into Maytree House she had known. This was not temporary, this was not another

152

of the places that could not cope. This was where Olive would stay, living and dying.

Lenny could have a dog now. Or two.

The house was quiet. Too quiet.

In the quietness, she remembered things she wanted to forget.

Twenty-six

He brushed his blond hair back and it flopped onto his forehead again and he remembered being fifteen or sixteen years old and trying to plaster it down. Now there was gel, of course, but now he didn't care, since this woman or that had told him they liked it as it was, flopping forward. But Rachel was not one of those women.

The Burleigh was an old manor house with a stylish modern extension at the back. In Simon's experience, there were two kinds of floodlights on hotels or pubs – cheap garish orange, and designer silver-white, like this one, but this one also had a touch of warmth which enticed you in, up the shallow flight of stone steps and into the hall. Pillars. Deep sofas and chairs arranged in corners. Lamps. Heavy curtains, drawn together. A small reception table, not a corporate desk. The office was out of sight. Flag stones. Rugs. It was much smarter than he remembered, obviously refurbished.

But the library bar was still there, up the stairs to the right. More discreet lamps. Dark green velvet sofas.

Rachel sitting on one, in the far corner. He looked at her for several seconds before she saw him. She sat quite still, not flipping through a magazine, not fidgeting, not putting her hand to her hair, not turning round. Just sitting.

Maybe when you see me you won't feel the same.

He felt the same, and yet it was not the same, because what he felt now was far more and it disturbed him so much he had an overwhelming fear that he would panic and run. He ought to walk away, this was the last moment in which he could make the decision, before he became quite unable to choose. He ought to leave now.

She looked up and straight at him. And then he could not leave.

'Hello.' She did not put out her hand or stand up. He saw that her expression was not as tranquil as it had seemed from a few yards away. She was very pale. Her eyes were the colour he remembered, the same deep violet, but anxious.

'Let me get you a drink. What would you like?'

'Anything. Lime and soda?'

'You could have one real drink. I shall.'

'Is that all right?'

'Yes. We can always have coffee afterwards if you're worried. But one is fine.'

'A small glass of white wine then, please.'

He touched her shoulder briefly. 'It's all right,' he said.

He had a single vodka, chose a good Sancerre for her. Asked for something better to eat than nuts and olives.

The drinks came first. Heavy glasses, a separate bowl of ice. Then the small tray of canapés. Good canapés.

Then silence. Rachel was looking down. He wanted to say everything and could say nothing. Drank.

'That was – very strange. The Lord Lieutenant's dinner . . . banquet,' she said. 'I know what you were doing there. Your job – you had to go instead of . . .'

'The Chief.'

'But what was I doing there? I still don't know. We were asked but of course Kenneth couldn't . . .' She stopped and looked down.

'Go on,' he said, after a moment. 'If you want to. Only if you want to.'

'I don't know if you want to hear.'

She looked at him. What is this? he thought.

'The thing is . . . Ken would like to have gone . . . of course he would. He used to enjoy all those things, dinners, public stuff, and now he can't, so he likes me to go and then come home and tell him everything about it. I suppose it's the next best thing to being there.'

'You paint the picture.'

'Yes.'

She hesitated. 'Some of it anyway.'

'Yes.'

'I've been to other things . . . dull dinners, the theatre occasionally, opera . . . I'm not very good at opera. I like ballet but it never seems to be the ballet. Then I go home and paint the picture for him. I suppose that sounds strange.'

'Not in the least. It sounds good. A good thing to do. Will you tell me about him? About home. No, probably you'd prefer not to.'

And he didn't know if he wanted to hear it.

Yes, he did know. He wanted the man not to exist. But he wanted to hear her talk so that he could look at her and listen to her and feel whatever it was he was feeling. It was important. Not small talk. Non-talk. False talk.

He had been sitting in the chair opposite but now he got up and moved to the sofa, beside her. She looked troubled for a second, but remained quite still.

'Tell me.'

'There's . . . I suppose a long version. And a short version.'

'Whichever you like. Start with the short one?'

'All right.' She drank her wine. He looked at her hand on the glass and wanted to touch it, though only to reassure her, or so he told himself. But he did not.

'Ken has Parkinson's disease. He's had it for six years now and it's a vile illness. It takes everything away little by little . . . dignity mainly. That's the worst. He could go out, even now, but he won't – he hasn't for a long time, because he feels ashamed. He hates the way it has made him look and sound. God knows he's no need to be ashamed or embarrassed, though he's every right to be angry. He has changed, you know? He is the same man but – not the same. I barely know him. So I feel ashamed of that. There, you have it.' She looked away. 'We've been married for nine years so there were barely three before . . . Ken is much older than me . . . so, you see . . .'

156

He did. He saw everything and took in what it meant.

'If I didn't go out to that sort of thing occasionally – like the banquet – it's not often, you know?' She looked up at him, as if she needed reassurance or even his permission. 'I need it. I have to be myself somewhere, to be me. Just me. God, how selfish is that?'

'Why? I don't see that at all. Does . . . your husband . . .' He couldn't say what he meant.

'I told you – he likes me to go instead of him, he says he likes to think of me at these things . . . but he likes my company too, a lot of the time. Someone comes in when I'm not there . . . he has a rota of carers – they're pretty good but he can't talk to them. It's not the same.'

She finished her wine and set the glass down but did not look at him.

'Can I ask something?' he said. 'You don't have to answer.'

'But I'll try.'

'You must sit next to all sorts of people at these functions.'

'God, isn't that an awful word?'

'Sorry. I'll never say it again. Now you've stopped me in my tracks.'

She was laughing. 'Perhaps I know what you were going to say.'

'Do you?'

'You were going to ask if . . . if this was something I'd done before. Met a person by chance and then wanted to meet them again, not by chance. And did it. Met them. That's what you were going to ask me, weren't you?'

'Yes.'

'No,' she said. 'I've never done it before. Absolutely not. I can't imagine how it would ever happen.'

'But it did.'

'Yes.'

'Would you like another drink?'

'Thank you. Lime and soda now.'

At the bar, he wondered how long they had, when she had to leave, when they could meet next, where they could meet . . . He was light-headed.

When he returned she was sitting very still again. She glanced up.

'You did believe me? About meeting people. I couldn't bear you to think –'

'I don't.' He put his hand over hers.

'I shouldn't be here,' she said.

The drinks came.

'You haven't eaten any of those.'

'Nor have you.'

He took one. Put it down again.

'But you *are* here. We are.'

'Yes. I . . . I don't understand what happened, Simon. I told myself all the way that I wasn't coming here to meet you . . . all the way. Turning off the road, up the drive . . . I wasn't coming.'

'Listen, it's easy for me. I'm a free agent – in case you were wondering about that. There's just me.'

'I know.'

'How?'

She flushed slightly. 'I found out. Asked people. I'm sorry, I shouldn't have done that but I had to know.'

'I'm glad you didn't turn round.'

'Yes.'

'Are you?'

'Very.'

'Can we have dinner?'

'No. I have to get back.'

'But not straight away. Please?'

'No. Tell me. Tell me about Simon.'

'What, work?'

'No. We talked about that. I mean Simon. Not his job. You are not your job.'

'I sometimes think I am. A lot of the time. I have to be.'

'And the rest of the time? Tell me about that.'

He told her, told her more than he had ever told anyone, told her not only about now, Cat and the children, his father, Judith, his flat, his drawing, but about the past, his mother, Martha, Chris, and then childhood, things he had almost forgotten but which bubbled to the surface as he spoke, leaning his head against the sofa back, looking at her sometimes, and sometimes away. He could not believe how much he told her and how she listened, very still, listened as he did not know anyone could, quiet, attentive, relaxed next to him, saying nothing though sometimes she smiled.

Other people came into the bar.

'Please have dinner with me. I won't talk about myself any more.'

'But I'd like you to.'

'Meaning you will?'

'I'll . . . need to make a phone call.'

'Yes.'

He wished he could have a second vodka. She had gone out of the bar to ring home and he waited with dread that she would return and say no, she had to leave. Or else not return at all but simply drive off and avoid him, and his calls and messages in future.

He did not dare think of any future, nothing beyond the next few minutes, the next hour. The intensity of his feelings bewildered him. He had known fun and diversion and pleasure and – and what? Affection. Yes. Desire, of course. But not this. This was unrecognisable to him and yet he barely knew her.

There was some laughter from a group at the other end of the room. The chink of glasses. He did not dare to look at the door.

She would not have dinner with him. She would not be able to or want to. What did she feel? Anything like this? Of course not. How could she?

But she had felt something. She had returned his calls. Come here. She needn't have done so. But she needed diversions. She had told him so. A diversion. God knows, he had had enough of them but he knew quite surely that this was not one.

'It's fine,' she said.

She was standing in front of him, but not smiling. She looked anxious again.

'Sit down. I'll go and ask if they can give us a table.'

159

He touched her arm lightly as he went. She jumped.

'Rachel,' he said, 'it's all right. This is all right.'

It was. If nothing else happened, if they never saw one another again, there was this and it was all right.

A time out of time, sitting at a corner table, troubled by no one, not noticed. They ate. Talked. Fell silent. He put his hand over hers and she left it there.

'Everybody else seems to have gone,' she said sometime later. The room was quiet. A waiter was hovering in the corner, folding napkins. Simon had no idea of the time.

Her car was on the other side of the drive from his and he took her hand as they walked to it.

'When will I see you?'

'Simon, I don't know . . . Leave it.'

'I can't.'

'I mean, leave it for me to work out . . . leave me to get in touch.'

'But will you?'

She looked at him but he could not see the colour of her eyes properly here. He wanted to take her back into the hotel.

'You know I will.'

He hesitated then put his hands on her shoulders. 'Yes,' he said. 'Yes. Yes.'

Rachel smiled.

He kissed her once, lightly, waited until she had got into the car. Closed the door for her.

They said nothing more to one another, she simply smiled at him again and drove away.

It was only ten fifteen. He wanted to talk to someone, tell someone what had happened, what he was feeling, ask for an explanation, ask for – he supposed he meant help. Cat.

No. No, for the second time.

He accelerated the Audi through the lanes. It was a quiet night. There was a thin paring of moon. Many stars. No traffic. A horse whinnied as he pulled into a gateway to check if she had already left him a message.

160

Five minutes later, having turned the car inside out, he realised he had left his phone at home. He was off duty but while he was working on a case like the present one, a message might come in at any time with some vital bit of information. How had he forgotten his phone, for God's sake? He had never forgotten his phone before now, never once.

He had never been meeting Rachel before.

'Si? What happened? Presume it's work but you could have let me know.'

Shit.

Cat. Supper. And he had completely forgotten that too. Something else he had never done before. He had had to cancel enough times because of work but never failed to call or send a quick text.

Shit.

He rang the station first but there was no one in the CID office and the duty sergeant was not aware of anyone trying to contact him. Then Cat. It rang four times. *'Hello, this is Dr Deerbon. If you leave a message I'll return your call when I can. The surgery number is . . .'*

He put the receiver down. She would be in bed, probably reading, but not wanting to answer the phone, probably furious with him. Rightly.

He went into the kitchen to find a beer, changed his mind and poured a whisky. Rachel's number was on the pad. When had he written that?

His phone was ringing.

'Serrailler?'

Silence for long enough for him to say it again.

'I . . . I wanted to say thank you. For dinner. Sorry, it's very late. I shouldn't have rung.'

'I'm glad you did.'

'Is it OK?'

'Of course. I was having a drink.'

'What? Tell me – no, let me guess.'

'Guess.'

'Brandy.'

161

'No, but warm.'

She laughed. 'Scotch then.'

'Scotch.'

'Malt.'

'Laphroaig.'

'Nothing like it.'

'It's good to hear you. Was it all OK – when you got home?'

'Yes. Yes, fine. The carers are very good – nice man, this one. Jon. He's the only one who – he talks a bit. Politics, business . . . and he and Ken play chess. So it was fine.'

'I'm glad. Rachel? I want to see you again.'

She was silent.

'Just a drink . . . that's possible, isn't it?'

'Simon . . . leave it to me? Please. I'll ring you.'

'Soon. Can it be soon?'

'I have to go. Thank you again.'

'Rachel . . . ?'

But she had put the phone down.

He rang Cat again.

'Hey, sorry, sorry about tonight . . . stuff, you know, and then I lost my bloody phone. Listen . . . can I come over tomorrow? Cup of tea? Feel free to kick my arse. Night.'

He lay awake, on his back, his hands behind his head. He could see the starless night sky. In his job, tiredness was a serious enemy, muddying thought and blunting judgement. He always urged his teams to go home and get proper sleep or they would be no use to anyone.

He had met her just twice, for heaven's sake.

Rachel. He closed his eyes and saw her.

Opened them. Saw her.

He got up and went to the kitchen, poured some water, stood in the half-dark, drinking it.

Rachel Wyatt. Married to a much older man who had an illness which was ravaging him, slowly eating away his life and most of his pleasure in it, which was probably terminal, but not yet, perhaps not for years. He should ask Cat.

Cat, who was angry with him and rightly so, but who would

162

be fine, forgive him, shrug it off as ever. He could ask her tomorrow. Today. Sunday.

How could he think like this? Wish a man dead? Of course he was not wishing a man dead.

Then what was he doing? He mustn't lie to himself. He had been looking forward to a time when Rachel's husband was dead. Come on, tell the truth. Madness. Wickedness. But the truth.

What did he expect Cat to tell him, that it could take months, years? That she did not know? That there were so many variables? All of that.

The phone woke him at seven. Ben. There had been two calls, from people who said they thought they recognised the second girl.

'There's no one in CID yet, guv, but I thought you'd want to know. One doesn't sound like anything but the other might be.'

'I'll have them both.'

'OK. You got a pen?'

He drank a quick, strong coffee and went out. The Cathedral Close was quiet, but the bell was ringing for the first service as he set off on his run, through the archway and down towards the canal. He preferred to go further into the country, but pounding the towpath would have to do this morning. It was deserted, a thin mist wreathing above the dark water.

To the beat of his running he heard Rachel's name, but after a mile or so, he began to think not only of her but of Chris. He did think of Chris often, tried to remember him as he once was, not as he had been the last time he had visited, just before he had died. Now, Chris was almost present, as if they were running together as they had often done.

Chris. Healthy, full of life, not even middle-aged, Chris, with a loving marriage and three children he adored, Chris, who worked so hard for his patients and got so much out of every day. Chris, dead, of a devastating tumour of the brain which had so quickly depleted him and everything that had made him Chris.

It had only taken a few months.

Rachel had a husband who had been dying for years, was still dying, and his illness was taking everything away from him too, only more slowly, eking out a half-life and taking life away from Rachel at the same time.

He ran faster because he was angry. He was angry in a way that surprised him, a cop, used to all the tricks of death, the whole array of lives cut short and other lives ruined in the process. He had always said that being angry somewhere inside himself was what kept him sharp, kept him wanting to do the job, and that was true. The anger spurred him on – it spurred them all on, made them determined, got the results. Now, though, he was unsure of where the anger was directed. Life? Mortality? The unfairness?

All of those, but most of all, he realised, as he ran over the bridge and along the opposite towpath, he was angry at himself, because somehow or other his guard had been down, and while it was, he had met Rachel.

At some moment he could not pinpoint but very soon after he had first seen her, he had been unguarded enough to fall in love. He leaned against a tree trunk to get his breath. Admission. He had stopped playing games in his head and now, he saw that it made things both clear and rather simple.

Simple, though, was not easy, was not straightforward. Simple was only the start of his problems. Their problems.

He ran through the centre of Lafferton, still in its Sunday quiet. As he slowed his pace in the close, people were coming out of the cathedral after the eight o'clock communion, including his sister, who stood talking to someone. He waved but he could hardly go over to them in his present state, sweaty and wearing running kit. He was sure Cat had seen him, which meant she would come up to the flat for coffee. He ran up the stairs two at a time, showered, dressed. Switched on the coffee machine, took milk out of the fridge and put it on to warm, waiting for the sound of her footsteps on the stairs.

They didn't come.

He was picking up the phone to call her when it rang. His heart jumped, but it wasn't Cat. Or Rachel. There had been a

164

flurry of calls about the young woman. Nothing looked urgent but they thought he ought to have an update.

Fifteen minutes later he was banging in through the doors of the station.

Mrs Angela Pilbur, 56 Laurel Grove, Lafferton. 'The face is quite familiar. I think I saw this girl a couple of weeks ago in the marketplace. She had a toddler with her. It's very like her anyway. I remember because she was telling the child off a bit roughly.'

Sally Gloman, 112c Wishart Road, Bevham. 'This is my friend Lu. She used to live in Bevham then she went abroad. I haven't seen her for ages, two years maybe, haven't heard from her. I wondered if anything awful had happened. This has to be Lu. Oh my God.'

Glen Robertson, by email. 'I happened to catch this on the Web. I'm British, living over in Berlin for a year. This is a strong likeness to a girlfriend I had who came from Sweden. She was blonde but this is her, maybe darkened her hair. It was a good five years ago but I thought I ought to contact you.'

Mrs Poynter, Handley Cottage, Fishhook, nr Lafferton. 'This girl used to live in the village here. Only for a short time. It was a while ago now. I remember her quite well. We spoke once or twice. She was foreign. Seemed a bit nervous. Not sure where she lived, but she said "in the village". Only it must have been, what, fourteen, fifteen years ago now. Before they built the new houses.'

Gerry Bright, 41 Pint Corner, Rimming, nr Exeter. 'I know this girl, she was an au pair with some people near here. I think she came from Romania or Hungary, that sort of place.'

Deena Wanowska, Warsaw. 'Is my sister. Came to England

1993. Never came back. Please say not. But is my sister, I know.'

There were half a dozen others from the usual insane or desperate attention-seekers. He read them again, deleting those whose dates did not match. He kept those from Exeter, Warsaw and Fishhook.

There was a message from the BBC producer with an update. The reconstruction was taking place in two days' time and the programme would go out the following Friday. Simon was to liaise with the crew at the Cadsdens' former house, from where they would begin filming.

The station was quiet. He could hear someone banging on a cell door, then stop. Start again. A phone rang. Nothing else.

He got out a clean sheet of paper. When he wanted to work something out carefully, he never did it on his computer. He could think best with a pen in his hand. An hour later two sheets were covered with a sketch map of Lafferton. He took a third sheet, and drew a map of where the two graves had been found, the bypass, the access road onto the site, the two lanes that led away, and their direction. He connected those to the area in which Harriet had last been seen, noted down landmarks, routes leading to and from Lafferton, Bevham, the villages closest to the Moor.

He studied it for some time after he had finished, tracing it over in his mind until he had a clear image which he would not now forget. Links and queries would come to him, and he would make mental notes and when he was here, sketch them in. There was something about the act of drawing it all out carefully which had helped him in the past, some sub-conscious process that went to work.

The canteen was closed and he had eaten nothing. The Cypriot café did not open on Sunday. Lafferton was a food desert, other than bar snacks in the pubs. He needed to think too. The country pubs were always packed at lunchtime on Sundays.

He wanted to drive to the farmhouse in the hopes of lunch. Usually, he would simply arrive, sometimes remembering to text that he was on his way, but today, he was unsure if he would be welcome.

He wondered about Rachel. Did she and her husband have lunch together? Did she cook? Could he feed himself? Where did they sit? What was the house like? Large. Yes. Almost certainly too large, like John Lowther's house. They had no children. Or did they? He realised that he had no idea. She had not mentioned any and people usually did. But perhaps not in this case.

He went to his computer and found her address. Their address.

The road had no sign and there were only a dozen or so houses, set well back. He drove slowly down and was about to turn when he saw it.

Knighton.

He parked.

It was quiet. No children. No animals. He edged towards the entrance and looked at the house. Her car was in the drive but there was no sign of life. He willed her to come out, knowing that if she did he couldn't speak to her or even let her know he was there. Years of hanging about outside houses when he was first in CID meant that he was good at concealment and at making a fast exit. But she knew his car, knew him. If she came out . . . If.

He waited. Waited longer. Waited forty minutes. She did not come out, no one did. Nothing changed.

But he knew where she lived. He could picture it, picture her there.

It was madness.

It was better than nothing.

Judith's car was next to Cat's outside the farmhouse. Simon cursed that he had arrived without warning, and now had to encounter his father and stepmother as well as an annoyed sister, but before he had got out, the front door had opened on Sam, Felix and the Yorkshire terrier Wookie, and Felix was hurling himself at Simon's legs, Sam standing back with his usual reserve but looking pleased.

'Didn't know you were coming. Mum didn't say.'

'She didn't know either. Hello, blasted dog, stop leaping up my leg.' He swung Felix onto his shoulders.

167

'Grandpa and Judith here for lunch?'

'No, it's just Judith, but she only came about half an hour ago. She seems to be a bit upset.'

'Oh Lord.'

Simon bent down so that he could get Felix through the doorway. He glanced in to see Cat and Judith sitting at the kitchen table and made a business of swinging Felix round and round, before putting him down.

'There isn't any food left,' Cat said. 'And actually, Si . . .'

He had not looked at Judith properly but now he did and saw that she was tense, her face strained and without its usual pleasant, happy expression.

'Sorry, I've obviously barged in . . .'

'No, Simon, it's fine.' Judith got up. 'Coffee? And I'm sure we can rustle up some food.'

'There isn't any,' Cat said. 'Molly's Rob finished off the joint and the last veg. There might be some crust of blackberry and apple pie. You didn't say anything about lunch.'

Judith looked at Simon. 'I'm having coffee.'

'Be great. Thanks.'

'Oh Felix, not again.'

Felix was staring ruefully at the chocolate ice cream all over his T-shirt and shorts.

'You have to ask me before takings things out of the freezer. Come on.' Cat turned her son round and propelled him swiftly out, banging the door.

'All because I forgot to turn up for supper?'

'I don't think so,' Judith said. 'She's feeling pretty low. Not your fault.'

'What's happened?'

'Nothing in particular. Being a single parent is hard, no matter how much help you've got. And she's had a big wave of missing Chris. You do. I know. I couldn't function at all sometimes, for years after Don died. She'll be all right. Let her come round.'

She poured water into the cafetière.

'What about you?' Simon asked, getting down two mugs.

'Me? Oh, I'm all right.'

168

He waited until she turned round. Caught her eye.

Judith shrugged. 'Nothing.'

'Dad?' He carried the cafetière to the table. 'Listen, I know Dad. If he's been – like he can be, don't put up with it, don't let him bully you.'

She said nothing.

Simon had had a tricky start with Judith, but once he had understood her real worth, her patience and gentleness, her ability to deflect his father's moods, her genuine love for him, her acceptance of his family and her care about them, her generous spirit, he had loved her and he was not prepared to see her hurt.

They sat down. Nothing more was said. The kitchen was quiet.

'The other thing is the hospice. Financial crisis there. They're going to have to close beds and put the expansion of the day care unit on hold. Doesn't help. There's something I want to say and you mustn't take it wrongly, Simon . . .'

'Go on.'

'Things aren't as they were. Well, you know that. When Chris was alive everyone relied on Cat, but she had him behind her. It's different now. Don't take her for granted.'

'Have I done that?'

'We all have.'

He shook his head. 'You've done nothing of the sort.'

But he had said he would come for supper and forgotten, called in now, as he had always done, expecting a meal, a drink, a bed, a listening ear, someone he could rely on.

'What shall I do? Do you think she needs a break – a holiday or something?'

Judith stirred her coffee thoughtfully. She still looked strained, unrelaxed – something. 'Not sure how it could work but a weekend away without the children perhaps.'

'Would she want to go on her own though?'

'I was thinking she and I might go somewhere. Molly has weekends, your father could help – do him good. And you could take Sam somewhere for an afternoon, couldn't you? Hannah always has friends to stay with. It's just an idea.'

'Good one. Ask her then.'

'Ask who what?'

Cat startled them. Felix was still trailing slowly down the stairs.

'So, do you want something to eat?'

'Listen, I'm sorry about the other night. I didn't let you know. I'm really sorry.'

Simon opened his arms and, after a second, Cat accepted his hug.

'Just a bit . . . you know. At the moment.'

'And the answer to eating is yes. Any leftovers?'

'Not really. I can do you bacon and eggs and sausages.'

'Let me.'

'I'd rather cook them myself, thanks, we've not long cleared up the kitchen.'

He threw a tea towel at her.

He could easily have spent the evening at the farmhouse but it was probably best not to outstay his welcome, though he and Cat seemed to have reverted to normal. But better if he left now, not hang about expecting supper.

Judith followed him, and at the cars he asked again if something was wrong.

'Yes and no. Come back to supper with me? There's a chicken pie that was meant for last night but we didn't quite get round to a proper supper . . .'

Judith had always tried to make sure that whatever happened during the day, she and Richard ate together in the evening.

'Dad?'

'Masonic. So I'd be glad to share the pie.'

'I'll follow you back.'

Simon gave her a glass of wine while he mixed the salad dressing and laid the table. Judith said little, but leaned back watching him. He found fresh candles and lit them.

'So what's happened?'

As he had intended, Judith didn't have time to control her reaction. He saw tears in her eyes.

170

'I hate it. I hate arguing with anyone, but most of all with him. I don't know how it started, that's the stupid part . . . something trivial, but before we knew it all sorts of things were being said. Hurtful things, I mean. We've never done that. What's going on, Simon? Suddenly there are resentments and jealousies we didn't know existed being thrown to and fro. If you'd asked me a week ago if that would ever happen I'd have laughed at you. But it did. And your father has been like a . . . I don't know. Cold and silent. Miles away. What's that like?'

'Like he always used to be but hasn't since he met you.' He poured her more wine. 'Leopards. Spots.'

'No, Simon. Please don't.'

He had never heard her sound like this.

'I'm sorry. Judith . . . ?'

'What we've had is a spat . . . nothing. It'll sort itself out. I love Richard and the person who is your father is a different man from the one I have come to know. I understand that. But I live with him in the present and our relationship isn't remotely the same as any he might have had years ago with all of you.'

'No. I'm sorry.'

'You don't need to be. I said I understood and I do. I hope I do.'

When they ate, Simon's mind was still on what she had just said, trying to adjust himself to what it meant, trying not to feel snubbed by it, aware that he was touchy.

He was about to say something else but Judith spoke instead, and caught him, in his turn, completely off guard.

'Simon?'

He glanced up.

'Something's happened to you. Hasn't it?'

Twenty-seven

'It's wrong. It all seems so wrong.'

'Why? What's the difference?'

'I thought the first thing was a consultation with the doctor, I thought he considered your case and made a judgement and then he let you know if he was . . . God, I was going to say "agreeable", but I mean "in agreement". This is just wrong.'

'You'd rather I had to make the journey twice? Wait and wait, not knowing? Would you rather that, Penny?'

'I'd rather not at all. I'm sorry. I know I promised I wouldn't say that. But this is surreal. I can't believe in this.'

'The coffee's good.'

Penny did not meet her eye. They were sitting outside at a café table. Opposite, trees around the perimeter of a park. There were other cafés, other people sitting at tables. Traffic. The world going by. The sun shone. She knew what Penny was thinking. But just now, when she had tried to pick up her own cup, she had not been able to grip the handle, her finger and thumb had not obeyed her brain. She had almost sent it crashing onto the tabletop. Penny had grabbed it and set it down. 'You see?' she had said. 'Don't try and hold it for me. Have you ever seen people holding cups while someone sips. Like a toddler. Like a baby.'

A couple of teenagers glided by on roller skates, arms folded, graceful boys with caps of dark hair, their bone structure not yet settled into adulthood.

She watched them.

Penny was right. It was surreal. They were a couple of tourists. They were on holiday. They were having a City Break. The coffee was so good. The cake was rich and moist with almond and butter.

My last cake, she thought. Last coffee. Last.

People say, there's always a first time but that is not true. There may not be one at all. But a last time. Yes. That is true. There is always a last time.

The appointment with the Swiss doctor was in an hour.

'I'd like to see a bit of the city,' she had said.

Penny had said nothing. Had not needed to, it had been written on her face.

'But why not? You'd like to see it, wouldn't you?'

Now the cake on the plate in front of Penny was barely touched.

'This is madness. This is insanity. Mother, what in God's name are we doing here? Come home. Get the next train. Come back home.'

'No,' Jocelyn said.

She was surprised at how calm she felt, how certain that turning back, going home, as Penny wanted, giving the idea up, was not an option. She had almost fallen that morning in the small hotel room, which had had a rug beside the bed. The rug had moved slightly and she had not known what was happening to her legs, they had splayed out and she had grabbed the end of the bed to save herself. Now, it was the cup of coffee she could not hold. The previous week she had not been able to swallow a spoonful of cereal, her throat had constricted, frozen, the muscles had seized up. She had managed to reach the kitchen and spit her mouthful into the sink.

It had not happened again. But it would. There was no time.

All the same though. All the same. She looked across at the trees in the park. The shaven grass. The glittering glass of the shop windows. A bus slowed. Stopped a few yards away. People got off. Others got on.

Life, she thought.

Normal life.

Everyday life.

A normal day in life.

In an hour she would see a Swiss doctor who would listen and take notes and prescribe phials of lethal medicines. They would wait. They would be given an address. A taxi would drive them to the clinic.

But then . . . she took a deep breath, knowing, picturing it. Understanding fully that this beautiful place would be her last. She knew about Swiss clinics because when she was a girl, a friend's mother had come to one for tuberculosis treatment – though that had been in the mountains. Her own mother had visited and described the place. A terrace set out with chairs and loungers, so that patients, well wrapped, could be outside in the glittering sun and air, breathing it, breathing it, healing their lungs. The rooms had had plain simple furniture of pale wood. Soft white curtains. Crisp white sheets and pillows and covers on the beds. Sunlight. A wooden crucifix on each small chest. A picture on every wall of snow, mountains, rivers, trees, waterfalls, green grass – some beautiful, tranquil landscape. That had been the word. Tranquil. 'It was so tranquil,' her mother had said over and over again. She had brought a postcard back, a watercolour painting of the clinic in the mountains, and Jocelyn had gazed at it for days, when it had been propped up against a lamp on the dresser, taken it down and imagined herself into that impossibly white landscape, touching that sparkling snow, breathing in the ice-cold air.

That was why she was perfectly calm today, she realised that, calm and – no, not happy. Of course not. She would rather be at home, rather never have had to come here, rather be getting on with her life. But that was the point, wasn't it? There was to be no life, not life as she had known it and hoped it would be for many years into the future. There was to be disability, clumsiness, the closing down of everything – movement, speech, swallowing. Breathing. One by one, it would all go and she would be a flickering, panicking mind trapped inside a dead shell.

That was why she was here.

She looked up. Penny was crying, the tears on her cheeks not wiped away, just left to gather. Her hand was palm upwards on the tabletop.

'No,' Jocelyn said, covering it with her own. 'You promised me you wouldn't do this.'

'That was before we got here. Mother, please . . .'

'No.'

'How can you sit there drinking coffee? I don't know this person you've turned into.'

'Yes, you do. Of course you do. I'm the same person.'

'You don't seem to have anything to do with me. You're a million miles away already, you're –'

'Stop it. Oh, do look, that sweet little white dog. What do they call them? I can't remember.'

'Shut up, shut up, shut up!' Penny stood. She had raised her voice. It was not yet a shout, but it might turn into one.

'I think we should go now,' Jocelyn said. 'Will you pay while I flag down a taxi?'

'No.'

'All right, I'll do both.'

'I can't do this . . .'

Jocelyn faced her calmly. Behind them, a couple of young men took their vacant table, pushing the empty cups and plates to one side, talking hard as they did so. The small white dog was sitting beside its owner while she too talked, talked.

Life.

Normal.

This is normal life.

The words ran like ticker tape through her head.

'Listen,' she said. 'I understand. I do understand. It's harder for you and maybe I shouldn't have let you come. But you came and you're here. So, you can come with me, or we can . . . part now. You can go home. I'm fine. But decide now and stick to that, Penny. I'm fine but I don't think I can cope with . . . you changing your mind, changing it again. Not knowing if you are going to be with me or not. That's harder than anything.'

'And what you are asking me to do is the hardest thing possible.'

'I understand.'

175

'I don't think you do. I have to live with this. Hear what I'm saying. I have to live with this.'

'Whereas I don't.'

They stood looking at one another and each saw the horror of realisation on the face of the other.

Then Jocelyn stepped forward and raised her arm and the taxi that had been spinning towards them stopped.

They could have walked. It was five minutes away from where they had had their coffee, one of the older apartment blocks, like private consulting rooms anywhere. There was an entrance hall. Reception. Telephone. Computer. Vase of flowers. Bland pictures. Waiting room. Plants. Low table. Magazines of a neutral kind, in German, French and English. General Interest. Cream paint. Double glazing, muffling the traffic sound.

The receptionist had hair piled up high, tied round with a black band. Formal smile. Perfect, accented English. Neutral, like the magazines, Jocelyn thought. Trained expression. Sympathetic but not involved. No. Never involved.

How many of us come here? Of 'us'? Plenty of people must come for other reasons but how many of 'us'? One a day? One a week? A month? More? Dozens more? Hundreds?

Her appointment was at eleven thirty and at eleven thirty she was ushered into the doctor's room. High ceiling. Tall windows. Wide desk. Photograph of a wife, two children. Plants. The room of consultants anywhere.

It took perhaps fifteen minutes, and of those, he spent several reading her notes, turning pages to and fro with a soft sound. He asked her about her symptoms. Movement. Speech. Throat. Hands. Grip. Touch. About changes. Then about thoughts. Mental attitude, she thought.

She expected him to try and persuade her against, to talk about hope and symptom control, about home and disability and care.

He said, 'It is one of the worst of many. Perhaps the worst.'

He riffled through the papers once more. Then turned to his computer. Typed briefly. Wrote on a sheet of paper and handed it to her in an envelope.

'You take this with you to the clinic. They now have the medication approval. You know what is to happen next?'

'I go to the clinic?'

'Return to your hotel and wait for the taxi which will call. It will ask for you by name and you go in that. They will check your details first, then take you. I am not sure exactly when.' He stood up and put out his hand.

She felt as if she were in a television play. The receptionist came in and ushered her back to the waiting room. It was a play. Penny stared at her, looking into her face for some sign, some answer, some relief.

'We go back to the hotel and wait,' Jocelyn said.

How long would it take? They were in the city centre and the clinic would be in the country somewhere. She had expected everything to take longer but was glad that it had not. She asked Penny if she wanted to have lunch in the hotel bar. An open sandwich. A salad. More coffee and cake.

'You should have a drink,' she said.

Penny did not answer. In the end, they sat in the room and waited. It seemed wrong to go among people in a busy bar. Jocelyn felt it would be wrong. She would be a bad omen. A death's head.

They waited for three hours and twenty minutes. In the end she dozed. Penny simply sat. The twin beds had pale yellow coverlets. Sunny. The room faced a side street. Jocelyn got up and stumbled. Her left leg was numb.

In the street, a man got out of a car. Lit a cigarette at once. Walked away. A woman with a suitcase on wheels went towards a house. Rang a bell on the side of the door.

'We didn't decide . . . how stupid. We should decide.'

'I can't stand this.'

'I brought so little but I do have . . . bits and pieces.'

Toothbrush and paste. Face cream. Lipstick. Foundation. Clothes. Underclothes. Nightdress. Diary. Purse. Phone. Bits and pieces.

'Are you going to take them back with you? Home, I mean. Or . . . you can ask them to . . . downstairs. Ask reception for a bag and . . . leave them. Rubbish. There must be a bin. Or just take them home.'

Home.

'It was a disgrace,' Penny said. 'How could that man tell anything from a few minutes?'

'It was more than a few. And he had notes. A file on me.'

'Did he read through them – every word?'

'Of course not, he would have done all that ages ago.'

'You think so?'

Penny stood up. Walked across to the bed and picked up her jacket and scarf. Bag.

'It isn't here yet.'

'You said if I wanted to go . . . if I couldn't do it . . . you said that.'

'Yes. I did. So you should go. Go to the airport. Just get there, look up a flight, you'll get one, surely. They'll change your ticket. You may have to wait a few hours. Still, at an airport – you can buy a book . . . have a meal . . . coffee . . . there are worse places to wait.'

'Yes.'

'So, go now. I should never have expected you to do this for me. It was quite wrong. I know what you said but I should never have agreed.'

'I thought I was . . . that I could cope with anything. See anything through. It seems I was wrong.'

'You're not wrong. You could see anything through.'

'Not the one thing. Do you know what it is?'

'Yes, of course. Fear. That's all. Are you surprised?'

'No. Not fear at all.'

'What then?'

The room phone rang.

'The taxi,' Penny said.

Of course she went with her. There was never any question. She got into the waiting cab before Jocelyn.

'Sorry,' she said. 'I'm sorry.'

Jocelyn touched her hand.

She did not know how long the journey would be but the taxi was comfortable. It wouldn't matter if it took an hour, which she supposed it could. This was a big city. They had to get out

178

of it, through the suburbs, before they were anywhere near open country. She wondered if they would go as far as the mountains, though it would not be like the postcard, she knew that perfectly well; this was not winter.

But Swiss mountains were not only wonderful in snow.

It was not even half an hour.

They had driven through the beginnings of suburban estates, block after block of flats, business parks, industrial units. The taxi slowed and swung left off the main road beside a long row of concrete garages. At the end, two more low blocks of flats, sharing a short approach. Green rubbish bins stood to the right. A Portakabin was parked.

'Thank you. Apartment second.' The driver was pointing. 'Ring top bell.'

He leaned over and opened the door without getting out, then faced forward again, as if he did not want to register either of their faces. As Penny closed the cab door the wheels were already turning.

'Now . . . that bell? Yes. That bell.'

But Jocelyn did not move.

'This is a terrible place,' Penny said.

'We can't judge the clinic by the surroundings.'

'Can't we? I can.'

'Inside it will be –' She hesitated. Nothing here was as she had expected. Imagined. Remembered from the watercolour postcard, even while she had told herself that was irrelevant, that of course she had not expected to be up in the snow-covered Alps. Of course not.

The apartment block was grey. Functional. Three storeys. Metal window frames.

'Mother . . .'

Jocelyn put up her hand. She saw that it was shaking. Why was that? It shook so hard she could not touch the bell. She turned to Penny.

'No.'

She reached her hand up again and this time managed to press the metal disc. There was an intercom on the wall.

'*Bitte?*'

179

'Yes . . . hello . . .' Her own voice sounded husky. Not like her own voice.

'Name please?'

'Mrs Jocelyn Forbes.' She cleared her throat.

'*Ja.*'

The intercom buzzed and the door moved a few inches.

'No,' Penny said again. 'This is a terrible place. You can't go in.'

Jocelyn went in. The hallway was not well lit. To the right was a lift. From above a voice called, 'Press for first floor.' A door slammed. Penny's face was ashen. They did not meet one another's eye.

On the first floor, the lift doors opened onto a landing. Two doors, both with chipped blue paint. Marks on the doorpost, as if someone had been chiselling.

A dog barked somewhere above.

The door immediately opposite them opened.

'Ah, yes. Come in please.'

The girl had short blonde hair. A pale green tabard like those worn by dental nurses. Jeans. She held the door open for them.

'Wait for a moment here.' She indicated a bench set against the narrow corridor wall, then went away.

Jocelyn did not look around. Not at the walls or the light or the floor or the ceiling. She looked at her own hands. Her own hands. In an hour, several hours, minutes – she did not know how long – they would be dead hands. She would not be able to lift them, move them. The blood would lie flat and motionless inside her veins. Her hands would change colour. How long would it take . . . ?

Penny sat as if she herself were already dead, barely breathing.

Someone coughed. A tap was turned on. Off.

Silence.

'Mrs Forbes.'

A man stood in a doorway. Older. White-haired. His shirt-sleeves were rolled up.

'Come this way please.' His accent was barely noticeable.

Now, she thought, now is the moment when we leave this place and go to the clinic itself. They should have a better – what?

180

Reception area? Shop front? More like the private doctor's. Flowers on a desk. Pale painted walls. Pictures. Magazines. The clinic would lead off here. The clinic with the pale walls, pale furniture, the crucifix, the tranquil white pillows, the soft music, the rug beneath your feet, the air of calm. Of reverence even.

It was a small bare room. There was a high couch covered in a plastic sheet. A sink. A wooden chair. A draining board with a cupboard beneath it. Kitchen cupboard. She thought, is that where they keep the tea, the coffee, the mugs. Or . . .

'You have your identity paper, please, your passport?' He held out his hand.

She fumbled at the front pocket of her bag but her fingers would not grasp the zip.

Penny sat, still motionless. Still barely breathing.

It took a lifetime. He did not offer to help her, simply stood, waiting. In the end, she got the pocket open, her passport, her identity papers that had come in the post.

He took them. Read every word. Turned the pages of the passport. Looked at her face. Then her photograph. Her face again. The photograph. He nodded. Put the papers and passport on the draining board.

'Mrs Forbes, yes. Now. I will tell you what will happen. I will go through this step by step and you must indicate at every point that you understand me.

'You will take off your coat and shoes, and lie down. We will make sure you are comfortable. You will be propped up on the backrest. The pillows. I will then mix the medication in front of you, so that you see everything I do. Your witness . . . your companion sees. It will be a glass of mixture. And I will unwrap a square of good sweet chocolate. I will hand you the glass and then I will say to you this. "Mrs Forbes, you have indicated your wish to commit suicide. If you drink this, you will die." You will tell me that you understand. Then you will hold the glass in your own hand and your own hand only. I cannot help you. Then you will drink it all and as it is bitter to taste you will eat the chocolate square. You will then lie down and after a moment you will feel drowsy and you will go unconscious. After some more moments, which you will not know anything

181

of, you will die. You will be dead. I will not have killed you. You will have committed suicide with the medication prescribed for you. That is all. Do you understand all of this?'

Jocelyn nodded.

'Say yes, please – the tape is to record this.'

Like the police then. The arrested person interviewed. 'For the benefit of the tape please state your name.'

'Yes. I understand.'

'Thank you.'

She realised how cold the room was.

The man had his back to them and was opening the cupboard, checking her paperwork again.

The young woman came in and spoke to him quietly. He nodded. She too looked at the papers. Picked up Jocelyn's passport and turned a couple of pages. Put it down.

That was not a check, Jocelyn thought, that was nosiness. How dare she flip through personal items like that.

Yet in a few moments, twenty, thirty, personal items would not matter. They did not matter now. Her passport would be obsolete. The passport of a dead woman. Dead.

The man had a glass vial in his hand and read out something in German to the girl. She took the vial. Read the label.

'Ja.'

A second vial.

'Ja.'

The two vials were on the worktop together.

The girl bent and opened the cupboard beneath the sink. Stood up again with a pack of small plastic beakers and slit the wrapping. Took one out.

Beside her, Penny seemed to be frozen. Her hands did not move, but were folded on her bag, white. Her face was stiff and without expression, but when Jocelyn glanced, she saw that her daughter's eyes had sunk inwards, and the hollows beneath them were deep.

For a second time stopped. Everything in the room stopped. There was a streak of sunlight on the far wall, like a patch of child's paint. The air was dense and thick so that she could hardly force it into her lungs. There was no sound. The two figures at the worktop were waxen and neither moved nor breathed.

Time stopped.

'Mrs Forbes.'

The young woman. Short hair. Fair hair. Pale green tabard. It shone faintly. Polyester then. Not crisp cotton. Jeans. And plastic clogs. Terrible acid-pink plastic clogs.

'If you will stand now please?' She held out a hand. Long fingers. Bony fingers. One ring. 'And take off your coat.'

Penny was still frozen.

For a second, Jocelyn had an image in her mind again, of the quiet room. The sunlight filtering through half-drawn curtains. A candle flickering, sending a slightly moving shadow onto the wall. The blonde-wood table. Cross. Bed. White pillows. White sheet. White coverlet. Music perhaps. Tranquil music. She had thought of bringing a CD of her own. It had been mentioned in the literature.

Music to die to.

The image flickered too and before it faded completely she had a surge of longing for it, longing to lie down on the white sheets and rest her head on the soft pillows. Look at the cross. Look at the candle. Look at the light sifting through the cotton curtains. Look at Penny, sitting quietly beside her. Penny holding her hand. Penny smiling.

'Mrs Forbes.'

The light went out and the room in her head was in darkness.

Jocelyn stood. The girl was still holding out her hand. The thin hand. Pale skin. One ring.

Jocelyn took a step back from the hand. The edge of the chair pressed against her. She looked round. The man had come to life. He had a bar of Swiss chocolate in his hand and was breaking off a section. Snap.

Hands.

'No,' Jocelyn said.

Twenty-eight

'I don't have good news,' John Lowther said. 'The director, the medical officer and I have gone through everything. We have tried to identify any hidden reserves we can free up. There are none. Savings? We're still in the process of identifying any more we can possibly make but frankly it's unlikely. Everything has been cut to the bone and beyond the bone. A couple of support staff have taken redundancy, one nurse is leaving and not being replaced. another is due to retire next month. We can't lose any more without compromising patient care and even endangering patient safety, which obviously we would never do. We have no other option. We have to close C ward – that is eight beds – and mothball it for an indefinite time. If we do that we can keep going, just about, for another three or four months, without an absolute financial crisis. The bank is being relatively accommodating – which in these days is quite something, you'll agree. The PCT is not. They have no more money for us and they cannot bring any forward. Indeed, they've told us informally that we're likely to have our support from them cut by 40 to 50 per cent next year. Cat drew in her breath and John Lowther nodded. 'I can't argue with your reaction,' he said. 'Other than that, we're cutting the opening hours of the day care centre. Looking at either two full or three half-days.'

'That's completely inadequate,' Cat said. 'Given the health and safety and staffing level limits on numbers already, we can't cater for much more than half the patients who would benefit

184

from day care, which in itself saves us money. Quite a few people we manage to treat by a combo of day care and home nursing would have to become inpatients. Oh, for heaven's sake, what are we doing here? Limping along. This isn't anywhere near a proper hospice facility.'

'I know.' John Lowther sighed.

'I'm sorry, John.'

'Please.' He raised a hand. 'Feel free to vent your feelings in here. I am as angry as you are. I hope none of us ever has to hold back what we really think and feel, around this table at least. But, let's look at something a little more hopeful. Leo Fison has begun his task. I am not going to speak for him but I feel a bit more optimistic about our finances now he's in charge of raising some emergency funds. Leo.'

Cat had had a patient with alopecia a few months earlier, a man in his thirties who had been desperate to have a wig rather than show himself to the world entirely bald. Cat had tried to persuade him that many men now chose to shave their heads, that it was fashionable.

'Bouncers and criminals,' he had said. 'I don't care what it costs. I'm not demeaning myself by being a bald man before my time.'

She had wanted to mention the number of women, young women, sometimes beautiful, who had become bald after chemotherapy and who had refused to hide behind wigs. But she had kept her mouth shut.

Now she looked at Leo Fison and wished she could have introduced him to her patient. He did not have a hair on his head and yet he was handsome, strikingly so. Some women would even find him sexy. She did not, but only because she had found no man sexually attractive since Chris, and doubted if she would ever do so again.

There were five of them round the table – several trustees had sent apologies this time. Meetings were not usually so frequent and they were busy people.

'I have to begin by stating the obvious,' Leo Fison said. He had a good voice, a clear, warm tone. He inspired immediate confidence, Cat thought, and if he was asking for money that

185

was an invaluable asset. 'At the moment there are far too many good causes chasing a shrinking amount of charitable money. Everyone has cut back and these are straitened times. You know that but it bears repeating because I don't feel I can be as bold as I might have been a few years ago. But that isn't going to deter me. One of the avenues which has closed up is the business one – corporate giving. Firms simply do not have the spare cash. Those local businesses which already support Imogen House very generously are looking at the amount they donate and finding they may have to reduce this. One firm which was a principal supporter – Jameson Studley Hines – has gone into receivership, another – Cole Brothers – has said it can't give us anything for the next year though they are adamant that this is a temporary situation. I have approached a few businesses which for one reason or another have never given to us, so far without success. They already donate to other local causes and they can't take on anything else. One spot of sunshine, however. A large, upmarket insurance firm, Hinchley, have relocated to this area. I had lunch with their CEO who is Mr Hinchley himself, Michael Hinchley – his father founded the company and he now heads it up. They are going to give us thirty thousand a year for the next five years, and he also said that he would make that fifty thousand for this year only, to help us out of our present crisis.' He glanced across at Lowther. 'I kept that one back from you, John. I thought I'd bring at least one nice surprise to the table.'

John Lowther's face, permanently creased into sadness now, lit up with a quick smile. 'Good man,' he said. 'Good news.'

'In addition – and I've got the list of names here, a copy for each of you – I've extracted another forty thousand, almost forty anyway, from here and there. A couple of trusts, someone I was at Cambridge with who's made a fortune from biotechnology, that sort of thing. So we have all but ninety thousand in the bank, though we need a good deal more, as you know. It's a very small start . . . but at least I don't come to the table empty-handed. I have one or two other notes but perhaps you might want to say something at this point?'

One by one ideas were thrown into the ring and thrown out again.

Leo asked how many volunteers the hospice had.

'It's an ever-changing number but we can count on a core of about twenty-five to thirty people who are generally available and then maybe a dozen more who sometimes help out, depending on circumstances.'

'So approximately thirty people we can call regular, committed volunteers?'

'Yes, I think that's fair.'

'Then rather than going down the bazaar and coffee-morning route, the sponsored this and that – which takes up a lot of time and not always for a huge reward – suppose we have a meeting with the volunteers and ask if they would each be willing to try and raise a thousand pounds, in a limited time frame. Two months . . . three? Do it any way they like – whatever they want to organise. Is that an impossible challenge?'

'Not at all, I'd have said.'

'Some might struggle.'

'Yes, but some would raise more so it would even out.'

'That would be another thirty thousand.'

Leo straightened his papers together. 'I think we must try. I'm going to London with John next week to see a few people. We have to knock on every door, frankly. No choice.'

On the way out, Cat caught up with John Lowther. 'We need to talk.'

'About having to close C ward. Yes.'

'You announced it without consulting me.'

'I know. I did mean to phone you yesterday, but I got caught up in other things.'

'We've four patients in C ward now.'

'I don't propose throwing them out on the street, Cat, you know that.'

She was angry, extremely angry. There had to be another way. She should have been asked, consulted, her opinions heard.

'I feel as if I'm incidental to everything,' she said, knowing that she sounded petulant and hating herself for it. She had been feeling tired and stressed for weeks, irritable with the children, short-fused at the surgery. Furious with Simon, way beyond

187

what he deserved simply for failing to turn up for supper and forgetting to let her know.

'I'm sorry, John, that was petty of me. Of course you had to say something. And it makes sense to try and make one major saving. Close C ward and we give ourselves room to manoeuvre for a while . . . Or we could simply close the day care unit altogether for the time being.'

They had reached the reception area. A couple were sitting together, holding hands. Two women were talking to one of the nurses. The phone was ringing. They went on down the corridor to Cat's tiny office. The phone was ringing there too. She took the call quickly, made a couple of notes.

'That would save on staffing, equipment, running costs – they're pretty high in the unit, you know. I'd hate to be without it, but it would mean the staff weren't so stretched, we could absorb the loss of two nurses better. Therapeutically, psychologically, practically, the day care unit is invaluable but it isn't indispensable. It's an extra for us. I still feel our expertise is in the wards. Pain control, the best nursing for terminal patients, the best possible palliative care. I'm still not fully convinced about hospice at home – I think we do better in-house, frankly. And the day unit could be regarded as icing on the cake.'

'How much would we save?'

'I'd have to ask Clive. He's the financial whizz, not me.'

'I meant to ask, what do you think of Leo?'

'I like him. He's got down to things, he's understood the urgency. I'm impressed. I'm glad you could persuade him, John. I went out to see his nursing home by the way, though it hadn't quite opened its doors then. I was impressed by that too. Leo Fison seems to be a good thing all round.'

John Lowther smiled. A sad smile, Cat thought. The smile of a man who has all but forgotten how a smile is done.

'Listen, John – what about you? How are you coping?'

The smile shrank back into the shadows and hollows of his face.

'It drags on. They have this television business tomorrow.'

'Yes. Will you go?'

'Oh no. No. I do wonder what use it can be at this distance,

188

you know. I hope this isn't just being made for – for voyeurs, for cheap thrills. I couldn't bear that.'

'I'm sure it isn't. My brother wouldn't have authorised it if he hadn't thought it was worthwhile.'

'I dare say you're right. Let me know when Clive has done his sums, would you? Then we can make a decision.'

'Yes, I will,' Cat said. 'Thank you, John. Thank you as ever.'

He raised his arm as he walked away.

Twenty-nine

There had been hundreds of phone calls to the police hotline immediately after the disappearance of Harriet Lowther. Computers had been in their infancy but most of the calls had been logged electronically, though some had been taken down by hand and put onto index cards, which were later entered into the database. Simon had asked for those that had been flagged up as containing material of use. Within them were a few which were marked with red asterisks. It was early evening, the station was quietening down, and he was going through them one by one. Somewhere, in here, he thought, sitting up and stretching his back and rolling his shoulders, somewhere might be the one vital nugget of gold. Might be. But probably wasn't.

There were two separate murder inquiries, he had stressed in a conference earlier – though 'conference' was giving a grand name to a meeting of three people. Cold cases were not a priority. Last week a driver had mounted the pavement in a 4 x 4, hitting a mother and her child in a buggy, and killing them both, before reversing, knocking over a man and leaving him with injuries from which he died, then fleeing the scene.

The following day, a house on the outskirts of Lafferton had been entered in the middle of the night, the elderly occupants bound, gagged and beaten, and a large quantity of antiques and jewellery stolen. The woman had subsequently died and her husband was in intensive care. It had been a thoroughly professional job, there were no fingerprints, no footprints and the burglar alarm system had been disabled, probably a couple of days before, by a man with an apparently bona fide ID coming to do an inspection after the 'reporting of a fault'.

These incidents were taking all the resources of CID and Simon was the SIO of the burglary. They were short of both time and bods.

'My name's Mary Salway. Can you reassure me that my name won't be made public please? I just think you might . . . you should know about the man – Ronald . . . Ronald Pyment . . . he was clipping his hedge, it said, when she went by – the girl who's disappeared . . . only he was cautioned for kerb-crawling . . . it's a few years ago now but it'll be in the records, won't it? Only can you make sure my name doesn't come out, we have to live with our neighbours.'

Which should have been picked up at the time, though Serrailler had found no mention of it. Now Ronald Pyment was dead.

'Joan Cook, 24 Pines Lane, Lafferton. I was on the bus. I remember seeing her at the stop, only . . . I've been thinking, racking my brains, you know, and I know I saw her at the stop, holding her tennis racket, but . . . this might be stupid but . . . I don't remember her getting on the bus. I suppose she must have and I was looking out of the other window, only . . . I just thought I should say. I don't remember her getting on. Sorry, this is wasting your time, isn't it?'

No. It was not. He put a 'check' beside it and went on.

'Er . . . I don't . . . I might have seen something to do with the girl. I might . . . she was at the bus stop. It was the girl who's gone missing, I'm pretty sure . . . I was . . . nearby. That day. She had fair hair in a ponytail, tennis racket . . . funny, I noticed the name on the cover, Slazenger, it struck me because I had one that same make – well, years ago . . . only . . . there was something else. I was . . . I was getting into my car . . . I saw her definitely. The thing is . . . I saw

191

the bus . . . I'm pretty sure it was that same bus. Only she didn't get on it. Definitely, she – I've got to go, sorry. (I don't think she got on it . . .)'

There was a note. *Caller wouldn't give name. Tried to get number to call back but was a public phone box in Bevham. DC J. Peters.*

The others were about a man who was a known paedophile living in the same village as the Lowthers and one from a clergyman who thought he had seen Harriet with a boy a bit older than herself, leaning against the wall outside his church and seeming 'intimate', on the day before her disappearance.

Details about the paedophile were noted but it took only a few minutes for him to find that the man had left the district altogether, to live in Spain. An A.T. Cook still lived at 24 Pines Lane. Simon could go there later. The last two callers were linked because both expressed doubt as to whether Harriet had actually boarded the bus. So why had no one checked them against each other? Perhaps they had, but if so the reports of interviews were not in the files, he was quite sure.

The anonymous caller might not have been traced but Joan Cook should have been interviewed.

It was little enough but it was something. If Harriet had indeed failed to get on the bus for which she was waiting, why?

He read over the call from the clergyman. Katie had wondered if Harriet might have had a boyfriend, though she doubted it; this call suggested she had been seen with one. Who was he? How serious was it – boyfriend, or friend who was a boy? Simon did not remember any other mention of a boyfriend in the files, but he made a note to himself to check back. Too much detail, too much reading and rereading.

The filming started early. He was there at seven o'clock, by which time the crew was assembled, and standing beside one of the BBC vans was a girl resembling Harriet Lowther. Right age, height, colouring. Simon looked at the girl. Her features were not the same as Harriet's. That didn't matter. But something niggled in his mind as he watched her. Something. There was nothing wrong, as far as he could tell. The clothes, shoes, hair, tennis racket, all seemed right. No, nothing wrong. So why the niggle?

They had managed to get hold of a bus of the same model as the ones used in Lafferton at the time – they had all changed four years ago, but a few towns and cities still had some of the old type in service and the one they had borrowed was now parked up in a lay-by. Most other traffic had been diverted around this section of the road but the greengrocer's van was beside the bus, and people who had been driving, cycling or walking in the area at the time had been urged to attend. There were not many.

In the Cadsdens' road, they had a man on a ladder, hedge clippings on the path.

Simon traced the route Harriet had taken, walking from the Cadsden house, past the hedge clipper, up to the main road and across it, and then along to the bus stop. The bus approached on its first practice run. The greengrocer's van was immediately behind. Anyone noticing Harriet Lowther waiting could have been on the same side of the road as her or on the opposite side, but once the bus pulled in, only a passer-by on the same side would have known if she had boarded it or not – the bus itself hid the view of the stop from the opposite pavement.

It wasn't much of a detail but he noted it.

Now, the girl playing Harriet was being walked down and positioned at the bus stop, the bus itself having been driven off and turned a couple of hundred yards higher up the road.

Serrailler looked at the double. Fair hair. Shorts, blue sweatshirt, trainers, small bag. Tennis racket.

Tennis racket.

He texted Cat. *'Medical query. Can teenager with 4 toes excel @ tennis? Good sprinter 2. Si.'*

Pines Lane was not a lane but a street of 1930s semi-detached houses that had seen better days. Hedges and several patches of lawn had been removed from the fronts, the occasional car or motorbikes parked there. But 24 was neat. A picket fence, a wrought-iron gate, clean windows.

He rang the bell, memories of door-to-door flooding back. Other people's houses, other people's lives – he had learned to look, take in, assess, store away, snippets of this or that, details seen or heard. They were useful.

The man was holding an electric iron and a plug.

Serrailler showed his card. 'I wonder if Mrs Joan Cook still lives here?'

'She does.'

'Is it possible to have a word with her? I'd like –'

'About that girl?' He held the door open. 'She wondered if you'd come. I said you wouldn't bother. Wrong as usual. Joan?'

There was a polished oak table. A standard lamp. A Turkey-red carpet runner. A small brass gong. It smelled clean. They could have been standing here forty years ago and everything would have fitted.

'You were right. This is a Detective Chief Superintendent. Do you want to go in the front room? I must get the plug back on this. Shall I make something?'

He wore a beige sleeveless pullover. She wore beige slacks. Grey hair. No make-up.

Forty years ago? Sixty. Nothing had changed in houses like this.

'Mrs Cook?'

The front room. Brasses. Fire irons. Another gong. A small bell. Indian civil service somewhere along the line. His father? Hers? More Turkey red. Moquette upholstery. An upright piano. Photographs in frames standing on a linen cloth.

'Do sit down. I knew you'd come. I should have telephoned again really, shouldn't I? But when I said to my husband, he thought not. It isn't that I have anything new to say. What I said when I rang at the time is all there is, I'm afraid. Poor girl.'

She sat on the edge of her chair, opposite to him.

'I can remember it very well. I don't know why it stuck in my mind at the time but once it had I couldn't get it out. That's why I rang of course. And then when I read about you finding her . . . I knew you'd come.'

The door opened.

'Tea or coffee?' the husband said.

Serrailler knew the sort of coffee he might get. 'Tea please.'

'Make a big pot, Peter. We'll all have it.'

The door closed.

'Can you tell me why you were on the bus that afternoon, Mrs Cook?'

'I can. I'd been to visit my aunt. She's gone now, went the year afterwards. She was getting on for ninety then. She was in the residential home – it's closed now – Leafield Lodge. I came out and walked up to the bus stop – that's about four or five away from the one . . . . where the young girl was waiting. The bus wasn't long coming.'

'Did you always get the bus to and from seeing your aunt?'

'Yes. We don't have a car. Neither of us drives. We've never seen the need for a car, we believe in public transport.'

The Cooks probably believed in quite a few things. And did not believe in even more.

'Can you tell me where you sat?'

'On the pavement side halfway down. I always try to sit in the middle of buses and trains. My mother had it that you were safer in the middle. Why is that? My husband says it's true of planes too but I've never flown in one so I wouldn't know. Yes, in the middle of the bus I'd have been.'

'I'm going to take this all down as a fresh statement, Mrs Cook. So if you remember anything new or want to change what you said originally, this is the time.'

But there was nothing new and she did not change anything. The statement was almost word for word the same as the one she had made just after the disappearance.

She had been seated on the left-hand side of the bus and as it had travelled down Parkside Drive she had seen a girl at the next stop, with fair hair and carrying a tennis racket. There had been no one else there. The bus had slowed down and had been overtaken by other traffic as it pulled in but she had not registered any vehicles in particular. She had been looking out at the stop, and became aware that the automatic doors had swung open but that no one had got on, and after a moment the driver had pressed the button to close them and pulled out into the road again. That was all. She had barely registered that the waiting girl had not got on the bus after all. It was only when she had read about Harriet's disappearance, and her description and last-known movements, that she had recalled her, thought about it, talked to her husband – and then rung the special police line. But if Harriet Lowther had not boarded the bus, Joan Cook had no idea what else she might have done or where she had gone. Nor had Serrailler.

Back in his office he pulled out the record of the call that had come in anonymously. A man. *I saw her definitely. The thing is . . . I saw the bus . . . I'm pretty sure it was that same bus. Only she didn't get on it.*

Why had no one linked these two calls at the time? They had been flagged up as possibly important but no one had visited Joan Cook or, apparently, made any serious attempts to trace Mr Anonymous – if they had, it would have been in the reports. Why hadn't they? Yes, there had been hundreds of calls, but these two had been singled out and yet not pursued. It was always in the detail, he thought, pulling his jacket off the chair. It was always somewhere in the tiny detail.

He went downstairs to see the press officer. For years there had been two of them, plus a secretary, in what had been a decent-sized office. Now, there was only Marianne in a cubby-hole. Things were never quiet but handling the usual daily events plus Serrailler's two high-profile cases was as much as she could cope with, and if she had not been efficient, experienced and very cool-headed, there would have been chaos.

'Can we put out a request? Is tomorrow morning possible?'

'Glad you don't want it now. Yes, can do.' She opened a new file on her computer. 'Did you go down to see the recon by the way? I won't be sorry to get them off my back – nice guys but . . .'

'Demanding?'

'You could say. Looking forward to the programme though.'

'Be interesting to see what it turns up.'

'The usual, I dare say. Where do you want this to go, Simon?'

'Everywhere. OK, here we go: "Lafferton Police, investigating the case of the missing schoolgirl Harriet Lowther . . . blah blah –" the usual general call for info – but then: "In particular they

196

are anxious to hear from the anonymous caller who contacted the special information hotline after Harriet's disappearance. The caller claimed to have seen her waiting at the bus stop in Parkside Drive, but he stated that he did not think she had actually boarded the bus when it pulled in. If you were this man, the police would like you to ring them again urgently. Please contact –" then give the hotline number and add my name as well, would you? I want to flush this guy out. He knows something or he saw something and he might respond to a name rather than a general request.'

'Anonymous usually does. I'll put it out to catch the local news bulletins first thing.'

'Wonder woman.'

It occurred to him as he went out that Marianne actually preferred to have the job, and the office, to herself, even if the work pressure was intense. She was one of the best of their civilian staff – and the best tended to like to hold the reins on their own. And it also occurred to him that, other than missing the extra pairs of hands in terms of time, he too preferred to have his job to himself.

The programme went out the following night. In the end, the other two-thirds of it were given more prominence than the Lafferton section and very little of the reconstruction was used, though what they did show – the girl waiting at the stop and the bus drawing up to it – was the vital part. Simon watched it, drinking a glass of beer, the window open onto the cool evening, and wondered if being a BBC producer was even more frustrating than trying to solve a cold case.

He remained slouched in front of the television, beating both Jesus College, Cambridge, and the University of Warwick on *University Challenge.*

'*What was the name given by the British to the metal foil used to baffle German radar during World War II?*'

'Window,' Simon said as his phone rang.

'Evening, guv, duty switchboard here. I just had a call, anonymous, about the Lowther case. He asked to speak to you personally.'

'Can you trace?'

'Trying, but he said he'd call again.'

'OK. When – if – he does, do your best to keep him. Can you replay him to me?'

'Hold on.'

The man sounded local, middle-aged, hesitant. He was not muffling his voice but he spoke as if he had his head turned slightly away from the receiver.

'It's about the girl . . . I saw the TV programme tonight. Thing is . . . when it happened – after she went missing, I mean – I did ring in then. I've never really forgotten about it, only . . . it's just that . . . hearing she's been found . . . I mean, she's dead, we know that now . . . not just missing . . . then seeing this . . . Can I speak to the man in charge? I don't want to say any more now . . . I need to talk to him, the Superintendent . . . the Detective Super, I mean . . . how do I get to talk to him?'

The operator replied, smooth, reassuring.

'If you'd give me your name, sir, and a contact number, I'll make sure your message is passed on to the Superintendent. I can't do anything if you won't tell me those details, I'm afraid.'

'Can you . . . is he there now? No, he wouldn't be, I suppose. Look, I'll call again.'

'Your details will remain confidential, I guarantee. I just need your name and a contact phone number, if you could let me have those, sir?'

'No, it doesn't matter. Leave it. I have to go, sorry.'

'Don't hang up, sir, please, your name won't be made public if that's what you're worried about. Just a surname is fine for now.'

'I'll ring in the morning.'

He rang off suddenly, as if someone had interrupted him.

Simon got another beer and stood by the window. It was quiet. He thought about the girl – both girls, though it was difficult to keep someone in mind if you could not give them a name, an age, an origin, any detail at all. Harriet Lowther he felt he knew – sporty, musical, friendly, just gaining a bit of independence, possibly enjoying the company of a boyfriend.

Was there a boyfriend? No one had identified one, not the Lowthers, or the Cadsdens. No boy had come forward, either to say he knew Harriet or even to say that he knew someone else who did. And it was simply not possible that anyone had been going out with Harriet Lowther without a single other soul in the world being aware of the fact. Girls confided in their friends. Boys did too, though rather less. Someone would have known.

Simon was as sure as he could be that there had not been a boyfriend. And Cat had confirmed that four toes on one foot would not deter a sporty teenager.

But if, as Joan Cook and the anonymous male caller seemed to believe, Harriet had not got on the bus for which she had been waiting, then perhaps she had changed her mind at the last minute and walked away. If so, in which direction? Heading out of town towards the country? But why would she do that? So had she headed to Lafferton on foot? If so, why? Because she felt like the walk? Then why not just start walking in the first place?

Had she seen someone on the bus she didn't want to talk to? Or someone who was not on the bus but whom she *did* want to talk to? Someone walking by? A friend? If so, had she seen them by chance? Or had they arranged to meet at the bus stop?

No one had reported seeing her anywhere other than at the stop – not walking in any direction, or standing talking to someone. And they surely would have done.

So had Harriet seen someone in a car? Had the car stopped? Had the driver spoken to her? Had she been offered a lift? Had she prearranged to meet someone in a car? Expected to be given a lift? Into Lafferton then? In which case why wait for the bus? Because the bus stop was a convenient place to wait for someone who would be collecting her?

He felt as if his head were full of bees. To get rid of them, he went to the table and pulled a drawing out of the folder, one of a series he was working on, of churchyards and gravestones in villages around Lafferton. But this one, of an eighteenth-century monument to a mother of three young children who had died giving birth to a fourth, he had drawn inside St Cuthbert's, Up Starly. It was a monument he loved, smooth, pale, distant and yet full of love and grief, the tiny marble children clinging to the idealised young woman's feet and arms, her hair streaming down her back, eyes closed, hand stretched out towards them. The churchyard group of drawings would be one of the focal points for his next London exhibition and this its centrepiece. The dead. And the living. The living would include some new drawings of Cat's children. But he knew he wanted Rachel there. She came into his mind now.

He wanted to spend hours sitting looking at her, drawing her. He wanted to be with her.

He looked down at the young mother, the clinging children, the graceful flowing lines of the whole monument, too good for an uninteresting village church – and yet why not? Why should a small ordinary village church not have a masterpiece of sculpture to commemorate someone once so loved and so alive?

He reached for a pencil from the row laid out neatly in front of him, but when he looked down at his drawing again, all he could see was Rachel.

Thirty

She wasn't going. She wouldn't go. There was no point at all in being there. Olive didn't even know she had been moved to another place.

It will unsettle her, Lenny thought, if I go. It's happened, hasn't it? Look how she was the last time. She saw me and started to cry, she took my arm and tried to pull me out of the room, out of the front door. She wanted to come home with me and I couldn't take her home, she didn't understand why and it tore me apart.

She wasn't going.

The room was a mess. She had opened a single window for half an hour and in that time a bird had managed to fly in, panic, skim round and round madly, dropping feathers. They lay on the floor, on the bookshelves, on the piano, on the stool, and droppings too, little greenish-white blobs on the keys and inside between the strings.

She needed to clean the house, not just this room but right through it, the kitchen, where the stove was crusted with brown dried grease, the grill that had been spattered with cold fat for months, with a silt of crumbs in the tray. The bathroom had soap scum, limescale; their bedroom, soft balls of grey fluff under the furniture, grubby pillowcases, stained cover.

Their bedroom. They had never slept in separate beds, not once since they had been together, until Olive had gone into the first home for a week, to give Lenny some rest. On those nights

Lenny had lain awake and put her arm out now and then to check that Olive was there and had not gone wandering, and when the other side of the bed had been empty, had sat up in alarm – and then remembered. Would Olive mind being alone in bed at night? Would she call out for her?

'To be honest, I don't think she even noticed,' the nurse had said.

But how could that be true? You did not sleep with someone for nearly thirty years and not notice if, without warning, without telling you why, they were no longer in your bed. Though Lenny had told her, time after time, tried to prepare her. 'On your holiday,' she had said, 'I won't be staying with you, O. I won't be there at all. You understand that, don't you? I'll be here at home, waiting for you to come back. You do understand that?'

Now she rang up Maytree House every day, and every day they said the same thing. She was settling. She was calm. She seemed perfectly happy. She was amiable. 'A lovely person.' Calm before the storm – Lenny knew that perfectly well. She was calm herself now, here in the cottage on her own. She could not face destroying that, going to find Olive shouting or screaming or grabbing hold of her and clawing at her, desperate to be taken away. Let her stay and be calm. Let her go.

She went outside to get the bird feeder. They had always had such pleasure in watching the birds, noting if one was absent, riffling through the books on the window ledge to identify something new. Olive had filled notebooks. Bird diaries. But gradually had simply sat in silence staring, or else wandered out into the garden ignoring them entirely.

The phone rang as Lenny was gently pouring nuts into the metal tube. It made her jump and spill them all over the floor. Olive had done that the last time she was home, not accidentally, but by taking the bag down and shaking the nuts and scattering them. Lenny had shouted – no, screamed – in anger and desperation. Olive had stared at her for a moment blankly before bursting into tears. A small child's tears.

'Miss Wilcox?'

So it had started all over again but more quickly this time.

They wanted her to come at once, they couldn't cope, Olive had to return home. She sighed.

'Are you all right, Miss Wilcox?'

'Yes. What's she done this time?'

'Nothing. Well, nothing to worry about. She's fine.'

'What's she doing?'

'She's just having a walk round the garden with Lorraine, one of the carers – it's such a nice day. No, it isn't anything to worry about really but we've got a bit of a puzzle we can't solve. And just now and again she seems worried about it – a bit agitated, if you understand me.'

She understood.

'It's a name . . .'

'What name?'

'That's the thing . . . we don't know. She can't tell us but she says it sometimes and then gets very upset and agitated. I thought you would know and maybe give us an idea of how we can calm her down. The trouble is she only mutters it, says it almost to herself.'

'What name?'

'It sounds like – Agatha maybe?'

'Agatha?'

'Yes. We've all tried to make it out. I repeated what she was saying – or what she seemed to be saying – but she got very upset. Perhaps it wasn't Agatha.'

'I don't know. I can't think of anyone called Agatha.'

'Well, whatever it is, it's the only thing that's disturbed her since she came here, so if you do think of what it might be . . .'

'Perhaps it isn't a name.'

'Perhaps.'

'Should I come to see her? I wanted her to settle down first. If she sees me she might get upset about – not coming home with me.'

'I don't think you'll find that now. They do move on a stage, you know . . . when some things just don't upset them any more.'

'You mean she might have forgotten me?'

'No, I don't mean that, or not yet anyway, though you can

never quite predict how things have moved on. But she might have forgotten home . . . where it is, what it means.'

'Is that a good thing? Is it?'

'Sometimes. Letting go can make them more peaceful . . . they come to an acceptance. But this is hard for you – it's always hardest for the ones looking on. If you ever want to come and talk to one of us about that you only have to ask. Dr Fison is very good at helping relatives come to terms with it all. You'd find him such a help if you ever need to get it off your chest.'

'Thank you. I'm fine. I'm quite able to manage.'

'Well, any time – the offer's always there. Are you coming to see Olive soon then?'

'Yes. I don't know which day. But of course I'll come – did you think I'd abandon her after all these years? Is that what kind of a person I seem to you?'

'Of course not.'

'Tell her I'm coming to see her.'

'I will.'

'I'll try and come later. Or tomorrow.'

She made it sound as if something might prevent her. Busy life. Things to do.

She had nothing to do. She could go now.

She went back to quietly filling the bird feeder. That was it. Quiet. It had not been quiet with Olive for so long, not without anger and anxiety and resentment, except during the brief times she had been in one home or another. Lenny looked out of the window. The birds were fluttering about in confusion, trying to find the feeder. There was no sound. She used to have the radio on most of the time but now she rarely did, the silence was so much more precious.

The phone rang again but this time she did not answer it.

'Come on, Olive. Let's go back into the house.'

Lorraine tried to steer her towards the steps into the sitting room but Olive simply stood.

'Olive? It's cold now, come on.' The girl tugged her arm gently.

Olive gave a series of little grunts.

It took almost ten more minutes to persuade her in, step by reluctant, shuffling step.

204

There were two other residents in the home, one of them in the sitting room, which was bright and light, airy and pale, and smelled of new paint, new carpet, new upholstery. But for how much longer? Lorraine thought, remembering the other places she had worked in, the smell that came at you however hard the rooms were cleaned.

She had hold of Olive's hand but, as they went up the last step and in through the open French windows, Lorraine felt a sharp tug and then Olive was on the floor.

'Olive? Oh, for goodness' sake, now what have you done? Come here, let's see if you're hurt.'

Olive had crumpled like a puppet inside her wide cotton skirt, but as Lorraine bent over her she pulled at her arm until the girl almost fell on top of her.

'Olive, don't do that. Come on now, I'm going to help you up, just take my hand.'

'Lorraine?' Moira Fison had been on the phone to Lenny only half an hour before. Now this.

'I'm not sure if she tripped or – honestly, I think she went down deliberately –'

'Olive!'

Olive suddenly put her hands over her face.

'Now, have you hurt yourself? Come on, let me look.' She touched the woman's hands, arms, legs. 'Sit up.' Olive took her hands and sat. 'There. No damage. Now stand.'

Between them they pulled her easily to her feet. She weighed as little as a bird.

'Right. Let's get her sitting down. She can go back to her room in a minute. Was she all right out there?'

'Seemed to be.'

'Did she say anything?'

'Not really. Only muttered under her breath a bit. That woman again.'

'Agatha?'

'No, it's not Agatha.'

'What then?'

'What's the other woman's name? Her – you know.'

'Miss Wilcox?'

'This Wilcox says she doesn't know an Agatha.'

Olive was rocking to and fro and moaning, and the moans were loud then soft, loud then soft.

'Where's Mrs Sanders?'

'Coming down before long – just cleaned up.'

'Right, well, Mrs Sanders really doesn't need this one upsetting her. Come on.'

'Do you think she should maybe have a rest now?'

'I'll see if my husband's about. He'll decide.'

Which meant, Lorraine thought, that Olive would get a rest. Give them all a break. She knew perfectly well what people thought about sedation but they weren't the ones who had to cope and it wasn't like giving chemical coshes to normal healthy kids who were just over-lively and needed some discipline. This place couldn't function at all if the patients didn't get a sedative now and again.

'Ahhhhhhh!' Olive shrieked so suddenly, and so loudly, that Lorraine and Moira Fison both jumped.

'Ahhhhhhhh!'

'All right, Olive. That's enough.'

They each took hold of her under an arm, hauled her up and walked her between them out of the room.

'A . . .' she whispered. 'Ag . . .'

'Can you get it now?'

Lorraine shook her head. 'I don't think it's a name. I think it's just noises.'

Olive went on making them, deep in her throat.

When Lenny arrived in the late afternoon Olive was asleep, lying on her bed, shoes off, the covers pulled loosely over her, groaning softly.

'Is she all right?'

'Yes. She had a bit of a fall this morning – she tripped over the step coming in from the garden so it was better to let her rest. Dr Fison looked her over and she wasn't hurt but you can't be too careful. Do you want to sit with her?'

Lenny touched the hand that was splayed out from under the coverlet. It was the colour of wax, the nails pale and cut short.

206

Her hands. She had loved those hands. Loved to stroke the soft backs of them, link her own little finger in one of Olive's.

'Should she be making that noise?'

'She's just snoring, bless her.'

'She doesn't snore.'

'Most old people snore.'

'I said she doesn't snore. I should know. What have you given her?'

'After a shock like that a wee sedative is a good idea – calming, you know.'

'You've no right to stupefy her with drugs. She can't protest, she doesn't know.'

Moira Fison spoke very carefully. Patiently. 'I would never use the word "stupefy", Miss Wilcox.'

'Oh, I would.'

'You see, Olive was very agitated earlier. She was worrying over this name – she was asking for Agatha.'

'There's no one called Agatha,' Lenny said, pushing past the woman. Behind her, Olive, lay too still, too deeply asleep, the yellow-white hand outstretched and limp against the covers.

He was coming up the stairs as she went down and Lenny would have pushed past him too. She had met him once, the day she had brought Olive, and had disliked him but only because she disliked all doctors, disliked the way they assumed power, claimed superior knowledge, passed judgement. He had talked plausibly about new ideas, new ways of caring for dementia patients, new approaches, stimulation, one-to-one care, small steps, memory hints, making the best of . . . Lenny could have trotted it all back at him. She hadn't believed much of it. Nothing here seemed different from any of the other places except that it was new, the carpets were still shedding fluff, the paint smelled. Give it time, she knew, give it only a very short time and it would smell of pee and Listerine and stewing meat, the same as they all did.

She got into the van. A treecreeper was going up the trunk of an ash tree nearby, a bird she had rarely seen and one that Olive had tried over years to attract to their own garden without success. This one was camouflaged against the trunk and only its deft, expert movement upwards gave it away. Lenny watched.

207

'Come here, quick,' she would have said. 'Look, O, isn't that what you've always wanted to see?'

And Olive would have come over, her movements neat and purposeful as the bird's, taken up the binoculars that were always on the window ledge, and focused them.

'It is, isn't it?' Lenny would have said, and after a moment's excited, waiting silence, breath held, Olive would have turned to her, lowering the glasses, her face lit with her particular smile, eyes slightly narrowed, as if against the bright sun – what Lenny had always called her 'giving smile'.

Thirty-one

'Rachel?'

'Oh . . .'

'Sorry, is this a bad time?'

'It's just . . . I'm on my way to Kenneth's room. He's in bed, he hasn't been well.'

'I'll hang up.'

'No, don't . . .'

'I can call you again?'

'No – I don't mean no, I mean, no, listen . . . don't go. Hang on.' Her voice was muffled. She said a word or two. Then footsteps. 'Sorry. I'm in the kitchen. Simon?'

'I'm still here.'

'I'm sorry.'

'What for? You don't have to apologise . . . I – I just wanted to hear your voice.'

'And me. Me yours, I mean. I hear enough of my own.'

'I can't believe that. Anyway, I'm sorry – I'd better go.'

'No, don't, please don't. It seems ages.'

'It is. Are you all right?'

'Yes. It's just, when Ken gets ill he gets more ill because of the Parkinson's – he only had a cold but it's now a chest infection. I was just taking him a drink. He's got so many blasted drugs he has to take . . . Sorry. You don't want to hear me talk about my husband.'

'I've told you, I just want to hear you talk. Can I see you?'

209

Silence.

'Rachel, I know I shouldn't ring you and I know I shouldn't ask to see you but I so want to. I so need to.'

Eventually, she said 'Yes', very quietly.

'When?'

'I meant, I want to see you. I need to. As well.'

'Can we?'

'I don't know . . . it's difficult at the moment . . .'

'Just a drink? Just for an hour?'

'It wouldn't be an hour though, would it?'

'It would. Anything you say. I can set my watch. Please.'

'I'll ring. You're busy, aren't you?'

'Yes, but I do get time off.'

'Can I ring then, when I see a way?'

'He'll be fine, won't he? Your husband. He's got antibiotics presumably . . . all that.'

'It takes him longer to recover . . . not like you and me.'

'No.'

'I'm always terrified for him.'

He was silent.

'Simon?'

'I understand.' He did but he hated that he did.

'Listen . . . he's my husband. I'm responsible for him.'

'I know that. Of course I do. What kind of a shit do you think I am? I know you have to put him first, I know that.'

'I don't think you're any kind of a shit, I think you're . . .'

'What? Rachel? What do you think of me?' It was the only thing in the world he wanted to know. Was desperate to know.

'I have to go. Sorry. I'll ring you. I promise I'll ring.'

'Simon, it's Judith.'

'Yes. How are you?'

'Your formal tone. Are you on duty?'

'I'm always on duty.'

'No you're not. You're annoyed with me and I don't altogether blame you but can we meet all the same? Always better to be annoyed face to face, I find.'

'I'm pretty up to my eyes.'

'Yes, but you have to eat. Your father's out tomorrow night so I wondered if you and I could have a quiet supper somewhere.'

'When you say "somewhere" . . .'

'I meant I could do without cooking and this house isn't conducive to our having the best conversations, is it?'

'I suppose not.'

'I'm sure not. So – may I take you out to supper at that nice Italian place of yours? It worked for us before.'

'You're making it sound as if we've fallen out over something.'

'I rather think we might have, don't you? Crossed wires and misunderstandings anyway.'

'Hmm.'

But she was right. He was just finding it hard to admit, as ever.

'I'd like to. Should be fine, but things are surfacing at odd times on this Lowther case so there's a chance I might have to cry off.'

'There is always a chance you might have to do that, isn't there?'

'I'll pick you up.'

'That would be lovely, then I can have a drink or two and get a taxi home. Thank you, darling.'

His mother had called him that. Now Judith. No one else, other than this woman or that, to whom the word came easily and meant little. It was not an endearment word he used himself.

'Is everything all right?'

'Talk about it tomorrow. You?'

'Talk tomorrow.'

He had told her about Rachel, and what he had not told, Judith had deduced, from his face, his tone of voice, and from the silences between the half-uttered phrases. She was the only person he could have told and he didn't know what reaction he had expected from her – certainly not anything like the one he would have got from Cat. She had listened with care and said little but he had sensed hesitation, a holding back of something – sympathy? Approval? He had needed both. He realised

211

that he always did. But Judith did not rush into anything and so he had flared up, wishing he had never spoken to her, tense and irritable and confused about his feelings. They had parted on abrasive terms.

She had dressed with some care, he thought, as they took her coat in the restaurant. His mother had dressed elegantly and strikingly, Judith was always well presented but drew little attention to herself with her clothes. Tonight, though, she had a black top with a deep red silk stole, a black-and-gold heavy necklace. People glanced round.

But when they were sitting opposite one another at his favourite table in the window, he saw that her eyes were sad, that she had concealed the shadows and hollows beneath them, that she had lost enough weight for it to show in her face – and she had not needed to lose it.

He ordered a bottle of prosecco.

'Peace offering?'

'Guilt offering,' Simon said. 'But we don't need an excuse.'

The menus came, the old-fashioned huge menus, with the slip of paper clipped to the bottom on which the specials of the day were handwritten, the menus that went with the time warp within which the restaurant operated to serve the best food in Lafferton.

They ordered a large dish of antipasti. The wine came. Bottles of water. Chunks of fresh bread. The bowl of deep green olive oil.

Simon waited. The restaurant was busy, as always, but at this table they could talk without being overheard, they had a space to themselves. The candlelight reflected in the window.

I want to be here with Rachel, he thought. I have to bring her here tomorrow or the next day, somehow I have to seal things by bringing her here.

Would she come back to the flat? It was not a question he had ever needed to ask. He had always decided if women he knew were invited there or not. It was not automatic, but if he did ask them, it had never occurred to him that they might say no. None ever had.

Rachel might.

Judith drank some wine before she said, 'It's easier here. You know I've never been a tearful person – I don't mean I've never cried – of course I have – but not very often in front of other people.'

'You mean you want to cry now?'

'I don't want to. I'm afraid I might.'

Her hand was on the table and he put his own over it for a moment, as much to steady himself as her. He had had a moment of sudden chill.

'Judith?'

They were silent as the platter of antipasti was set down.

'Not often comfort food is also such good food,' she said. 'It's all right, darling, don't look so stricken, I'm not about to announce a divorce.'

'Now that's a relief.'

'Did you really think . . . ?'

'For a second.'

She shook her head. 'I love Richard. I do love him very much. I love him in quite a different way from the way I loved Don – when I married Don, I was twenty-two, he was the first man I ever looked at seriously, and we had over thirty years and two children together. Of course it's different.'

'I'm coming to the conclusion that's always true. All love is different.'

'In a sense. But something happened and it's shifted the ground on which our marriage stands. That's your phone.'

He went outside to take the call. It was a mild evening and there were people strolling down through the Lanes, couples, groups of the young, two girls pushing bikes. It was a world into which nothing harmful should intrude.

'Guv? Woman on the special line. Wants to talk to you. Wouldn't tell me any more. Sounded agitated. Said she'd seen the recon. Hung up.'

'You got a number?'

'No, trying to trace the call. But she's going to ring again later tonight.'

'Did she say when?'

213

'No. Could be any time.'

'OK – listen, I'm eating out. If she calls again ask her if she'll ring back at ten o'clock tonight. I'll be home. Put her through to my landline. And keep tracing. Anything else?'

'A few other calls, nothing that sounds up to much.'

'Thanks.'

As he turned to go back into the restaurant the phone rang again.

'Simon? Paula Devenish. Any chance you could come and see me tomorrow morning?'

'Of course. How are you?'

'Stir-crazy, but threatened with dire consequences if I set foot in a police station. Half past ten?'

'Sorry, Judith.'

'I got them to hold back our main course but they'll bring it now. Unless you have to go?'

'No. All in hand.'

Her halibut and his *fegato alla veneziana* arrived with a flourish. Simon topped up her glass. He looked directly at her as she drank.

'So. You should tell me,' he said.

'Yes.' Judith flushed slightly, not with the wine. 'Right. You know how your father can be – he says something, apparently out of the blue, though it rarely is. I've learned that he will have been brooding about it for hours – days sometimes. The more significant the thing, the more he is inclined to drop it from a great height. It can make him seem insensitive.'

'He *is* insensitive.'

'No, Simon, he isn't. I know how it is between you two and I wouldn't dare to tell you that you don't know him, or that you are wrong about him. The man you have known since you were born is the man you know in a way only you can – well, you and the other two. But I know him pretty well now, and the point is, I know him differently. I haven't the childhood baggage and that makes for a clearer view.'

'Whatever. But now he's said something which has clearly upset you. Doesn't sound sensitive to me.'

'He isn't good at timing. I'd just had a long phone conversation with Vivien, who keeps going from one unhappy relationship to the next, and right after that, one with Emma – you know, she has the new bookshop? – and she appears to be doing exactly the same.'

An image of Emma flashed into Simon's mind. He'd found her attractive – but not very. And that had been before Rachel. Emma? He couldn't even remember her last name.

Judith was looking down at her plate.

'So I was feeling a bit battered. He must have known – he must have heard me. I came off the phone and put the dish of lamb chops on the table and he said, "Martha's death wasn't natural, you know. I can't remember if I've told you this. Her mother took the decision that Martha's life was no life."' She spoke so quietly that Simon had to lean forward to catch every word. 'He told me that you knew.'

'Yes.' He finished half his glass of wine in one go, before he could trust himself to say anything and his hand shook as he did so. 'Yes,' he said. 'I knew.'

'Simon . . .'

'But I can't believe he told you.'

'Well, I'm his wife now, aren't I? Maybe it's as simple as that.'

'If that's the case, why didn't he tell you before now? Why not even before you were married to him? Had you been talking about Martha?'

'No. He never talks about her. Simon, your father has barely so much as mentioned her name in all the time I've known him. I don't know why he came out with what he did, let alone at that particular moment or in that way, but I know I wish he hadn't. I so wish that. He should never, ever have said any of it. That should have remained something between him and Meriel. But not me. It's a family matter in which I have no part and I shouldn't be made to have one.'

He knew she meant it. She had never attempted to discover things about their past nor felt that she had any right to be told them. So far as Judith was concerned, her life in the Serrailler family began with her marriage to his father. It was

215

one of the things that, once he understood it, had brought him round to liking and respecting her – albeit late in the day.

'What did you say to him?'

'I was very angry. I have never been so angry. I couldn't sit down at the table and eat with him, I had to go out . . . I just stood there in the dark, I didn't know when I might be able to go back into the house and face him.'

'When did you?'

'I don't know – it must have been half an hour. It was a long time. I walked around . . . I was shaking so much . . . I couldn't think. The worst part was when I went back – he'd eaten supper by himself, he'd cleared away and gone off into his study. I went to bed . . . I was trying to read but not taking in a word. I knew we'd have to talk but I couldn't face it that night. I just turned over and pretended to be asleep. That old one.'

'Did he try to wake you?'

'No.'

'Next day?'

'He got up and made the tea – just brought the tray up as usual, and the newspaper. And . . .' She looked at him.

'And,' Simon said, 'he carried on as if nothing had happened.'

'Yes.'

'Jesus, don't I know that one. I know every word of the script. God knows it was played out often enough at home. I don't know how my mother stood it. I couldn't, nor could Ivo. It's what my father did time after time – dropped something in the middle of a perfectly pleasant normal occasion, breakfast or Sunday lunch or when everyone was in the garden, anything, so long as we were all together and happy. And bang. Crump. The sound of a bomb going off, scattering everyone, shaking us up, horrifying us . . . you see? You see what he's like? I thought you'd changed things.'

'Yes,' Judith said. 'I thought I had too.'

'Have you talked to him about it since?'

'No. I can't. For the first time, I don't know how, I don't know where I could possibly begin.'

They finished the bottle of prosecco, had coffee. Several tables emptied, other people came in to fill them. Judith turned the conversation, asking a few questions about the Lowther case, then about Sam, who had been in detention twice at school recently.

'And that's not like him.'

'Bad work or bad behaviour?' Simon asked.

'Behaviour. He works hard. But Cat has enough on her plate at the moment, she doesn't need this.'

'I'd better have a word with him. Try and dig a bit.'

'He likes going walking with you.'

'I'll drive up to Wales with him, stay overnight in a B & B, climb. Trouble is, I don't know when.'

Judith stirred her coffee. She did not ask the question but it was in the air between them. He wasn't sure if he wanted to answer, to talk about Rachel at all. He had never felt himself to be on such ground before, so important, so uncertain.

'Darling, you have to go home and take a call, I am dropping with good food and wine and tiredness, so if you would walk me to the taxi rank . . .'

'When is Dad back?'

'Tomorrow. I want a long sleep and a good lie-in tomorrow morning while I do some thinking.'

'Are you going to talk to him?'

'About Martha? No. But I need to think about it – or rather, about why he told me and what he might have been expecting to come out of it. What he thought my reaction was going to be. I just don't know. I don't understand and that makes me feel . . .'

'Unhappy?'

'Not so much unhappy as – bewildered, I suppose. I thought I knew where I was. I don't. Insecure is more the word. And I shouldn't feel that, not by now.'

Walking along towards the cab rank, Simon felt another surge of anger towards his father. 'He doesn't bloody well know what he's got,' he said, 'he doesn't know how lucky he is and he doesn't deserve you. Listen –' he opened the taxi door, but put his other hand on Judith's arm – 'listen, don't let him bully you. He bullied us, he bullied my mother. I won't have him doing it to you, Judith. Neither Cat nor I will. We care about you.'

She kissed him and got quickly into the cab without saying

anything else. In spite of her best efforts to conceal it from him, he saw that she was crying.

The call came seconds after he had sprinted up the stairs.

'Serrailler.' There was a silence. 'Simon Serrailler here. You've been put through directly to me and no one else is on the line.'

Silence.

'How can I help? Do you have some information about Harriet Lowther?'

Silence.

'Listen, I'm on my own and nobody else can hear this.'

Which was not true. The call was being recorded.

'If you don't talk to me I can't help you.'

He waited. She was there, he knew. She hadn't replaced the receiver. But it was another thirty seconds or more before she said, 'Hello?'

'Hello. This is DCS Simon Serrailler.'

'I don't want to give my name.'

'That's fine. But please understand that if you don't it makes it harder for us. I'm trying to solve a serious crime. I need you to give me any information you may have about this, and I might need to get back to you. That's hard if you won't even tell me your name. Listen – this is a murder investigation. I am trying to catch a killer who is still out there, after sixteen years. A murderer.'

He heard the slight reaction to the word as he emphasised it but then there was a silence again.

'It's my job to find this murderer, and I will, but it isn't easy and every bit of information, every tiny detail and snippet, might be the vital bit that links things together. So if you have anything to tell me, however small or apparently irrelevant it is, then please tell me. If it isn't important and it doesn't lead anywhere, how can that matter? It can't. But what if it is? You don't know. It's my job to decide, my job to follow it up. You'll have done your bit. Only, if you don't tell me, and it does turn out to be the one missing piece I need – how would you feel? Can you live with that? Now – please talk to me. Will you talk to me?'

There was a small sigh and then the woman said, 'It's probably nothing. I'm sure it's nothing. But . . . well, like you just said.'

'Yes. I'd rather hear about nothing than miss something important. What's worrying you?'

'The television programme . . .'

'Yes.'

'They showed that day – well, they made it look like that day.'

'The reconstruction, yes. You saw it?'

'Yes, I was watching – I was actually in the middle of watching the programme when he – when Steve came in. My husband came in. He started watching it . . . we watched about ten minutes, I suppose, but then that bit of the programme came on . . . about the girl. The reconstruction part. And he . . . he just behaved . . . well, it was odd. I don't know. It is nothing, isn't it?'

'Just go on telling me what happened, Mrs . . . ?'

'Foster. Oh.'

'Mrs Foster. Will you tell me your first name?'

'I didn't mean to say it.'

'Mrs what Foster?'

She sighed. 'Noeline. Born on Christmas Day of course.'

'Did your husband say anything while he was watching the programme?'

'No. He just got up, and changed chairs, then he seemed – I don't know – fidgety. He picked up the paper to look at what was on the other channels . . . he found the remote and flicked over but then he went back and sat watching really . . . really intently, you know? As if he was afraid to miss any of it. He sort of – leaned forward as well. I've never seen him do that.'

'Did you say anything?'

'No. Yes, yes, I think I said how awful it was, or "that poor girl" or something like that.'

'Did he answer?'

'No. It was as if he was – sort of transfixed by the television.'

'And when it finished?'

'He got up and went upstairs. He almost ran up. He didn't say anything at all. And then I heard the bathwater starting.'

'Did he say anything later on?'

'No. I tidied up and did the doors, then I went up to bed. He didn't come for ages. He stayed in the bath for such a long time. He never does that. I was reading a magazine but I'd put it down when he came to bed. I was almost asleep. I'd been going to ask him about it . . . the programme. Only I was so tired, I just didn't.'

'And the next day?'

'No. But he wasn't himself.'

'In what way?'

'It . . . it's not easy to say. Only . . . there was just something. It's all rubbish, isn't it? I feel stupid.'

'No. I don't think it's rubbish and you are certainly not stupid. I don't know why your husband – Stephen, did you say?'

'Steve. Well, yes, Stephen, only he never is.'

'He was obviously affected by the programme for some reason. I'd like to talk to him.'

'Oh no, you can't do that, you mustn't come round here, he'll know it was me, that I said something to you, won't he?'

'No. Can you just give me the address please?'

'It's 60 – No, no, I won't, sorry. I shouldn't have made this call. I . . . sorry. Forget it all. Stupid thing to do. Just stupid.'

'Mrs –'

But she had hung up. He jotted down 'Stephen Foster, 60? Lafferton?' and added 'Noeline'. And the time of her call.

220

Thirty-two

'There are warnings of gales in Viking, North Utsire, South Utsire, Forties, Cromarty, Forth, Tyne, Dogger, Fisher, German Bight, Humber, Thames, Dover, Wight, Sole, Lundy, Fastnet, Irish Sea, Shannon, Rockall, Malin, Hebrides, Bailey, Fair Isle, Faeroes and south-east Iceland.'

Jocelyn wondered which was more comforting, the voice of that night's continuity announcer reciting the shipping forecast, or being safe and warm under her duvet while the gale raged round Lafferton.

Both were, but she knew that the deepest satisfaction came from the simple fact of being here at all, in her own bed, her own house. Alive. She looked around the room. There were three new library books on the bedside table beside the lamp, another on the quilt. The bedlinen was fresh. The photographs of Penny as a child, of Carol's wedding, of Tony in his uniform, of Lottie, the old spaniel, with Penny again, arranged in one large frame on the dressing table. The reflection of the soft pink wallpaper in the mirror.

Alive.

She closed her eyes for a moment and the horror of what she now thought of as the Death Room was there in every detail.

Alive.

Since they had returned she had had nightmares of such horror and ferocity that she had made an appointment to see Dr Deerbon again. The nightmares woke her several times, or else attacked her just as she slipped down into sleep, and she came out of

221

them shaking and sweating, her heart pounding so fast and hard she was afraid it would burst out of her chest.

How did people go through with it? She had asked Penny a dozen times on the journey home – because they did, many of them, people who had travelled, as she had, a long way, to the terrible apartment block, who would then lie down in the dingy room on what had looked less wholesome than a veterinary couch and accept a glass of fluid which would kill them. Had those people been more honest? Had they confronted the facts first, not fantasised about a tranquil room with clean crisp white bedlinen and a gauzy curtain fluttering in the breeze, gentle music, low lighting and sweet-faced nurses? Had they found out what it was really like and yet gone through with it?

She opened her eyes on her room again and at once she felt safe. It had not happened after all, she had run away and she would never go there again. She felt as if she had escaped from Death Row and been transported home on a magic carpet – for even though the actual return had been tiresome and fraught with delays and discomfort, it had been transformed into the most wonderful journey of her life, because of her relief and happiness. She and Penny had clung to one another for most of it, in a way they had never done before, holding one another's arms, and even clutching hands at one point, crying together and sharing a packet of tissues, and then laughing and drinking their little bottles of wine on the plane, their hearts light, unable to believe they were both on their way home.

Alive.

She tried to pick up her book but her fingers would not tighten on it. Earlier, she had gone out to post a letter and felt herself shuffling along the pavement. The symptoms were manageable but they had definitely grown worse. She noticed every tiny change, recorded it, worried about it.

Alive.

Yes, but the reprieve was only temporary. She knew what was going to happen and neither her escape nor this respite made that knowledge easier.

She pulled the book closer to her, scooped it up somehow with one hand, but the fingers felt nerveless, thickened and inert, and she could not turn the page. She abandoned it and switched off the light. The wind gathered itself and hurtled towards the house. A gate banged further down the street. There was a full moon and the clouds scudding fast across it made strange moving shadows on the wall. It was like being a child again, warm and safe in her seaside bed, while the waves crashed onto the shingle and the gale roared and the street lamp outside flickered.

Safe.

Sheltered.

Alive.

When the phone rang she reached out for it automatically but her hand would not grip the receiver and she ended by knocking it onto the floor. By the time she had managed to switch on the lamp, get out of bed and retrieve it, the caller had rung off.

Since returning home she had been twitchy, anxious about callers and the telephone, worrying about the security settings on her computer – though Penny had checked them and pronounced them perfectly adequate. Her illness made her vulnerable. It had been one of the reasons she had gone to the clinic. Vulnerable older people with medical conditions were prey to intruders, scams and hoax callers as well as to accidents. She had always been a woman of nerve and practical common sense. This new feeling of frailty and the nag of anxiety that was always in her mind disturbed her. She did not know herself any more.

But she was herself, that was the point. She was herself now, warm under the bedclothes while the wind raged outside. Herself.

The lamp had a dimmer switch and she set it to Low, then, with the light softened to a glow, she turned her head on the pillow and sank into sleep.

The phone woke her again, a little before eight. The wind was still high and although it was fully light, the clouds were so heavy that at first she thought it was not yet dawn. She was slightly disorientated, slow in movements, so that by the time she had registered the phone and managed to sit up, the ringing had stopped.

1471.

'You were called today at . . .'

She dialled Penny.

'Mother, I was just about to step into the shower. Is it urgent?'

'Someone keeps ringing me – they rang late last night and again just now.'

'Who is ringing you?'

'I don't know. Number withheld.'

'Well, I'm not sure I can do anything about it. I'm in court this morning, and even if I weren't . . .'

'I was a bit unnerved, that's all.'

'Have you had your tea yet? That's sure to help. Go and do that and get back into bed with the paper, Mother. I'll try and call you at lunchtime.'

'Penny, do you think . . .'

'What?'

'I just wondered . . . I mean . . .'

'Mother . . .'

'It's illegal. What we did. What I did.'

Penny snorted. 'And the police or the CPS make "number withheld" calls at strange times of the night about this sort of thing, do they? For goodness' sake, stop it. Go and make your tea. I'll talk to you later.'

When she opened up her computer, she found an email from the woman Hazel Smith.

I happened to hear that you had aborted your visit to
Switzerland and wondered if there was anything I could do
for you, any help I could give. I have counselled several
people who have found it a difficult journey and one woman
who, like you, could not go through with her plan. If you
would like to talk to me do please ring and we could perhaps
meet? I would so like to know how you are feeling, how you
are facing up to things, whether you have another plan in
place. Don't hesitate to call, will you?
    Warm regards,
    Hazel

Jocelyn began to shake. The message nauseated her, with its false sweetness of tone, its offer of help which she found sinister, its intrusiveness, its unpleasant assumption of a friendship there had never been and could never be. The woman had seemed genuine, slightly detached, willing to be a paid companion and take a certain risk in doing so. Now, she was apparently trying to insinuate herself, trying to extend her business arrangement further, ready to advise and counsel. Jocelyn deleted the message. Then, because it felt as if it were still a stain, contaminating her computer and the whole desk, the room, the house even, she emptied the recycle bin. So it was gone. It could do no further harm. She would have nothing more to do with Hazel Smith.

But the memory of the woman and her message lingered, souring the air, weaving in and out through her thoughts. And she wondered if the phone calls might also have come from her.

Getting dressed took longer now. By the time she had done so, driven to the supermarket and talked to her next-door neighbour for ten minutes on her return, she was exhausted. She was also frightened. As she had turned out of the car park she had not been able to feel her foot as it touched the brake and pressed down too hard, almost bringing the car to a shuddering stand-still. People had hooted, one man had shaken his fist out of the window as he had overtaken her.

So how long would it be before she had to give up driving? How long before she became entirely dependent on other people to fetch and carry?

'You were called today at . . .'

Thirty-three

'I didn't think you'd come.'

Rachel smiled. 'You said that the last time.'

He looked at her, astonished that she should be with him, that she hadn't hesitated when he had rung but said, 'I'll be there.'

'Ken is away in Oxford until tomorrow. He goes to a clinic once every three months to get treatment.'

'Bevham General no good?'

'Bevham General is fine but this is alternative stuff . . . acupuncture, herbal medicine.'

'Ah. That.'

'There's a practitioner he trusts. He listens to Ken. I think that's the point really, don't you?'

'My sister listens to her patients. She reckons it's important.'

'It is. Look, for what it's worth I don't think these treatments do any good . . . but it helps him to go there, he thinks they're doing him good so maybe they are.'

'I don't buy that.'

'He has two days of people making him feel he's important and that they can do something for him. He believes in it, he feels better when he comes home – mentally better, more able to cope. That's worth paying for in my book. Why are you so hostile?'

'Maybe because of a local acupuncturist who murdered

226

quite a few people? Maybe because of all the cranks and quacks who colonise Starly? Maybe because my sister has had to pick up the pieces from some of these snake-oil salesmen? You tell me.'

They were standing in the car park of the Cross Garters at Cobwood, ten miles out of Lafferton to the west, where Simon rarely came, though not for any particular reason. But he had wanted to bring Rachel somewhere which had no memories or associations and with little chance of his meeting anyone he knew. He had rung her without hope of her being able to come.

'You look beautiful.' He heard himself and realised it was something he almost never said, not because he failed to notice – he always noticed – what women looked like, how they wore their hair, the colour of their eyes, their clothes, their tone of voice, but because compliments did not come easily from him. Perhaps, he had often thought, in this, if in nothing else, he was exactly like his father.

'Thank you.'

He smiled. Thank you, she had said. Not disagreeing, not being embarrassed, not turning away his words. Thank you.

'I hope we weren't arguing just then.'

'What, about quacks? Hardly worth it.'

'Hmm. Aren't you working?'

'Yes. Are you hungry?'

'Not very. Maybe if we walked up to that spinney and back I would be.'

They crossed the lane, went through the gap beside the footpath sign. The spinney was on the crown of the slope ahead. A pair of buzzards soared over it, flat wings widespread.

'They look like the *Angel of the North*,' Rachel said.

He took her hand and, for a second, she paused, so that he was sure she would take it away. But in the end, she did not, and said nothing, walked on.

The breeze coming downhill blew her hair, and as she turned to shake it out of her face, Simon felt a strange sense, not of déjà vu but of the opposite – a snatched moment in the future, months, even years ahead, when they would be here, walking up the slope, her hair blowing in her face.

That is what I want, he thought. I am seeing what I want to happen.

He had never felt such a thing in his life and he had no idea how or why he did now. Rachel Wyatt. He barely knew her. He had met her less than half a dozen times. She did not know him. She had not seen where he lived, met anyone he knew. But they had talked, and that talk had included so many lines of subtext, about their feelings, their wants.

He knew her. She knew him.

They knew nothing.

The breeze was a wind as they reached the shelter of the spinney. Rachel sat down on a fallen tree trunk and looked towards the village and then turned to the west, where the Mynt Hills rose, like a distant back of a blue whale.

'On a good day . . .'

'Have you ever been over there?'

'No. Sometimes you don't see the hills at all . . . it's as if they're just faint clouds on the horizon. Are they very high?'

'No . . . I'll take you. We'll climb the Mynts.'

'I wish.'

'Why not?'

'You know why not, Simon.'

He sat down next to her. 'It would only be a day out.'

'Not easy.'

'This is a day out.'

'No, it's an hour or two. But that isn't the point, is it?'

He was silent. Rachel stood up and turned away from him.

'I don't know what's happened,' Simon said. 'How or what or why.'

'Oh, there's a word for it.'

'Yes.'

'The French put it well.'

'I don't know what – what to do with it either. Sorry, that sounds crass.'

'No. I'm the same. What do I do? I'm not a free agent. You are. It's very different. A different place.'

'You could be.'

She turned. 'No. No, Simon, I couldn't. That is the one sure thing.'

He said, 'I only know about one sure thing.'

'Yes. But . . .'

Now he was the one who turned away, and started to walk out of the crown of trees and back down the track. He didn't trust himself to speak or to look at her. His mind was a swirl of thoughts and words, things only half said but wholly felt.

He heard her footsteps behind him, soft on the grass, and paused until she was beside him, but he did not take her hand again.

They found a window table at the pub and sat with plates of soup and salads in front of them but not eating, saying little. Simon wanted simply to look at her, see the light change her eyes from pale to deep violet blue, with the darker rim around the iris, to look at the curve of her lower lip and the way her hair curled into the nape of her neck.

He put his hand on hers for a second but she slid it away and picked up a spoon.

'I shouldn't have come.'

'Why? Why do you say that?'

'It's not sensible.'

'Sensible.'

'Or – fair. Not fair to you. Not fair to either of us. Or to –'

'Oh, Rachel, what's "fair"? What's "sensible"? What kind of words are those?'

'Useful ones.'

'Are you happy as you are? Just tell me that truthfully. Because it isn't enough. This isn't any sort of life for you.'

'Ken doesn't have any sort of life either.'

'I need to see you.'

'Need.'

'All right, want. Need. Anything. I'm in love with you.'

She looked straight at him. 'Yes.'

'What does "yes" mean?'

'It means . . . it means I know. And . . . yes.'

'If I can't . . . I don't want to say all this here. We need to be on our own.'

'It's good that we're not. We're in a public place and it prevents us.'

'I can't do that. Stop – stop saying things to you, stop myself wanting to say them. That's a warning, I think. Yes.'

'I can't let this happen. I won't let there be any more.'

'So why did you come? What are you doing here?'

'Don't interrogate me like that.'

'Sorry. I'm sorry. But I don't understand what you're doing. You say this but you're here. You rang me. You sent me a text. You came to the hotel. All that. But you seem to be telling me you want – well, what? I don't know.'

'Friendship?'

'Is that what you're offering me? Is that what you want? Because all right then, yes, if that's all I can have, I'll take it because I can't have nothing. I've just realised that.'

Rachel got up without a word and went across the bar to the cloakroom. She had long legs. Long, slender legs in smart jeans with a creamy linen jacket, hair tied loosely back.

I've blown it. He almost said it aloud. Telling her he would have friendship because he couldn't bear to have nothing had made him sound desperate and desperation was never attractive, desperation repelled. She could walk out now and never return a call or a message, simply avoid him from this moment on. It would be easy enough.

They hardly knew one another.

He had asked Judith if that mattered. No, she had said. But had warned him, all the same.

'Simon, I'm not being judgemental, I'm being realistic. You're not talking about a relationship which could go somewhere. She isn't free. I don't even mean "she's married". It's more than that because of his situation. Isn't it? How long you've known her is neither here nor there, is it? Not set against that.'

He could see her as she had said it, hear the words. More than a marriage.

Thirty-four

This time it was half past nine in the evening. Jocelyn was sitting with a cup of milky coffee and a couple of buttered crackers on the side table, watching the last episode of a historical crime series set in the Victorian underworld, but the violence had become so sickening that she was relieved when the phone rang.

'Mrs Forbes?'

Not a cold call, surely. The voice was older than most call-centre operators and more . . . she couldn't think of the word.

'Yes.'

'Good evening. I hope this isn't an inconvenient time to have a word with you?'

'Who is this?'

'And I don't want to intrude, so perhaps you would just hear what I have to say for a moment, and if you feel that I am indeed intruding then please say so, and I promise I will ring off at once.'

'All right,' she said carefully. Educated. That was probably the word. A well-spoken, educated man, and an older man, not a twenty-something insurance salesman.

'Is this a convenient time to have a word with you?'

'Yes . . . yes, this is all right. But . . . are you the police?'

'Emphatically not.'

'Or some sort of lawyer?'

'Again, I am not. No.'

'Because –'

'I am a doctor.'

'Oh God, are you from them? From the clinic? Bene Mori?'

'No. I am most certainly not and let me reassure you that, in my view, Bene Mori should be closed down. Their methods, the way they run their operation – those are despicable, beyond disgraceful. The whole place, the whole organisation, brings shame on the movement.'

'The movement?'

'The movement to make assisted suicide legal, to help those who wish to end their own lives with dignity at a time of their choosing . . . those of us – and I am one – who want this to be properly and very strictly regulated, but to be legal in this country – frankly, we are all ashamed of this Swiss operation. But unfortunately, what happens in another country with different laws – well, we can bring pressure to bear on their medical authorities, even on their governments, but we can't actually have them closed down. If they were in this country, of course, it would be a different matter.'

'Doctor . . .'

She waited but he did not reply.

'Why exactly have you rung me?'

'For this reason. I know what a dreadful experience you had. Believe me, I've met others in the same situation. You aren't the first and, sadly, you won't be the last. I want to advise you and give you every possible assistance – but only if that, at some point in the future, is what you yourself want. If not, then you tell me so and you will not hear from me again. I want to help you.'

'Help me?'

'First of all, I'm offering my services as a fully qualified doctor, to counsel you in the aftermath of the trauma you went through at the Bene Mori clinic. I can listen to everything you have to tell me and try to put it all out of your mind, help you recover. If you're having stressful thoughts, panic attacks, nightmares. Anything like that. I can help you deal with it. And then we could look at your medical condition, reassess it, and if, at any point you wish to consider the route of dying with dignity at a time of your own choosing, then I can help you there too.'

'But that isn't possible in England. It's illegal.'

'There are ways we can help, nevertheless. I am in the business of helping people, Mrs Forbes. I became a doctor to alleviate pain and suffering, it's what I've spent my working life trying to do . . . but in these later years of my career I have decided to concentrate on this one area of therapy. It is so essential, and yet we have no proper way of handling these situations here. Travelling to a country where it is not illegal is a stressful, miserable, lengthy, expensive and often very shocking way to proceed. As you discovered.'

'Oh, I did. I can't tell you . . . it was the most awful, horrible shock – to find out that the whole thing was . . . Not that I have had experience of one, but I imagine it was like backstreet abortionists used to be and probably still are in some countries.'

'Exactly right. That is how they conduct their business, in spite of the smooth, shiny, reassuring front they present. We don't want that here. I'm trying to ensure that people in this situation – your situation – are able to experience something very, very different.'

'It's so necessary . . . what I saw, what that place was like . . . I wake up shaking sometimes, to be frank, I can't get it out of my mind.'

'Have you talked to your GP?'

'I haven't really . . . I wasn't sure . . . well, how she'd take it. I'm not sure she approves. I did try to bring the subject up with her – when I first . . . when I was contemplating . . . you know? But perhaps I should.'

'If you feel you can talk to her, I think you really ought to do that.'

'She's a very good listener, that's not in question.'

'No . . . But she has a duty to preserve your life, to help you deal with your illness, to give you every sort of pain relief. That's her job. Is that what you want?'

'Well . . .'

'If you find it difficult, you can come and see me and talk about this at any time, you know.'

'The thing is . . . I haven't quite gathered . . . well, you say you're a doctor . . .'

'I do apologise. How do you know I'm a doctor? I could be anyone. Of course, of course. I assure you I am a fully qualified doctor, but the way to check is this – I am going to give you a phone number. Call it whenever you like. That's my consulting-room number, and if I'm not there my secretary will answer. She will make an appointment and give you the address. If you're not happy, please, do nothing. I want to help you.'

'Is this . . . ?'

'A scam? No. Is this someone from Bene Mori? No.'

'I was going to ask if this would be – a professional consultation. You understand?'

'You mean, do I charge? Not for the initial consultation, no. That is entirely free. After that, if you wish to make a full hour's appointment, then yes, I do charge. And if I feel you are coping well, then we go no further. If in my professional opinion you would benefit from a further counselling session, then I set out a plan – a treatment plan and, indeed, a payment plan. But once we've met and talked, if you're not happy about anything, please just don't come again, don't even make contact with me again. I'll respect any decision you may come to. I'm not in the business of persuading anyone to do anything, Mrs Forbes. That would be unethical and immoral.'

'That is reassuring, I have to admit.'

'Good. There is one thing which I know you'll understand as you've already taken some steps along this road . . . What we are discussing . . .'

'I understand.'

'You know that it is against the law in the country and I will ask you to sign a short statement that you are fully aware of this. It's for your protection and mine – I hope one day it won't be necessary but at the moment . . .'

'Yes. Yes, I understand. Can I ask you . . . ?'

'Ask me anything at all.'

'It seems . . . well, I wonder how many people come to see you. I mean – it isn't an everyday situation, is it?'

'Ah, this takes up only a small part of my professional time, Mrs Forbes – I see patients for quite different reasons as well. Though having said that, you might be surprised at the number of people in your situation who want to discuss this – and the numbers are increasing. People aren't prepared to put up with the present situation in this country, they want to take control of their last days and hours – they know it is possible elsewhere, so why not here?'

'I agree. I think you're right, Doctor . . .'

'Goodnight, Mrs Forbes. Sleep well. And think about what I have said. And, if you want to see me, please make a note of this . . .'

He gave her a Lafferton area telephone number before wishing her goodnight again.

She went back to the television but the programme was over. It was news time and she had made a point of not watching the news since returning from Switzerland. Everything presented a crisis or an emergency which was distressing but which she could do absolutely nothing to solve, everything cast her into despair, every item was war and pestilence, famine and drought, floods and espionage, corruption and incompetence, sickness and death. She had always felt under some sort of social or moral obligation to watch the news and current affairs, but now her own state of health and peace of mind were paramount and she put those first.

She switched off and sat in the quiet room.

She had liked his voice. It was courteous. It invited her to confide. It was charming but not over-familiar, educated but not over-refined. A consultant's voice, she thought, the old style of consultant.

She would not tell Penny. That was a given. But whether she would do as the doctor had suggested and talk to Dr Deerbon she could not decide. Her gut feeling was that she would not, that her GP would try to persuade her to put the whole euthanasia question from her mind and focus on the quality of life she still had and the possibility that she might have a remission from her symptoms.

Jocelyn knew that her end would be every bit as terrible as she feared, with every aspect of her dying and death way beyond her own control. Dr Deerbon was a wonderful GP but she could not work miracles. Talking to her would lead only to a bed in the hospice.

She looked at the number she had jotted down. She would ring in the morning and make an appointment. He had emphasised that she need proceed no further if she wasn't happy, so what had she to lose? If nothing else, she might put an end to her nightmares and daytime flashes of dreadful memory if she went through every detail with this doctor.

Penny would tell her to be sensible and cautious, to ask questions, to query why the man had rung her, what he hoped to gain from the appointment, to try at least to discover who he was and something about his background before seeing him. Which was one reason, though by no means the only one, why she intended to tell no one about the doctor, his phone call, or any appointment she might make, and to keep Penny, above all people, in the dark about it.

She felt happier when she went to bed, calmer and less afraid that her sleep would be jagged with nightmares about the clinic. The phone call had reassured her. She did not ask herself how he had found her name and number, how he knew about her aborted trip to Switzerland.

Thirty-five

'Mrs Foster? Simon Serrailler.'

'Oh.'

'Please don't hang up. Just listen to me.'

'I don't –'

'Is your husband going to be at home this morning?'

'He usually is Saturday mornings, though not in the afternoons, not usually Saturday evenings either. He coaches junior football and then he's at the pub.'

'Fine. I'm going to call round this morning, I need to talk to him.'

'I didn't tell you where we live.'

Serrailler said nothing.

'Yes, I see. Nothing's private, is it? Nothing's confidential from you lot.'

'I'll come between ten and eleven, but I'd be grateful if you didn't mention this to him.'

He could have called on the off chance and risked finding Stephen Foster out of the house but he preferred it this way. Noeline might warn her husband about his impending visit. His behaviour then would say a lot. If he knew nothing, and certainly if he had done nothing, then he might well stay put. If he was at all anxious or felt guilty, he might decide not to be in after all, or, at the very least, work out a story and rehearse it carefully. And in Serrailler's experience, only those who had something to hide went to the trouble of doing that. He had Foster in his sights. Whether that was because at the moment he had no one else there he would have found it hard to say.

It was a small detached house in a short avenue of similar houses but smarter than most of them, freshly painted, the windows shining after a recent clean, the paved front area set about with pointed miniature conifers in a careful pattern. A silver Ford Focus was parked at the gate.

Foster was in his fifties, well spoken, neat grey hair, even good-looking, Simon thought. A well-set-up figure of a man. But he wore old, paint-splashed cords and his feet were bare.

He looked at the warrant card, before meeting Serrailler's eye for only a second.

'What's this about? I was just going out actually.'

'I hope not to hold you up too long. May I ask where you were going, Mr Foster?'

'Just out. You'd better come in here.'

A neat sitting room, with a hideous orange and brown carpet, and amateur paintings of orange and brown landscapes on the walls.

'Do you paint?' Simon asked, going closer to one to look at the signature.

'My wife. Doesn't do it so much now.'

'Africa?'

'Well, yes, but she does them from postcards.'

'Right.'

Simon turned round quickly, to catch the man's expression. There was no panic. The most it could be described as was wary. But who wasn't wary when visited by a detective wanting to ask them questions? Wary was normal.

'I'd like a word with your wife after we've spoken.'

'She's gone out.'

'Where to?'

Foster shrugged. 'Shops, I suppose. Don't think she said.'

'Is she usually out on Saturday morning?'

'Sometimes is, sometimes not.'

'And you?'

'Me?'

'You're usually here on Saturdays?'

'In the morning I am, generally. Yes. Later on I do a bit of soccer coaching. Listen, what's this about, Mr . . . ?'

'Detective Chief Superintendent Serrailler. Simon Serrailler. May I sit down?'

Foster hesitated, then sat on the edge of a straight chair himself. Simon took the tightly upholstered small sofa with blood-red covers.

'Sixteen years ago, a young girl vanished from a bus stop at which she had been waiting on Parkside Drive in Lafferton. Harriet Lowther. You telephoned the special line at Lafferton Police Station to say you had information about her disappearance. That was the next day – Harriet went missing on a Friday afternoon and you telephoned the hotline on the Saturday.'

Foster's colour had heightened and he was staring at his hands. But then he looked up and directly at Simon.

'Why do you think it was me who did that? What makes you come here, what gives you the right to attach some random anonymous phone call to me, to my name, my address, all these years later?' He was blustering.

'I didn't say the phone call had been anonymous.'

'Well, it must have been, mustn't it?'

'Why is that?'

'Well, it wasn't me so it was either anonymous or someone giving my name . . . a false name. Using my name.'

'Why would someone do that?'

'Or just coincidence. Stephen Foster. It isn't the most unusual name on the planet, is it? I wonder how many of us there are in the world. Hundreds probably.'

'And in Lafferton?'

'Got to be others. Almost bound to be. That's what it would have been.'

'We do have a recording of the call, you know. Everything is on tape.'

Alarm flashed across Foster's features before he controlled it.

'Where were you on the afternoon of 18 August 1995, Mr Foster?'

'Was that the Friday?'

'It was.'

'I'd have been at work then.'

'Where is that?'

'Was. Hummings.'

'The printing firm?'

'Yes. I worked there for eleven years. I was there then. In 1995.'

'What exactly did you do?'

'Sales.'

'A sales representative?'

'Yes.'

'Not a job that kept you in the office full-time then.'

'I was in the office a lot.'

'And out on the road a lot, visiting clients and so forth.'

'Out of Lafferton mainly.'

'Right. So on that afternoon, were you out of Lafferton?'

'No.'

'I can easily check.'

'I don't think so.'

'What makes you sure of that?'

'Well . . . It's years ago. I left not long after. They wouldn't keep a record of an ex-employee for all that time.'

'You'd be surprised. Firms are obliged to keep all sorts of information.'

'And in sales you make your own timetable, pretty much . . . I could have been anywhere. But I was in the office.'

'Why are you so sure of that, Mr Foster?'

'When I read about the girl of course . . . I searched my memory.'

'Why?'

'I should think every man in Lafferton did – every woman too for that matter. Had they been anywhere near, had they seen her maybe. Look, when that sort of thing is all over the television and on posters . . . a young girl missing . . . you automatically wonder, you think, Christ, where was I?'

'Do you?'

'I bet even you did.'

'I was based in the Met at that time, so no. But just to go back. You could have been in the office for part of the afternoon and out of it as well.'

'I could but I wasn't.'

'Where would your nearest client have been at that time?'

'Nearest . . . Gatley and Scholes, they're technical publishers in Bevham. Were. They relocated to Oxford. But they were nearest to the print works and a big client.'

'So you went to see them how often?'

'Maybe once a month?'

'And how would you have got to them from the print works?'

'Bypass obviously.'

'Not down Parkside Drive?'

'Wouldn't be a sensible way to go, would it? Add about three, four miles. Why would I do that unless the bypass was shut or something?'

'And was it?'

'I don't know. I mean, no, of course it wasn't, how could it have been if I used it? Why would the bypass be shut anyway?'

'You tell me.'

'What?'

'You didn't use the bypass at all, did you?'

Foster was silent.

'You were in Parkside Drive that afternoon – why I don't know, but I'll find out. No reason on earth why you shouldn't have been there except, as you say, it would have been an odd way to get to the east side of Bevham, which is where Gatley and Scholes, were located. But you weren't going to Gatley and Scholes, were you?'

'No.'

'You were in Parkside Drive, at about the time Harriet Lowther was waiting at the bus stop. That's what you said when you called the information line the next morning.'

'I didn't call the information line.'

'We've got your voice on tape, Mr Foster.'

'No. No, you haven't. You've got someone's voice but it isn't mine. It can't have been.'

'Why can't it? If you were in Parkside Drive –'

'I wasn't –'

'– that afternoon and saw Harriet Lowther, which you were and you did, why wouldn't you call the line? Very public-spirited of you. You did the right thing. You said you saw her waiting at the bus stop, from the other side of the road. You saw the bus come. You saw it pull in and stop. But you were pretty sure that Harriet did not actually get on it. That after it pulled away again, she was walking on down the road. Only a few yards probably, but she wasn't on the bus. That's what you said when you rang.'

'No.'

'And it was very useful information. Very useful. Vital even. It could be the one bit of vital detail we need.'

'Could it?'

'Oh yes. Absolutely it could. Everyone naturally assumes that when a young girl is waiting at a bus stop and a bus comes, she gets on it. Of course. Why else would she be waiting? There's only one number bus calls at that stop on Parkside Drive, the 73 into Lafferton, so she couldn't have been waiting for another number bus, going somewhere else. She didn't get the bus and you said as much in your call to the hotline. Your anonymous call. But what I can't understand is why you wouldn't give your name and address and a contact number? That's why I'm here, asking all this. It isn't that you did anything wrong in calling us – on the contrary, as I just said. This is vital information. Maybe you've thought about it since and remembered something else?'

'No.'

'Nothing else?'

'No.'

'But once you'd rung us – well, you know how it is, Mr Foster. Things are remembered later . . . one thing stirs up others . . . something else, some little detail . . . '

'No.'

'I can assure you it does, very often. No, I applaud your remembering what you saw, that Harriet didn't get on that bus, and you did absolutely the right thing in ringing us. If there was any problem, it was the time lag. I could wish you'd rung earlier, not left it till the next day.'

242

'I didn't know until the next day that the girl had disappeared.'

Simon leaned back on the uncomfortable sofa and looked steadily at Foster. There was nothing else he needed to say.

Stephen Foster went to the window and stood for a few moments, hands in the pockets of his cords, head bent, then turned, looked at Simon, turned back. His face was flushed again.

Yes, Simon thought. Yes.

He waited for a long time in the silence.

Suddenly, Foster went out of the room, closing the door. Another door closed somewhere. After a moment, a lavatory flushed.

Simon doubted if the man was going to run out of the house. He hadn't even put a pair of shoes on his feet. But it was not only that.

'Coffee?'

'Thanks.'

Foster looked slightly surprised.

'A splash of milk, please, no sugar.'

There was a serving hatch in the wall. Simon could hear the man fill and switch on a kettle, the chink of china, the opening of a jar, the tap of a spoon.

Gut instinct told him that Foster had nothing to do with Harriet's disappearance but he had certainly been in Parkside Drive and had seen her. Why else would he have phoned the hotline? He was not a time-waster or an attention-seeker, he seemed perfectly sane. Criminals sometimes did unexpected things, phoning with false information in order to steer the police away from the truth, or because they could not resist putting themselves in the spotlight of an investigation when prudence would recommend they stay as far from it as possible. But Stephen Foster did not fit that profile.

He came back with a small tin tray and two mugs of coffee.

Simon waited, watching him put it down, move it, put it down on a different small table. Foster did not meet his eye. But he had put on brown leather slippers. He stood with his back to the window, holding his mug.

'Would you sit down please, Mr Foster?'

243

'Sorry.'

Something had happened. His voice sounded slightly different, the confrontational, even hostile, tone had gone, he spoke more quietly, seemed subdued. Now, he sat down in an armchair. There was no trace of bombast or defiance about him now.

Simon sipped the instant coffee. Waited. Foster put his mug down. Leaned forward, hands on his knees. Stared down at the carpet. The house was very quiet.

'The thing is . . .' He stopped. Picked up his coffee again. Set it down without drinking any. 'Are you . . . charging me with anything? Are you thinking I had something to do with her disappearance?'

Simon shook his head. 'No, to the first. As to the second . . . Did you have something to do with it?'

'No! No, I didn't, I wouldn't . . . I couldn't. God, what happened to her? Poor kid. You finding her bones like that, just dumped in some soil anywhere . . . left to rot. I didn't see her for long, I didn't . . . but she was . . . how can I describe it? – she looked so bright – you know? – bright in the sunshine. Does that make sense? Yes. Bright and young and happy . . . you could see that, even just catching sight of her standing at the bus stop, you know? It struck me and it stayed with me, only I suppose if nothing had happened it wouldn't have stayed. But then when I read she'd gone missing, saw her photo . . . it set it in my mind. And it's never left it, never left it. I can see her now.'

Simon sipped his coffee again. Waited. He would need all this in a statement later but he wanted the man to talk it out, tell him everything without the sense that it was being recorded, taken down, set in stone. In so far as he could, Foster needed to relax into trusting Simon enough to tell him the truth, whatever that truth was.

'Is it an offence – I mean, have I done something you can charge me with, ringing up the hotline and refusing to . . . to give my details?'

'No. Not on the whole.'

'Not on the whole.'

'There could be circumstances . . . if someone rings an info

244

line with a tall story, a pack of lies, which leads us off on a completely false trail, spending time and resources . . . and if that person hasn't given a name or contact number but we track them down, as we often do, then we can charge them with wasting police time. But simply refusing to tell us your name – that's not an offence. The problem is, why would anyone do it? If you've witnessed something and it could be of help to us in an investigation, why tell us but remain anonymous? It would remain confidential – we don't make details of callers public. Not unless there's a very good reason for us to do so and that would be unusual and only come out at a much later stage.'

'Right.'

'Did you watch the TV programme about Harriet's disappearance?'

'No.'

'Really? I'm surprised.'

'Well, I was probably out. Not sure I even knew there was a programme, to be honest with you.'

'Ah. There was a reconstruction of Harriet's last-known movements. It could have been very useful if you had watched it.'

'Why?'

'Because you were there, weren't you? You might have spotted some discrepancies, something not quite right. Could have been very helpful. Pity. I'm surprised you weren't interested.'

'I would have been, I suppose. If I'd known about it. Probably would have watched it, yes. Was it handy? I mean, did anyone come forward afterwards, give you anything new?'

'We had a lot of calls and a lot of very helpful information, yes. Recons generally do produce good results. You'd have found it interesting.'

'Pity then.'

'Did your wife watch it?'

'No.'

'How do you know?'

'Well, if I didn't, she wouldn't . . . what I mean is, if she had, I'd have known, wouldn't I?'

'You always watch television together then? The same programmes?'

245

'Not always. I don't watch all that much actually. I'm out a lot . . . well, a bit. In the evenings.'

'Ah yes, the soccer coaching. Do you play yourself?'

'Not now. I ref, but I mainly coach juniors. Kids' team, you know.'

'Do you have boys yourself?'

'No. No, we haven't any kids. Unfortunately. No.'

'What's the team?'

'Sorry?'

'The name of the team?'

'It's . . . doesn't really have a name. It's just a bunch of kids, a few dads . . . we meet on the Rec, play there, you know, there are some pitches, anyone can use. Book them up, you know?'

'I presume you are CRB-checked for this coaching?'

'Yes, yes. I know all about that.'

Simon made a quick note.

'That's all in order, isn't it?'

'I'm sure it is. Everything will be on record, won't take a moment to pull up the details on the computer. That's made a big difference since the original investigation of course.' He put the top back on his pen.

'What has?'

'Computers. Speeded everything up. There was so much taken down by hand, taken down on typewriters . . . filing cards, record sheets. Still is a lot of handwritten stuff of course, but it's the data. We can access data in a minute that would have taken days to dig out.'

'Obviously.'

'Why did you get the sack from Hummings?'

'I didn't get the sack. I was made redundant. General cutting back, you know?'

'Even in 1995? Thought things were pretty rosy then.'

'No, no, we were just coming out of a bad recession, nothing was rosy.'

'So where did you go?'

'I went out of the print business altogether. Well, more or less.'

'Into . . . ?'

'Wholesale newsagent. Sandis and Baker.'

'Is that where you are now?'

'Yes. Well, no. Still in the same line of business, different firm. Taylor's.'

'How long have you been there?'

'Listen . . . what are all these questions about? What have they got to do with the girl who disappeared?'

Simon finished his coffee and set down the mug.

'What car do you drive?'

'It's outside. The Focus.'

'How long have you had it?'

'Well, it's a company car. Since I started at Taylor's.'

'Which was?'

'Two years ago. Nearly two. Yes.'

'Before that?'

'What?'

'Your car?'

'I always had company cars.'

'What were you driving when you were with Hummings?'

'Vauxhall Cavalier.'

'Colour?'

'Listen –'

'Black, wasn't it?'

'No, light blue. What –'

'Was that the car you were driving the day you saw Harriet at the bus stop?'

'It would have been –'

'Where were you parked? How far away from the bus stop?'

'I was on the other side.'

Simon looked at him steadily.

And then Stephen Foster crumpled. His head went forward and he put his hands over his face. But after only a moment, he jumped up and came to stand in front of Simon. His eyes were wild, his face even more deeply flushed.

'All right, I was there, I was parked there, I saw her, I admit that, and I phoned because the second I found out about the girl going missing I knew I had to. I had to. Anybody would have to. But I was on the opposite side of the road the whole time, I didn't speak to her, I didn't go near here, I just saw . . .'

'Yes. So you'd better sit down, and then tell me first of all exactly what you did see and then why you wouldn't give your details on the phone – either originally, or the other day when you called again. You did call again on the new hotline, we know that.'

'Yes.'

'Yes. And you'd better tell me what you were doing in Parkside Drive that afternoon, why you lied about it, why you said you were in your office, and why you also said you hadn't watched the television programme when I know that you did. You did watch it, didn't you?'

Foster's voice was hoarse. 'Yes.'

'OK. You tell me everything, every last detail, and it had better be the truth and I had better believe you, because if I don't, if you lie any more, if you give me any bullshit, we'll be talking again in an interview room and I'll be asking you why you killed Harriet Lowther.'

Thirty-six

'Sam, have you finished your homework?'

Sam slid *Right Ho, Jeeves* expertly under his maths textbook before calling out, 'Nearly.'

'How long?'

'Er . . . ten minutes.'

His mother appeared in the doorway of his room.

'Hmm.'

'Why?'

'Supper in half an hour but I've got to make a couple of calls, and one of them might take a while, so Molly's doing yours, OK?'

'Whatever.'

'I wish you wouldn't say that.'

'Whatever.'

She came and glanced at his maths book. 'Is that all tonight?'

'Yup.'

'So is there a chance you could read to Felix?'

'No, there is no chance. I have some French and then a poem.'

'French what?'

'Verbs.'

'Which verbs?'

'Haven't looked yet.'

'What poem?'

'Ditto.'

'Sam . . .'

'Sorry, need to pee really quickly.'

He shot off his chair, and out, knocking the maths textbook to the floor, revealing *Right Ho, Jeeves* as he did so.

'SAM . . .'

Cat sat down in his chair. The desk lamp threw a bright circle onto her son's maths exercise book. She stared at the figures, remembering. She had been good at maths, and at physics, bad at chemistry, best at biology. But she had resented the need to concentrate on sciences to the exclusion of everything else. Now, they could get into medical school on a broader range of subjects – Molly had done English A level, with biology and maths, her boyfriend Rob had done history. It was better, it gave doctors a broader base, it stopped them from becoming narrow scientists with a narrow scientific outlook. She had continued to read throughout her Cambridge and medical school years because she loved literature and could not imagine life without it, and because she believed it deepened her understanding of the people she dealt with in her surgery. But it had been a struggle sometimes, and there had always been time constraints, always the weeks on call as a junior doctor when she didn't open a book. During those periods, she had missed reading novels as if they were cool water and she had a permanent, raging thirst.

She picked up *Right Ho, Jeeves*. Sam had inherited his love of P.G. Wodehouse from her father, who was quietly delighted by the way he had grasped the point of him immediately. It was a passion that had skipped a generation. Neither she nor Simon, who both read omnivorously, could bear PGW. Their triplet brother Ivo never read books at all.

She was not going to complain to Sam about the Wodehouse. Nagging about homework was counterproductive, and in any case, Sam was bright and worked pretty hard, it was not a problem. But he had others. A note had come from school saying that he was barred from the school sports teams for one weekend's matches because of 'unruly behaviour'. More detailed explanation was not forthcoming and she did not feel able to ask. No, untrue – she felt perfectly able, just unwilling. She didn't want to confront what Sam had done, or said, didn't feel she could deal with any of it. It was weak and cowardly to opt for ignorance and she blamed herself. But there were times, and they were becoming more frequent, when she felt inadequate as the single parent of an early-teenage son. And it would get worse before it got better, she knew that. Sam was headstrong, he could land in all sorts of trouble, he needed a loving but firm hand and he lacked a father. Simon was full of good intentions but rarely had much time to give his nephew, her father was not the right person to deal with any problems – he had not coped with his own sons well.

'Oh.'

Sam was standing in the doorway.

'I thought you had phoning and work stuff.'

He came and stood at her shoulder. 'You OK?'

'Tired, that's all,' Cat said.

'You haven't got a headache, have you?'

He would not get any closer in asking for reassurance. His father had had appalling headaches. His father had died of a brain tumour.

'Absolutely not. But Sambo, listen . . . people do get headaches for quite ordinary reasons, you know. They're very common.'

He did not reply.

'I see patients with headaches every week. Ordinary headaches that go away by themselves and don't have a serious cause, OK?'

'Yup.'

'How much longer do you think you'll be? Honest answer.'

'Is Molly in yet?'

'Sam . . .'

'Twenty minutes?'

'Fine. If Molly isn't back by then could you read to Felix once he's in bed?'

Sam sighed. 'Look, OK, but not *Mr Strong* or *Mr Messy* . . . actually, not *Mr Anything*. They're so boring.'

'Yes, but he's too young to know that.'

'I don't mind reading *Peace at Last* or *The Gruffalo*.'

'It's his bedtime, it really ought to be his choice.'

251

'Yeah, it can be, only just not a Mr Men.'

'Hi . . .'

Sam leapt up, hearing Molly come in and dump her bag and cycle helmet on the kitchen floor.

'Hi, Moll, you don't mind reading the Mr Men to Felix, do you? Only I've got this absolute load of homework.'

'Better get on with it then, hadn't you?'

'Do you want testing on the nervous system later?'

'No thanks.'

'Tropical diseases?'

'Nope.'

'Eruptions of the skin?'

'Sambo, will you get back in there? This is your last warning.'

'Molly . . .'

But she was on her way to her room, waving a hand as she did so. Sam made a face.

A couple of hours later, the kitchen was quiet, all three children in bed, Felix asleep. Hannah had persuaded Molly to let her paint her fingernails with the clear varnish Molly used. 'Granny Judith has scarlet – she's even got one that's dark purple and one that's black.'

'Cool.'

'She doesn't let me have that. She *is* quite cool, isn't she?'

Molly had put Hannah's hair in a dozen small plaits, which would make it wavy when she woke up and took them out, and for an hour afterwards, before the tendency to absolute straightness reasserted itself. But an hour of waves, in Hannah's book, was worth the tedium of the plaiting.

Supper was eaten, the dishwasher was full. Mephisto and Wookie were curled on the sofa in relative harmony.

'You revising?'

Molly's finals were a month away.

'I guess. Tired of it.'

'I remember. But you're with me tomorrow and Wednesday which has to be more interesting than "What are the contra-indications for the insertion of a catheter?"'

'Are there any?'

252

Cat laughed. 'You want a coffee?'

'Let me get it.'

'Sit still. Are there any others in your lot interested in spending a day shadowing me?'

'Not sure. Jamie might be. He was getting aereated about the withholding of treatment last I heard. But he gets bees in his bonnet. He was on about the twenty-four-week rule before that.'

'I wonder why.'

'Well, twenty-four weeks is viable, isn't it, there are plenty of –'

'Yes, but I meant palliative care. Just wondering why not many are interested. We need new blood. Hospice care is going to get more important still with an ageing population.'

'I think it's to do with – well, we go into this wanting to save lives, make people better . . . which means, terminal patients don't figure, I guess.'

'You make their lives comfortable, and pain-free, you help them to the best quality of life you can obtain for them and then you help them to a death without pain or distress, with dignity and care and attention and . . . with love. You make the end of a life as good as you possibly can and you help their relatives to an acceptance and an accommodation with that death too. That in itself is a healing process to which you are devoting your time and contributing all your skill. It's ultimately the most satisfying, rewarding medicine I've ever been involved in, Molly.' She put the two mugs of coffee on the table. 'Here endeth the sermon.'

'No. I like you to say stuff. I need to hear that.'

'Well, if nothing else you'll begin to understand what a crying need there is for Imogen House and what a scandal it is that we're living from hand to mouth and under threat of closure every day of the week. Which reminds me, you ought to meet Leo Fison too. You should come with me to his care home.'

'Would I be able to shadow him?'

'Don't see why he shouldn't have a student for a day or two. Dementia care is another branch of medicine that's bound to grow during your career – ageing population again, and it's a thriving research area too.'

'Another thing none of the others seems to want to do.'

'What do they find sexy, then?'

'A & E. Intensive care. Paeds. Cardiac.'

'*Plus ça change*. Obs and gynae was pretty highly rated when I was training.'

'Yeeuch, no.'

'Now, the thing is, are we watching the rerun of *Foyle's War*? I'm not fit for much else.'

But car headlights swept across the kitchen blind, and a moment later, Wookie was hurling himself at Simon in a frenzy of noisy affection.

Molly picked up her pile of textbooks and went out.

'You don't have to go, Moll. You live here, Si doesn't count.'

But she was already halfway up the stairs.

'We've eaten,' Cat said.

'Didn't come for that. Can I have a coffee?'

'Since when did you need to ask?'

Cat sat on the sofa and stroked Wookie's ears, at the same time as she watched her brother. There was something but she couldn't quite put her finger on it. He was preoccupied, but that was usual when he was in the middle of a big case. He had a look about him. Distant. Distracted. Something.

Something.

'Any leads on the two girls?'

'Lots of calls. Nothing useful. Well – having said that, there was one to the line today . . . someone was sure she remembered a girl coming into the village post office she used to keep. Said she came in about twice a week, sometimes more, did bits of grocery shopping, posted stuff. Talked about the war once or twice.'

'The *war*?'

'Former Yugoslavia – Serbia . . . that one. And that fits her profile – she could have come from that region, according to the experts.'

'Have you been to the village?'

'Not yet. Post office closed not long afterwards, and this caller moved to Derbyshire but she obviously keeps her eye on the Lafferton news, she had the newspaper, all the stuff about the girl, and about Harriet – she'd seen the television programme.'

'Going up to Derbyshire?'

'Not yet.' He sat down at the table and looked down into his coffee.

Something.

A look.

The shadow from the lamp fell across his face. Simon had always looked rather younger than her and Ivo, but now Cat suddenly saw that middle age was about to settle on his features, though she could not quite identify how. Perhaps it was just an expression. Temporary. Something.

'Not many girls would have come here from that part of the world surely. Not in 1995.'

'You'd be surprised. There were a heck of a lot of au pairs from Yugoslavia.'

'Is that what she was?'

'Could have been.'

'Bit of a long shot.'

'So is everything.'

'Nothing on Harriet?'

'Possibly. Possibly on Harriet.'

'What, someone in your sights?'

'Possibly.'

She knew when not to press him.

'About Sam,' she said instead. 'I know you're up against it but you did say you'd find a weekend to take him climbing.'

Simon sighed.

'Listen, it doesn't matter right now, there are the summer holidays, but you don't even play so much cricket these days and he misses being around you.'

'I know, I know. I tell you what, if I absolutely guarantee it, can it wait till July or August? I'll have so much leave owing me. I'll take him up to the island. I said I would and never did. Then we can walk and climb and he can go out in the boats.'

'You mean it? Because . . .'

'Well, other things being equal.'

'Ah, that. Other things.'

'How do I know now if this case is going to be done and

dusted by then, or trailing on or blowing up in my face? Be reasonable.'

'Be reasonable? Me, be reasonable? Si, he's your nephew, you're his father figure now, he's always adored you, you're his role model, you —'

'Listen, stop dumping all this on me, would you?'

'*What?*'

'I'm his uncle, OK, I do my best, OK, but it's hardly my fault his father's dead.'

His words fell heavily between them. The dishwasher clicked off and there was a dreadful silence. After a moment it was broken by Mephisto's faint snoring.

Simon knew what he should have done, knew perfectly well. A swift step across to his sister, arms round her in a long, tight hug. He would not have needed to say anything, neither to explain – there was no explanation or excuse – nor even to apologise. She would have taken his embrace as all of those things.

Why did he not do it? Why did he simply stand where he was, coffee mug in hand, staring at the floor to avoid looking at Cat, who was hunched up, head down, motionless and silent?

It was Molly who broke the terrible spell, running downstairs and into the kitchen, but then hesitating, as she sensed the tension.

'Sorry . . .'

Cat waved her hand. 'It's fine, Moll, Simon was going.'

Simon didn't move. Molly picked up a book from the chair and fled. Silence again.

In the end, Cat got up and went past her brother without looking at him. Put her mug in the sink. Emptied the cafetière. Rinsed it. Set it on the draining board.

'I had supper with Judith.'

'Oh –'

'I knew Dad would revert to type sooner or later and sure enough.'

'Revert to type?' She sat down at the table with a glass of water in front of her. Did not drink it.

'You know.'

'Do I?'

'To his old self. He upset her. Did she tell you? She was here that day – she must have been talking to you.'

'She was. But I don't expect her to disclose the intimate details of their marriage.'

'Don't be pompous.'

What happened next was shocking. Cat got up, came round the table to where he was standing, and slapped him hard across the face, making his skin sting. Then again. As she did so, she drew in her breath and seemed to be about to say something, but did not.

He put up his hand to his cheek. 'I suppose I deserved that,' he said.

'And more.'

He went to the sink and splashed cold water on his face. Cat had not moved.

'I don't think I've ever hit anyone before,' she said quietly.

'Yes you have, you punched me when we were seven. Your hamster escaped and I laughed.'

It should have lightened the mood but it did not.

'Dad . . .'

'Yes,' Cat said. 'You know what? I never thought you had anything much of Dad in you, but you have. It was buried, but it's surfacing. Is it the job? Is that it? You see and hear such appalling things every day that it's hardening you, it's making you as cruel as some of the people you have to deal with? You used to keep it all separate. The policeman wasn't the man. But maybe that's no longer true. You'd never have said what you said to me just now a few years ago.'

'No. Listen –'

'Why? Why should I?'

'I was only going to ask what you thought about all this stuff with Dad and Judith.'

'What about it?'

'I just wonder what his motive was.'

'Now there's a word.'

'You know what I mean.'

'Oh, I do. Motive. Dad's motives are as unfathomable as yours. I told you – it's coming out.'

He wondered whether that was true. Was he turning into his father? He was like Meriel. He had always been like Meriel. He had felt alien to his father every day of his life. It was not possible that he was now becoming like him.

'Why would he tell Judith about Martha?'

'What about her? There's nothing to tell. Judith knew all about Martha long ago, way before they were married. Probably before they had anything to do with one another, before Mother died. Everyone knew about Martha. That she was . . . handicapped. That she . . .'

'Well, yes, obviously, but I didn't mean *in general*, did I?'

'I don't know what you meant.'

'Of course you do!'

He might have wondered at that moment, might have hesitated to ask himself, but the thought was barely there, if anyone had asked him he would have denied that he had any doubt at all. Of course she knew. She had probably been the first to know. She was a doctor, like their parents, she above all people would have known. He was the only one who had been kept out of the loop for so long. The moment when he might have stopped himself from saying it flared up and was gone.

'He told Judith about Mother giving her the injection.'

Cat's face registered something – some subliminal awareness, some shock, some fear, her eyes were on him, asking, asking.

She cleared her throat. 'Mother . . .'

'Yes. Giving her the injection that killed her. Come on, what other injection would I be talking about? Can't remember the name but you know . . .'

'Si . . .'

'Potassium. Don't know why I forgot, because oddly enough there was a case last month, in the Midlands somewhere, only this was a nurse – you've must have read about it. She saw off about half a dozen that way, but no reason or excuse with her of course, it wasn't –'

He stopped. Cat's face was grey. She had not taken her eyes off him all the time he had been talking.

Silence. This kitchen has never known such silences, he thought. Never known such vast terrible distances between people who are close. Were close. Need to be.

'Jesus,' he said. 'Jesus Christ, Cat. You didn't know.'

Thirty-seven

He switched off the electric razor.

'Serrailler.'

It was ten past seven.

'This . . . It's . . . Stephen Foster.'

'Right.'

'I need to see you.'

Don't make it easy. Give him a hard time. This morning, Simon would have given anyone a hard time.

'I'll be there in half an hour.'

'No . . . I don't want that. I want to meet you somewhere.'

'Sorry. Your house or nowhere.'

'I can even come – come into the police station.'

'No need. Half an hour.' He rang off and went on shaving.

He had driven away from the farmhouse just after midnight. Cat was shaken and angry, partly out of professional pride, he thought, that she, doctor among doctors, should be the last to know what had happened, but mainly out of the inevitable distress at what their mother had done. Mercy killing.

At ten to eight, he was at the Fosters' front door. Foster answered it, barefoot as before.

'Is your wife in?'

'No.'

They went into the orange and brown room.

'Right,' Simon said, 'this time, you tell me.'

'Can I get you a cup of tea?'

'No thanks. Talk.'

Foster walked up and down the small room a few times, stopped by the window, stopped by the chair on which Serrailler was sitting, notebook out. He rarely wrote anything other than a name or a date but the open page itself often focused the mind of someone reluctant to talk.

'Listen, this doesn't go any further.'

'Depends what you're going to tell me. You must know you can't ask for any sort of immunity once you start making confessions.'

'Who said anything about a confession?'

'Didn't you?'

'Not . . . right. If you think I rang you because I killed that girl and thought better of denying it, you can forget it. I wasn't near enough to lay a hand on her. I was on the other side of the road.'

'Why?'

'I'm coming to why. I said I wasn't anywhere near, that I was at the print works because . . . I shouldn't have been in Parkside Drive . . . anywhere near Parkside Drive.'

'So why were you?'

Foster stopped by the window again and turned his back to Simon. 'I . . . I was going to see someone.'

'Who?'

'A friend.'

'A friend.'

'Someone . . . my wife doesn't . . . didn't know about.'

'I need her name.'

'I don't want to give you that. I don't want her involved.'

'Where did she live?'

'I don't want –'

'Name. Address. Don't mess me about.'

Foster sighed. 'Elaine Morner. 8 Parkside Drive – it's a block of terraced houses pretty much opposite the bus stop.'

'How long had you been seeing Mrs Morner? Mrs?'

'She's divorced. But Mrs, yes. Then? Only a few months. Not quite a year.'

'How often?'

'Quite often. Afternoons . . . evenings. When I could.'

'So you didn't want to admit you'd been in Parkside Drive because you were having an affair with Mrs Morner? Understandable. But you could have told us that. We're not in the business of divulging private information which isn't relevant to any inquiries, and it probably wouldn't have been, would it?'

'I don't know.'

'No. If you're telling me the truth, *why* you were in Parkside Drive, when you happened to see Harriet Lowther at the bus stop is irrelevant. The fact is that you saw her. You almost gave us some vital information, but you decided not to, and to remain anonymous and not to call us back. Why was that?'

'Obviously . . . I was afraid of it getting out. In spite of what you just said. These things do.'

'And did it?'

'No. I don't think so.'

'So, tell me what you saw. Never mind about your affair, I'm not interested. Tell me exactly what you saw. You refreshed your mind when you watched the television reconstruction, didn't you, it's all come back to you. I need to know.'

Foster sat down and leaned forward, hands on his knees.

'I came out of Elaine's house. It was just after four – ten past, maybe a minute or so before.'

'Yes. Harriet was waiting for the four fifteen bus.'

'Right. I walked to my car – I always parked it away from Elaine's house, at the end of the block. I happened to look across the road and saw the girl . . . she was standing on her own at the bus stop. I'm sure she was on her own.'

'Sure it was her?'

'As soon as I read her description in the paper, yes. She had blonde hair in a ponytail, she was carrying a tennis racket. About fourteen or fifteen – she was fifteen, wasn't she?'

'Yes.'

'I just thought – this will sound odd – but the sight of her – well, it just somehow cheered me up . . . gave me a kick, you know what I mean? I don't go for girls or anything like that, wouldn't dream of it, but . . . she was so . . . bright-looking . . . sunny-looking . . . her hair, her expression . . . holding the tennis racket . . . she just looked young and full of life, full of . . . well, sounds daft, but, full of sunshine, somehow. I remembered thinking that. When I read about her. I remembered it straight away. It seemed so – awful. Shocking. Her looking like that and then . . . just . . . gone.'

'Then what happened?'

'Well, I saw the bus come almost as soon as I saw her – it must have been travelling down the road – and next thing, I saw it pull into the stop. I unlocked my car but while it had been parked there the sun had moved round and it was too hot to get inside . . . I opened the doors and waited for a minute, so that's when I was just looking across, without even realising I was doing it, I suppose . . . and I saw the bus pull in, then after a minute, it pulled out again. Only she hadn't got on it.'

'How can you be sure? You weren't on that side of the road and Harriet could have been sitting on the far side of the bus.'

'Yes, but she wasn't, because I saw her walking away from the stop and on down the road.'

'Which direction was she walking in?'

'After the bus. Lafferton direction. Just seemed odd at first that she'd been waiting at the bus stop but hadn't got on it . . . that she'd started walking.'

'Odd at first?'

'Yes. Only then of course she got the lift.'

Simon's stomach flipped. 'She got the lift?'

'Yes. She was . . . she glanced over her shoulder a couple of times and then a car came up alongside her and stopped and she got in. But then a white van got in between, overtaking, and I turned back to my car. I didn't see any more.'

'Can you explain that?'

'I got into my car – it was a bit cooler – and when I looked again, they'd all gone . . . '

'They, meaning . . . ?'

'The girl, the car she got into, one of those Ladas it was, the white van, the bus . . . you know. All of it.'

Simon let out a slow breath. 'This is important information. Do you realise that?'

'I suppose.'

'You suppose it's important or you suppose you realise?'

Foster did not answer.

'After sixteen years, you come up with information that might have saved Harriet Lowther's life. Think about it, Mr Foster. Just sit there and think hard.'

'I know. I . . . listen, the minute I saw that television programme I knew. I suppose I'd pushed it away before . . . and then years have gone by, you forget.'

'Harriet's father hasn't forgotten.'

'No. Only . . . when I saw the TV it was pretty good, quite accurate – surprising that. And then I thought –'

'Pity you didn't "think" sixteen years ago.'

'I know, I know. I'm sorry. I've got to live with that.'

'What happened to the woman you were having the affair with? Elaine – Morner? You didn't want your wife to find out, presumably.'

'I still don't.'

'Sorry?'

'I still don't want my wife to find out. I still see her. We're still . . . . . . Elaine. Nothing's changed. That's the thing.'

'You're still having an affair with Elaine Morner? You've been having an affair with her for sixteen – seventeen years? Is that what you're telling me?'

'Yes,' Foster said. 'That's right.'

The doors of the hatch into the kitchen burst open with such a sudden bang that both men leapt up.

'I heard that. I heard you. I came in and I heard . . .'

'Noeline . . .'

She burst into the room now, her face twisted with anger and pain.

'I used to wonder, I used to think . . . there were always things, only I told myself it was rubbish, and then I stopped wondering, I was ashamed I'd even thought you might be having an affair with someone. I was ashamed! I haven't had that thought for years – and I come into my kitchen and hear you saying . . .

saying it's been going on since . . . hear you telling him. I can't believe what you said. I can't believe this . . .'

Noeline Foster put her hands up to her face and began to take ragged, sobbing breaths.

Simon looked at her husband.

Helpless, embarrassed, flushed with guilt.

'I'll leave you to sort this,' Simon said. 'But I want you at Lafferton Police Station at two o'clock this afternoon.'

'I can't –'

'If you're as much as ten seconds late, I'll have someone round to arrest you. Do you understand?'

Foster nodded. His wife had sat down but her face was still covered with both hands.

'I'll want a full and frank statement, every detail.'

'I don't want Elaine brought into this.'

'I am not,' Simon said at the door, 'interested in your affair. I am not interested in your mistress. I am not interested in how you sort out your marriage. I'm interested in the probable abduction and subsequent murder of Harriet Lowther, about which you are going to make a statement. Two o'clock.'

He did not look back.

Thirty-eight

The press officer had said that *Bevham Gazette* reporter Jed Mulligan was new and bright and would have a fresh take on the Lowther case, which was why Serrailler was now sitting in a coffee bar in the Lanes with a double espresso, waiting to meet him.

'You want him to focus on this new info,' Marianne had said, 'though he'll have to fill in the background. But the point is, he isn't a jaded old hack who'll just regurgitate his last dozen pieces before going to a liquid lunch.'

'I thought liquid lunches were a thing of the past.'

'Not on the *BG* they're not. But this guy is impressive, he'll be going places. He's done some great reporting on the drugs ops.'

Simon groaned.

'Yes, I know your opinion, but he has and it's woken people up – not the same old, same old.'

'Which is what drugs ops always are?'

'Meet him. Give him everything you dare. Mulligan's your man.'

He spotted him as he came through the door. Leather jacket. Jeans. Hair gelled and spiked. Dark glasses. Local reporter masking as a bit-part actor.

'Jed?'

'Hi. Green tea, thanks.'

That figured. The guy probably didn't do wheat or dairy either.

'So . . . you've got new stuff. I saw the telly. Interesting.'

Jed Mulligan drank his tea, apparently untroubled by its being scalding hot, set down the glass and took out a small recorder. 'Shoot,' he said.

Simon smiled. Yes, he thought. But he's quick, he's sharp. He'll get it right. The nationals will pick up on it because he'll make sure they do, he'll be on the phone the minute he's filed his copy. Ambition shows.

Mulligan got it right, the Press Association picked up his feature-sized article, which came with several photographs, and the nationals ran follow-ups, albeit shorter and without the background details.

He had written the piece cleverly, so that the new information came first and last but was interwoven with older material and background facts so that anyone unfamiliar with the story would get all they needed on the one page. Everything about Harriet and her disappearance, the subsequent investigations and the finding of the skeletons was there. But what Stephen Foster had come up with the previous day was what readers would notice and, with luck, might remember and think about.

Question. 'What's the difference between a Lada and a Jehovah's Witness?'

Answer. 'You can shut the door on a Jehovah's Witness.'

So went the old gag and dozens more like it, about the world's most laughed-at car. But in spite of that, some people actually owned and drove Ladas. One person in particular. It was a Lada in which 15-year-old Harriet Lowther took a lift on the hot, sunny afternoon of Friday 18 August 1995. That was the day on which she disappeared, and was not seen or heard of until her skeleton was found in a shallow grave the day after the recent Lafferton storm.

Until yesterday's dramatic new development, it was thought that Harriet was last seen waiting for the Lafferton bus on Parkside Drive around four o'clock that afternoon. Several witnesses saw the pretty teenager, fair hair in a ponytail, tennis racket in hand, standing at the stop. But after the recent television reconstruction and calls to the police hotline, it is now known that Harriet did not get on the bus.

Instead, she was seen walking slowly away from the stop after the bus had left. As she walked she glanced over her shoulder a couple of times, until she spotted the car she was looking for. It slowed beside her and stopped, and Harriet got in. Then it drove on.

The car was a blue or possibly green Lada. The model was probably a Lada Samara.

Detective Chief Superintendent Simon Serrailler, of Lafferton Police, who is now heading up the investigation said: 'This new information from a member of the public gives us an absolutely vital breakthrough in the Lowther case. No one has come forward until now to say that not only did Harriet Lowther categorically not get onto the Lafferton bus she had apparently been waiting for, but that a car picked her up.

'Unfortunately, our informant did not see the driver of the Lada and cannot give us any description, but it is clear that Harriet was not abducted. She got into this car of her own volition and by the report of her glancing over her shoulder down the road she was obviously expecting its arrival. Perhaps the bus stop had been the arranged meeting place but when the car did not arrive on time, she started to walk slowly on, sure that it would soon pick her up. Was this a prearranged lift into Lafferton? If so, did she arrive there? Or was she expecting to be taken somewhere else?

'One thing is certain. Lada cars were not that common by 1995. Their heyday, such as it was, had been five or ten years earlier. So anyone who knows of a Lada, a blue or possibly green Lada Samara, which belonged to a neighbour, someone in their family, a friend, may well remember it clearly.'

The DCS continued: 'I can't stress strongly enough how significant this new piece of information is. It's a real breakthrough and I'm very hopeful that we will get more, which will lead us to the person who killed Harriet Lowther and subsequently buried her body.'

Mulligan had also interviewed Sir John Lowther and obtained a couple of emotional quotes, and ended the piece with an appeal to

the people of Lafferton and its surrounding villages who have longed for a resolution to this terrible tragedy, to think, think, think back. If you lived here when teenage Harriet, with all her life ahead of her, vanished, think hard. Did you know anyone or live near anyone or work with anyone who owned a Lada Samara? Did you perhaps see one regularly parked in a street near you? Or in a lock-up garage next to yours? If you did, please call the special hotline. You could be the person with the key to finding Harriet's killer. Don't let them get away with it any longer.

Simon went down to the communications room.
'Anything?'
The girl manning the hotline pushed her headphones aside. 'Every other car on the roads of Lafferton in 1995 was a blue or green Lada.'
'Of course.'
'There are a couple might be useful.'
'Ping them up, will you? But listen . . . if in doubt, it's important, OK?'
'What, even "my Uncle Ron had a Lada done out of flowers for his funeral – he didn't actually own a Lada, he just loved the jokes"?'
'Go on then.'
'What do you call a Lada with a sunroof?'
Simon went out of the door, almost closed it, then glanced back and said, 'A skip.'

Thirty-nine

'We've time to grab a coffee before we do the last three, Moll. I'll go over their notes but, if you want to say anything about what you've seen so far, now's the time.'

There was a warming plate and a jug of fresh coffee in the small staffroom.

'And decent biscuits.' Cat pushed the plate towards Molly. 'Small perks of working in here. Relatives are so generous – you'd pile on pounds if you ate all the chocolates and cakes and biscuits people bring in. Help yourself.'

Molly sat at the table looking thoughtful. Cat recognised the signs. Seeing half a dozen terminal patients, one after another, two of them quite young, was a shock and there was no way of preparing any student or junior doctor for it, they had to plunge in and cope. The important thing was that they had a vent for their feelings afterwards.

'So . . . thoughts?'

'I'm just – impressed. It's so different, isn't it? Everything, everything's different.'

'But what most of all?'

'Time. You know what a ward round is like in the General – one two one two, good morning, this is Mr Smith, being prepped for a lung operation later this morning, stats are as follows, treatment has been this, how are you feeling, Mr Smith, fine, fine, nothing to worry about, right, ladies and gentleman, on we go, keep up, keep up.'

Cat laughed. 'Nothing changes.'

'Here, you sit down, you listen, you answer their questions properly. The nurses do the same. You tell them about this or that treatment option, how they might feel tomorrow . . . you just . . . yes. It's that one word, isn't it? Time.'

'It's a luxury in a general hospital. It's an essential here. It's perhaps the most important part of the palliative care process because if we spend enough time we can help them towards peace of mind. A lot of the treatment isn't physical, though that's vital – especially pain and symptom relief – it's mental, it's emotional. And that takes time. I can change the dose on a syringe pump in twenty seconds. I can spend an hour before I get a patient to admit they're terrified of choking to death or of dying when no one is with them.'

'Pain control isn't difficult, is it?'

'I wouldn't say that. Sometimes it's straightforward – people respond well and we can keep them quite comfortable. But what about intractable bone pain? What about intracranial pressure? Not so easy. Pain isn't obsolete yet unfortunately.'

'Nausea. So many people in a general hospital are nauseous for one reason or another, but somehow it's regarded as nothing much, no one hurries to sort it out.'

'I know, but anyone who has ever had morning sickness will tell you what kind of priority it ought to have.'

'Chemo?'

'Almost always makes people sick, but there's no need for them to suffer it, we've got a whole cabinet of anti-nausea drugs. You can't give anything to pregnant women but you sure can to cancer patients.'

'There's something else I noticed. Listen, I know you're a Christian and all that and I really don't think I am, I'm not anything, I just couldn't reconcile any sort of God with the stuff I'm seeing most days. But . . . I don't know why but there's something in this place . . . I suppose it's calm and peace but it's more than that . . . It's something spiritual and I don't do spiritual.'

'But you do. Obviously. You've just said so.'

'No. I absolutely don't.'

'Molly, I'm not trying to convert you or convince you. I understand what you mean, that's all. I've never been into a hospice which didn't have this sense of – tranquillity, you could call it. Spiritual is the right word, whatever you happen to believe.'

They finished their coffees companionably and went back to the ward to see the last three patients. C ward had already been closed and mothballed. ·

'Mrs Mary Stalker,' Cat said, outside the door. 'She's eighty-nine and has one of those long, slow-growing cancers of old age. She's been in and out of here half a dozen times in the last year for pain relief and general care – she lives with her daughter who is seventy herself and not very fit, so the respite times are important for them both. But I'm not sure if Mary will ever go home again. She's been pretty sick this week.'

'Where is the cancer?'

'Everywhere now – started in the bowel, but they didn't want to start chopping her about and she's done quite well without any treatment to speak of. We just kept an eye on it and it only started to spread quite recently.'

Mrs Stalker was propped up on two pillows, her eyes closed. Her skin was yellow-tinged and there was almost no flesh left on her, but when she heard the sound of the door she opened her eyes and they glittered like black beads in the skull. Her wisps of white hair had been combed and arranged across her head by one of the volunteers, her nightdress was set off with a pink lace bed jacket.

'I hoped I wasn't going to miss seeing you,' she said to Cat, 'by dying before you got round to me. Now who's this?'

'This is Molly. She's shadowing me today to learn how we work here. If you'd rather see me on my own, Molly won't mind going outside.'

'It's all the same to me, Doctor, bring them all in, we'll have a party.' She scrutinised Molly carefully. 'You look a bit young to be a doctor. You look a bit young to be out by yourself, come to that.'

'I'm not quite qualified yet – I take my final exams next month.'

'I hope you pass them, my dear. You won't look any older if you do though.'

'How's the pain in your back, Mary? It was troublesome the other day and I changed your medication around a bit. Did it help?'

Mary Stalker made a face. 'So-so, but what I do to it is a lot better than any of your drips and tablets.'

'Whatever do you do?' Molly asked, glancing at Cat.

'I give it a good talking-to. By the time I've finished it skulks off into a corner.'

'Are you eating and drinking much?'

'No. Don't see the point. A fat corpse isn't any use to anyone.'

'Mary . . .'

'Am I shocking you?'

Molly looked embarrassed.

'Listen, my dear, when you've been a doctor a few years and you've seen a lot of old worn-out coats like me, you'll understand a bit better. I'm dying. I know it, Dr Deerbon knows it, they all know it. So now you know it. I'm dying and I don't mind, I've had a very good innings. The only problem is I'm not dying fast enough. I've been in here expecting never to come out I don't know how many times – how many times is it, Dr Deerbon?'

'Quite a few.'

'Yes. And much to my surprise, I've been off out of those doors again. But not now. I'm a bit further gone. And that's the way things are, you see. You get old, you die. If you didn't how would there be room for the next lot coming on?' She looked at Cat. 'There's one thing driving me mad, though, and I don't see why I should put up with it as well as with dying.'

'Tell me.'

'Itching. My skin itches. It's like creeping things all over it and I scratch until I bleed – look, here.' Mary stretched out an arm. The yellowing loose skin was dry and flaking and there were marks where her fingernails had scratched through it and brought blood, which had then dried.

Cat lifted the arm and turned it gently. 'Is this on your legs as well?'

'It's everywhere.'

'Did the nurses not give you any cream for it?'

'Oh, I didn't bother them. I thought I'd wait till you came round.'

'Mary, that's just silly . . . it's what the nurses are for, they could have saved you scratching and making yourself bleed like this. It's probably because of the drugs, I'm afraid, but I'll give you some tablets and a cream and that'll stop it in its tracks. You don't have to put up with this sort of thing, you know.'

'I've put up with a lot worse.'

'I dare say, but please let us do what we can for you, Mary – or are you up for some sort of bravery award?'

Mary laughed, showing half a dozen stubby teeth sitting like ancient tombstones between the fleshy gaps.

As they were leaving, Mary held out her hand to Molly. 'Let me hold it,' she said. Molly put her own hand into the old woman's. Mary stroked it. 'I like that,' she said. 'Lovely young soft skin. I like that. That cheers me up.'

She patted the back of Molly's hand and let her go.

Outside, Cat said, 'If everyone was like Mary . . .'

'She's very philosophical, isn't she? She seemed to be almost happy to be dying, which can't be true.'

'Why not? She's had a long life and I guess quite a hard one. She only has one daughter who is crippled with rheumatoid arthritis and can't really cope. She's been in awful pain, her symptoms are making her uncomfortable – the itching, the nausea, the loose bowels, the cough, the backache . . . she's had enough. She's tired.'

'Is she religious?'

'No. We had a chat about that once. She says she isn't looking forward to another life, one's been quite enough. She's ready to go.'

Molly shook her head.'

'Now, this is a difficult one. Roger Flynn. He's thirty-seven and he has non-Hodgkin's lymphoma. His outlook is grim, the chemo made him very ill – he's had severe allergic reactions to just about every drug in the book – he's had a terrible time. He was married just under a year ago and he was diagnosed not long afterwards. It's a bugger and he is very, very angry – he's angry with the illness, with himself, with me, with the nurses, with God . . . probably more than with the rest put together.'

'I don't blame him.'

'No. But he's an evangelical Christian, very born-again, converted in one of those mass rallies in a football stadium. He gave his life to Jesus and he became an evangelist himself, he's a preacher, and then he started to heal people, or so it seemed. He had a ministry at one of the evangelical churches in Bevham, laying on of hands, charismatic healing . . . you know the sort of stuff.'

'Yes and it gives me the creeps. Actually, if he's angry, I'd be angrier. I just don't know how people can fall for that sort of thing.'

'Discussion for another time but basically I agree with you. Mass hysteria is a dangerous thing. But now, of course, Roger is up against it. He really expected a miracle. His congregations expected a miracle. Half the charismatics in the country have been praying and expecting Roger to be healed – and he hasn't been.'

'Well, of course he hasn't.'

'If you believe God is a magician up in the sky who favours only you and your kind then it comes as a nasty shock.'

'But you're a Christian, Cat.'

'Yes. Only I don't think God is a magician.'

Roger Flynn was tall and lay straight as a felled tree trunk in the narrow bed, his head turned to the wall. He had a small fuzz of hair on his scalp, his skin was reddened and scaly, his eyes sunken down. His hands were clenched on the sheet.

'Hello, Julie,' Cat said. 'Roger. This is Molly, she's following me today. Do you mind her being here? You only have to say.'

'Of course not.' Roger's wife was pretty, round-faced, with bubbly curls, but her expression was lifeless, her voice flat, her eyes almost unseeing. She looked exhausted and as if she could not face anything else that might happen but fully expected it to do so, and then worse.

'Thank you.' Cat went round to the far side of the bed and took Roger's hand. He let it lie in hers but did not respond. 'How are you today?'

'Tired. So what's new?'

She looked at his chart. 'How's the fever? They gave you some paracetamol in the night.'

'Sweating like a pig. Do pigs sweat?'

'I'll look it up. Are you more comfortable now?'

'Not really. But I'm not going to be, am I? How long is this going on?'

'Roger . . .' his wife said, but it was a token protest.

'I don't know, Roger. I know it's what I always say and that it isn't very helpful but I'm afraid it's true.'

'Get me out of this.'

'I wish I could.'

'What use are you then?'

'I understand.'

'No, you don't. Can't you give me something?'

'What's it for? If it's pain, I'll check your dosage.'

'No. Something to put me under. Like dogs and cats.'

'Roger . . .'

'If vets can why not you? Our vet put the cat down just because it was old. I give you permission. I know it happens.'

'No, it doesn't.'

'Happens every day.'

'Not in this hospice it doesn't.'

'It should. Put the lot of us down. Nice injection, fall asleep, that's what the vet did. Shit.'

A tear pushed its way out from under his tightly closed eyelid. He wiped it off angrily and went on wiping.

'I'll make sure you're not in pain, though you'll be sleepier. Just go with it. Relax, Roger.'

'Fuck off.'

Julie looked anxiously at Cat, who shook her head, then bent down and gave the young woman a hug.

As they left the room, a nurse came down the corridor and raised her hand to Cat.

'Mary,' she said. 'I just popped in to see if she wanted anything . . .'

'Oh no. She seemed fine.'

'She'd just dropped her head down on her chest and gone. Not a murmur.'

Cat glanced at Molly. 'All right?'

'I don't believe it,' Molly said. 'I . . . We only just left her . . . I was planning to come and see her again. I don't believe it.'

'No,' Cat touched her arm. 'When death happens like that you don't, quite.'

Two nurses were on a break in the staffroom. A chocolate cake had appeared on the table with 'Thank You' iced on it in cream.

'Are you all right, Molly?'

'Yes. I just couldn't take it in. Mary. I still can't.'

'The difference is that you see the occasional death in a general hospital but mostly you're dealing with the living at all ends of the spectrum. Here, we are only at one end and it's relentless, there's no balance. You have to learn to deal with it carefully or it affects you too much – it pulls you about emotionally working here and it's right it should. I wouldn't want it to be any other way. But you have to look after yourself. Do you think you could do it?'

'I'm not sure.'

The chocolate cake was sliced into, more coffee brewed. One of the nurses had a daughter getting married the following week. The talk turned to frocks and flowers. It was how they dealt with it every day, Cat thought, how they stayed sane. Coming in here, leaving the ward and the patients, pain and distress and bereavement at the door, eating cake, chatting about everyday events, about the news or the weather or, as her mother would have said, 'the price of fish'.

Her mother. She had tried to put what Simon had told her out of her mind, and while she was working, she could, but the moment she stopped thinking about a patient or a drug dose or the effect of the day unit closure, she was back there, with Meriel, with a syringe of potassium, with her sister Martha. With killing. Mercy killing. But killing. And Si had known. When had he known? He had not said. If it had been before his mother had died, he might have taken action, but what action? Reported it. And then what? Arrested her? Of course not. For Cat, human life was sacred. For Simon, it was all about bringing criminals to justice. Yet he had failed to make certain that justice was done when the perpetrator was his own mother.

Cat could not decide if she wanted to talk to her father about it or not, whether there would be any point at all. Ill feeling. Anger. Resentment. There would be all of that. Knowing Richard, he might even refuse to discuss the subject at all. He was perfectly capable of remaining tight-lipped and silent. He had told Judith, without warning, and upset her considerably. Why? Judith had no reason to know. Now, it would be there for good, troubling her. What is known can never be unknown.

Unless everything else is, she thought suddenly. Dementia. The gradual dismantling of what you once knew. The unknowing of everything.

She looked at Molly, fresh-faced and laughing now, chocolate icing round her mouth. Molly. Twenty-four. Facing a working life of dealing with dying and death, with unravelling and unknowing.

She shook herself. There was a lot more to it than that and much of it more positive. Watching people get better, relieving serious pain, preventing this or that serious illness, diagnosing something in time, helping a baby from womb to world, saving a life in an emergency, confident of your skills.

'Come on, Molly. We're going to the pharmacy. The first principle of palliative care – appropriate and adequate pain relief.'

But the image was in front of her eyes as she opened the door. Her mother. Martha. A syringe of potassium.

There was no unknowing.

Forty

Free later 2day. Maybe we can meet 4 a drink?

The text had come an hour earlier and he had still not replied.
The case was opening out and at last he had the sense that something important was going to emerge, some new lead. Cat had
only replied briefly to the message he had left on her phone, and
in the cool, non-committal voice he knew, which meant that she
was being distant with him. And now Rachel. He sat in the Cypriot
café with an empty coffee cup. He picked up the phone on the
table in front of him.

'Guv?'

'Ben, I need you.'

'I'm on this burglary, out at Pyrbeck. Another with the same
MO, couple and a visiting daughter beaten up. You getting
anywhere?'

'Yes,' Simon said.

Outside, he read Rachel's text again. He wanted to see her
but seeing her was never straightforward, never just a drink or
dinner for two people, it was full of emotional tension and
frustration; unanswered, perhaps even unanswerable, questions
hung in the air between them, messing things up, distracting
them. Just now, he couldn't afford it.

*Sorry, up to eyes. Have to leave seeing you till case is wrapped up.
Will be in touch. Miss you. S.*

He hesitated only for a second before clicking on Send.

* * *

Message received. Rachel had started to empty a drawer in the kitchen as soon as she had sent the text to Simon, to give herself a distraction, but emptying a drawer did not stop her thinking, imagining, wondering. Panicking. The drawer was on the table, beside it a carrier bag into which she was sorting the rubbish, the broken paper clips and dry biros, old labels and bits of string and unidentifiable small plastic objects. She did it on autopilot, her mind on Simon. Kenneth was asleep in his chair beside the open sitting-room window. He slept a lot during the day and not always well at night and there was nothing she had so far been able to do to reverse the order of it.

Message received.

She read it. Read it again. Zapped it.

Her hand shook.

She shouldn't have sent the text, shouldn't have asked him, should have waited for him to make the next move, should . . .

Should. Shouldn't. Ought. Must.

The text was perfectly clear. The subtext of the text that was. Yes, he was up to his eyes in his case but that was not the reason. Whatever he felt, seeing her was too fraught with difficulty. She was married, he was reluctant to involve himself further, and who would blame him? He would be in touch when his case was closed. Except that there would be another case and then another. Of course he would not be in touch.

It was the right decision.

The decision she should have made herself if she had been principled enough. Strong enough.

She looked down at the small metal bottle opener in her hand. It was bent at the edge. Why had it been kept? Why had most of this junk been kept?

He was in her mind, his tall frame, his features, his steady look, his hands. Beautiful hands. She had noticed his hands before anything else, as he had reached to pour something or hand her something, at the banquet. His hands and his extraordinarily fair hair.

What had happened between them had been as final and as definite as anything in her life, and it had happened then, that evening, when they had sat next to one another and talked and looked with astonishment into each other's eyes and quickly away, terrified.

He could not mean this. The words were not his words. He would not use such brisk, dismissive, polite words. *Will be in touch.*

She could not bear it and she could not wait. *Will be in touch.* When? In a week, or a month? How long? Cold cases took years to solve and so might this.

Will be in touch.

'Rachel . . .'

She always got up automatically when Ken called her. He was awake, he was too cold or too hot, or uncomfortable in some way or other.

She went to him, her mind elsewhere.

He asked for a drink but Rachel knew that it was her company he wanted. She felt guilty for tidying out a drawer, texting Simon. Thinking about Simon. She felt guilty about everything. It was her condition. And Ken's condition was misery and there was no end to it. His limbs, his sight, his hearing, his mind, his breathing, his digestion, his bowels, his mood, name it and it was affected by the illness, and he bore it, for the most part, with great stoicism. He was not cheerful. No one could be in his state and feel cheerful. But he complained little, apologised when he did so, tried not to let her know about his lowest moods, tried not to call her to do this or bring that. He sat in his chair, or propped up in bed, listening to the radio, occasionally watching television, sometimes wanting music. He had been a reader and he still had books beside him but it took such a long, slow time to get through them now, he had almost given up. Rachel read out the reviews from the weekend papers, asked if he would like this biography or that history, and if he showed a flicker of interest, ordered them for him. The pile of books on the table in his room had doubled in the last few weeks. Sometimes she read aloud to him, which he liked, but when she had suggested audio books, he had refused. Pride. She did not always understand.

One or other of the carers was there at half past seven every evening to help her put Kenneth to bed. If she was going out, they then stayed with him, using the spare bed in the small den adjacent to his room.

Tonight, when the slow business of undressing, washing, toilet, pyjamas, guiding into bed, was done, Jason, that day's chirpy helper, was going off. Jason was the youngest of the three carers, the most cheerful and upbeat, black, full of talk about his twin baby daughters, his mother, his brothers, his music sessions. Kenneth listened to him in a bemused way but Jason delighted him, with his jokes and his patois and his swift, expert, gentle handling.

When Jason had gone, Rachel and Kenneth watched twenty minutes of television, but it was poor fare and Kenneth was dozing. She switched off, kissed him, turned out the light and left the room.

The house became very quiet. Rachel made coffee. Ate the remains of some ham. Wandered into the sitting room and looked at the TV listing but found nothing she wanted to watch. Wandered out again. She could have a bath. Get into bed early. She had bought a pile of books earlier in the day, from Emma at the new bookshop in the Lanes. The latest Joanna Trollope. *Wolf Hall*. A replacement copy of *Middlemarch*, as she had lost her own. Joseph O'Connor's *Ghost Light*. A book of poems by Elizabeth Jennings. The shop was tempting. Emma managed to find books no one else seemed to stock or even to know about, treasures from small publishers, reprinted classics. Rachel looked at them on the round table now. She spent evening after evening reading, often in a chair beside Kenneth's bed while he slept, sometimes in the day when he liked her to be near him but was happy not to chat. She had a vision of herself in ten years' time, still sitting, still reading beside him, when he would have deteriorated further but still be alive. She was not yet forty. Kenneth was seventy-seven.

The drawer was emptied, wiped out, relined, replaced, the few things that ought to be kept put back neatly inside it, the rest in the bin.

At twenty past ten she had picked out the book she wanted to read first, made a cup of camomile tea, was going to lock up.

A surge of desperation and longing stopped her on the way to the front door.

Kenneth was asleep. She checked. She went back almost on tiptoe. Checked again. His breathing was never good but it was regular and he was propped up on two pillows, as comfortable as he could ever be. She wiped a dribble of saliva from the corner of his mouth.

Then she went upstairs and changed out of her shirt and jeans, combed her hair, swapped her useful flat shoes for high heels.

Ten minutes later, she was turning the car out of the drive.

Kenneth Wyatt, barely sleeping, heard her. Glanced at his clock, the face always backlit when his room was dark.

Rachel went out in the evenings, to supper with this or that friend, occasionally to a film, even to London then back on the last train. She went to the odd official dinner or cocktail party, once or twice a year to a banquet, to which they were always both invited. She went to be his eyes and ears, to help him feel that he was somehow still part of public life, in the swim, merely excluded temporarily, as if he had broken a leg or was recovering from a bad bout of flu.

But not at this time. If she was going out, she usually left by seven, was home by midnight.

She did not take the car out at a quarter to eleven.

He lay back. He did not mind Rachel being out, was acutely conscious that she gave up such a lot of her life attending to him. He had sometimes wondered if she would meet another man. If she had already done so. But if she had, she had never given the slightest hint, there had been nothing to make him suspicious.

Suspicious. No. Early on in his illness he had made a promise, not to Rachel but to himself. He had told no one. He had promised that he would not criticise or object, not even comment, if it became clear that she had a lover. She would not leave him. He loved her. But she was a young, beautiful woman and he was almost forty years her senior with a long-term, unattractive, debilitating illness. Might she not with good reason look for another man?

* * *

283

The roads were quiet and the centre of Lafferton deserted. As she drove through the archway the cathedral clock struck eleven. The lamps in the close were ancient, carefully preserved over a hundred years or more, listed now and making the place look like a waiting film set. They cast soft light onto the cobbles and the grass. St Michael's itself was floodlit until midnight.

She knew where the building was, although she had never been to it, had a strange sixth sense which guided her directly up to the far end. Everything was in darkness around it. The first three floors were dark too. But at the top, light shone from the long windows.

She did not park in the bays directly in front but some distance back, beside one of the sets of legal chambers. *Judge Davitt* the board read in front of the designated space. But she would be gone long before His Lordship came in the next day.

She walked slowly up the path. The great bulk of the cathedral, like a docked ocean liner, reared up to her left, the eighteenth-century houses, set back behind the wide grass verges, stood pale-fronted and decorous. And always ahead of her, beckoning her on, the rectangles of light from his windows.

When she was twenty she had been in love with a man, almost as much in love as she was now, and had come out after dark in just this way, to stand outside his house, looking at the gate, the path, the hedge, the porch, the windows. His car. Looking until her eyes blurred, looking until each thing transposed itself onto the next. She could see them even now, they were so imprinted on her mind, though if she tried to recall the features of the man himself, Tim Scully, she could not. She had stood outside the house night after night. Once, he had come home late and his headlights as he turned in might have picked up her figure if she had not ducked and crouched behind the gate-post of the house next door. She had watched him get out of his car, put his key in the lock. Go in. Heard the door shut. Seen lights come on. Hall. Front door. A side window. Upstairs. Watched the curtains blot the lights out one by one.

She felt as if she had no skin. No pride. No shame. He had sent a note which was as clear as it could be that he did not want to see her again. She should have left it at that. What man wanted a woman hanging about on his doorstep, unable to take no for an answer?

Simon. She was sure. Simon wanted it. It was not something casual or temporary, without strings, without commitment on either side, this thing that had happened between them. It was rare, she knew that, rare and precious and not to be spurned. How many people experienced it and knew it for what it was?

She walked slowly up to the house. The air was mild. She could stand here all night, just to be near to him. But that would not be near enough.

What would he say if she rang the bell? She saw that there was an intercom. He had to let her in at the main door. He would tell her he was working or about to go to bed. He had someone else with him. She could not have borne that.

He could be angry or irritated, and she would creep away, humiliated and chastened and angry with herself.

But then there were all the other possibilities.

She hesitated. Went up to the intercom. Hovered her finger above the bell. Took it away.

She rang, pressing the bell hard, urgently.

Simon knew who it was the second he heard the ring, though why or how he could not tell. But he had been thinking of her as he had sorted through some sketches, picturing her here in the room, sitting, reading or simply watching him, legs curled beneath her, glass on the table beside her. He had regretted the text the moment he had sent it, had thought of it over and over again. He should have sent another one immediately. But he had not. A sort of terrible paralysis had overcome him. He was uncertain quite what to say and so had said nothing, no words at all. An hour earlier, he had thought that he would send her not a text message but some flowers and a card. But how would she explain the arrival of flowers? Would she have to? He did not know the way things were arranged in her house, how much her husband saw, knew, what questions he asked.

And so the flowers had not been sent either.

There was a moment's silence after he pressed the intercom. Of course it would not be Rachel and he knew better than to open the door automatically.

'Serrailler.'

'Simon?'

'It's open.'

She came running up the stairs.

Ten minutes later, a bottle of wine open, poured, they lay half in, half out of each other's arms on one of the sofas, saying little, intent on one another, disbelieving.

'Happy?' Rachel said.

'Yes.'

'I couldn't bear it. If you'd meant what you said.'

'I didn't. You should be able to recall texts.'

'And emails.'

'And letters.'

'And faxes.'

'Good God, faxes.'

Simon leaned over and kissed her. 'I was right,' he said. 'At the banquet. I was right. There's nothing else to say really.'

'So was I. And no. But there is, isn't there? That's the trouble.'

'Not now. Not tonight.'

'Simon . . .'

His mobile rang.

'Bugger.'

'Someone's just come in on the hotline, sir . . . think you ought to hear it.'

'Who is it?'

'Woman from California. Regarding the ID of Skeleton 2.'

'OK, thanks, put the recording through, but on the landline, it's clearer.'

He switched off and turned to Rachel. 'Sorry, sorry . . .'

'No, absolutely don't be. Of course you must.'

'Important.'

He topped up her wine glass. Leaned forward again and kissed her.

The phone rang.

'Here you go,' the duty telephonist said. 'Not a brilliant line.'

'Have you got contact details?'

'Everything.'

'Fire away.'

'*Lafferton Police special incident line.*'

'*Oh yes. Thank you. Hi there.*' The voice was English with an American overlay.

'*Can I help you?*'

'*It's more – can I help you. I have something you should know. I . . . we only just looked at the local newspaper online. We used to live near Lafferton but it's some years ago now and we don't check back too often.*'

'*May I have your name please, madam?*'

'*Sure, of course. It's Ryman. Celia Ryman. Mrs Ryman.*'

'*And where are you calling from please?*'

'*My address, you mean?*'

'*If you'd give me that, yes please.*'

'*It's 1446 Surfway Boulevard, Santa Monica, California, USA.*'

'*And the phone number?*'

She gave both her landline and cell numbers.

If every caller, with or without useful information, could be so efficient.

'*Thank you. Can you tell me what your information is regarding, Mrs Ryman, please?*'

'*Sure, it's about – as I just said, my husband was glancing through your online local news and he came across the photo . . . a facial reassemblage of a young woman whose body I think was found?*'

'*Yes.*'

'*My husband called me to look, and the second I saw it, I agreed with him. We're not in any doubt really.*'

'*Did you recognise the young woman?*'

'*Well, we used to live in a village outside Lafferton, pretty village called Bransby. We were there for nine years – the Old Forge, in Bransby. Both our children were born in the Bevham Hospital – Bevham General – and when they were around three and four – they're very close together – we had an au pair, from one of those places that changed their name – Balkan states. It used to be Yugoslavia, you know? Former*

287

Republic of Yugoslavia. So I'm not sure what it would be now, I'm sorry.'

'Don't worry, we can sort that out. What was your au pair's name?'

'Agneta. Agneta Dokic. And this is her. I'm absolutely as sure as I can be. This is Agneta's face.'

'When did you last see her?'

'She left us in a bit of a hurry actually – under a cloud, you'd say. I caught her stealing money, let her know that if she did it again I'd have to lose her – which would be a real pity, she was a great au pair, the kids loved her, she was very reliable, very trustworthy. Or I thought she was. Only then one or two other things went missing – I bought a bracelet for a bridal gift and it just vanished. Then a pair of my own earrings went missing. I found them in Agneta's room, in her make-up bag, and that was that.'

'You sacked her?'

'I didn't have time. She was out, it was her day off. I put the earrings on the kitchen table with a note, asking her about the bracelet and saying I would talk to her in the morning. But when I got up around seven thirty, it turned out she'd already gone. We never saw her again.'

'What about her things? Didn't you have to forward anything to her?'

'No. She'd taken her handbag and a sort of canvas tote bag she used but left most of her other stuff. She never returned. I never saw her again. I thought she'd been too scared to come back and face us, maybe just run off. It was odd she hadn't taken more if that was the case though – she didn't have a lot of clothes, but there were some, and books.'

'Did you ask any of your neighbours if they'd seen her?'

'Yes. She used to work for someone else in the village because once my kids had started nursery she had free time, so I said it was fine by us if she wanted to give someone else a hand. And so she got a job with some other people in Bransby, not au pairing, just general household help. She was very good, she'd do cleaning, cooking, shopping – and she could drive. So she worked for them two or three hours here and there, and as soon as I found her things gone I rang, but they hadn't seen her, they didn't know anything. I wasn't surprised. But interestingly, they said they had wondered if she had taken things from them – money had disappeared, and a silver ornament. But they were *a bit – I guess you'd say chaotic, so I'm not sure how reliable that was.'*

'Can you give me their names and an address please?'

'The address was Tadpole Cottage, and I've been racking my brains to remember their names but I just can't. My husband can't either. We didn't really know them.'

'And you never had any communication with Agneta again? Or with her family? Did you have an address?'

'Yes, but it was a PO box and I didn't want to send her things there, so when we left England to come out here I gave all her stuff to the charity shop. No, we heard from nobody. No one got in touch with us, but I wasn't really surprised. Only of course now, now I find out what happened, which is truly awful, well, seems odd that no one did make contact. Her family must have had our address. You'd think so. She was a good girl, a nice girl, you know . . . this thieving was the only thing, and maybe it was . . . I don't know. Maybe she'd problems at home, maybe she'd suffered some sort of trauma. I'm sure we could have talked it through, maybe sorted it all out. I feel very bad about that.'

'I don't think there's any need. Thank you very much for contacting us, Mrs Ryman, it's extremely helpful. I'll just read back your details to check I have them down correctly and someone will be in touch.'

'Only don't forget, it's a nine-hour time difference. It's early after-noon here.'

'Thanks for the reminder. Now, you are Mrs Celia Ryman, you live at . . .'

The duty operator came back on the line. 'And that's it, guv.'

'Terrific. Absolutely terrific. Good work.'

'Thanks.'

'Send it all across to my email please.'

'Will do.'

As he turned away from the phone he looked over at Rachel, sitting with her feet up, head resting on the back of the sofa. This is love, he thought. I have never known it before but now I do.

It seemed the simplest thing in the world.

* * *

289

Kenneth Wyatt woke out of a nightmare that he was drowning and could not breathe. Awake, he still could not breathe. His lungs seemed to be full of water, his throat was tight. But there was oxygen. There was Rachel. Rachel always woke on the instant.

He pressed the bell which was attached to his headboard, never out of reach. No response. He pressed again. The house was absolutely still. Dark. Silent. Jason had not stayed – he remembered that now. But where was Rachel? Out in the car. He'd heard her drive away. Drive away, leaving him. Leaving him alone.

He kept his finger on the bell. Heard it ringing, ringing.

He could not breathe, his chest was tight now, as well as his throat, his heart racing. Then he managed to draw a breath, but it was painful, the air dragged up from his lungs like water over shingle.

His finger weakened on the bell, but he had the mobile phone, tied to the headboard, switched on. One number to press.

'Stay,' Simon said, holding her face in his hands. Her eyelids had the faintest blue tinge, like the eyelids of babies. He breathed her.

'My phone,' Rachel said. He let her go at once.

'Ken. It's too late for anyone else.'

She fumbled about in her bag.

Simon poured the last of the wine into his glass. Waited. Because he could not bear to listen or think of Rachel talking to her husband, he went over in his mind what he would say to Mrs Ryman in Santa Monica, California. If he had not been with Rachel now, he would have got onto it the moment the station operator had rung off. But he would not feel guilty. Could not. It was a cold case. The girl had been dead and anonymous for sixteen years already. She could wait another day.

'I have to go, Simon, I'm sorry . . . I knew something would happen if I left him on his own, I should never have done that, it's the most appalling thing . . . I'm so sorry . . .'

'Rachel . . . listen . . .'

'No, please, leave me, don't touch me, don't stop me.'

'I wouldn't dream of it but you have to calm down for a couple of minutes or you won't be safe.'

'He could be dead in a couple of minutes. *Please let me go.*'

'Let's ring for an ambulance.'

But she was out of the door and flying down the stairs. He wanted to follow her, if only to check that she arrived home safely, but he had had more to drink than she had, he dared not get into the car.

'Rachel . . .' He raced down the stairs.

She was fumbling with her keys, dropping them on the grass, letting out a shout of frustration. He jumped forward and retrieved them. 'Listen – ring me. Tell me how he is. Ring me.'

She got in, looking quickly at him, her face full of anxiety, spinning the wheel as she reversed out of the space.

'Ring me.'

He saw the dust kick up behind the car as she went fast out of the close.

The oxygen cylinder was on the other side of the room. He could not have reached it, could not have used it by himself. Someone had to help him. Someone had to help him with everything. He was trapped. It came with the illness. But he minded that Rachel was trapped by it too, so he could never blame her if she went out. He did not blame her tonight.

She would come. He did not know where she had been, how far away she was, but she would come, she had said so, she was on her way the second she heard his voice.

Even that had calmed him, her voice, so that by the time he heard the car, her key, her running steps, his breathing was easier. She came flying through the door of his room, her violet eyes full of panic.

'I'm so sorry, darling, I'm so sorry. You're fine now. I'm here, it's OK.' As she talked to him she was moving the oxygen to the side of the bed, hooking up the tubes.

She bent to kiss him. Rested her lips on his forehead. He smelled her. Something fresh. Sweet. Her forehead was damp. He moved his hand to touch her.

'I'm so sorry.'

The mask was over his face, and he was breathing easily again. Rachel sat on the bed and took his hand.

'I am so, so sorry.'

He moved his head. No, he was saying. No. He pulled the mask down to speak but she replaced it gently.

'No. I'm going to call the doctor.' Though she knew that all she would get would be advice over the phone at best, that if she was seriously concerned she should ring for an ambulance. But she was not. It had happened before. He woke and found himself alone, perhaps trying to cough, could not, panicked, his breathing tightened. Sitting with him, calming him, the oxygen, was all he needed. Then sleep. He always slept, from relief.

But she had never left him before. What if he had not rung her? If he had perhaps pulled the phone accidentally off the headboard or his coughing had become choking, his lungs had filled up and he could not clear them? She would have stayed with Simon. She knew that. Perhaps all night, certainly for several hours. She could have come back to find Kenneth dead, alone.

She tightened her back against the shiver that ran down it.

Kenneth's eyes were on her face. His breathing was normal.

'I can take it off now. You're fine.'

She did so, and gave him a sip or two of water. As she held the glass, he lifted his hand slowly, and put it shakily on top of hers. Rachel bent her head to touch it. The hand did not stop shaking. No part of him ever stopped shaking, even while he was sleeping.

'D-don't,' he said. 'No . . .'

Later, when he slept, exhausted, she gazed down at him, a ruin of a once fine-looking, tall, strong man. She had married him when she was not thirty, he sixty-seven. She had loved him then, depended on him. And even as the illness tightened its grip, she had come to like, respect, honour, care for him. These had been good grounds for a marriage, she had discovered, far better than she deserved. Any diminution of passionate love on her side had not seemed relevant. Until now.

She thought of Simon. The quiet, calm flat. The lamps in the close. The cathedral bells. Simon's drawings on the white walls. On the long elm table.

Simon's hands. His mouth. His tall frame.

Simon.

She would have been there still, she knew that, and if he called she would be there again. She knew that too.

She felt deeply ashamed, and powerless to change anything.

Forty-one

Simon waited for an hour. Rang. Rachel's phone went straight to voicemail. Rang the landline. The same. He sent a text but there was no reply.

After midnight was mid-afternoon in California.

Celia Ryman answered almost at once.

'This is Detective Chief Superintendent Simon Serrailler.'

'Hi, I was thinking you'd probably call.'

'Thank you for ringing us earlier, Mrs Ryman, It was extremely helpful. I wonder if I could ask you a few more questions?'

'Sure, please. You know, I haven't been able to get her out of my mind. We had a bit of an upset but she was a lovely girl, really, underneath, the kids were so fond of her, she was great with them . . . I'm just so shocked by this.'

He went over the ground. It was all there. No discrepancies, nothing new. She was anxious to be as helpful as she could.

'You said Agneta worked for someone else in the same village?'

'That's right, and we've been struggling to remember the names . . .'

'This was another family?'

'Not exactly – it was a couple – well, it was a couple of women, you know what I'm saying? They were – well, together, you know?'

'Can you remember anything at all that would help us trace them?'

'I remember the cottage . . . funny, ancient old place, roof sort of wavy in the middle. Tadpole Cottage. That name really suited it. The two of them used to be in the garden a lot, very keen. But we didn't really know them, the cottage was tucked away, they weren't often around the village. But I just don't remember either of their names. I wonder if they still live in Bransby. They might do. They seemed staying-put kind of people, you know?'

It was ten to one. He had to see Rachel. He had to know how her husband was.

He was unlikely to sleep but he knew he should try. He set his alarm for six. Woke at four with a headache, so unusual for him that he had not even basic aspirin in the flat.

He showered, drank coffee. At twenty five past five he was walking along the corridor to his office. No aspirin. He went to the CID room. Empty. Down to the canteen. A couple of weary uniform were talking to the pretty Hungarian behind the counter. He bought tea, toast. Aspirin.

Is everything OK? Call me, txt me. Please. Love S.

He hesitated, then sent it. She would be angry with him. Angry with herself. Would not reply.

Might reply.

He needed to see her.

The tea was good, fresh and hot. The toast was cold and soggy. He left it.

The village of Bransby was quiet. Once, there would have been a couple of working farms, cow manure down the main street from the early-morning journey to milking, a cockerel crowing, the smell of pig. People about.

No one was about. He found Tadpole Cottage, up a narrow snicket between low hedges, and then he smelled not pig, but honeysuckle.

Perhaps this one cottage had not changed a great deal. The thatch was moth-eaten, there was a rusty old water pump to one side, a shed with broken windowpanes. A cat stared at him from the step up to it, then half closed its eyes lazily, face to the sun.

The gate was at the side. Just beyond it, in a small turning space, an ancient grey van was parked. Serrailler walked up to it. The back doors did not close fully. The body was dirty but not rusted, the tyres in order. It was not locked. The fabric of the seats was worn away here and there. The floor was a silt of paper, wrappings, plastic bags, a funnel, a piece of rubber hose, some half-torn cardboard boxes. The driver's seat had a canvas backrest on a metal frame. The passenger seat was set as far back as it would go. The keys were on the dashboard.

He made a note of the number, removed the keys and locked the van and walked back to the wooden gate.

The cat's eyes gleamed briefly before the lids half closed again. Disdain, he thought. It was the look Mephisto had when he glanced up at anyone. Superiority and disdain.

The kitchen faced the front and the sound of Bach came from a radio on the open windowsill. He looked inside. No one. Walked round. Creeper with small white flowers hung down over small windows. He cupped his hands to peer in. No one. The garden was untidy but someone had once loved it, someone had planted it with care. Someone had known what they were doing.

He pushed aside an overgrown bush and edged his way up the side, coming out onto a terrace of uneven old paving stones. The back door was open. A woman was sitting in an ancient basket chair, reading a newspaper, a basin of eggs on a table beside her. Half a dozen hens were scratting round behind some netting.

'Miss Wilcox?'

The woman leapt up, sending the paper flying.

'I'm sorry. I didn't mean to startle you.'

'Well, you did. Who are you? What are you doing in my garden?'

She peered at the warrant card he showed, coming closer to him and reading it intently. He saw that her hair was thinning, enough to show the scalp here and there.

'I'd like to ask you a question or two, please. May I sit there?'

She hesitated, looking at him with an expression that was both angry and suspicious. And fearful.

'All right.' She picked up the paper and folded it roughly together.

He sat. Waited. Watched her.

'What's this about? I'm quite busy. I don't like intruders.'

'What can you tell me about a young woman called Agneta?'

'I don't know any young woman called that.'

'But you did.'

She stared him out. He waited.

'Oh, that girl. A long time ago. She helped a bit in the house. I don't remember anything about her.'

'Why did she leave?'

'She worked for some other people in the village – that was her main job, she only helped us out a bit now and then. She just upped and went.'

'Why?'

'I – she stole. They caught her thieving, so did I. She was confronted. She went. That was that. Never saw her again.'

'You said "she helped us out".'

'Yes.'

'Can you tell me who else lives here?'

'No one. Not now.'

'You read the papers.' He glanced sideways at the one on the table. 'The *Guardian*.'

'Yes.'

'Do you see the local paper?'

'No.'

'Do you watch television?'

'Don't have it. I listen to the radio.'

'So you won't have seen this?' He took out a copy of the press release with the image of the missing girl and passed it to her. She hesitated. Glanced at it, then away. Picked it up again and looked at it closely.

'Is that Agneta?'

She drew in a slow breath. 'It looks like her. But I don't remember her well and this isn't a proper photograph, is it?'

'No. It's a facial reconstruction done by computer.'

'Oh, well . . .'

'From her skull.'

297

She did not move. The hens scratched about. The sun was warm.

'The other family she worked for in the village have confirmed that it is a strong likeness.'

'They moved away.'

'Yes, but we have been in contact with them. They're sure this is Agneta Dokic.'

'They're probably right. I don't know. If they say so, why do you need my opinion?'

'Confirmation. And you didn't see her again after she left?'

'No. I think the people rang and said they'd caught her stealing – and I agreed that she'd taken things from here. So that was that.' She stood up. 'I can't tell you any more.'

'Thank you.' Simon took out his card. 'If you do remember anything else . . .'

'I won't.' She did not take it.

'May I have just a couple of details from you? Your full name, the name of anyone else living here.'

'I told you. There isn't anyone else. Unless you count the cat.'

'So you're a widow? Your husband died?'

'What's that to do with anything?'

He waited without replying.

'Not a husband,' she said. 'If it's any of the police's business.'

'I just need to tick all the boxes.' It was the kind of ridiculous phrase he would never normally use.

'My partner has dementia and is in a home . . . and do not *dare* tell me that you are sorry.'

He did not.

'If that's all, you can leave, I'm going there now, actually. Have you ever visited someone you love but who no longer knows you?'

'No,' he said. 'Not exactly.'

She looked at him with contempt.

The cat had moved, following the sun.

Simon stood in the lane and rang in the number of the van for a check, which came back within the minute as registered to Miss Leonora Dulcie Wilcox, clean licence, up-to-date insurance.

'Sir John? Simon Serrailler.'

'Good morning. Beautiful morning.'

Simon was startled. He had not noticed anything whatsoever about the day.

'Yes indeed.'

'Been out in the garden since half six. I even took my morning tea out there – But you haven't rung for this. What's happened?'

'I wonder if you can answer a question for me please.'

'Anything. Has there been a development?'

'Possibly. You said Harriet was very musical.'

'Yes. Though what does that mean in a young girl? I've no idea if she had any sort of exceptional ability but she did love it . . . loved playing her instruments.'

'Which were?'

'The piano first, she started at seven, then the clarinet – she wanted to play the guitar too but we didn't agree.'

'Why was that?'

'Three different instruments to practise – takes up a lot of time, you know. She had to concentrate on her schoolwork. So the piano and the clarinet were fine, nothing extra.'

'Where did she go for lessons?'

'School. It had good music teachers, that school. It's closed now, of course – sad. Just not enough fee-payers to keep a girls' day school like that going these days. Harriet had her music lessons there.'

'Do you remember her teachers?'

'I'm afraid not . . . oh, wait. Yes, of course. The clarinet was Mr Winder, which became the inevitable bad joke as you may imagine.'

'And the piano?'

'No. I don't remember any name. Sorry.'

'Presumably whoever it was wrote on Harriet's reports at the end of term?'

'Yes. And if you'd asked me a few years ago I'd have told you I would look them out, but after Eve died I cleared out all of that sort of thing. It suddenly seemed pointless to keep it. All the paperwork, all her toys and sports things and tapes and clothes – everything Eve had wanted to keep. I couldn't bear it. It went out, the hospice shop, the bin. I'm sorry. Is this important?'

Forty-two

An hour before she left home, Jocelyn Forbes made a pot of tea and a round of toasted fruit bread and took them on a tray into the conservatory. It was another of the clear blue, warm, daffodil-golden mornings that had started over a week earlier and she wanted to enjoy watching the birds before she got ready to go out. Five minutes later, she was bent over double, choking, unable to swallow a piece of the toast down or to cough it up and spit it out, paralysed both in her throat and with terror. No one else was in the house. No one would hear her because she was making no sound, though an odd, thin whistling noise came out of her mouth once or twice.

Her heart raced and she reached out to hold onto the back of her chair, but could not grip it, her hand was as useless as her throat.

She saw the bright room swirl round in front of her eyes, inside her head.

And then, abruptly, her throat pushed the lump of food up and out. She heard herself retching, heard her breath rasp. She stumbled backwards to find the chair and sat down heavily, her body shaking.

It was as much as she could do to get herself ready and she called a taxi, feeling unsafe to drive, wondering if that was that, if the previous day's short foray to the supermarket was the last time she would ever take out her own car.

Everything was slipping out of her grasp.

* * *

For a moment, she was reminded in Switzerland. The consulting rooms were in one of Lafferton's Edwardian houses in Sorrel Drive, many of which had become either flats or dental surgeries and solicitors' offices in the last few years. But the entrance hall was light, the walls and doors freshly painted white, the magazines new. She tried to look at one but her hands would not turn the pages and she was still shaky after her earlier fright.

She looked out of the window onto the trees that lined the road, old trees with thick trunks and heavy canopies of leaves.

I will not see any of this again, she thought. The thick lushness of the leaves, the shady green, the sunlight filtering through here and there. I will not see an autumn or a winter either.

And it occurred to her that she was glad, that however much she had wavered in Switzerland and immediately after coming home, she now felt the old calm resolution returning, the sense of decision, of having a choice and making it.

She did not want to go on.

'Mrs Forbes?' The voice was familiar, though the appearance was not and took her aback slightly.

This was a light room too, with a high moulded ceiling, a recent partition across one end.

He had a sheet of notes in front of him on the desk but he did not look at them, he looked at her, leaning back in his chair, calm, still, waiting.

'Something happened, just this morning,' Jocelyn said, and began to talk. He listened, as she had rarely known anyone listen, listened, without interrupting, looking at her steadily, his eyes thoughtful and full of sympathy. She talked about the onset of her illness, the symptoms, the fears, the creeping dread of becoming dependent, the terror of dying in the way she might have died this morning. She recounted everything about the visit to Switzerland, told him about Penny, told him about her own changes of mind and heart. Until now.

'Now,' he said when she had fallen silent at last. 'Now, today. Where do you find yourself?'

'Decided. Absolutely. If I could only be sure that there was somewhere even a little like that place in my mind. The one I imagined.'

'Not like a shabby apartment in a suburb of Switzerland where the bed was more like a none-too-clean examination couch.' His voice was filled with disgust. 'That is a complete scandal and a disgrace and I cannot tell you how many of us would wish to have the place closed down. The whole organisation closed down.'

How many of us. Who? What did he mean?

'One of the few things we are managing to do in this country is rescue people such as yourself once they have fallen into – and, thankfully, out of – the clutches of these criminals – because that is what they are, I assure you. We have some efficient ways of tracing their victims – I don't use the word lightly, Mrs Forbes – and offering an alternative to at least a few.'

'How?'

He put his fingertips together and glanced down at his desk. 'Let's just say there are people prepared to pass on information. But the point is, as I know you are aware, for the time being we have a legal problem in the UK. All of this is strictly against the law – in short, it is criminal. That is a crime in itself, in my view – a crime against common humanity and an infringement of basic human rights. One day, we'll win the battle, I have no doubt about that. It's a moral battle, not merely a legal one. But in the meantime, we have no alternative but to be very careful, very circumspect. Before you leave here today I will ask you to sign a statement which will not only help you but will be essential to me and to my staff should there be any future legal challenges or problems. Do you understand? I'm sure you do.'

She thought of Penny. Penny could not know.

'For this reason, among others, if I do offer you an appointment in my clinic, you will not be allowed to bring anyone with you – no relative or friend. It is better to involve no one else at all. I have staff who will look after you and be with you every step of the way to the final step – who will take the place of that relative or friend and are specially trained to do so.'

'Are they not at risk of prosecution?'

'Yes in theory, but they believe as passionately as I do in our work, so they are prepared – brave enough – to take the risk. And we are very, very careful indeed. Now, you've told me about your condition. It's plain that it is deteriorating and you're right to fear some of the things you do. But I would urge you, even so, that care for motor neurone sufferers, in hospices for example, as well as in hospitals, is increasingly sophisticated. There's no cure but there are many ways in which symptoms can be controlled. You should leave no avenue unexplored, you know.'

'I haven't. I appreciate what you're saying to me but I am very clear now about what I want to do. Very clear. Going to Switzerland put me off in one sense. I would never go back there and I'd deter anyone else from going, with the last breath in my body. It was a terrible experience. But you assure me that you have something quite different to offer.'

'I like to think that my small facility is as – well, yes – as perfect – I won't be afraid to use the word – as I can make it. As peaceful, as calm, as tranquil, as spiritual, as beautiful – and as professional. All those images you had which you have called "fantasies" of a place of great peace and acceptance in which to die with dignity – all those images are true. You will see.'

'So I would be able to visit in advance?'

'Ah, no – I'm afraid not. That is part of our having to be so private and secure – it's a risk we couldn't take. Not at the moment. You can imagine . . . word would only have to get out after an unscrupulous person decided to "visit in advance" . . . I hope you understand. I wish this were not the case, I really do.'

'What should I do?'

'I can't tell you that, Mrs Forbes. This is your decision. Your illness. Your life.'

'My death.'

He looked directly at her without any embarrassment.

'Yes,' he said. 'It is. You should go home and think everything through. Think it through again, from every point of view. Make the decision – to remain alive until death takes you in its own time. Work your way through that in your mind, looking at every possible outcome, every sort of care you might opt for, every medical help. The positives and the negatives. Then do the opposite. Make the decision to come to the clinic and take your death into your own hands. See how you feel about that. Look at that from every point of view.'

'Should I talk to anyone else?'

'That's up to you. My own feeling is that you should not – this is your decision, no one else's. In any case, as the paper you will read and sign makes clear, you should under no circumstances talk to anyone about this consultation, or our clinic – this has to be totally confidential. Do you understand that fully?'

She understood. She understood that he was protecting himself, his staff, his clinic, that he could be prosecuted, struck off the medical register, imprisoned – she did not know exactly. But it occurred to her that if she were to go out into the street now and telephone the police, she would be able to prove nothing.

She read the statement, signed it. He gave her a card with his telephone and email contact details. The telephone number was not the same as the one she had had previously. 'I so dislike this cloak-and-dagger,' he said, 'and roll on the day when it is no longer necessary.'

But it did not feel like cloak-and-dagger, she thought, walking out of the consulting room to her waiting taxi in the bright sunshine. It did not feel sordid, or backstreet. Illegal. Wrong. It felt right. She felt right.

She almost tripped, climbing into the back of the cab. She could no longer trust her body. It was time to leave it.

Forty-three

Frances Cadsden came out of her front door wearing a tracksuit and carrying a sports bag as Simon stopped outside. She looked slightly annoyed.

'It won't take a minute.'

'It's just that I go to a fitness class and then I meet a friend for coffee. But of course, come in . . .'

'No need. It's only a couple of questions.'

'About Harriet?'

'She was musical. Played the piano, played the clarinet.'

'Oh yes, and loved them both, really did . . . she loved her music. Right from when she and Katie were first friends.'

'Was she very talented?'

'That's hard to say. I'm not musical, Katie didn't play any instrument so . . .'

'Do you remember anything about her parents trying to stop her playing the piano?'

'I do actually. You'd better come in, hadn't you?'

No neighbours were about, no one looked out from behind net curtains here. It was not that sort of road. But he had Frances Cadsden down as a dignified person who would not want to chat to anyone at all on her doorstep.

'Yes,' she said, putting down her sports bag, and closing the door, 'we had talked about this – probably during the summer term. Harriet had been staying the night – it was a Saturday, she was only allowed to stay on Saturdays during term – and she was saying there was a concert coming up and she had been asked to play her clarinet in part of it but she wasn't sure she could because she didn't have enough time to practise. Then she spilled it out about wanting to learn the guitar, wanting to do more music, wanting to go for Grade 8 piano, but her parents were against it. She got quite upset and Katie was telling her to go for it, I was saying no – not just that, but at least maybe have another chat with her parents. It seemed such a pity. Don't you think so? It still seems a pity to me. She was so good at music, so keen, and then to have them be so negative.'

'Did they want her to give her music up?'

'No, I don't think so. But they said she was doing quite enough music, she had GCSEs coming, she had to concentrate on her schoolwork, not on extra stuff. I think they saw music as "hobbies department". A lot of parents do, don't they? Sport, art, drama . . . all that. Nice hobbies, nothing to do with getting A grades and a good career.'

'I know Katie didn't play an instrument but is there any chance that you or she could remember who taught Harriet music?'

'I wouldn't know, I'm afraid. I don't suppose I ever knew. Katie might. They were pretty close at that age. Try asking Katie. All I know is that the whole subject was a bit of a bone of contention in the Lowther household. Poor Harriet.' She looked down silently at her sports bag, and the bright, neat hall was filled at once with the memory of a blonde girl carrying a tennis racket.

Bevham General was like an airport, he sometimes thought, with the all-important shopping mall, the check-in desks, the lifts, the uniforms, the people, the muzak, the big windows and the general hum. And upstairs, the quieter areas, where people waited. He had grown familiar with it over the times when Martha, his sister, had been in and out of emergency rooms and he had sat with her for hour after hour, talking to her, holding her hand, drawing her. Waiting. She had always recovered somehow, always gone home, though home had not been Hallam House for years. But she had been happy in the nursing home, loved and spoiled. Until there had been one more crisis. Until their mother . . .

'Is Katie Morris here?' He showed his warrant card.

'She's in ICU. Is it urgent?'

'Yes, but it will only take a minute.'

'I'll see. You may have to wait. Relatives' room?'

Not his favourite place. He had been in too many with the shocked and the suddenly bereaved, the traumatised and the fearful, as they sat grey-faced, holding someone's hand, cups of tea left untouched, the air thick with grief and bewilderment.

But this one was empty. He looked out of the window onto the main forecourt where the ambulances were pulling in, unloading, driving off. It was high up. The people walking about in white coats were like tiny figures on a child's construction set, the cars toys.

His family had spent most of their lives here one way and another, his father in the old, small building long since demolished, an Edwardian house extended and expanded, with Nissan hut wards running at every angle. Cat had not trained here but had come back to do her house jobs, where she had met Chris; Ivo had trained here before heading off to Australia the minute he qualified; Meriel had been on every committee and board, in her day the strongest force to be reckoned with.

What would it have been like if he had trained here, worked here too, a cardiac surgeon, an obstetrician – a bench scientist researching into vaccines, say? He had started out, dutifully, on the family path, but always going against the grain, always feeling he was in the wrong place, among the wrong people, never enjoying a single day, a single aspect of it, always ill at ease, always looking round for his escape route.

'Sorry you had to wait, I can't spare you long.'

'That's fine. Thanks for finding a moment.'

'What's happened? You've found out something, haven't you? I can see it in your face.'

Could she? How? He was startled, never expecting to be so transparent.

308

'It's very possible, yes. And you can help, Katie.'

'Anything. I was thinking about her only this morning, you know? Where would she be now, what would she be like? Would we have kept up? I think we would but you can never be sure.'

Simon sat opposite her on one of the Scandinavian-looking chairs.

'It's this. Harriet was musical, played two instruments.'

'Yes, piano and clarinet. I never quite got it, the music thing, typical Walkman-in-ears girl, me, but she liked playing more than anything. Piano best, but she wanted to try the guitar as well as the clarinet, only that wasn't on, of course.'

'Her parents weren't keen, I gather.'

'You could say. They wanted a little brainbox though they pretended to be laid-back, but you could tell. They should have let her follow her own star. All parents should in my view.'

'And mine. Do you remember who taught Harriet music?'

Katie smiled. 'Mr Winder, the wind, er, instrument teacher.'

'I heard that one. And piano?'

'Miss . . . God, what was her name, what was her name? I can see her now. She lived with another woman. She never taught me but Harriet got on really well with her because she was so good at the piano – star pupil. Yes, and I remember now – Harriet wanted to have extra lessons, you know, private ones, out of school time, but they wouldn't have it.'

'Her parents?'

'No. God, it's all coming back . . .'

Keep it coming, Simon thought, keep it coming, Katie. But he said nothing. She would recall better without being pushed or prompted.

'Harriet wanted extra piano lessons but that was no-go as well as the guitar – the Lowthers just put their foot down. But Harriet was one of those quiet people who can get quite stubborn, quite determined, and she told me she'd fixed up the lessons anyway. I think it was only one a week and she was going to the teacher's house for them. She made me swear I wouldn't say anything – sweet, really. That's not the kind of thing you usually swear not to tell about – extra music lessons!'

'And she definitely didn't tell her parents?'

'Absolutely not.' Katie looked thoughtful. 'She just told me. My God, is this important? Is this something I should have remembered before and told you?'

'You weren't to know, Katie. The main thing is, you've remembered now.'

He did not wait for the lift.

Forty-four

'AGAAAAAGAAAAAGAAAAAGAAAAAGAAAAAGAA
AAAGAAAAAGAAAAAAAAAAAA!'

It was difficult to tell if the scream was of rage or pain. Molly
had been helping with a check of the controlled drugs cabinet.

'What's happening?'

'Don't worry, it's only Miss Mills.'

The screaming went on, and after a moment of listening
intently, Sister Fison locked the cabinet and gestured Molly to
follow her. 'The trouble is, they don't like going to her so they
always try and leave it to someone else – usually me – which
means she gets worse and worse and then the other patients are
upset. I wish they would just deal with it.'

She crossed into the small dining room where the early lunch
was being served. Miss Mills was standing in the middle of the
room holding her arms out and screaming what might have
been the name Agatha, now barely to be made out, in the high-
pitched uninterrupted noise. She held a fork in her right hand.

The dining-room attendant was standing near the door
looking bemused, two other patients huddled together, chairs
pulled tight up to tables. One of the carers was reasoning with
Olive but standing yards from her and glancing every few
seconds towards the door.

'Right,' Moira Fison said, 'Lorraine, get on with your job.
Kelly, will you please help the others? – they've been left alone
in fright and bewilderment and this must not happen. Go on.

311

Molly, give me a hand, please. Olive, please put the fork down, you haven't got your lunch plate yet. Let me have it.' She took a single step to face the screaming woman and held out her hand. 'You needn't shout any more, my dear, it's all been dealt with. Just give me the fork and we can carry on with lunchtime as usual.'

Molly edged round until she was at Olive's back, and waited. She could feel the heat of rage coming from Olive's body.

Olive was still screaming. She ignored Moira and did not let go of the fork.

Molly reached up without warning, took Olive's raised arm and pulled it swiftly down. Olive swung round, her mouth open but the scream dying into silence.

'Drop the fork on the floor,' Molly said calmly.

Olive stared at her in bewilderment. Dropped the fork. Fell on Molly, arms out to be caught. Molly caught her.

'Good,' Moira Fison said, taking her other arm. 'Well handled, Molly. Thank you. Now, just help me lead her out of here into the sitting room. The others will be having their lunch in five minutes. We can't do this here.'

'What triggers it off?'

'No idea. She does it a lot but sometimes this name, Agatha, comes out. No one knows who Agatha is. She can't tell us, of course, but Miss Wilcox doesn't know, either. That's the other woman – partner, whatever you want to call it. Right, in here. Come on, Olive, don't try and fight me. Take a firm grip on her arm, Molly.'

Years ago, Molly's youngest sister, Leonie, had had tantrums, which had started up for no apparent reason and involved similar hysterical screaming and aggression. Dealing with Olive was like dealing with the three-year-old.

'Sit down here, Olive, we want you nice and calm. Can you roll up her sleeve? She doesn't understand what you mean if you ask her to do it. I've rung the bell for my husband, he's on a call.'

Olive was quietening, her hand in Molly's, her body trembling slightly. Molly stroked her arm and murmured to her. Leonie. Yes. It was the same. They had soothed Leonie in the same way until she had surfaced from her tantrum like someone waking from sleep.

'It's like reverting to childhood,' she said.

Moira Fison shot her a look. 'More troublesome though. Ah, here he is.'

She should not find someone without a single hair on his head so unsettling. Molly had told herself that several times since she had started her three-day work experience. He had had alopecia. A disease. So what? Not his fault.

But it made her shudder. She was ashamed. She forced herself to look at him as he came into the room and not to look away at once. People must look away too often. Somehow, a head bald because of disease was not the same as a head bald from choice. It was the smoothness of the skull, the way it shone. The complete absence of absolutely any hair at all, any down or blue-grey shadowing beneath the skin. So get over it, she thought. It could happen to you.

'How long since the last time this happened?' Leo Fison said, drawing up a syringe from a vial of liquid.

'Two days. It's getting worse.'

'Yes. I'll up the morning and evening dosage and add another at two o'clock. Thank you, Molly, if you'd just hold her arm firmly. She doesn't usually fight it though. Too exhausted with all the shouting.'

Speak to her, Molly wanted to say to him. Speak to her, look at her. She's alive. She can hear you. She understands your tone of voice.

He drew the needle out. 'OK. We need to get her upstairs to bed straight away, Molly, it's quick-acting. You support her on her right.'

Chemical cosh. It hardly seemed like the new revolutionary treatment for dementia sufferers, the talking, one-to-one therapy, the memory class, the constant support from fully trained, sympathetic staff. In the old days it had been the Brompton cocktail to keep them quiet. This was no better. Molly was due a session going over her time here at the end of tomorrow. She planned to ask some questions.

They helped Olive onto the bed, took off her shoes and her

313

spectacles, turned her onto her side. Molly covered her with a quilt. She lay, snoring very slightly. Her features settled and she looked less disturbed, more like any other human being calmly settling down to sleep, no longer hysterical, no longer with wild, vacant eyes. Molly stroked her hand.

'Let's get back to the drugs check,' Sister Fison said. 'She won't bother anyone for a while.'

But as they got downstairs, the sister was called to the phone. Molly went along the corridor in search of something to eat but hesitated near Dr Fison's office, feeling roused enough to go in and challenge him now, query the injection he had given Olive, ask what he planned for her future treatment. It would be fair to hear what he had to say before telling Cat what was happening, asking for her opinion.

His door was ajar.

'. . . But Mrs Forbes, you agree with Hazel that this country has a misguided attitude to assisted suicide. Easy enough to condemn ending a life which has become pain-filled and intolerable when you don't have to deal with the reality of it day in, day out. What about a single parent with a desperately handicapped child? What about the loving partner of someone in great agony? . . . Yes, Hazel Smith . . . Yes, she gave me your number . . . She was very concerned about you. She told me she felt powerless to help you.'

There was a pause.

'Hazel is a mutual friend, that's all . . . Well, that's my point. Hazel believes the same as you and I do . . . Yes, that's why I am trying to . . . Listen . . . I want to make sure that the facility we offer in this clinic is absolutely the best because it's only when we give the best that we will win the argument and get the law changed. Meanwhile, I'm going ahead on my own as I told you . . .'

Molly walked on towards the kitchen to collect a salad and a drink from the fridge. In the staffroom, Teresa, one of the carers, was drinking a Coke and doing *Take a Break's Wordsearch*. She glanced up.

'When do you get to be a doc?'

'Couple of months.'

314

'Then what? GP?'

'Not sure yet. Don't think so.' She sat down and peeled the cling film off her salad.

'You won't be going into this lark though. Who would?'

'Don't you like it? You're good with the patients, I've watched you. I watched you with Olive.'

'Poor Olive. She's got something buzzing round inside her head and it's driving her mad trying to swat it. Well, you don't get anything back, do you?'

'They trust you. They rely on you.'

'Nothing back. Nice enough place though. They keep it fresh which is more than you can say for some homes. I've worked in places you wouldn't keep your cat.'

'I don't always . . .'

'What?'

Molly stuffed her mouth with ham and tomato to avoid having to answer.

'He's all right, you know. He's not bad. It's her I can't stand. He has these ideas only she doesn't bother to try them out. Started these memory books, you know? Memory books, memory boxes – and showing them short films of what it was like in their own day, when they were kids, when they were in their twenties . . . get them to try and talk about it. It was good. Only she doesn't bother to keep it up.'

'Maybe they're beyond it.'

'No. Well, two of them aren't, I started with them, it made a difference, you could tell. Dr Fison came round, he was quite impressed. Only we haven't done it for a couple of weeks and I can't organise a session if she isn't backing me up. I didn't come here just to sit them in a chair and leave them to stare at the walls.'

'Or to be drugged into shutting up.'

'What, Olive? She's the only one they do it with. They can't cope, you know, it is quite difficult with someone like that. She gets beside herself with rages. She bites and kicks, she spits, she screams, she lashes out. You saw her with that fork. She'd have stabbed someone with it in one of those moods. She could injure one of us, injure herself. So what do you do? Easy to say.'

315

She scored neatly through a line of words.

Molly finished her salad. She wanted to tell Teresa about the phone conversation, to ask her opinion, to find out if she was on Fison's side. Because was she herself on it? She knew the arguments perfectly well. She knew Cat's passionate opposition to any change in the law which would allow assisted suicide, any suggestion that doctors should be allowed to administer lethal drugs in doses which would end life. They had argued about the difference between ending a life and not making strenuous efforts to prolong it no matter what. Cat had explained the difference patiently. Molly had listened and still been unsure.

'You'll discover,' Cat had said. 'When you've been doing the job for a few years, you will gradually learn and you will know.'

'But will it be enough? Is it enough?'

'Yes,' Cat had said. 'Yes, Molly. I can't tell you how much I believe that. It has to be or we are no longer human.'

It was warm. Sunny. The old part of the garden, and the meadow beyond it, was beautiful, with some handsome mature trees, avenues of shrubs, paths leading towards the field. Only the newer areas nearer the house were still raw in the aftermath of the building works. A couple of sturdy old sheds had names and messages scratched on the wood panels. The place had been a school, she remembered, a Catholic convent. Girls had sat in the sun here lifting up uniform skirts to try and get their legs brown, had walked arm in arm between the trees and chatted on wooden benches. Girls had carved their names on the sheds.

She wandered towards a small copse of silver birches and Scots pines, along a stretch of newly surfaced road which ran up to the trees, then turned away to the right, out of sight. A squirrel raced up one of the pine trunks and leapt across to the next level of spreading branches, high up.

She was not expecting to come upon any other building. This was single-storey, with a window at each side. A white door. New paint.

Molly glanced round. The squirrel had leapt to the tree next to her and was peering down. Black bead eyes.

There was something, just something, some sense, some instinct. She walked round to the back of the building. A barred window, high up. A pair of wooden doors. A path leading to a gravel turning space. The trees had been felled here so there was a clearing. A small brick-built shed stood to the right. She expected it to be locked but it was not. A small generator was installed, full of diesel. It looked new. Unused.

She hesitated. There was a slight soft crunching sound. Footsteps snapping a twig, walking on dry leaves.

Molly edged behind the shed. Waited. The footsteps came nearer. Long strides. Stopped. A key in a lock. The faintest creak of new wood moving as the door was opened.

But not closed.

She moved away from the shed.

There was complete silence.

She did not know what the building was for or what was inside it. Possibly it was a mortuary, but surely a small nursing home would simply send for the undertaker and had no need for body-storage facilities.

It was a teaspoon of suspicion and a large measure of simple curiosity that urged her on towards the white door, which had been left slightly ajar, and to push it.

She was in a small lobby with a second door ahead which was half open. She put out her hand and touched the door until it opened an inch or two further, then edged round it. Ahead of her was what she took to be a single room. She heard a metal drawer being opened. A cough. These sounds came from a screened-off area.

The room was light, with pine panelling halfway up the walls, white paint above. A pine table held a pair of candlesticks in which stood new wax candles, on a white linen runner. There was a straight-backed but upholstered new bedside chair. On the walls several large pictures of tranquil country scenes, lake-side and meadowland in spring, photographs which had been expertly enlarged so that when looking at them you began to feel that you might actually step into them through the frames.

There was a bed, single but not too narrow, and made up

317

with fresh white linen and several pillows. A cream rug on the floor beside it. Nothing else. It did not seem as if anyone had used the room. But it was a long way from the house for a patient to be assigned to it, and the whole building was too small for any other rooms. Something scraped against the floor behind the screen, then someone came smartly out from behind it, almost knocking her over.

'Ah,' Leo Fison said. 'I had a sense that someone had come in. Do you ever have that, Molly? The sensation of being watched or that someone is just behind you, even though you've seen nothing and heard nothing?'

She stammered that she had mistaken the path, had thought this was the storeroom from which she had been asked to collect something, had no idea why she had strayed as far as this.

'I'm sorry. Sorry. I didn't mean to barge in. Sorry, Dr Fison.'

Molly was furious with herself for being on the defensive and apologetic. She was not that sort of person. She did not see that she was doing wrong. He might have understood that she was either innocently exploring, or coming to find him, having seen him walk in this direction.

He stood quite still, arms folded, silent, waiting for her excuses and half-explanations to peter out. She felt as if she were twelve years old again, up in front of the head for instigating some sort of stupid prank.

'Right,' he said at last. 'You had better listen to me because I am going to trust you. I think it's a good idea that you should learn one side of an argument of which you almost certainly, as a medical student, have only heard the opposite. Who knows – I certainly don't – you might agree with me? You might be entirely of my own way of thinking. Now you've come as far as this, you'd better come further. Come here.'

He pushed the screen aside and beckoned.

There was a window high enough up to make the area light but not to afford any view. A long wall cupboard, with a bunch of keys hanging from the lock. A clinical table. A wooden chair. A sink. Antiseptic handwash dispenser. Soap dispenser. A blood pressure monitor. A digital clock.

Fison opened the cupboard. 'See?'

She looked. A small pharmacy was on two shelves. Phials. Boxes of medication. Syringes and latex gloves.

'Do you know what these are for? Why not look?'

He gestured her to go nearer, stood back so that she could read the labels. As she did so her heart began to thump. Leo Fison was standing so close to her she felt his breath on her neck.

'And through here . . . you've already looked in here, haven't you? The only thing I have not yet set up is a sound system for playing DVDs. Headphones, too, of course, if people want to be even closer to their music. Headphones mean you can have what you like almost inside your head, inside your brain. Don't you think?'

Molly felt nausea gush up through her stomach into her chest but no further. She would not shame herself by actually being sick.

The room was utterly silent. The window was tightly closed. No rustle of the trees or sound of any birdsong, animal or human movement could penetrate from outside. She saw that it was double-glazed and sealed round the edges.

'The undertaker's van comes in through a separate entrance, which is off the back lane and unmarked,' Leo Fison said.

Molly turned quickly to look at him. His face was completely expressionless. His absolute baldness gave him an oddly neutered look.

'So, Molly. What do you think?'

She could not speak. Her mouth and throat were dry.

'What do you deduce from all this?'

She dared not deduce anything.

'Come. You're a bright girl.'

She shook her head.

'Tell me what you know about Bene Mori? I assume you've heard of it?'

She nodded.

'And? Do you think it is a sympathetic operation? Do you think people travel there to die in peace and tranquillity at a time and in a manner of their own choosing?'

319

She realised that she had no clear idea, only knew what she had picked up on odd television programmes and in a newspaper feature.

'I – I don't know.'

'But you ought to know, don't you agree? You'll be a fully qualified doctor shortly. You may have patients who want to discuss the subject with you. Who may want to take themselves there? What would you say?'

Molly glanced quickly round.

'Do you want to go back? You seem anxious.'

'No.'

'Good. Then tell me what you think. Come and sit down here.' He gestured to the bed and the chair beside it.'

'I should get back. They need me to help with things.'

'It's your lunch break. There's nothing to help with, they'll all be asleep. What is this room for, Molly?'

'I . . . for a patient who has to be kept away from the others?'

Fison smiled. 'Like the old isolation wards you mean? History of Medicine, Part 3. Come, you know, don't you? You know what I am setting up. You know because you were listening outside my door earlier.'

'No, I . . .'

'I have a mirror in front of my desk. I could see you.' He had folded his arms and was standing in front of the white-sheeted bed, his eyes never leaving her face.

Anything might have happened. Or nothing. He might have taken hold of her, or not, attacked her, or not, blocked her exit, or not, gone on talking, asking her questions, or stayed silent, arms folded, and looking, looking at her. She did not think, or hesitate, or give herself a chance to find out, she turned and ran, out through the door, and out, down the narrow path, between the trees, over the grass, round the corner to the back of the main house. She was fit. Her heart pounded so much that it burned inside her chest but not with the strain of running. With panic. With fear.

At the corner, she glanced over her shoulder, expecting to find Fison on her heels, just emerging from the trees. But the way behind was deserted. No one else was about. Molly stopped, in

320

the safety of the side door and looked back again. But he had not followed her. There was no sound of footsteps.

She was on her own. She bent forward and vomited onto the gravel.

Forty-five

Simon called in at the Cypriot deli on his way out, picked up a good espresso. He checked his phone but there were no messages.

'Beautiful morning,' John Lowther had said, long ago. And now, at last, Simon noticed it. The air was warm, there was no cloud, the trees were a thick new green. They had mown the banks on the bypass. Simon opened the car roof and smelled the fresh sap.

His phoned beeped a text but he was cutting fast up the outside lane, then turning off and looping back down a couple of side roads and a long avenue towards Rachel's house. It was several minutes before he could check.

'*Best if we don't meet again. Unfair to K. Unfair to you. Please don't try to see me. Don't reply. But with love, R.*'

He clutched the small ordinary phone as if it were a lifebuoy and he seconds from drowning. He was about a hundred yards away from her.

When it rang the phone seared his palm.

'Serrailler.'

'Guv. Remember a Deena from Warsaw? Deena Wanowska. Well, she phoned. Name before she married was Deena Dokic. Sister of Agneta Dokic . . .'

Simon's tyres scorched the drive so that the housekeeper was at the door before he had reached it.

'You've found someone,' she said. 'You've come to tell him you've found someone.'

'Mrs Mangan –'

'And now Sir John isn't here, he's on a plane, he's flying to America. He's only just left. This would happen when he wasn't here.'

Yes, he thought furiously, oh yes, he would be flying to America.

'Can we go inside for a moment?'

'I do apologise, yes of course, Sir John would want me to ask you in, I know that. Can I get you a cup of tea, Inspector?'

'Tea would be wonderful.' He needed the housekeeper on his side. 'And maybe a biscuit?'

'I can do better than a biscuit. Would you mind coming into the kitchen?'

'I'd prefer it. Kitchens are always more friendly, aren't they?'

He waited until a pot of tea, a fruit cake and a plateful of shortbread were in front of him before he asked her.

'Have you been with Sir John many years, Mrs Mangan? It feels as if you have.'

'Why is that, Inspector?' She sliced a thick wedge of the fruit cake, poured the tea.

'I just got a sense that you'd belonged with the family for a while. I'm right, aren't I?'

'Twenty-four years.' She stood back, pride and satisfaction on her face.

'So you were here . . .'

'I was. I was here when she went missing. Yes. I came when Harriet was a little girl of eight. She and I spent a lot of time together, one way and another, with her father working, and going away a lot. Mrs Lowther – well, she was Mrs then, before he got to be Sir John – she went with him on a lot of his business trips, especially abroad, so Harriet stayed with me. We were very happy together, we used to play all sorts of board games, we used to cook, I taught her to knit, I taught her to crochet . . . I was married for twenty years until my husband passed on, but we had none of our own, and Harriet was like mine, felt like mine. They trusted me with her. They were my family to me. Still are. Well, Sir John is. This isn't where I work, this is my home, Inspector. So yes, I was here.'

Serrailler set down his cup and nodded as she lifted the pot to refill it.

'And I used to say I'd give anything or do anything to get her back safe and sound and then, when you found her poor little body, even though we didn't know exactly what had happened, but it was obvious it was something terrible, then I said what I keep saying, and I'll say to you, that I'd give anything and do anything to find out who harmed her, and if I could put him to rot in hell myself, put him there with my own hands, I would. There now, I've said it.'

She turned away so that he could not see the expression on her face. But he could picture it.

'Mrs Mangan, I need to find something urgently. Sir John said he had cleared out most of Harriet's things, after her mother died.'

'That's true, and I couldn't blame him, you know. Lady L had wanted everything kept, she believed Harriet would come back and just walk into her room again and expect to find everything, just as she'd last left it. She wouldn't have anything moved or changed round or touched, but I knew he found it hard, I knew he wouldn't leave it. When she died, he started clearing out her things, all the old Christmas and birthday cards she'd painted and made when she was little, you know how children do, all the models and the drawings, and then all her stories and schoolwork, her reports and certificates and so on. He burned all of those. He gave her books and clothes away but he burned the personal things. "No one wants these, Mrs Mangan, and I don't want them to go to anyone. These are for the bonfire."'

'Did everything go? Absolutely everything?'

'I think it did. He kept her clarinet and some little bits of jewellery she'd had – christening presents, he kept those, a little silver bracelet she had for being a bridesmaid. Bits and pieces.'

'Nothing from school at all? Magazines or things about the school? Her school reports?'

'No. All that went. And of course the school closed down anyway, it closed a few years ago.'

'Where would the things he did keep be?'

'In a drawer of the dressing table in her room. That's the only place. Did you want to look? I'm sure it would be in order for me to show you, Sir John would want me to. I don't know that you'd find it of any use though.'

'No,' Simon said, getting up, 'I don't either but I need to try.'

'What is it you're looking for exactly?'

'Names,' he said. 'Names, addresses, phone numbers, pencilled notes about teachers, friends. A diary maybe.'

Mrs Mangan led the way up the wide flight of stairs. 'You won't find anything like that. She never kept much of a diary and anything on paper went on the bonfire in any case. There were postcards and letters from school friends, the sort of things young girls keep, birthday cards and so on, but they all went. This was her room.'

He had been into enough of them, the rooms of the dead, the rooms kept like shrines and the rooms stripped of every trace of them. This was almost but not quite the latter. The window looked out to the side garden. The bed was unmade but had a plain blue coverlet. No pillows. There was a desk. A chair. A dressing table. A set of empty bookshelves, and a display shelf on the wall, also empty. He lifted the lid of the desk. Nothing was inside. A picture of a pony in a field was on the wall. A photograph on the dressing table, of the Lowther parents somewhere on holiday, wearing sunglasses.

'Nothing left,' Mrs Mangan said. 'But it's still her room to me. Or it was. Funny – once you found her, it started to slip, that feeling. That sense of her. Funny.'

'You said her clarinet was still here?'

'Yes. That's down in the sitting room in its case. I can show you.'

'Please.' Though he was unlikely to get anything from a clarinet in a case.

There was a piano, the lid propped open. A long stool. A music stand which was empty. Shelves of books. An armchair. A clarinet in its black case was on top of the piano.

'No point in it being here, is there? I don't know anything about them but surely someone could get a use from it?'

Simon opened the case. He knew nothing about them either.

325

The clarinet looked new. Well cared for. He lifted its pieces out carefully. Turned each one over in his hand. Inside the case was Harriet's name and telephone number and the name of her school, on a metal tape printout glued to the lid. Nothing else. He put it back.

'Did anyone else play the piano? Lady Lowther?'

'She had as a girl apparently. This was the piano she had from her own home, I was told. She always said it was a nice instrument but I don't know any more about them than about the clarinet. She didn't play at all by the time I came. Just Harriet. She loved her piano. Loved it. She was always in here, tinkling away. Sounded so lovely.'

'Did you know her music teachers at all?'

'Oh no, they were at the school, same as all her other teachers. She just did her playing practice at home on her own.'

'Did Sir John give away all her music as well?'

'There's some left in the stool compartment but he gave most of it to the charity shop, like all Harriet's books.'

He lifted the lid of the upholstered piano stool as far as it would go. It had a double compartment with music in each. LRAM Examinations Grade 5 Piano. LRAM Examinations Grade 6 Piano Chopin Waltzes. J.S. Bach: *The Little Book of Anna Magdalena*. J.S. Bach: *Preludes Book 3*. John Rutter: *Christmas Music arranged for Piano*. *Christmas Carols arranged for Piano*.

He flipped through the piles. Harriet Lowther. Harriet Lowther. H.P.E. Lowther. Harriet P.E. Lowther. Harriet Lowther. All the music was named in pencil on the top right-hand corner. Schubert: *Eight Pieces*. Harriet Lowther. Then: 'Wednesday 9th, 3.30'. Harriet Lowther. H. Lowther. Jenny R. and Katie. Sat. Harriet Lowther. Miss W's copy. H. Lowther. Harriet Lowther. Different handwriting and red pen not pencil. L.W. 486990. Harriet L . . . Harriet Lowther . . .

He flipped back. Quickly. Handel: 2 *Concerti Grossi arr. for Piano*.

'Mrs Mangan, may I borrow this?'

'One of the old music books? How can that be any use? Is it for fingerprints? Even after all this time? You'd only find Harriet's, and maybe Eileen's, she was a cleaner we had . . . she might have moved stuff when she was doing the piano.'

Simon wrote quickly on the back of one of his cards, stating what he had taken and signing it.

'I'll confirm it with a full receipt. Keep this for now.'

He went out fast, Mrs Mangan behind him, puzzled. Alert to everything. At the door he said, 'Thank you for your help. You've been wonderful. And for that delicious cake.'

'Should I let Sir John know you've been? If he rings me later. He usually does to let me know he's arrived safely. He's a very considerate man.'

'Just tell him I'll be in touch, would you?'

'Shall I say when?'

Simon shook his head as he started the car.

He stopped again beside the village green. Took out his phone.

The music was beside him on the seat. He drew a deep breath. Knowing. Sure. So near. Surely, so near.

486990.

'The number you are calling has not been recognised.'

He dialled again slowly. The same.

Bugger. Number changed then.

No. He had dialled the Lafferton code. But it would be on the Bevham exchange.

Again, with the different prefix.

It rang for a long time, but no machine cut in. He was about to give up when a woman answered.

'Hello?'

He disconnected quickly. Dialled again. He had to be sure.

This time, it rang only twice. 'Who is this? Please have the politeness to give your name.'

He disconnected without speaking, then rang the station. Gave the name and address. 'Get me details of all vehicles registered to this owner going back to 1990? And it's urgent.'

When he hit the bypass he took the Audi up to eighty-five in the outside lane.

Forty-six

The message came through as Simon pulled up in the lane. He wrote it down.

'Just what I wanted to hear. Thanks very much.'

He punched the air.

The van was still there, in exactly the same spot. The hens still scratted in their patch of grass among the groundsel. The sun had come out again. It was warm. And very quiet, except for the soothing sounds of clucking and pecking.

How was she going to react? Calmly, one way or another, whatever she chose to tell him; he was sure she would not show anger or panic.

The kitchen door was open, and as he approached, she came out, carrying a couple of wet towels in a plastic bowl, and, calm or not, she jumped as she saw him. The bowl fell.

'Let me.'

Lenny said nothing as he picked it up and set it on the table behind him. She watched.

'This number isn't in the phone book,' she said.

'I need to talk to you again, Miss Wilcox.'

'I told you everything about her.'

'About who?'

'I told you. She stole from me, from the other people, she was caught, and she did a bunk. Nothing else to say.'

'We could sit out here and talk? In the sun.'

'I don't want to sit in the sun, I've got plenty to do and I've told you everything there is to tell you about her. Agneta. I don't know why you're here again.'

'It isn't Agneta I want to ask you about. Not just for the moment.'

A flicker across her face. Her eyes wary. But then gone.

'Oh?'

Simon sat down on the metal bench and indicated the basket chair to her. In the end, she sat, but forward, as if wanting to be ready to get up again any second.

'You teach music, Miss Wilcox?'

'No.'

'You did.'

'Once.'

'When did you give up? Retire?'

'Years ago. I went on too long as it was.'

'How many years ago?'

'Six? Seven? What's this to do with anything?'

'Did you teach Harriet Lowther?'

He looked at her intently as he asked. Her expression did not alter.

'I taught lots of girls. Hundreds of girls probably.'

'Yes. Including Harriet Lowther.'

Silence. She stared in front of her, her body rigid in the chair.

'I'm sure you know that Harriet was missing for sixteen years until her skeleton was found after the storm had shifted the earth in which she'd been buried. And that we found what we now know is the body of Agneta Dokic in the same area, in a shallow grave.'

Silence.

'You gave Harriet private music lessons, didn't you?'

Silence.

'You taught her at school, of course.'

Silence.

'Was she very talented? Is that why you felt she should have extra piano lessons? Out of school hours?'

'What makes you think I know anything about this girl?'

'She was having private piano lessons.'

329

'Well, there are plenty of others. I'm not the only local teacher. It could have been half a dozen.'

'No.'

'Of course it could.'

'You taught her the piano at school.'

'Doesn't mean I taught her outside it.'

'So you *did* teach her at school?'

She flicked her eyes to him and away. 'For goodness' sake, man, I taught dozens of girls. I was at that school for fourteen years.'

'Which school?'

'Freshfield.'

'Which Harriet attended and where you taught her the piano.'

'I've said. I could have done. It's a long time ago. How am I supposed to remember?'

'Not remember the girl who disappeared while waiting at a bus stop sixteen years ago? The girl there was a huge national appeal about, a massive local search for – face in every paper, on posters, on television?'

'We don't have a television.'

He waited. The hens clucked and scratched. She had her hands on the table now. They were not the hands of a woman who gardened and cleaned out hen houses and did domestic chores, they were not the hands of a woman of her age, they were hands with long, well-shaped, well-flexed fingers, carefully rounded short nails. Clean.

'Tell me about her,' Simon asked, putting his left leg over his right knee and clasping it. Eyes no longer on her face. 'It must be quite rare for a piano teacher to have a gifted pupil. A teacher of anything, actually. Most of them must grind away, hating every minute of it, never practising. I know my sister did. Her teacher asked her to give it up, she was so hopeless. So I can guess it must be a joy to find a pupil like Harriet. You'd offer her extra lessons like a shot.'

'Her parents were philistines,' Lenny Wilcox said at last. 'Yes, she was talented, though who knows how she would have done in the long run. You have to be more than just talented. But she wanted it. She loved it. She would have played and played all

330

day, her lessons were always too short, she said. I never had another pupil who said that to me. Never. She asked if I would give her extra lessons and I was thrilled, absolutely excited about it, I knew just how much I could bring her on, how much she would love it. Value it. And then the damn parents. Hobbies department, they thought. She played the clarinet as well, she was good at that, though the piano was her instrument, she'd never have gone far as a wind player. Damn parents.'

'So she asked if you'd give her the lessons without telling them.'

'No, she didn't, I suggested that. I said I would give her an extra lesson a week, a good long lesson, an hour and a half, here, on my piano, which is a Steinway, and I wouldn't charge her a penny.' She looked him straight in the eyes. 'That doesn't mean anything.'

'In what sense does it not?'

'So – I gave her some lessons. Here. Without her parents' knowledge or consent. Doesn't mean I know what happened to her. How would I know what happened? How did you find out that she had lessons with me?'

'When did she last come here?'

'How would I remember that?'

'Did she meet Agneta here?'

Alarm on her face, a shadow across the sun.

'What day did she have her lessons here? Saturday?'

'No. Or – she may have done once or twice.'

'How did she get here? Obviously her parents didn't bring her.'

'On the bus, I suppose. I didn't ask. Or on her bicycle. Probably on her bicycle.'

'Harriet didn't have a bicycle.' It was a shot in the dark. He did not know.

'So it was on the bus.'

'During the holidays she could have come any day. So it was Friday afternoon, wasn't it? The last time she came. The day she disappeared. The Friday you arranged to meet her. The Friday you picked her up on Parkside Drive.'

'No.'

331

'Did you arrange to meet her at the bus stop? Or did she realise it wasn't a good place for a car to pull up so she walked on a few yards down the road?'

Silence.

'You came along and she glanced round and saw you. You stopped by the kerb. Harriet got in. You drove away.'

'No. This is all invention. I didn't realise the police invented things but of course I should have done, we're always hearing about it.'

'You were seen.'

'What?'

'Your car was seen that afternoon. Harriet got into it. You drove away. We have a witness who saw you quite clearly. What car do you drive?'

'The van. The one out there. You've seen it twice now.'

'How long have you had the van?'

'I don't know. Years. That's why it's so unreliable. I can't afford a new one.'

'You drove a green car then.'

'I can't remember what colour car I had all those years ago for heaven's sake. Cars get you from A to B. I'm not interested in them otherwise.'

'Let me remind you. We have a witness.'

'What sort of witness remembers a green car sixteen years ago? What sort of witness is that?'

'He saw Harriet get into your car. I've traced your car ownership from 1990. You don't change your cars often. A blue Ford. A green Lada. And the van that you have now. One green car, a Lada. The one Harriet Lowther got into at four ten on that Friday afternoon. Friday 18 August 1995. Did you come straight here to this cottage?'

Lenny Wilcox was so still he could not see her breathing. He hardly breathed himself. And suddenly, he felt in no hurry. Sooner or later, she would talk to him, tell him, give him an account of it in the sort of detail people always remembered for ever after such an event. It was going through her mind now, picture after picture, sound after tiny sound, words spoken, and cries. Silences.

He could wait.

A vein pulsed in her neck.

Simon's phone rang. Lenny barely noticed. It stopped. Rang again.

She turned her eyes to his face and looked at him steadily but did not speak. She was in no hurry either.

Forty-seven

The side door led to a passage which led to the kitchen stores on the left, the main house to the right. No one was about. There was the distant sound of someone singing in a thin, high, voice.

> 'Oh my love is like a melody
> That's sweetly played in tune.
> And fare thee well, my only love
> And fare thee well, awhile.
> And I will come again, my love
> Though it were –'

And broke off.

Molly stood, taking slow, deep breaths, gathering herself, calming down. She needed to think it all through, but if the panic and tension were easing in her body, her thoughts were jagged and broken, like crazy paving, and seemed to jump here and there, from one thing to the other.

She knew what she had seen. Nothing explicit had been said but she was utterly clear about it. She did not know what Fison planned for her, whether he would send for her, threaten her, bribe her, to make sure she kept silent. This was her last day. If he meant to talk to her he would have to do it in the next few hours. Perhaps he did not.

She would go back into the living areas or the staffroom, the kitchen, to Sister Fison's office, follow anyone, ask for a job among the patients or with one of the carers, move about so that she was not alone anywhere. She was afraid of him, afraid of what he would say, afraid of her own reactions. Afraid of what she had seen. Afraid.

She turned and went towards the sitting room, where one or two of them sat after meals, turning the pages of magazines without taking in anything on the pages, Mrs Overthorpe crocheting and unpicking what she had crocheted, over and over again, smiling.

The sun shone into the room, catching the jar of flowers on the sideboard, making the smooth china of an ornament gleam. The doors were open onto the garden. Someone was a few yards away, by the flower bed. No one was in the room itself.

Molly reached the doors and was about to step down onto the gravel when there was a shout and the person she could see swung round and held out her arms for a second, before flinging herself forward, head down, running, running in a blind, confused way, like a bull that had been goaded, and roaring in the same way too.

At the same moment, she heard a step behind her. A voice. 'Ah, yes. There you are again, Molly.'

Something hit her in the chest, the throat, the face, arms flailing, a head hard down into her as she was propelled in the small of the back, lost her balance, fell forward across the step. She knew what was happening but not in any order, knew someone had cannoned into her and that someone else was pushing her so hard from behind that she had no strength to resist them, to turn, to keep her balance. She fell slowly, as she might fall in a dream, until the pain as she hit her face, her head, rushed up not as pain but as an enveloping blackness.

Forty-eight

'Tell me about Miss Mills,' Simon said.

Lenny was like a pillar of stone beside him. The sun had moved round and the hens were basking in it, digging out bowls in the dust and rubbing themselves down into it.

'Nothing left to tell.'

'But there was once.'

'Oh yes. Olive.'

'Talk to me about her.'

'Why? Olive has nothing to do with it.'

'When did you meet?'

'Years ago.'

He waited.

Lenny stared ahead. 'She was never beautiful but she had a – a spark. Life. Olive was full of life. She was like a Catherine wheel. Fizzed. It was very attractive. Volatile but very . . . I don't have that. Now it's all gone.'

'When did it start?'

'Forgetting? It's hard to know when it does. She was unpredictable, she didn't operate like you and me, remembering things, putting them in order, she was all over the place, here and there, things didn't connect with her the way they usually do. So I missed it at first.'

'Years ago?'

'I suppose so. Dementia. Being demented. I used to tell her she was demented, sometimes. How cruel.'

'You weren't being cruel.'

'No. But it feels like that now.'

'Did Olive meet Harriet Lowther?'

She stiffened. Said nothing.

'Was she here when Harriet came for her lesson? Was she always here when your pupils came?'

'Nobody else did come.'

'Just Harriet?'

'I told you. Harriet was exceptional. I didn't want the cottage invaded. Girls here at home. This is home. It was our home. Now it's my home. Just mine.'

'Tell me about that day.'

'What day?'

'You know what day.'

Her mouth twitched. Her fingers twitched. Then went still. She said nothing for a long time. She would. He knew perfectly well now. It was all there. He just had to wait.

'I'd like a cup of tea. I suppose you would.'

'Very much.'

'Or gin. I have gin.'

'Tea.'

'I could have gin.'

'If that's what you'd like, why not?'

She turned to him, her blue eyes bright with a moment of amusement. 'Is that allowed?'

'It's your gin. Your home. Why would I stop you?'

'Ah.' She sighed deeply, and then got up.

He filled the kettle. Found the tea. Milk. A china mug with a picture of Tintagel.

'Cornwall,' Lenny said. 'We loved Cornwall before they spoiled it with tourists. We swam in the sea. We went out in fishing smacks. Cottage overlooking the harbour. Every year. Then it started to fill up. Visitors. Gift shops. Yes, all right, I bought that in a gift shop. We had half a dozen. That's the last.'

'I'll be careful with it.'

'Why bother?' She sat down at the table and poured a single measure of gin. Topped it up. Creeper hanging down over

337

the kitchen window and a couple of pots of geraniums on the ledge made the kitchen dim. The sun was on the other side now.

Simon put a splash of milk into his tea. It struck him that he had never taken an interview so slowly, never let it run on for so long. But he could not push. Sometimes pushing, jostling, putting on the pressure, was the way. Sometimes it was the last thing to do. It could take hours. He would get there, all the same.

'She was a pretty girl,' Lenny said. 'Fair hair. Pale skin. She had a composure you don't often find at that age. Not the awful shoulder-shrugging. Can't be bothered, not interested. Just composure. A quietness around her. That's what singled her out, that's what gave her the extra quality she needed. Perhaps she could have had a bit more fire as well. They can go together, you know. The very best musicians have a fire in the belly. I don't have any. Not sure she did. It was what would have held her back in the end. But the calmness gave her something else. I picked her up. She had no other way of getting here, you're right. I'd have dropped her back at the bus stop into town.'

Simon lifted the mug of tea to his mouth but barely sipped it. Held his breath.

Lenny had finished the gin in a couple of mouthfuls but she did not pour herself any more.

'It was her second lesson here. Olive had seen her the first time. She was trimming the forsythia. She turned round and she looked at Harriet, took in everything. She would. She saw.'

'Saw?'

'Saw her. Saw it all. Her prettiness. Her calmness. She wouldn't miss anything. Never missed anything. Agneta wasn't here that first time. She came irregularly. But that afternoon she was here, cleaning the windows. Olive wouldn't get up on the step-stool, it wasn't a job she would ever do, and since I'd broken my leg I was wary of clambering about. Still am if it comes to that. Agneta would do them, she was fearless, did anything, climbed up anywhere. She was very willing, very capable. Useful.'

'You liked her?'

'Agneta? Yes I did. Olive didn't but that was only jealousy.'

'Jealousy?'

'Oh, there was nothing to be jealous about, never had been for all those years, never would be. But jealousy isn't rational, is it? Olive was born jealous. So when she knew I liked Agneta . . . anyway, Harriet was playing Schubert. Perfect composer for her. It was a new piece to her. Tricky. The bass hand is tricky. If you don't get the fingering exactly right . . . It's unforgiving, music like that. I had to show her the fingering. But she went on getting it wrong, getting it wrong, not listening properly, not taking any notice of what I was saying.'

'That doesn't sound like Harriet.'

She ignored him. She was speaking faster.

'I was annoyed with her. I gave her a push, I was so annoyed, and the push made her lose her balance. She slipped off the piano stool and she hit her head on the corner.'

'The corner?'

'Of the hearth.'

'She . . .'

'Yes. Hard. She hit her head hard and I screamed, and as I screamed Agneta came in. Agneta saw it all. She rushed over to Harriet and she screamed as well. There was a lot of blood everywhere. Agneta was shouting and screaming at me that Harriet was dead, that I'd pushed her and killed her.'

Lenny had been looking down into her empty glass, her hand rubbing the table top to and fro, to and fro, in a repeated movement, but now she lifted her head.

Serrailler caught her gaze and tried to hold it but her eyes slid away at once.

'I – pushed her, she was screaming and shouting so much. I pushed her and she fell as well. Agneta fell. You wouldn't think it could happen like that, two people pushed, two people hitting their heads, two people dead, you wouldn't think it could happen, would you?'

She stood up. 'There,' she said. 'I killed Harriet by accident, I killed Agneta deliberately. There isn't anything else you need to know, is there? I've told you. You have to arrest me now, don't you?'

She was speaking quickly. But it was the odd, pleading note in her voice that made Simon hesitate. Something was out of joint about what she had told him – the haste of it all, the way the story had tumbled out. He had heard enough false confessions to be wary.

He needed time, more time to calm her down, get her to go over her story, one thing after another in careful order. He needed to ask and ask again, to pick up minute details and get her to repeat them, to question how she remembered so much, whether she remembered other things. It might take the rest of the day. It might take longer.

'Could I have another cup of tea?'

But as he asked her, his phone was ringing. Cat. He went into the garden. He had a clear view of the kitchen door, the path, the gate. A few yards and he would catch up with her easily. But she would not run. He was absolutely certain of that.

'Hi.'

'Si, I'm sorry if you're caught up in something –'

'I am.'

'Sorry, but it's urgent. Molly has been taken to hospital. She had an accident, fell and hit her head . . . only I don't think accident covers it, something happened and I can't get to the bottom of it.'

'Where is she?'

'In A & E. I'm on my way there now.'

'Get off the phone then, and call me when you get there. I'll come when I can but it might not be for a while. Where was she exactly?'

'Maytree House. Moira called me. When I got there the paramedics were getting her into the ambulance. I talked to Leo Fison, I talked to one of the nurses, but they were cagey. Said she'd just tripped. I don't believe it.'

'Why? People do.'

'One of the helpers was talking about a patient who kept having sudden rages and attacking whoever was in her sight. There was an air of panic, you know, a lot of whispering and people looking at one another.'

'Is she badly hurt?'

'She's got a nasty head wound and she wasn't conscious. Those things can either be nothing much and she'll come round

340

quite quickly, or be pretty serious. I'll find out more when I get there but I had an odd feeling you should know about it.'

'Good. I'll get someone onto it. They need to go and ask questions. If it's a genuine accident they'll know. The home has to fill in accident forms and so on for their insurance.'

'Where are you, Si?'

'Trying to make sense of something that doesn't. Bit like Molly's accident.'

Lenny was sitting at the kitchen table, her hands in front of her.

'Interruptions,' she said, not looking at him.

'Always.' He sat down and glanced at his mug.

'Want some more?'

'May I?'

She gestured behind her to the kettle but did not move.

'There's something I don't understand.'

Silence.

'Why would you push Harriet so hard that she fell off the piano stool and hit her head? Teachers can get very annoyed by badly behaved pupils, I know that, but Harriet wasn't badly behaved, she was calm and conscientious, she wanted the extra piano lessons, she was keen to do well.'

'It happened.'

'Why? What had she done?'

'I don't know, I don't remember. Made some stupid mistake, wouldn't listen to me.'

'Harriet? I don't believe you, Miss Wilcox. I've come to know Harriet very well, from the statements, from what people have said to me. Making a stupid mistake is possible, but one bad enough for you to push her off the stool onto the floor? Not listening to you? Really? She wanted you to teach her. She'd asked you specially. So she was going to listen, wasn't she? I just do not believe what you've told me.'

'Suit yourself. It's what happened.'

'And then Agneta came in and saw her lying there and started to scream, you said.'

'Yes. Awful noise. Couldn't shut her up.'

'People do panic, they do scream, they become hysterical. If

341

that had happened you might have slapped her. To calm her down.'

'I told you.'

'Two girls, pushed over, in a small room, both hitting their heads so hard that the fall killed them? Harriet, making some stupid mistake bad enough for you to lose your temper and shove her very hard; Agneta, coming in and seeing her lying there, becoming so hysterical you had to slap her so hard that she also fell. Both girls dead.'

He rinsed his mug. Made more tea, unhurriedly. Took it to the table. Sat down.

'Now,' he said gently, 'you're going to tell me the truth.'

He had sat for long periods in interview rooms, waiting for someone to crack, to break down, give in to the pressure and start to talk. But this was different. Lenny Wilcox said nothing at all. An hour, then an hour and a quarter, passed in silence. They sat at the kitchen table. Nothing happened. No one dropped by, no one phoned. Neither Simon nor Lenny moved. He finished his mug of tea. She did not drink anything. There was no change on her face. She did not cry or even fidget. She did not seem to be going through any sort of conflict inside herself.

They might sit here for another hour, more, the kitchen growing dark, the silence thickening and spreading between them.

He tried to calculate the advantages of leaving now and coming back the next day. Lenny would not run – he was confident enough to take that chance. But what else might she do? He stood up. 'Thank you, Miss Wilcox. Thank you for the tea, too. Don't get up.'

She looked at him, her eyes full of confusion, even panic. 'Where are you going?'

'Back to the station. I don't need to bother you any further today.'

'Don't I have to come there with you?'

'No.'

'Don't you have to arrest me?'

'No.'

'I told you what happened. It was all my fault, I killed two girls. I've *told you.*'

342

'You've been very helpful. I appreciate it.'

He walked out without glancing back.

The garden smelled sweet, the early evening after a warm day. The hens had put themselves away in their house.

He hesitated beside the parked van.

Risk it?

Go with your gut feelings.

Forty-nine

Molly was in ICU but likely to be transferred the next morning. She was conscious. Her face was bruised, the palm of her right hand badly grazed where she had reached out as she fell. But the brain scan had shown no damage.

The pillows had slithered down on the metal backrest and Cat was trying to rearrange them without disturbing her too much.

'Rob came into A & E,' she said, 'but you were still out for the count. He'll be here soon.'

Molly smiled.

'How's the headache?'

'It aches.'

'They have to be careful what they give you for the next few hours. As you will know. They might do you a cold compress if anyone finds the time. God, they're overworked and under-staffed in here. I hadn't realised how bad it was. Apparently there was a big RTA just after you were admitted and those always take over.'

'How long have I been here?'

'About an hour in here. The ambulance brought you in around half past three.'

Molly frowned.

'What?'

'Did I have any lunch?'

'I should think so. What time is lunch there?'

'Early. Twelve? Half past?'

'It always is. And tea at five thirty, hot drink at eight. Same as hospital.'

'I don't remember having lunch.'

'You'll be confused for a while, but that's normal. Don't fret. What do you remember? Falling?'

'No. What happened?'

'Apparently you were walking through the French windows into the garden and you tripped over the step. That'll have health and safety running about like headless chickens.'

Molly still frowned.

'What do you remember?'

She closed her eyes. A white bed was in her mind. A freshly made bed. Then a tree. The tree merged into the bed. She opened her eyes and looked at Cat. 'Nothing. It's a muddle.'

'It might have gone altogether. It doesn't matter, Moll. Things sometimes come back weeks later, months even. Or they never do. The tests were fine.'

'Yes.'

She closed her eyes again. Cat sat without speaking, touched her hand, adjusted her bedding. Molly slept.

She was still asleep when there was a tap on the door.

'Cat . . . Glad you're here. How is she?' Leo Fison slipped into the room.

'She'll be fine. Scan clear.'

'Thank God for that. We'd never have forgiven ourselves – that step is dangerous, a patient could have fallen over it, a nurse . . . the doors have to be kept closed until we can make it safe.' He spoke in a low voice, glancing at Molly a couple of times. 'I can't tell you how awful I feel about this.'

'What exactly happened? Molly doesn't remember.'

'Nothing at all?'

His voice was raised slightly in what Cat thought was anxiety. No wonder. They'd been lucky. But Molly could sue. She might not be well enough to take her finals. The home wasn't out of the woods and Leo knew it.

'No.'

'The trouble is, no one knows. She was on her own. Someone

345

just found her lying there – one of the carers when she came in looking for something. Damn good job she did. It's always quiet for an hour or so after lunch. Molly might have been lying there for much longer.'

'Do you know how long she was there anyway?'

'No, I don't. No one has said. Not sure we can find out now if Molly has amnesia.'

'It might come back of course. She could remember it all quite clearly in a day or so.'

'Yes. Well, let's hope. Has she said anything else?'

'What about?'

'Oh, you know, the morning, if she found it useful being with us . . . anything at all really.' He was looking at his watch, then at Molly again.

'No,' Cat said. 'I haven't quizzed her either.'

'Of course not, I didn't expect it. Just wondered . . . sometimes people come out with things when they've had a knock.'

'Sometimes.'

'I have to get back, I'm afraid. Some relatives to look us over. They like to meet us both. I like them to get the best impression.'

He was restless, anxious to be away, Cat thought, anxious to put Molly and her accident to the back of his mind.

'Better make sure those doors are locked,' she said.

'I have. I will.'

'What?' Molly was stirring and muttering. 'What is it?'

Cat went to the side of the bed and put her hand gently on the girl's forearm. 'It's all right, Moll. You're just waking up. I'm here.'

Molly opened her eyes and, as she did so, saw Leo Fison who was at the foot of the bed. Cat saw a look cross Molly's face as she recognised him. It was a look of pure fear, then anxiety, panic. And then it changed to one of bewilderment, before she closed her eyes quickly, as if to shut out the sight of the man.

He had seen it too. Cat knew it. He saw, and then he turned and left, giving her a slight wave of his hand, but not looking in her direction again.

Cat set her chair closer to the bedside and took Molly's hand. She pulled it away, but then opened her eyes again.

346

'Oh,' she said with a sigh. 'Oh.'

'Yes. Moll, what is it?'

'I . . . don't know.' She looked fearful.

'You seemed frightened.'

'Did I?'

'Are you?'

'I don't know.'

'It was when you saw Leo Fison.'

'I don't know.' She looked completely bewildered. 'I'm frightened because I felt frightened but I don't know what of or why and I'm frightened because I don't remember anything at all. Has my mind gone?'

'No, not at all. You've had concussion. You'll be fine, this is quite common. Your brain isn't damaged.'

'I'm quite thirsty.'

Cat helped her to drink, then lowered her backrest a couple of notches and dropped the window blind.

'Have a sleep now. Best thing you can do.'

'It won't be hard.' Molly smiled at her wanly as she went out.

Simon was coming in through the main hospital doors as Cat left.

'How is she?'

'She'll be fine. Doesn't remember anything about it. No permanent damage though.'

'Sorry, I haven't yet had a chance to send anyone up to ask questions but if she's going to be OK maybe it's not necessary. Listen, at a rough guess, how many nursing homes would there be in the local area taking people with dementia?'

'Well, Maytree House does for a start.'

'The one where Molly's been?'

'Yes. I told you – run by Leo Fison who's bringing us in a fair bit of dosh for the hospice. Lot of good contacts too. He might have saved our bacon.'

'Any others?'

'A lot of care homes refuse to take Alzheimer's sufferers. I've got a list in the surgery . . . half a dozen maybe? Not more. Why?'

'I need your list. I need to track someone down. Molly doesn't remember anything but presumably she will . . .'

'Not necessarily. She might. Hopefully she will.'

'But someone with Alzheimer's won't remember anything?'

'Depends. It's short-term memory that's affected – so people might remember a whole poem they learned when they were eight or nine, not what they had for lunch an hour ago or even if they had lunch at all. That sort of thing. Eventually, the long-term memory goes too of course.'

'Someone with dementia now – say they've had it for five or six years? Would they remember something from ten years before?'

'I can't answer that. It's like Molly. They might, they might not. It's random.'

'Would it depend on what it was? Say it was the memory of being attacked? Or of being in a car crash? Something that sears itself on the mind.'

'I can look up some articles. But I think the answer is likely to be yes, a dramatic incident – one full of emotion – that could well be remembered longer than a mundane event. There's no guarantee though.'

'Can you get me that list of care homes?'

'Come back to the surgery now, I'll find it in two minutes.'

'I'll follow you.'

'You can start with Maytree.'

'I thought you said it was new.'

'Opened last month.'

'Then she won't be there – she's been in a home for several years.'

'Right. I'll get the list. See you there.'

Twenty minutes later, Simon sat in his sister's office, telephoning his way down the names of care homes which accepted dementia patients. There were seven of them. It didn't take long to track the sad trajectory of Miss Olive Mills.

Molly woke and lay for a moment looking at the white blind drawn down over the window. Puzzled. Uncertain where she was.

What the blind was. Why it was there. Her head ached. She had a drip attached to her left arm. Why? The door opened.

'Ah, you're awake? How do you feel now?'

The nurse looked at the drip. Adjusted it. Checked her temperature. Pulse. Looked at her head wound. Hand.

'My head aches.'

'I'll give you some painkillers in a few minutes. You're doing fine.'

'What happened? I don't know why I'm here.'

'You had a nasty fall. Hit your head and knocked yourself out.'

'Where?'

'The care home . . . don't you work there?'

'No. What care home? I'm a medical student.' She remembered that quite clearly.

'What, here in BG?'

'Yes. Finals in a few weeks.'

'Right. Good for you. Have you had anything to eat?'

'No . . . I had lunch.'

'What did you have?'

'A salad.'

'So you'll be ready for the delights of hospital shepherd's pie.'

She straightened the bedcovers. Went out.

Salad. Was that right? Had she eaten salad for lunch? Where had she? 'You had a nasty fall.' Where? She tried to think. To picture anywhere she might have been when she had a nasty fall. Off her bike? No. 'The care home,' the nurse had said. Care home.

She had no memory at all of anything. 'A salad.' Why had she said that?

Her head ached ferociously. Trying to think made it worse and in any case it was pointless. Nothing happened, nothing came. She remembered riding her bike up a long residential road on a sunny day. But that could have been weeks ago. Nothing else.

Molly closed her eyes again.

Simon parked in the lane beyond the gates of Bransby churchyard. As he did so, his phone beeped a message.

'You are the love of my life. I don't know what this means.'
His hand shook.

Should he believe it? He could not believe it. Would not. What had happened between them was too rare. It mattered too much. Her husband mattered too. And, for now, Simon knew he had to be without her.

To wait.

He wondered how he was going to do that.

Leo Fison walked between the trees in the darkness, away from the brick building. The grass was slightly damp, the sky pricked over with stars. He had locked the door behind him, bolted it, secured the windows.

Would the girl remember? Who knew? It was a worry and he could do nothing. Wait. Hope.

The woman Jocelyn Forbes had sent an email saying that she would not visit after all. She had changed her mind. She would be consulting Dr Deerbon. Her daughter was moving in to look after her. She felt sure she had made the right decision.

He was not worried about Jocelyn Forbes. She would say nothing. Hazel would say nothing. And nothing was written down, there was no trail that could conceivably be followed to his door.

Had the way he had grabbed Molly caused her to fall over the step? No. It was the sudden way Olive had come crashing into her like a bull. Olive was known to be violent. And strong. It was amazing that she had come round so quickly from the injection he'd given her.

No one else had been there. Olive would not remember anything. Molly might not. And if she did?

There was no evidence. Nothing.

He went towards the house. But he felt no relief. No sense of luck, no triumph at having had any sort of escape.

His mind was uneasy as he went inside, and closed and bolted the door.

Wait. That was all anyone could do. Wait.

At first, Tadpole Cottage seemed to be in darkness, but when he walked round the back, past the parked van and the quiet hen run, Serrailler saw a low light shining through the drawn curtains of the kitchen. He could hear the sound of a piano being played inside the house.

It took a long time before she came to the door. When she saw him, she merely held it wider and walked away.

'I need to talk to you again,' he said.

Lenny shrugged. Her back to him.

'May I sit down?'

Silence.

He did so.

'Sit here, please,' he said.

'I'd rather stand.'

'Fine. Your partner, Olive Mills, was here that day, wasn't she? The day Harriet Lowther came for her piano lesson.'

Silence.

'Where is Olive now?'

'I told you. She has dementia. She's in a home. She'll never come back here.'

'Maytree House care home.'

She looked at him. 'She won't be able to tell you anything at all. She's way past remembering.'

'Not quite.'

'Have you been up there? Have you been pestering her? Pestering her with questions when you've been told what happened? You'd no right.'

'She remembers Agneta. She says her name quite often. The staff had thought it was Agatha but when I said "Agneta" Olive knew. Her eyes told me she knew the name perfectly well. She said it once or twice while I was there.'

'Doesn't she have enough without you pestering her, upsetting her?'

'Yes, she was upset. She became very agitated. They had to calm her down. She was actually quite angry. When I said the name. She has fits of rage apparently. Was that always the case?'

Silence.

'Did she fly into a rage that afternoon?'

'She wasn't demented then, she was herself, it was years ago.'

'Sixteen years. Yes.'

'Olive was perfectly well.'

'But she had a temper. She was liable to throw a fit of anger sometimes – when you said or did something that made her feel threatened, or annoyed. What really happened that afternoon, Lenny? You should tell me. You've told me half a story. I know that Harriet was here. That there was an incident. It involved Agneta too, didn't it?'

Silence.

'Tell me, Lenny. It won't make any difference.'

'What do you mean? You didn't arrest me earlier. Are you going to do it now?'

'I don't know. I have to decide that after you've told me the truth.'

'You ought to. I ought to rot in hell for what I did.'

'What exactly did you do?'

'I . . .'

'I know what you told me, but that wasn't the full story, or even some of it. I wonder if any of it bears an approximation to the truth.'

'Of course it does.'

Simon looked at her steadily. 'Tell me. Olive can't. That was very obvious. She knew the name Agneta and it sent her into a rage but she doesn't really remember the girl, and when I said "Harriet" she blanked it completely. Her eyes didn't flicker. I said it several times. Nothing. There was no point in continuing to ask her questions. There won't ever be any point and you know that. So you're the only one who can help me get all this right. Tell me the truth, Lenny.'

The bulb in the lamp was a dim one and the shade was thick, a waxy yellow, so that the kitchen was in the half-dark. The sky outside was ink blue. He could see a couple of stars. Nothing moved.

After several minutes, Lenny Wilcox sighed. Then sat heavily down, as if she was suddenly exhausted. He knew the signs. She had had enough. She would tell him now.

'I met Olive nearly thirty years ago. It was instant. Instant. I knew there would never be anybody else, from those first days with her. Her. She was everything. It was the same for us both.

But Olive never believed me, not really. She was a terribly insecure person. And it became worse. Everyone I glanced at was a threat. Everyone I knew – if I went to a concert with a colleague, if I was friendly with someone, that was a threat. I couldn't have stopped it. I came to believe she *had* to be jealous. It seemed to satisfy something in her. She *needed* to be jealous. She was jealous of the girls I taught, other women I worked with, there was row after row about it, but in the end I gave up bothering. Nothing I could do. When Harriet came here, Olive was very angry. School was one thing but pupils didn't come here, she wouldn't have it. Harriet was special though. Talented. And a very sweet girl. A pretty girl. I was sitting next to her on the piano stool, showing her some difficult fingering in the Schubert piece and Olive came in. Just banged in through the door. That was what she did. She was suspicious. No reason to be but she was and there I sat with Harriet, next to Harriet, at the piano. She went berserk, absolutely flew into a rage. Olive's rages were frightening. Harriet looked at me in terror. Who was this woman, what was happening? I put my hand round her shoulder to reassure her that it would be all right, I'd deal with it, and then Olive lunged forward, grabbed her by the arm and shoved her very hard at the same time. I had no chance to stop her, you see. No chance, it was all in a few seconds, and Harriet hit the kerb of the hearth, the stone kerb, right beside the piano. I heard her head crack against it. I've heard it every day since. And the next minute, I realised that Agneta was in the room.

'She'd come very early that morning, around eight o'clock, saying she wasn't needed any more at the other house, they'd thrown her out. She walked straight in and started clearing up the kitchen, getting out the mop for the floor, just working, working all that day. I suppose I just accepted it. I should have rung them there and then. I mean, why didn't it occur to me that it was odd they'd dismissed her at such an hour? But I didn't. I was glad to have her. Olive hated housework, I hated housework. Agneta did it, and everything else. She cooked, she shopped, she just worked. Just worked. I let her stay without a question. I suppose I didn't want to know anything.

353

'I'm not sure exactly when she'd come in. I was in a panic, Olive was raging at me. Agneta must have heard the commotion, probably saw Olive knock Harriet onto the floor. And she saw Harriet lying there. I knew she was dead. You do know, don't you? There's a terrible stillness. She wasn't breathing. Blood was pouring from her head. Agneta just stared. I can see her face. Stared at Olive. At Harriet. She put her hand to her mouth. And I looked at Olive and somehow, without either of us saying anything, we knew what had to happen. I was screaming at Olive that she'd killed Harriet, Agneta was looking at us and she knew everything and we panicked. Olive picked up a heavy brass bell that was on the table. Agneta turned towards her and she . . . hit her. She hit her on the temple, very hard. She was still shouting, shouting at me in a rage about Harriet – it propelled her. It made her hit out. But I could have stopped her. I know that. I didn't.' She was completely still, hands on the table in front of her, face in shadow, eyes oddly bright. 'That's what happened.'

'You had to get rid of two bodies,' Simon said. 'That won't have been easy.'

'It was terrifying. Don't let anyone tell you that sort of thing can be done calmly. In cold blood? We were raging with fear, both of us. Only a mad person could have done it without being in fear and dread, trembling with it. We did it and it took a long time. That's not easy either, carrying dead bodies, lifting them, burying them. They kept on about the shallow graves. Why is that surprising? We didn't have strength left to dig down six feet, for God's sake.

'When we got home that night – in the middle of the night – we drank a bottle of brandy between us and still didn't sleep. The next day I remember thinking we had no right to be alive. I felt so ill. I didn't leave the house for almost a week. I couldn't. Every time I took a step beyond that door I almost passed out. Don't believe anyone who tells you it's easy. Don't believe a word of it. It almost killed us as well. Cold blood? I don't know what that means. But when nothing happened, no one came to the door, when it was clear no one knew, it gradually got easier. We started to learn to live with it. With the secret. And so that went on, for years and years. And then Olive began to forget. We never mentioned it, never referred to it at all from that day. It just lay there between us but we never spoke of it once. So it was a long time before it dawned on me that Olive actually didn't remember. She didn't remember that, and then, she didn't remember anything.'

They sat on in the half-dark and in silence for a long time.

In the end, Serrailler said, 'Why didn't you tell me this afternoon?'

Lenny said with infinite weariness, 'She's helpless.'

'Yes.'

'She has no chance to defend herself.'

'Nor does she have any need.'

'What do you mean?'

'Lenny, I've seen her. I've spoken to her. She is totally unfit to plead. What purpose would it serve?'

'So you'll arrest me.'

'No.'

'I saw it all. I should have rung the police then. I buried two bodies and I said nothing about any of it for sixteen years.'

'There are no witnesses and it's too long ago for there to be any forensic evidence.'

'Olive knew Agneta's name. She says her name.'

'Olive can't be questioned. The case wouldn't even get to court. She doesn't understand what any of this is about.'

'Now what?'

'Now?' Simon got up. He looked at her and felt huge sadness, and pity, and regret. Lenny would go on living with the memory. Olive would not.

He touched her arm gently. 'Don't forget to lock up the hen house,' he said. 'I know what foxes can do.'

A chilling ghost story by the author of *The Woman in Black,* which is now a major film starring Daniel Radcliffe

THE MAN IN THE PICTURE

978-1-59020-091-9
HARDCOVER

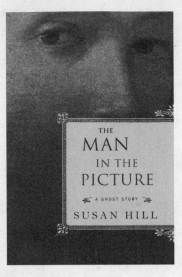

"A master class in the art of dread. . . This is scariness at its most convivial." —*The Independent*

"The story unfolds at a thriller's pace, and the setting is reassuringly contemporary. . . in the capable hands of Hill, the Gothic novel, that venerable but undeniably pensionable genre finds a new lease on life." —*The Times*

"Susan Hill knows exactly how to please. This small, smart, elegantly printed little notepad of a book is a delicious Victorian ghost story, nostalgically and expertly comforting."
—*The Spectator*

THE OVERLOOK PRESS
NEW YORK, NY
WWW.OVERLOOKPRESS.COM

THE VARIOUS HAUNTS OF MEN

978-1-59020-027-8
PAPERBACK

"Hill knows how to keep those pages turning."
—*Chicago Tribune*

"Susan Hill has always been able to tell a good story. . . and we should be delighted that she has turned her formidable talent to crime writing. This is the first of what promises to be a splendid series."
—*Daily Mail*

THE PURE IN HEART

978-1-59020-085-8
PAPERBACK

"This is realistic, gritty, and gut-wrenching crime fiction, but it's also a poignant and thoughtful character study. An outstanding read that will stay with readers long afterward." —*Booklist* (starred review)

"A gripping and unusual procedural. . . A must-read." —*Kirkus* (starred review)

THE RISK OF DARKNESS

978-1-59020-290-6
PAPERBACK

"Flawless." —*Spectator*

"An outstanding crime thriller from one of Britain's best writers. Taut, inventive, tragic, intriguing, and full of unexpected twists, it's a must-have for all mystery collections." —*Booklist* (starred review)

"Hill blends just the right measures of darkness, tension, and human interest . . . Well-crafted plot and believable characters make this a welcome addition to the series."
—*Library Journal*

Susan Hill's Simon Serrailler series is available as ebooks

THE OVERLOOK PRESS · WWW.OVERLOOKPRESS.COM

THE VOWS OF SILENCE

978-1-59020-442-9
PAPERBACK

"It's the intelligence of this brooding series that rivets a reader's attention." —Maureen Corrigan, *The Washington Post*

"[Hill] presumably did not set out merely to follow in the footsteps of P.D. James or Elizabeth George or Martha Grimes. Instead, she appears to have had a much darker goal in mind."
—*Los Angeles Times*

THE SHADOWS IN THE STREET

978-1-59020-085-8
PAPERBACK

"As every Trollope reader knows, English cathedral towns can be hotbeds of viciousness and vice. And so it is in Lafferton, where Susan Hill sets her thoughtful mysteries."
—*The New York Times Book Review*

"For the first time in years, P.D. James has serious competition."
—*Literary Review*

THE BETRAYAL OF TRUST

978-1-59020-280-7
HARDCOVER

"Susan Hill's second foray into the realm of crime fiction is a very British whodunit that unfolds in the cathedral town of Lafferton, with Simon Serrailler back in action. Like Ruth Rendell, the characters are as important as the circumstances, and the result is a psychological thriller, full of sharp details and finely crafted prose."
—*Seattle Post-Intelligencer*

"This is a crime series that specializes in side-stepping conventions, always to exhilarating effect."
—*Independent*

Susan Hill's Simon Serrailler series is available as ebooks

THE OVERLOOK PRESS • **WWW.OVERLOOKPRESS.COM**